BAD AT LOVE

Authors Note

Hey, ladies lets first give glory to God. He's so faithful. I'm so happy to be giving you this anthology. A lot of things jumped in my way with me putting this book out and I was very close to not releasing it. But I love you ladies and without you all I wouldn't be the same. Writing is everything to me. These stories were too good to not be released.

To the ladies that checked on me, I have to send a special shout out to YOU. I'm fine I really am. My biggest thing is blocking out the noise. I have to stay focused and not let outside people get me down. We all have a story to tell ladies and one day soon I'ma tell you mine.

I wanna send a Very special shout out to the women in my reading group! My author friends that have become my real friends and my readers that have become my real friends. Books are amazing because it connected me to some great women! Side note: Women I want nothing but the best for and I can't wait to see what God has in store for them!

To many of you this has been a long time coming but for the ladies that are new to me, these will be new characters. If this does well I will do another one.

Remember how the last series was kind of mellow? I mean it had the drama, but it was at a slower pace. Well for this anthology I switched gears. I write what the characters tell me to and some of these ladies were on a hundred. This anthology is filled with drama, but I love it and it suits the stories well. Some of the problems they face are things a lot of women are dealing with right now. I hope you all enjoy the stories. Like always stay up to date with me. Don't forget to leave a **REVIEW**, ladies!

Some people are going to leave you but it's not the end of your story. That's the end of their part in your story....

Can I love again?

Bahja

Prelude

The beat of her heart was so loud she wondered if he could hear it? She was done. Sick and tired of being alone while being with someone. Her eyes traveled his way as she watched him search the room for his wallet. It was now or never.

"I can't do this anymore," she said breaking the silence. Forcing him to pay attention to her. Something that he once gave her freely was now something she rarely received.

Times had drastically changed.

Dave snatched his keys off his dresser and frowned at his wife. He was tired and in need of a drink. Once again Bahja was looking for a reason to fight with him and he wasn't in the fucking mood for it.

"Can't do what?"

Bahja stared at Dave wondering where it all went wrong with them?

"This, us, this marriage."

Dave was shocked at her reply but didn't let it show. His pride wouldn't allow for him too.

"What are you saying Bahja? Just like that, you want a divorce?"

Bahja sighed. Did she? Could she? No words were strong enough to fall from her pouty lips. She ran a ragged hand through her chocolate strands. This was a man she'd given her all to. She'd chosen him over her family now she only had him and her sons. While she loved her kids, she was no longer happy with her husband. He was content with them merely co-existing but Bahja needed more.

She craved more.

She wanted passion. It had been a time when Dave would stare at her with so much love and adoration it would set her body ablaze. Somehow, he'd forgotten about her. She was no longer his priority and for years she ignored it, but she couldn't anymore.

"Dave, I love you. You know that. You also know how I feel about love. I've waited for years, done counseling and everything I could think of, yet you still ignore me."

Dave groaned and shook his head. He was handsome. Tall, dark and sinfully sexy. Bahja still remembered the day she'd seen him at the Underground Mall. He'd been with his boys bullshitting around while she'd been at her father's jewelry store. He owned twenty at the time which later turned into fifty.

Bahja gave Dave her heart and her body the first year while being with him. They began a relationship that was frowned upon by Bahja's family. Bahja was asked to choose and she chose Dave without having to give it a second thought.

Dave took her in, they were soon married, and three people showed up for the ceremony. While Bahja's Albanian family frowned on her union to an African American man Dave's family didn't show because he'd neglected to mention Bahja, however, once they did meet her they let it be known that she wasn't their cup of tea.

Bahja and Dave's sons ended up being turned away by both families because of the color of their skin.

Bahja sat on her bed with her eyes on Dave. She felt like he could possibly still love her, but she wasn't sure. He hadn't said or shown it in years.

"Are you in love with me?" she asked quietly.

Dave's angry eyes glared over at Bahja.

"Of course, I am. What would make you ask me some silly shit like that?"

Bahja's eyes watered.

"Because I haven't felt that love in a very long time, Dave. I want a divorce," Bahja replied.

Dave nodded. The sadness he felt from her response showed on his handsome brown face. He dropped his head and sighed deeply. When his eyes lifted and fell on her he shrugged.

"I do everything I can to please you. I don't know what else you want from me so if that's gonna make you happy then do what you have to do Bahja," he said before exiting the bedroom.

Bahja's tears were immediate. She fell back on her bed and pulled her covers up over her body. Her eyes landed on a picture of her and her husband and she could feel her chest tighten. She'd given him her everything. So much and all she wanted in return was his love. She didn't feel like she was asking for the impossible.

"He didn't even fight me on it," she mumbled with her tears clouding her vision. Bahja shook her head as she cried harder. "He didn't even fight me," she said again.

One

Are you okay? Should we come get you? We could all do something together. Maybe hookah or go shopping? Vashti was even asking about you.

A small smile covered Bahja's face at her friend's words.

Life had been hard. It hadn't always been that way however. She'd been born to wealthy parents and lived a perfect childhood. It wasn't until she met her late husband that things took a turn for the worst. He was everything her family didn't want for her. She was young and in love and when she chose to keep a child with him she lost her family.

Bahja was Albanian and her family frowned upon her relationship with an African American man. They simply wanted her to marry the man they had been preparing her to be with, but she didn't want that. In return, she lost them.

Bahja swallowed hard as she replied to Neveah's text.

I promise you I'm good. I love you all so much for it though. Please don't worry. I will be fine.

Bahja put her phone away and took a sip of her wine from the bottle. She sat on the bed with her eyes watery. She missed her husband. She might not have been in love with him anymore but to have him die unexpectedly and know that the last thing on his mind was her wanting a divorce hurt her. Dave was also her friend and the father of her two small sons. They no longer had him. Were too young to remember him and that was what hurt Bahja the most.

Bahja found herself homeless just months after losing Dave and was tossed out onto the street. She had no help from her family or Dave's and was sleeping in her car then finally a shelter. The shelter was where she'd met Neveah. Neveah had been a light of love in her life. She'd gone from being her friend to her family. Bahja loved Neveah and all the people that had come with her.

Neveah ran a nonprofit charity called Black Love with her fiancé's mother and Bahja worked with Neveah closely on the charity. It gave Bahja so much joy to help women and families in need. People like her.

Bahja had recently moved from Atlanta to Detroit with Neveah and was living in a beautiful home in the suburbs of OakPark. She shared the home with Neveah who was in the process of moving into a new home with her fiancé who was also there with them.

"Don't be mad. I caught them leaving out with the boys and I stopped in. I just wanted to check on you."

Micah's deep voice startled Bahja. She dropped her wine bottle on her leg and winced out in pain. He rushed over to her and picked it up as she rubbed the tender spot the glass bottle had fallen on.

"You scared the shit out of me! Micah today isn't a good day," she said frowning.

Micah nodded with his eyes on her. He sat the wine bottle on the dresser and helped her stand up. Bahja avoided eye contact with him as he pulled her into his arms.

For two years she'd been without a man. Without affection and she missed everything that came from having the opposite sex by your side. Bahja closed her eyes as Micah tenderly rubbed her back. She'd met him through Neveah and from the start he'd been intriguing to her.

9

He was handsome. Tall, charming and always smelled so damn good. Micah had impeccable style and lived up to his street name Pretty Boy with ease. However, it was the things that they had in common that made Bahja interested in him. Micah too had been homeless. They shared a lot of the same struggles and that made it easy for them to relate to one another.

It was Micah's not so friendly ex-girlfriend Rian that made Bahja back away from him. Bahja had unexpectedly been attacked by her and after spending hours in jail decided to walk away from the situation. She liked Micah but until he could guarantee that she didn't have to deal with that type of shit she was good on him.

"I missed your pretty lil ass," Micah expressed staring down at her.

Bahja sluggishly rubbed her face to clear her thoughts. She went over to her bed and laid down. Her head was spinning from all the wine in her system. Bahja could usually drink like a fish but had been killing bottles since she'd woken up and was now feeling it.

"Micah please," she mumbled with heavy lids.

Micah kicked off his sneakers and joined her in the bed. He pulled her into his arms and her head fell on his muscular chest. Bahja studied his handsome face as he stared back at her. Micah was the kind of man your mom warned you about. The type that looked so good you just fucking knew he would break your heart. He possessed smooth tawny brown skin with a few tattoos on his forearms but nothing major. The one tattoo that he did have that stood out the most was the heart on his chest with his mother and sisters name in it. It was extremely detailed and shaded in a way that showed off the tattoo artist's immaculate talent. Micah rocked his silky thick hair in a low cut even fade and he also had a full beard that wasn't outrageously long. He kept it groomed at all times.

The slant of his dark eyes along with the fullness of his lips always drove Bahja wild. She often lusted over him but hadn't taken it there because she did feel bad. Dave was gone and a part of her felt like it wasn't right to want someone else so soon.

"You wanna talk about him?" he asked.

Bahja smiled weakly. Micah was always so attentive to her.

"No but thank you. Let's just sleep," she murmured.

Micah began to rake his fingers through her soft strands. Bahja closed her eyes and his lips pressed against her forehead.

"It's not gone be that easy," Micah said quietly.

Bahja opened her eyes confused by his words.

"Huh?"

Micah looked down at her beautiful face and licked his lips.

"It's not gone be that easy to get rid of a nigga. I know my ex-was out of line. All that drama and shit was too much but I want this. I want you and I liked what we were building. Don't walk away from that ma. Your worth fighting for," he replied and Bahja had to close her eyes.

She hugged his body tighter as her thoughts drifted to her late husband. Micah wanted to fight for her and it had only been months, yet Dave was willing to walk away without a fight.

"I didn't love him anymore. The last thing I said was I want a divorce. He left to go have a drink and, on his way, home he was killed in that accident. Life is so short," she said quietly.

Micah continued running his hands through her hair.

"We all living to die. I hate that happened though ma. I'm sure he would be proud of you. Proud of how far you came and how good you're doing. Focus on that. I know you a little lush and shit when you wanna be, but you bent right now ma. That's not a good look," he told her.

Bahja rolled her eyes.

"I'm not a lush. I just like a good drink. I've been drinking since I was fifteen. My grandfather used to give it to me with my dinner. In other countries teenagers can legally drink so don't worry about me," she replied. "*I mean just because I have one, maybe two drinks don't make me an alcoholic*," she repeated sounding like Eddie Kane off of the Five Heartbeats.

Micah cracked up laughing.

"Something wrong with your ass but I'm just making sure you good. Just cause you not fucking with me don't mean I'm not fucking with you. I can't stop thinking about you," he revealed to her.

Bahja looked up at him searching his eyes for the truth.

"And what about Rian?"

Micah frowned.

"This is about us. You know I'm not with her and I made it clear that I'm not fucking around. If she pops up on some crazy shit it won't be good. She's not gone force a nigga to be with her," he said getting upset.

Bahja closed her eyes again with so much on her mind it made her head hurt.

"I just don't want any drama coming my way. That won't be my life," she let him know in a tired voice.

Micah tugged on her hair gently and she gazed up at him.

"And it won't be. Just give me one more chance to make you smile. I promise you won't regret it," he said and kissed her lips.

Two

"This is cool."

Micah nodded coolly. Always so handsome and laid back with his shit. Bahja watched the women in the line stare at him as he kept his attention on her. While she wore ripped jeans with a white cami and multi-colored kimono he was the star of the show. Micah had on black jeans with a white and black collard Gucci shirt that had the g's on the collar. On his feet were a pair of Gucci sneakers while a black cap covered his head. He held her hand tightly as Bahja glanced up at him.

"What sexy?" he asked and chuckled.

Bahja smiled. Since he'd popped up at her place they been back tight and so far, drama free. She'd missed him and was happy to be in his presence.

"Nothing, just happy to be around you. How was your trip to Dallas?"

Micah shrugged as they moved up a step in the line. Micah's eyes couldn't stop glancing at the woman in front of them and he paid her so much attention that it made Bahja look her way. The woman happened to glance back and when she spotted Micah she quickly walked over to them.

"Hey! I was just talking with Rian the other day. What's going on?" the attractive woman asked Micah.

Micah cleared his throat and Bahja took notice of how nervous he was acting.

"Ain't shit. Gina this is Bahja, Bahja this is Rian's friend," he said introducing the two women.

Gina looked Bahja up and down and immediately rolled her eyes. She'd only come over to be messy. She had no intentions on playing nice with the hoe that ruined her friend's relationship.

"Anyway, when you gone come to your senses?" Gina asked Micah.

"Come to his senses about what exactly?" Bahja asked looking Gina's way.

Gina looked at Bahja and laughed.

"Sweetie if I fought like you I would just keep quiet. Unless you done had some lessons."

Bahja looked Gina over and smiled at her.

"And if I looked like you sweetie I would just be fucked. What I would never want was for my girls or myself to have to beg anyone to be with me. It's rather pathetic any way you look at it. Rian knows the truth, she knows I had nothing to do with whatever happened in her relationship and at this point, I really don't care. What I won't deal with is disrespect. Clearly, your mom never took the time out to teach your ass some manners, so I'll give you some pointers. It's best to mind your own fucking business in life. Speak to people, be nice and if you're not that cute at least have a good disposition to you. Just doing little things like that can get you far," Bahja replied and wiping the smile off of Gina's face.

Micah pushed Bahja behind him as he frowned at Gina. Bahja walked away as he let Gina have it. Being around Gina and hearing her speak on the fight she'd had with Rian pissed her the fuck off. Fighting had never been her thing and she was okay with that. Bahja had never lived a life where it needed to be a necessity, so she wasn't ashamed of her lack thereof when it came to scrapping. What Bahja did know was that regardless of how good she could fight she would do it every time to protect herself.

"Hey, come here," Micah said walking up behind Bahja. His arms wrapped around her waist and instead of letting her go to the bar he took her back outside. Micah led Bahja over to the line they'd just been standing in and he grabbed her face. Bahja frowned as he peered down at her. "Don't let these bitches get to you. You know where I'm at and where I wanna be," he said before kissing her tenderly.

Micah kissed Bahja passionately as people looked on including Gina who was all in even making sure to take a picture for her friend. When Micah pulled back Bahja's lips were swollen from how hard he'd been kissing her. Micah slapped her ass and kissed her again.

"This the "D" baby. You gotta let these hoes know you not the one."

Bahja broke his gaze and looked Gina's way.

"Or you handle it so that they don't even walk up to me with the bullshit," she replied making Micah chuckle.

"And I did," he quickly added before pulling her to his side.

For hours Micah and Bahja played at the CJ Barrymore's as if they were little kids. Once they were done they headed back to Bahja's place to chill out and have a few drinks.

"Did you have fun?" Micah asked as Bahja sat on his lap.

Bahja smiled at him as his hands did things to her ass and back that made soft moans fall between her lips.

"I did. Did you?"

Micah nodded. The weed he'd smoked had his eyes hanging low. He stood up with Bahja on his lap and laid her back on the bed. Bahja's heartbeat picked up as Micah unbuckled her pants.

"Micah..." she said quietly.

Micah shook his head as his phone began to ring.

"I just wanna taste," he said and silenced the call on his phone. Micah sat his phone on the dresser before taking off Bahja's pants. Micah then took off Bahja's black thongs and his erection became so big that Bahja could immediately see it through his jeans as it begged to be freed.

Micah's phone rang again and Bahja groaned.

"It's her," she told him.

Micah turned his phone off and pulled his shirt over his head. He then leaned down and kissed Bahja passionately on the lips while staring into her eyes.

"This is about us, baby. Let me make you feel good," he said and kissed her one last time before opening her legs.

Bahja's head fell back as Micah began to suck on her center. She hadn't felt it in so long that she nearly came the minute his tongue made contact with her.

"Oh god," she said in a shaky voice.

Bahja's cell phone began to ring repeatedly. Bahja touched the top of Micah's head and he glanced up at her. His thick lips were coated in her juices as his eyes connected with her's.

"What's wrong?" he asked and began to slowly finger her.

Bahja whimpered but before she could enjoy the moment her phone rang again. Micah grabbed it before she could, and his face fell into a frown.

"Why the fuck are you calling her phone? Matter of fact fuck all of that shit. Don't ever fucking call her Rian!" he yelled and ended the call. Micah turned off Bahja's phone and sat it on the dresser.

Bahja tried to pull her legs back and Micah held them down tightly.

"Don't. You know where I been at. You know who I want and that's why the fuck she so mad. I promise you she will never call your shit again. I'll handle it. Okay?" he asked and added two fingers to Bahja's snug opening.

Bahja shook her head. She wasn't for the drama. She had so many questions and with every turn of Micah's fingers, she slowly forgot them. She closed her eyes as her body began to quiver. She was going to cum.

It was right fucking there.

Micah knew it as well. He leaned down and with the tip of his tongue flicked it rapidly against Bahja's clitoris. Bahja fisted the comforter and within seconds was releasing all over his fingers.

* * *

"Thank you for coming. Any woman that was good enough to grab my brother's attention is somebody I *have to know,*" Amor said with a smile.

Bahja stopped sifting through the clothes at Mickey's Rack to look at Amor. Micah had begged her to go shopping with his sister. Amor was a good college girl that Micah said was about her business. So far Bahja was enjoying her time with the young beautiful Amor that was even more attractive than her handsome older brother.

"Well, Micah isn't someone you can ignore. I'm sure he told you about Rian."

Amor nodded while frowning.

"And I never liked that bitch! Micah bends over backward for her and she kicks him in it every time. When he told me he'd finally put her out I swear I could have cried. Micah's special," Amor stopped talking and swallowed hard. Like Micah, she remembered the hard times her family had. To Amor, Micah was not only her big brother but the father figure she so desperately needed. So, at times she felt bad for all of the things she was hiding from him. She simply knew that once he found out he would be ready to kill her.

"I heard and I'm still in shock. Rian does have a habit of playing with Micah's emotions, but she isn't violent. I think it was everything combined that made her react that way. Please don't use that against my brother though. He isn't a bad guy," Amor replied running to Micah's defense.

Bahja took in everything Amor said but still wasn't so sure if it was all worth it. Micah had kept his word and Rian hadn't called Bahja again. However, Bahja was curious to know how she'd gotten her number in the first place and Micah had told her that Rian was just crazy.

"I know he isn't but the whole situation seems messy to me. I'm not used to that."

Amor smiled. She could tell that Bahja was cut from a different cloth.

"Are you rich?" she asked but not in a condescending way.

Bahja quickly shook her head.

"My parents are but I'm not. What made you ask me that?"

Amor shrugged. Bahja's wavy hair held a sleek shine to it. Her nails and toenails were done and while she wore plain jeans with a cream strapless bodysuit she still screamed money.

"No disrespect. I wasn't trying to be funny. I just get that vibe from you. You have so much class. I love that, and you seem sweet. I guess only time will tell if that's true."

Bahja looked at Amor and they both laughed.

"And your brother made you out to be the Virgin Mary but like you said only time will tell how true that is," Bahja retorted smiling at Amor.

Amor laughed harder and Bahja mistakenly backed into someone. She stumbled over her heels and he caught her at the waist. His alluring cologne teased her senses as he spun her around. Bahja stared up into the handsome man's dark-skinned face and lost all train of thought. She'd run into him at her home months prior because he knew her friend Neveah's fiancé. Back then she'd been caught off guard by his good looks. As he stood before her wearing black and red while sporting a cocky smirk she realized that it hadn't been her imagination.

Jigga was fine as fuck and the way her body came alive at the sight of him was startling.

"Look at fate. Sometimes she can ruin a niggas day or bring him a blessing. How you doing shorty, remember me?" he asked in his usual deep tone.

Bahja took a step back and Amor smacked her lips.

"I thought you said you were going to Cali for the weekend? What the fuck are you doing at the mall? You back cheating nigga!" Amor said loudly making Bahja and Jigga turn her way.

Bahja noticed that Amor was arguing with the man that was a few feet away from Jigga. The man was handsome as well but looked much older than her.

"I didn't tell you shit like that. Calm down with all that rowdy shit," Zayne told Amor.

Amor stared him up and down angrily before reaching up and slapping the taste out of his mouth. Bahja's jaw fell as Jigga rushed over and grabbed his cousin. He whispered something in his ear as Amor grabbed a nearby hanger and began to hit Zayne in the face with it.

"I knew your ass was back cheating! I'm pregnant with your damn kid and this is how you do me, nigga!" she yelled angrily.

Bahja quickly grabbed Amor and pulled her out of the store. They went to Amor's Range Rover and got in. Bahja stared at Amor not sure what to say and Amor laughed nervously. She smoothed down her honey blonde extensions and exhaled. Her heart was racing, and she was still mad as hell at her so-called man.

"I don't usually behave that way. I promise you I'm not ghetto," she said smiling at Bahja. When Bahja didn't crack a smile Amor's eyes watered. She dropped her head while breathing hard. "All my life my brother has been telling me about how I should be treated. How a good man was on his way to me and for a while I believed him. I believed that I could find someone like him until reality set in. The men I want. The fly ass niggas with the money, good looks, and big dicks aren't easily attainable. They're not Prince Charming. They aren't loyal, and they give no fucks

21

about breaking your heart. After getting fucked over by this punk ass college boy I met Zayne. He was at his brother's dispensary and I immediately fell for him. He was so fine and was saying all of the right things. He helped me out with my school work and even waited half a year to have sex with me. We always use condoms but one of them broke and I recently discovered I was pregnant. I'm ten weeks and when I found out it was like the mask was lifted. Bahja he's a whore. He would fuck you if we let him. I hate I ever fell for his bitch ass! And he lied about his age. Like what grown ass man lies about their age? *Zayne's* bitch ass that's who. Shit, he actually lied about his name too but let his real name slip up one night while we were drunk as hell. Please don't tell Micah. He's so proud of me for staying in college and I know this will crush him."

Bahja sighed in frustration. She'd only intended to do some shopping not get placed in the middle of Amor's bullshit. Bahja rubbed Amor's arm and smiled at her.

"People will only do to them what you allow. Be it a man or a woman. To get more you have to demand it. If your baby isn't here yet and already he's showing his ass, then that should tell you all you need to know about him. I'm not saying get an abortion, but you need to look out for Amor. No matter what don't drop out of school. A man can break your heart but don't let him ruin your life. Get your degree so no matter what you can provide for you and your child. Trust me it's the worst feeling in the world to not be able to do that," Bahja replied thinking of her own situation and how badly she struggled when Dave was killed.

"Thank you for that," Amor replied and hugged Bahja.

* * *

"How was the mall?"

Bahja watched Micah cut her youngest son Benji's hair. She hated keeping secrets from him but also didn't feel right telling business that wasn't her's.

"It was...*eventful*," Bahja replied with flashes of her time with Amor replaying in her mind. She also thought back on running into Jigga and her cheeks darkened. Bahja cleared her throat and glanced Micah's way. "Your sister is really beautiful and sweet."

Micah stopped cutting Benji's hair to peer up at her. His hooded eyes stared at her intently as he stood in her bathroom as if he belonged there. As if it was his home. He'd made it clear that he wanted a wife and a family. Bahja wasn't sure if she was ready for marriage again but she did feel blessed to have a man in her life that was looking for what she already had.

"You sure? You sound funny?" he asked.

Bahja smiled at him as her phone rung from the bedroom.

"Yes, I'm sure. We had fun and I'm going out with her this weekend."

Micah began to cut her sons hair again.

"Oh yeah? Where y'all going?"

Bahja noticed how sexy he was looking in his black basketball shorts with his white beater and she licked her lips.

"To some club in Royal Oak," she replied and walked away.

"She might be a bad influence on you!" he yelled.

Bahja laughed.

"If you only knew," she mumbled. She went into her bedroom and grabbed her cell off the dresser. She had several missed calls from her mother. She hadn't spoken with her mom in a year. Was shocked that she still knew her number. Her breathing picked up as she called her back.

"Honey, how are you?" her mom asked immediately answering the call.

Bahja cleared her throat.

"What do you want?" she asked in a tone that was everything but friendly.

"It's your father. He was in a bad car accident, but he survived! He's okay it's just he's different now. He says that we should speak to you. Check on you and the boys," her mom replied.

Bahja's emotions bubbled over and her tears fell. For years she wished to hear those words from her mom. However, as she stood in her bedroom they did nothing for her. She ended the call and placed her mom on the block list along with her father's number.

"You good?" Micah asked walking up behind her.

Bahja quickly wiped her face and nodded. She put her phone away and he pulled her into his arms. Bahja sighed as he hugged her tightly.

"The kids hungry. I thought we could hit up Flemings and get you that steak you been wanting," he said to her.

Bahja smiled. She had to admit to herself that it did feel good to have him back around.

"I would love that. How was your day? I know you said you were looking to buy that strip mall."

Micah let her go and looked her up and down in a way that set her body on fire. He gently touched her hips and gave it a light squeeze. Bahja was wearing the fuck out of some jeans and he was finding it hard to keep his eyes off of her.

"Yeah, shit is moving good. Hopefully, I can have it soon, so we can get that motherfucker up and running. I'm good now that I'm with you. Can I stay the night?"

Bahja nervously glanced around the room. She didn't mind him staying over when her sons were gone but with them being back she wasn't so sure.

Micah saw the look of uncertainty on Bahja's face and pulled her back into his arms. His hard body pressed against her's as he gazed down into her eyes.

"I know the kids here. I'll be on my best behavior. Maybe just rub it a few times. Make you feel good and shit," he said lowly.

Bahja's cheeks darkened and she slowly nodded. Micah slapped her ass while smiling.

"Bet let me go wash up," he said and walked away.

Bahja washed up her son's in the bathroom across from their bedroom and changed them into clean clothes. She then turned on their favorite cartoon movie and quickly changed into some black jeans with a white lace off the shoulders top. Bahja put mousse in her hair to wave it up and applied powder to her face and sheer gloss to her full lips. She sat with her sons once she was done and watched them while smiling as she thought of how lucky she was to have them.

"Mommy missed you two," she said and they both smiled at her before turning back to their movie.

"Emory's mom is so mad your taking them to the daycare full-time. She loves them so much already," Neveah said peaking her head into the big bedroom.

Bahja smiled at her. Neveah was carrying her pregnancy well and it showed with the beautiful glow on her face.

"I know she does. I just wanted to make it easy on all of us. I love how you all have taken us in, but it isn't her job to watch my sons. I can afford daycare now. *Thank God.*"

"Aye its, not about that. We family and my mom love them little dudes," Emory, Neveah's fiancé said walking up.

Bahja smiled at him and watched as Neveah gave him a lusty gaze.

"Well we're about to go watch Martin and lay down," Neveah said and damn near dragged Emory away from the door.

Bahja laughed.

"That's why your ass is pregnant now!" she yelled messing with her friend.

Neveah had gone through hell and back with Emory. Their story was unconventional, but it was theirs. Bahja was happy that they had made it to the other side.

"Y'all ready?" Micah asked walking up.

Bahja's sons jumped up at the sound of his voice and rushed to his side. Bahja watched him play with them before turning his attention to her. Micah wore all black with a Detroit fitted sitting on his head. Around his neck was a Cuban link chain and on his wrist was a Breitling covered in diamonds. He was clean like always and Bahja prayed she was making the right decisions. She saw the happiness in her sons' eyes whenever they looked Micah's way. She didn't wanna let them or herself down.

"Yes, let's go," she said and stood up.

Bahja walked over to them and Micah slapped her ass when she moved passed him. They left the house and got into Micah's Range Rover.

Micah took Bahja and her sons to Flemings in Livonia. After waiting for twenty minutes they were seated. They quickly ordered their food and while the boys played with each other. Bahja sat next to her oldest son while Micah sat beside her youngest son who was in a highchair. Micah smirked at Bahja as he peeped a few niggas looking her way. No matter where they went Bahja was always the center of attention.

"You looking beautiful like always ma. You working tomorrow?"

Bahja blushed. It felt so domestic to be with him and her sons in the restaurant. She nodded and smiled.

"I am, and I also decided to sign up for school. It's something I always wanted to pursue but I held it off for their dad. I let him chase his dream and I chose to stay at home with the kids. It's never too late to go back, though right?"

Micah licked his lips. He sat up and leaned across the table. His strong hand brushed against her's lovingly.

"Nah it's never too late for that. I'm proud of you. What you going back for?"

Bahja's eyes connected with Jigga's and she squirmed in her seat. She quickly brought her attention to Micah but the look he gave her was cold. He removed his hand and glanced across the room. He spotted Jigga and some nigga he didn't know sitting down with two beautiful women at their table and he chuckled. Micah looked back at Bahja and noticed she was staring down at her phone.

He knew they weren't exclusive still the idea of her entertaining anyone besides him pissed him off.

"You wanna go speak to him?" Micah asked with a slight attitude.

Bahja smiled as she set her phone down. She sipped her wine and relaxed as the cool liquid slid down her throat.

"Micah don't but I wanna go to school for journalism. I would love to start my own mommy magazine. For women that don't have it all together. I think that would be nice," she replied.

Micah stood up and went around to her side of the table. He leaned down and kissed her cheek. Bahja could feel the butterflies fluttering in her stomach as he caressed her neck.

"Anything you do will be amazing. I believe in you ma," he whispered and sealed his words with a kiss.

Micah went back to his seat and as he sat down Bahja's eyes inadvertently connected with Jigga's. He shook his head before turning his attention back to his people. Bahja looked back at Micah and was relieved when she saw he was answering a text on his phone. Bahja's phone vibrated on the table and she picked it up. Her stomach knotted up when she saw she had a message from an unknown number.

I'm trying to not step on that nigga's toes, but you can't be staring at me looking so fucking beautiful and not expect me to wanna come take you away. Don't ask how I got your number, instead ask yourself if you gonna use

28

mine? It's not a coincidence that we keep seeing each other shorty.

"You good?" Micah asked Bahja making her jump.

She quickly exited Jigga's text and looked at him. Micah was attractive, and she did feel a strong connection with him. Juggling men had never been her thing, so she chose to ignore Jigga. She blocked his number and put her phone away. She smiled at Micah and he relaxed in his seat.

"Yes, just ready to eat and go home," she replied.

Micah chuckled.

"Shit me and you both baby," he replied and Bahja made a real effort to not look Jigga's way for the rest of the night.

She wanted Micah to have all of her attention.

Three

"I see Micah pretty much spends his nights with us now. Which is a good thing because Emory and I found a house. We actually closed on it the other day. It's gorgeous Bahja!" Neveah said excitedly.

Bahja smiled and hugged her friend. They were inside of the offices of the Black Love Charity that Neveah ran and closing up for the night. After preparing for their first fundraiser they were both beat and ready to head home.

"I'm so happy for you! Where is it at?"

Neveah went over to her desk and grabbed her purse. She'd gained quite a few pounds, but it suited her well. Neveah and Emory had learned a month prior that she was carrying twin girls and weren't as surprised as everyone else. When Bahja asked her why she wasn't shocked, Neveah simply said her love angel had given them a heads up.

"I believe he said it's in Northville. Its huge and I wish you and the boys were coming with us," she replied with a pout.

Bahja waved Neveah off. She pulled out a shot from her tote bag and Neveah rolled her eyes.

"And I'm pissed that you get to drink, and I don't. I'm happy to be carrying these kids but it's like my life is being put on hold for months because of this. I keep telling Emory that wine won't hurt the babies. Hell, people smoke crack and their kids come out fine. I'm sure some red wine won't cause any damage," Neveah joked.

Bahja laughed and tossed back her drink. She threw away the empty bottle and looked at her friend.

"For your babies, you have to be at one hundred percent. Going eight or nine months without liquor is worth the health of your child. You'll get used to it and when you hear the babies cry in that hospital room you'll know that it was all worth it. I love my liquor now but with both of my kids, I was a health nut. It's women wishing they could have kids, wishing they could experience what you're feeling right now. You and Emory are being blessed with two little princesses. That's so special Neveah. Don't take that for granted," Bahja told her.

Neveah sighed while rubbing her belly.

"I won't. I swear you always know the right things to say. Are you and Pretty Boy a couple now? And did you fuck him last night?"

Bahja fell down into her seat and twirled it in a circle. She'd tossed back two shots and was feeling good. She wasn't drunk but had a nice buzz which was what she was aiming for.

"Neveah, I have a confession."

Neveah went over to her and sat on the edge of her desk.

"I'm all ears. Was it that bad?"

Bahja rolled her eyes.

"I kind of thought of Jigga while he was eating me out. I know it's wrong, but I couldn't help it! He's like always on my damn mind."

Neveah's hand shot to her mouth. She grinned at Bahja before they both started laughing.

"I'm not surprised. Jigga is that nigga. Every time he comes around I just stare down at the ground. It's like if I even take a chance and look at him my nipples might get hard. Plus, it doesn't help that Emory be watching my ass like a hawk and shit. But Pretty Boy is fine too. I thought you were falling for him."

Bahja shrugged. She was, then the drama with his ex-happened and she found herself getting turned off from him.

"I was but something changed. It was Rian and her bullshit."

Neveah stood up and rubbed her steadily growing belly.

"Or Jigga and his big ass imprint. You don't have a ring on your finger, so you should date them both. Hell, men do it all of the time. You need to know for sure who you want. Play the field before you make any huge decisions," Neveah advised her.

Bahja stared up at her.

"But what if Micah gets mad? I'm not trying to hurt him."

Neveah nodded.

"You're a good honest person. You also can't help how you feel. Put Bahja first not Micah. Shit if he wanted to be back with Rian I promise you that's where his ass would be. Don't let him bully you into being with him. Be with him because he's the only man that makes you feel good on the inside. Not because he was the first Detroit nigga that you met. I would take my time if it was me."

Bahja wished that it was that simple. After leaving work Bahja grabbed her sons from daycare, fed and bathed them before taking a hot shower. She finally climbed into bed and Micah called her. She knew that he was itching to come over, but she wasn't particularly in the mood to see him. For the last week, he'd been stuck to her like glue and she was relieved to have a break from him.

Bahja yawned as she scrolled down to Jigga's name. She unblocked him and called his phone. She closed her eyes as she listened to the line ring. Bahja also couldn't ignore the way her heart thumped wildly in her chest at the thought of talking with him.

"I hit big at MGM then you hitting my line. It's gotta be my lucky night. How you been?" he asked answering the call.

Bahja exhaled. His voice just did something to her.

"I've been good. I'm tired," she replied with her eyes still closed.

"Damn you sound like it. Wish I could come over and rock your sexy ass to sleep. Do you have a job?"

Bahja laughed lightly.

"Yes, do you?"

It was Jigga's turn to chuckle.

"Something like that. Can I bring you breakfast to your job tomorrow?"

Bahja cleared her throat. She thought of Micah and felt guilty for even talking with Jigga on the phone.

"I don't know. I am seeing someone."

Jigga laughed again.

"But you wanna be seeing me. We both grown as fuck beautiful. You don't have to sugar coat it. You feel the same shit that I do, and you interested in me. Shit I know I'm feeling the fuck out of you. I'm not into begging or pleading though sexy. That's never been my style. How about when you're looking to see me face to face by yourself you hit me up? How that sound?" he asked.

Bahja smiled.

"I like the sound of that," she said quietly.

Jigga sighed.

"And I like the sound of your voice. Got me wondering how you sound when other shit's being done to you. You have a good night beautiful. Just don't waste too much more time. I'm itching to have you. You like the next big drug and shit. I keep talking about you to my people. Dreaming about your ass and shit. Its real out here," he said making them both laugh.

Bahja's line clicked with Micah and she exhaled.

"Well I'll let you go," she told Jigga and clicked over. "Hey, you," she said talking to Micah.

Micah sucked his teeth.

"I won't go from one fucked up situation to the other. All I ask is that you keep it real with me baby," he replied.

Bahja sat up in the bed while frowning.

"Where did that come from?"

"I'm not stupid ma. Can you open the door for me?" he asked.

Bahja raised her brows.

"So, you just gone pop up at my home? It's like that?" she asked getting out of the bed.

Micah chuckled.

"I'm serious about you. Maybe you don't feel the same way and if that's the case let a nigga know. You wanna fuck with somebody else Bahja? Do you?" he asked.

Bahja's heart beat faster. Did she? Jigga was sexy, fine, handsome, anything in the category of looking good that you could name but what else did she know about him? She was actually building something with Micah and wasn't ready to let that go. She left out of her bedroom and walked down the stairs. Bahja ended the call and opened her front door. Micah stood on the other end holding a little blue Tiffany's bag along with some of her favorite wine and a to-go bag filled with her favorite seafood. Bahja's stomach growled at the smells wafting her way.

"You never answered my question," Micah said stepping into the house.

Bahja stepped back and gave him a quick once-over. Micah was wearing navy jeans with a white tee that had a white and red Pistons jersey tossed over it. He was sporting a fresh haircut and smelling better than the food. She watched him step out of his shoes and look her way. Micah always stared at her like it was his first time seeing her.

"You look tired," he said noticing her red eyes.

Bahja stood before him in a two-piece pajama pants set with her hair in two loose braids. She walked up to him and hugged his side. He seemed upset with her and the last thing she was trying to do was hurt him.

"I am. Did you miss me?" she asked him.

Micah chuckled. He grabbed her ass with his free hand and cuffed it in a way that made her cream her thongs.

"Yeah but you ain't miss me. Dodging a nigga's calls and shit. I see what time it is. If you wanna fuck with these other niggas out here just let me know Bahja," he said letting her go.

Bahja walked away and he stared down at her ample ass as he followed her up the stairs. They went into Bahja's bedroom and he stripped out of his clothes. Bahja climbed into her bed and waited on him. Micah went to the opposite side and sat down. He began to eat and the longer he ate the seafood without offering her any the angrier she became. Bahja started to breathe heavily and Micah fell out laughing.

"You not eating shit with me. You didn't even want me to come over," he said turning to her.

Bahja acted like she was about to hug him, and she grabbed his tray. She hungrily tore into the food as her cell phone started to ring. Micah grabbed the phone because it was on the nightstand beside him and he looked at the screen. He'd upgraded her to the iPhone X a month prior and it was trivial but still worked his nerves that she had niggas calling on a phone he'd paid for.

"Here you go," he said tossing the phone to her. He'd taken the liberty of picking up the call.

Bahja stopped eating her shrimp to look down at her phone. Jigga's name was displayed on the screen but the call had ended. Bahja tried to grab the phone and Micah quickly picked it up. Angrily he looked at her as he stood up.

"What's the deal with you and this nigga? You need to be telling me about that shit right now or I'm gone," he told her.

Bahja sat the tray down on her nightstand. She stood up and went over to Micah. She touched his chest and he backed up. Micah shook his head as he passed her the phone.

The only reason he was keeping his composure was because her sons were home. He wasn't trying to scare the kids.

"What the fuck is up?" he asked again.

Bahja fiddled with her shiny black phone.

"We talked once on the phone," she replied nervously.

Micah swallowed hard.

"And."

Bahja shrugged. She looked at Micah as he stood in front of her in his red Ethika boxers with his sexy body on display. Her eyes couldn't help but fall on his imprint. He might have been upset with her, but his dick wasn't as it begged to be freed from the pricey boxers.

"Bahja what else," Micah asked noticing her staring at his dick. He chuckled as he stared her way. "You just looking for any nigga to make you smile, is that it? Cause if that's the case then I can leave. You beautiful as fuck, of course, you got options but don't get this shit confused ma. A nigga not hard up for no bitch. I got options too but I'm choosing to be here with you. If you confused on who you wanna fuck with then I'll make the decision for you. I ain't got time for these fucking games," he said and went over to his clothes.

Bahja felt like shit as she watched him toss on his clothes. She went over to him and grabbed his face. Micah tried to pull back and she stood on the tip of her toes to kiss him.

"It's you and I'm sorry. I wanna build something with you," she whispered against his lips before kissing him again.

Micah took a few minutes to give in but when he did Bahja found herself on her back naked with her legs wrapped around his waist. His thick mushroom shaped head poked at her opening before he gently pushed in. Bahja moaned and her back arched up off the bed.

Micah grunted and closed his eyes. His heart raced as he felt his dick being hugged by Bahja's wet walls. She was tight as fuck.

"Damn you tight," he said and slowly started to move.

Bahja whimpered. Her body hadn't felt that type of pleasure in way too long. She opened her legs wider and Micah looked down into her eyes. The way she felt was unbelievable. Velvety soft with a snug grip and he was in pure bliss from being inside of her.

No condoms stood between them and he was able to feel all of her essence.

"You feel so good. This dick doing its job Bahja?" he asked fucking her harder.

Bahja nodded weakly. Her body was starting to shake all over. Micah felt her walls contract around him and he smirked at her.

"Yeah, it is. Relax and cum all over me," he coached pushing her legs back further.

Bahja cried and Micah began to kiss her as he fucked her so hard that he was pushing her up the bed. Between her climaxing, his girth and stroke Bahja was in heaven. Her eyes leaked with tears of joy as he finally released on her belly. Micah breathed hard as he gazed down at her.

"Block that nigga from calling you," he told her with his heart pumping wildly in his chest.

Bahja weakly nodded.

"It's already done" she whispered, and he licked his lips.

"That's what I like to hear. Let's take this shit to the shower," he said and picked her up. Micah tossed her over his shoulder and carried her away as her limp body clung onto him for dear life.

Four

"I can't believe I'm doing this," Amor said wiping her eyes.

Bahja rubbed her leg. She was a woman and she wouldn't judge.

"You're doing what you have to do. It's only if you agree, however. Do you really wanna have this abortion?" she asked her.

Amor nodded with her eyes closed. Zayne had disappeared on her. Only then did she realize how much she didn't know about him. Besides his brother's business, she had no other way to get in contact with him. All she wanted was support and he refused to give her that.

"He's a fuck nigga I swear. I asked him could we co-parent and he sent me back the eye emojis. After that, his ass has been missing in action. His brother is always nice when I see him, but I can tell even he's getting tired of my pop-ups. I refuse to bring a kid into this toxic ass situation. I can't, and I won't. I pray God forgives me for this. I feel really bad. I do," Amor replied sadly before leaning on Bahja.

Bahja rubbed Amor's arm feeling bad for her as well until the urge to turn around became so great that she had to see what was trying to get ahold of her attention. Sitting in the doctor's office was none other than Rian. Her eyes connected with Bahja's and instead of coming off angry she looked scared.

Amor looked up with Bahja and frowned when she spotted her brother's ex-girlfriend. Amor's eyes fell on Rian's stomach and she jumped up from her seat.

"Are you really about to sneak and kill his baby? Wow, how fucking cruel can you be?" Amor asked and pulled out her phone.

A few people glanced their way as Bahja stared down at Rian's very round stomach. Bahja gathered she had to be right at the limit to get an abortion.

"Amor don't! This has nothing to do with your little-spoiled ass," Rian said coming over to them.

Amor walked away and Bahja ran a rough hand through her hair. It was always fucking something with Micah. It never failed. She started to count up the weeks in her head and Rian sat beside her.

"It's his. He came over one night to tell me to leave you alone and it happened. We were both drunk, I was hurt, and he was honestly fucked up. He probably doesn't even remember it, but I do. I don't care why you or Amor is here. All I care about is handling my business. I won't bring a kid into my broken relationship," Rian said sounding defeated with the situation.

"My brother is on his way, Rian. He said that if you go through with this he's fucking you up," Amor said coming back into the room.

"Miss you all will have to leave. This is a private facility," the nurse said walking over with a doctor.

Rian stood up with Bahja and she glared at Amor.

"You little bitch. I should slap some sense into your dumb ass. He can't force me to have this kid and just why are you here?"

Amor grabbed her bag and glared at Rian.

"To get a check-up hoe," she lied and pulled Bahja away.

Bahja, Amor, and Rian walked out of the clinic and found Micah pulling into the parking lot damn near on two wheels. Bahja stood back quietly as she watched him jump out of his Range Rover and walk over to them angrily. Micah looked down at Rian's big bump and shook his head. The anger that covered his face was enough for all of the women to stay quiet. Neither of them wanted to make him angrier.

"I can't believe you would even take your big ass up in there to try and have that shit! That's fucking murder. What the fuck is wrong with you!" he yelled making Rian jump.

Rian began to cry and the whole scene was all too much for Bahja. She walked away, and Amor followed after her. They quickly got into Amor's car and Amor pulled off. Bahja glanced over at Amor and cleared her throat.

"I like you, Amor. Your immature but that's to be expected. You're young and with age comes wisdom. What you did today wasn't right. You were just asking me to not judge you and the first thing you do is call your brother when you see Rian. She had a right to make her own decision as well. Granted I wouldn't have gone if I was that big but who are we to judge her? Just take me home," Bahja said tired of the bullshit.

Amor shook her head.

"Micah is my everything. All he ever wanted was kids and I wasn't about to let her get over on him again. My brother adores the ground you walk on. Even with that baby, he will still want you so don't be worried about that," Amor replied wanting to reassure her of Micah's love for her.

Bahja laughed lightly. She pulled a small wine bottle from her bag and popped the cap on it. She glanced over at Amor and realized that she had a whole lot to learn about life.

"Amor I wasn't worried about that. Even you can see that a baby won't keep a man so that was the furthest thing from my mind. We have to treat people how we want to be treated. I can't stand Rian. I met her and immediately I let her know about your brother and whatever it was we had going on because I didn't want drama. I didn't come into that situation as a mistress. When he came to Atlanta he told me they weren't together. Still, she showed her ass, attacked me and everything. Since then she's been a fucking nightmare to deal with. I get it they have years under their belt but that's on them not me. Even with all of that being said calling your brother never entered my mind. It wasn't our business to tell. You up there about to get rid of your baby yet you tell on her. That was foul so just take me home," she repeated getting irritated with the situation.

Amor rolled her eyes while sucking her teeth.

"That I can do," she replied and quickly took Bahja home.

Bahja walked into her place with a frown on her face. Neveah was gone with Emory to Atlanta for the weekend to see her parents and the boys were still in daycare. Bahja didn't have to get them for at least four more hours so she decided to take a quick shower.

She made herself some chicken salad and instead of laying down got on her laptop. She bought a website and after watching a few tutorials began to build her mommy blog. It wasn't a magazine, but it was a step in the right direction. And within the comfort of her own home, New

Age Mommy was born. It was a blog about anything pertaining to motherhood.

Bahja had to step away from her website to pick up her sons and cook dinner for them. Micah walked into her home with Neveah and Emory hours later when the boys were asleep and Bahja was slightly peeved. She understood that he was family with them but still that was her place of peace. He didn't have the right to just walk up in her shit like he was paying something on the bills.

"You wasn't picking up your phone. We were worried ma," Micah said stepping into the living room.

Bahja closed her laptop and peered up at him. Micah had on workout gear with a black Detroit fitted. She watched Neveah stare at them questioningly as Emory hugged her from the back.

"*He* was worried. I figured you were sleep. Are you gonna come to see the house with me in the morning?" Neveah asked.

Bahja nodded while still staring at Micah. It was the way his eyes bored into her that made her nervous. The situation with Rian made her very uneasy.

"Sure," Bahja mumbled and Neveah and Emory walked away.

Micah came over to Bahja bringing with him the strong stench of weed. He leaned down and kissed her cheek.

"Come take a shower with me," he whispered. He grabbed her hand before she could respond and took her upstairs. While Micah undressed Bahja made sure her sons were still sound asleep in their bedroom. She joined Micah in the bathroom and silently took off her clothes. He turned on the water and led Bahja into the large shower. Bahja grabbed the loofah and Micah took it from her. He pulled her to his hard, tattooed body and she gazed up at him.

Bahja felt such conflicting feelings as she looked up into his eyes.

"It's your baby?"

Micah swallowed hard.

"I slipped up once when I went to check her about fucking with you. We weren't committed to each other at the time but still, I'm sorry."

Bahja looked away from him and his strong hands grabbed her face. They slid down her body to her hips and effortlessly he picked her up. His dick seemed to immediately know where to go as it started to poke at her opening. He tried to push in and Bahja shook her head.

"Micah no," she protested. "You're running back to her unprotected then coming over here. Put me down."

Micah kissed her neck. The last thing he wanted to do was put her down.

"I'm sorry and it was only that one time. That's not where I wanna be," he whispered while teasing her opening with his head. "This changes nothing baby," Micah promised and slowly slid inside of Bahja. Bahja closed her eyes as he filled up her tight walls. "Damn baby, you wet," he said and groaned.

Bahja whimpered, and Micah tossed her legs into the crooks of his arms. He pressed her against the shower wall and Bahja cried out. He was so deep she felt like it would split her in half.

"Baby don't let this run you away," Micah said and groaned. Bahja's wetness was driving him delirious.

Bahja kept her eyes closed not wanting to see his face and it wasn't long before they were both falling apart inside of the steamy shower.

* * *

"This place is huge! I'm so happy for you two," Vashti said looking around.

Vashti was Neveah's fiancé sister. Neveah beamed with pride as she showed Bahja and Vashti around her five-bedroom home. She took them into the master bedroom that was halfway furnished and over to her closet. It was the real definition of a walk-in closet. It housed separate sections, a sitting area along with a vanity and makeup corner. Bahja looked around at all of the boxes and shoes that needed to be put up and shook her head.

"This is just so beautiful. I'm so happy for you!" she told her for the millionth time.

Neveah smiled but it didn't quite reach her eyes. She shifted from one foot to the other as she stared at Bahja.

"I heard Micah telling Emory that Rian was pregnant. What the fuck is that shit about?"

"She's what?" Vashti asked shocked by Neveah's revelation.

Rian was once a stylist at her salon and a friend of her's until Rian learned about Micah moving on with Bahja.

Bahja sat down in the chair at Neveah's vanity and dropped her head. All night she'd tossed and turned as Micah rested beside her. He'd placed his phone on vibrate but it hadn't stopped it from ringing all night long. Micah never picked up but Bahja was certain it was Rian blowing him up.

Bahja looked up at Neveah and Vashti with watery eyes. She wasn't necessarily crying over Micah. It was the situation in a whole that had her drained.

Already.

"Bahja," Neveah said and Bahja shook her head while holding her hand up.

"Long story short I ran into Rian yesterday. I won't say where I was because it's not my business to tell just know she was very pregnant. She was about to get an abortion and Micah was notified of that. Not by me. He shows up acting a fool on her and I leave. He told me last night after popping up with you guys that it's still about me and him. How he is invested in making things work with me. How it was only one time. *Blah blah blah.* He said Rian is twenty-four weeks pregnant with his son. I honestly don't know how to feel. All I can think about is how ignorant she was before. I don't wanna deal with her but then I feel guilty for feeling that way because he's so good with my kids. I'm confused on what to do guys," she revealed.

Vashti found a seat on one of the ottomans in the room and Neveah sat beside her on the floor. Neveah rubbed her belly as they stared Bahja's way.

"That's bullshit! Why leave her if you're gonna go back and fuck her! Hell, you were attacked by this girl and spent the night in jail and his way of handling that was to put his dick in her?" Neveah asked.

Bahja shrugged.

"I don't know. He never said which time it was. All I know is that she's pregnant and now I feel like I need to run for the fucking hills. Then I look into his eyes and I wonder if cutting him off is the right thing to do. Micah makes me happy. He's good to my sons."

47

Vashti nodded smiling at her.

"And you like that feeling that he provides right?" she asked.

Bahja smiled. She thought of the security that came over her whenever he was near.

"I do," she admitted quietly.

Neveah looked her way.

"But it's nothing another man can't give you. I like Micah too. We all see how he cares about you but aren't you at least curious to know if this baby will push him back to Rian?" Neveah asked her.

Bahja looked at her friends and shrugged.

"If that's the case then he never really was mine anyway. But besides him, I started a blog. I signed up for school in the fall and I'm taking some journalism classes. It's my goal to have my own mom magazine," Bahja said changing the whole tone of the room.

Vashti and Neveah grinned at her words.

"What! I love it! Bahja yes," Neveah said and kicked her leg playfully.

Bahja laughed.

"Listen I would have jumped up, but you know I picked up some weight. I can't just be hopping up like I used to. Probably pass out or some shit," Neveah joked and they all laughed.

"No but seriously, we're both proud of you and you have our support with anything. You can even throw your website launch party at the salon. We're so happy for you!"

Vashti said standing up. She hugged Bahja and Bahja smiled at her two friends lovingly.

She'd gone years without the love from her immediate family and God had found a way to still placed people in her life that loved and cared for her. She was very grateful for them.

"I love you all too. We need another church date in the near future," she told them.

Neveah nodded while smiling and Vashti stared their way.

"Just without the fighting!" she blurted out making Neveah and Bahja start laughing again.

The one time they'd gone to church together they'd ended the day in jail after fighting with Rian. It had been a day that Bahja would forever remember.

Hours later Bahja sat outside of the shelter in downtown Detroit. She'd spent two hours passing out food and helping clean up. Being around people in need and helping them was still a passion of her's. Never would she forget the days when she couldn't feed her kids let alone herself.

"Look at you," Jigga said taking a seat beside Bahja.

Bahja stopped staring at the street and glanced his way. She'd once again hit him up and like before he talked to her with no problem. She'd called Micah a few times and all of her calls had gone unanswered.

"I shouldn't have called you," Bahja said admiring Jigga's masculine beauty.

His dark skin had a natural shine to it. The black jeans that he wore with a white crew neck looked appealing

49

on him and the jewelry decorating his body was simple yet stylish. Jigga smiled at her revealing his pretty white teeth and Bahja had to look away to keep herself from drooling at the mouth.

"But you did. I told you I'm ready for you whenever you are. What's going on with this little setup?" Jigga asked and glanced back at the shelter.

Bahja looked back at him and swallowed hard. She wanted to touch his face and see if it was as soft as it looked. Rub her hands across the beard lining his jaw and finally press her lips against his full ones. She was very attracted to him.

So much so that it frightened her.

"Could you date someone that was expecting a baby with another person?" she asked changing the subject.

Jigga sat forward and placed his elbows on his knees. It was then that Bahja was able to see the tattoos covering the side of his neck.

"I wouldn't flat out say no but I wouldn't want to be in some shit like that. I don't have any kids, but I see the bond that it places on people. That's a lifetime commitment. If you know for sure that the people don't wanna be together then you should be good but if it's any doubt, there I would say to watch out for you."

Bahja received everything he was saying, and she smiled.

"I need to get my shit together," she said with a laugh to keep from crying.

Jigga scooted her chair over to him and he placed his hand on her thigh. Bahja closed her eyes as he gently rubbed her leg back and forth.

"Sometimes you have to step out of a situation to see it for what it is. Pray on it beautiful then let him handle it. You know I'm ready to take you anywhere you wanna go but that's only if you ready. I know one thing. A nigga is supposed to do everything but make you sad. I don't know what part of the game that shit is," he said and they both laughed.

Bahja didn't either but what she did know was that sitting with Jigga outside of the shelter had been the highlight of her week.

Five

"This is different," Vashti said sitting downstairs with Bahja.

Bahja nodded thinking the same thing. They'd hosted Neveah and Emory's shower two weeks ago and was glad they'd gotten it out of the way because Neveah had woken up that morning in labor. Neveah and Emory had moved completely into their new home and was having a home birth for their girls.

Bahja and Vashti weren't aware that you could have home births for twins but apparently, you could as long as you weren't due to have a caesarian.

"Right, this nigga got food here and everything. This some Hollywood shit," Hayden, who was Emory's cousin commented sitting downstairs in the living room with everyone.

It was only a small crowd of Neveah and Emory's closest relatives. Neveah's parents were on a flight headed to Detroit while Emory's parents sat downstairs with everyone. Bahja looked at Vashti as she held her sleeping son and she smiled. Vashti's man was serving time and Bahja was proud of how well Vashti was handling things.

"How have you been?"

Vashti smiled at Bahja. Over the last few months, they'd grown really close. It had been hard at first because Vashti felt incredibly guilty for Rian attacking Bahja, but she'd learned to not place what grown people did on her. She accepted the fact that she was no longer friends with Rian and had welcomed Bahja into her life with open arms.

"I've been hanging in there. Some days are easy then some days I struggle to even get out of the bed. I miss him," Vashti replied with sadness clinging onto her every word.

Bahja rubbed her leg.

"And I'm sure he misses you as well. Try to remember the good times when that depression falls over you. You have to know that nothing lasts forever. Not even his sentence," Bahja told her.

Vashti smiled always ready to receive words of encouragement from Bahja.

"I'll do that. What about you, where is Pretty Boy?" she asked calling Micah by his street name.

Bahja shrugged. That was the million-dollar question. She seemed to see less and less of him as the days rolled by.

"I'm not Rian. I won't chase any man. Ever. If he wants to see me he will have to show it. I won't run after him and I'll leave it at that."

Vashti laughed.

"And I would never expect for you to."

"Aye she wanna see Bahja and Vashti," Emory said walking downstairs.

Vashti passed her son to her mom and stood up with Bahja. They followed Emory upstairs and into his large master bedroom. In the center of the room was a pool. The water was being poured into it as Neveah sat on a birth ball with a frown on her face. She wore a hospital gown with her hair pulled to the top of her head. Emory gave her a quick kiss before going to the bathroom to change his clothes for the birth.

On the side of the room was four midwives assisting Neveah with the delivery. Because she was carrying twins the center she was working with wanted extra hands available at all times. They were also checking her regularly to make sure the babies were breathing, making sure they weren't breached and also checking to make sure she was dilating how she should be.

With twin home births you always had to be extra cautious and so far, everything was going as it should be.

"Aww Neveah," Bahja said with her eyes tearing up.

Neveah smiled weakly at her friends.

"I'm so mad at you two. You bitches lied! These fucking contractions hurt," she said making every woman in the room laugh.

"You were in the room with me so don't even try it," Vashti replied walking over to Neveah.

Emory stepped out of the bathroom and went over to his lady.

"She good, she's almost there. You want some drugs?" he asked her lovingly.

Neveah whimpered as another contraction rolled around her waist like a painful tidal wave.

"No," she said quietly. "I want my mom. Emory let's just see if I can push," she said taking the pain as best as she could.

Emory caressed her neck and kissed her on the lips.

"I love you," he whispered to her while Bahja smiled on.

That was what she wanted. For a man to love her so much that everyone near them could feel and see it.

"We'll give you two some privacy," Bahja said and walked away with Vashti following her.

The two women went back downstairs and Bahja was shocked to see Micah in the living room. He looked up from his phone as she approached the sofa he was sitting on and he smiled.

"Hey baby," he said pulling her down beside him.

Bahja smiled at him and he pulled his phone back out. She tried to not pry but could see he was texting Rian.

"Bahja I heard about the blog and we are all so proud of you," Emory's mom Erykah said glancing her way.

Bahja thought of her blog and smiled. It had been doing really well and she was now getting things sent for her to review just because of the influence she had over moms on the web.

"Thank you. I can't believe it's doing so good though."

Erykah waved her off.

"We knew it would be," she replied as Bahja looked back over at Micah.

He was still texting on his phone while smiling. Bahja stood up and decided to step outside to get a breath of fresh air. Her first thought was to text Jigga, but she decided not to. He was a good ass dude and she refused to only fuck with him when she was mad. That wasn't fair to him. Instead, she went to her blog app on her phone and decided to update her followers on what was going on with her.

She titled the blog post. **Lost in translation.**

In a quest of finding myself, I found this blog. I also thought I had found new love. It wasn't easy to open my heart up to someone new. My late husband was all I had ever known but I took a chance. Things were good in the beginning but now they aren't. Something that I thought was so promising isn't anymore and I'm lost trying to figure out what's next? A good situation as somehow translated into a bad one for me. I'm not sure what to do.

Almost immediately women started to comment on the post but the answer that stood out the most was from a **King Jigga**. Under his name read the response.

Sounds to me like it's also time to find a door for that man to walk out of so that I can walk thru.

Bahja smiled to herself as she watched her women followers like his comment and even reply to him saying that he should do all that he could to make Bahja his.

"She's pushing!" Vashti said stepping outside.

Bahja put her phone away and quickly went into the house. She waited downstairs and thirty minutes later they were joined with Neveah's parents. Neveah's mom was ushered into her room while her father stayed behind with everyone else.

"This shit got me excited for my little man," Micah said to no one in particular.

Bahja found herself rolling her eyes and scooting closer towards the other side of the couch. Micah picked up on her mood and scooted over to her. He threw his arm over her shoulder and kissed her cheek.

"You been okay?" he asked her.

Bahja looked at him and smiled.

"If you have to ask me how I've been then it's a problem," she replied and stood up.

"They're both healthy and so beautiful. Eden and Ella," Neveah's mom Ladonna said walking down the stairs with happy tears covering her cheeks.

Bahja's own eyes watered and she began to cry. She remembered the nights her friend would call her in shambles behind the situation she was in with her fiancé. She remembered telling her to pray and know that things would be alright. Then, of course, like always God came through. Bahja was trying to stay hopeful and know that in the end, everything would work out for her as well. Bahja didn't want to be one of those people that preached things that she didn't believe in herself. No, she wanted to say that God had her and believe it, so she shook off the sadness consuming her body. She shook off the fear of being alone, the fear of never having that one true love and she gave it to her God.

She knew that if nobody else could help her that he could, and he was the perfect man for the job.

Six

Two Months Later.

Sorry I couldn't take that flight with you. Rian has been sick as fuck lately. I had to be there for her. Don't be mad ma.

"Thank you for coming. They are so handsome."

Bahja put her phone away choosing to not reply to Micah's text. She looked at her mom briefly before looking around the formal living room that she'd sat in millions of times before as a child. Everything was still the same. Even the décor which was kind of shocking to her but the condition of it was pristine. Not a dust particle in sight and it smelled of lilies.

Bahja's two small sons sat on the floor playing with their new toys in their matching black polos and khaki shorts. They were both handsome and replicas of their late father. Bahja could see her mother staring down at them with a big smile on her face. She wanted to still be angry with her family. A part of her never wanted to forgive them for what they'd done to her.

"We missed you and we're sorry," her mom Bina said making her look her way. She stood up and went over to Bahja. Her mom someone who never wore the same dress twice bent down in front of her and touched her legs. Bahja's mother was in great shape and looked more like her sister than her parent. "Please forgive us. Please, Bahja we want all three of you back in our lives and we're so sorry about Dave. The things we did, the things we said. My goodness, we can't take them back, but we can make up for them. Please," her mom begged now crying.

Bahja dropped her head and her father's hand was placed on the top of her shoulder.

"Please baby," he begged in his deep tone. He'd faced death, saw it coming for him but his life had been spared. He could now see the error in their ways. He'd been ignorant and so had his family. To know he'd placed his own flesh and blood out onto the street broke his heart. They didn't deserve her forgiveness, but he prayed they still got it.

"Mama," Bahja's son Benji questioned when he saw she was crying.

Bahja smiled at him and held out her hand. Her two sons stood up and joined her on the sofa. Her mom stood and Bahja looked up at her.

"Benji and Bryan this is your grandparents," she said making both of her parents smile through teary eyes. Bahja had so many reservations. She could still remember the nights she'd slept in her car. The days she had to wash up in the public restroom because she had no home. Things of that nature placed hate in her heart towards her family. When she'd needed them most they'd let her down. However, it was at that moment that she could hear the Lord. He told her to let go. He told her to forgive. Vengeance was his. Bahja knew that it wasn't her place to condemn them. She knew that her parents would have to answer to God for all that they had done to her. She chose to forgive and let go. She was happy. Her pain hadn't been in vain. She still had come out on the other side. She wouldn't act as if nothing ever happened, but she would be open to rebuilding a connection with them especially for the sake of her sons. As long as their intentions were good then she would consider it.

"Thank you, baby, now give them here!" her mom said excitedly and grabbed her oldest son while her father grabbed the smallest one.

Hours later Bahja sat with her father on the back terrace. Her parents had a main estate in the suburbs of Atlanta in Buckhead that sat on five acres of land. Everything from a golf course to a pool house sat on their property. Bahja and her father sipped on his favorite brandy while staring out at the vast backyard.

It was through her father that she acquired her love for liquor. They weren't addicted to it, but they often indulged in it and Bahja knew how to pick a good wine out in her sleep. Her father had a cellar filled with expensive wine.

"I've missed you so much. You're so beautiful baby and those boys of yours are something else. They're bad and they could use a spanking," he semi-joked. "But they are handsome young men. This woman that helped you, tell me about her," he said.

Bahja smiled as she thought of Neveah.

"She's the sister I've always wanted. She took me in daddy and so did her family. I will forever love them for that. The car I have belongs to her. The home we stay in is all thanks to her. Hell, even my job. I met her at the shelter."

Bahja's father frowned. His handsome face covered with confusion.

"The shelter?" He repeated quietly.

Bahja sipped her drink and glanced over at him.

"Daddy after Dave died I had nothing. I paid for his service and a few months later I lost our home. We had no money in the bank. I never had a job besides working for the family, so I wasn't qualified for anything. It wasn't until we were out on the streets that I was able to find one. I did odd jobs and sometimes I would make enough to afford a motel and other times I didn't, so we would sleep in the car."

Bahja's father abruptly stood up. Hearing the hardships his daughter faced due to his ignorance was too much for him to handle. He stared up at the sky as pain shot through his heart. He'd failed her and his grandsons tremendously.

"I'm very sorry," he said full of remorse before walking away.

Bahja decided to give him his time and finished her drink. She attempted to call Micah as she climbed into her bed but was blindsided by a text message from Rian. Bahja's heart pounded as she stared at photos of Micah laying in Rian's bed. He was fully clothed with his hand on her round belly. Bahja sent her back a smiley face not willing to play into her game and Bahja sent her back an emoji with the woman shrugging.

You might as well just let him go. He can't seem to stay out of this bed. Are you big mad or lil mad? Let me know boo.

Bahja forwarded the photo to Micah and blocked Rian's number. She received another text only this time it was from Jigga. Bahja hadn't seen him since the shelter but had been texting him sporadically. It wasn't anything serious just friendly chatter.

Woke up with you on my mind and shit shorty. All I can think about is how sad you was looking the last time I saw you. It fucked me up to see somebody so fucking pretty look so hurt. Trust when I say that shit it's not all physical.

61

It's something about you that just makes a nigga uneasy and shit. Like my body knows you the one and shit. Still, I won't pressure you for nothing you not ready for. You don't have to text me back I know it's been some weeks since we text and shit. Just wanted you to know that you got people pushing for you. Shit, I don't even know your full fucking name but I'm praying for you. Have a good night beautiful.

Bahja's face turned into a smile as she read over his text several times. He seemed to always know when to text or call. She licked her lips as she text him back.

Hey you. Things are better for me. I'm just getting my shit together like I told you I needed to. I didn't know you prayed for me but thank you and know after hearing that we'll be praying for each other. It's Bahja Sarkissian.

Minutes later a text from Jigga came in.

Yeah, we gotta make that Bahja Akachi.

Bahja found herself grinning at her phone before putting it away. She rested her head on her pillow as her father stepped into her room. He placed a check on her pillow then gave her a chaste kiss on her forehead and she gazed up at him.

"Nothing can fix what we've done but like your mom said before we will die trying to make things right. Even if you don't want the money take it for them. Give them the financial security that they need sweetie. I also want Neveah's parent's number, but I can get it in the morning," he said before leaving out of the bedroom.

Bahja looked at the check and her stomach knotted up. The zeroes seemed to be endless. Her father knew her well. She didn't want their money. For most of her life she'd depended on them and when she'd needed them most they'd let her down. Now she was back on her feet without the help of them and it felt great. However, Bahja thought of her sons. For her kids, she would put her pride to the side and cash the check. She'd place the money into trust funds for them and also buy a car. Finally, she could give Neveah back her Beamer and give her the money for the house. Bahja smiled to herself and closed her eyes. She had so many things to be thankful for that Rian and her stunts were irrelevant.

"Thank you, God. Thank you," she whispered.

Seven

"I'm overly joyed right now. This blog turned into something amazing. I never knew that I could relate to so many moms but here I am. With the help of my family, I have created a magazine out of it. This magazine means so much to me. These last two months have been hectic. From finding a building and employees down to what kind of paper I will use I have been stressed. I mean in between all of that I had to still be a mom," Bahja said and everyone laughed.

Bahja grinned as her eyes scanned Vashti's salon that had been transformed into her magazine launch party. With the help of her loved ones, she'd made her dream a reality. It hurt Bahja to step away from Neveah's charity, but she had to chase her own dreams and Neveah was loving enough to understand that. Bahja now employed six people and they worked out of a small office space in downtown Detroit that she rented out. She'd been on two morning news shows and had close to a million followers online thanks to her blog. Women gravitated to her. They understood the struggle. They loved her spirit and it made her blog a hit. She was excited about the things to come and feeling overwhelmed by her sudden success.

Bahja looked around the room once more for Micah and sighed.

He was a no-show. Rian was well into her pregnancy and Bahja found herself talking to him through text more than she felt she should have been, but it was like she'd told Vashti months ago. She refused to beg for his time or attention. Instead, she'd given her all to her kids, family and new magazine. And by putting herself first she'd done something that she never thought she could do. God had truly been good to her.

"So, let's drink this wine because you all know I love a good wine and let's celebrate women. Women don't get the credit they deserve. Moms never get the accolades that they should. It's not easy and if anyone could do it then everyone would be doing it. Let's celebrate us!" Bahja said and raised her glass.

"You did good sis. We proud as fuck of you," Emory said walking over.

He was without Neveah. Their kids were doing well but with the girls being so young Neveah chose to hang back with them and Bahja completely understood. Neveah was one of her biggest supporters and she knew that her girl always had her back. Bahja also knew that being a mom was something that needed to always come first.

Bahja smiled at Emory glad to see he'd been able to show up. She gave him a hug and when he stepped to the side her breathing picked up. Jigga stood beside him holding a dozen pink roses. He wore all white and it looked amazing on his chocolate skin. Jigga's fade was freshly cut, he wore wood framed Cartier glasses with a Cartier watch. The way his eyes slid up and down Bahja made her swallow hard.

"I'm proud of you shorty," Jigga said in a sonorous voice that made her knees go weak. He pulled her into a hug and her body caved into him. Bahja hugged him tightly as his presence gave her a feeling she'd never felt before.

"Are you?" she asked quietly.

She'd been spinning him. Every now and then they would text but for the most part, she'd cut him off. Bahja had wanted to focus on her goals but also, she wasn't looking to lead him into anything until she was completely done with Micah. Something that she saw happening in the near future.

Jigga rubbed her back in slow deliberate circles. Bahja was wearing a cream pantsuit that stuck to her skin. Brought out the curves on her body and complimented her olive toned skin. Her hair was in loose flirty curls and her makeup like always was flawless.

"Hell, yeah I am. So, you ready for me or are you still trying to be lonely and shit?" he asked making her smile.

Bahja cleared her throat in an attempt to regain control of her nerves that he had going haywire.

"What the fuck is this?" Micah asked angrily as he walked up with flowers as well. His arrangement was so large he could barely hold it in one hand.

Jigga let go of Bahja and Emory shook his head. With Rian being pregnant he hadn't seen Micah in months. No one really had, so he was surprised to see him at Bahja's opening. Truthfully, he thought Micah had gone back to Rian.

"What's up nigga," Emory said trying to dap him up.

"Emory, I see what kind of fake shit you on," Micah said to him.

Emory chuckled. Micah was his people. They'd grown up together, so he wasn't looking to fight with him. He also wasn't going to take the shit talking either.

"You know a nigga ain't never been fake. I can't stop nobody from coming to some shit that's not mine," Emory replied staring Micah's way.

Micah waved him off and glared at Jigga. Jigga smirked at him and grabbed Bahja's hand.

"I can't take somebody that's not taken nigga so chill out with the looks and shit. This about Bahja ain't it?" Jigga asked pulling Bahja to his side. He'd played it safe in the beginning, but he saw how Micah was moving and felt like he was wasting Bahja's time. Jigga was ready to give her all of the love that he felt she deserved. "It's clear you don't appreciate her so why the fuck you wasting her time?" Jigga asked Micah.

Micah watched Bahja hold another man's hand and anger filled him up immediately.

"Why the fuck you speaking on some shit that don't concern you motherfucka! How many times do she gotta tell you to get the fuck out of her face?" Micah asked making a few people look their way.

"Aye now isn't the time for all of this," Emory said trying to calm Micah down.

Micah ignored Emory and shoved Jigga hard as he could making him fall back with Bahja.

"What the hell!" Vashti yelled as she watched Bahja fall on top of Jigga.

"This fuck nigga," Jigga cursed as he stood up with Bahja. Bahja was pulled to the side by Vashti as Jigga was attacked by Micah. Women screamed as Micah and Jigga tore apart Bahja's magazine launch party.

"Micah stop!" Bahja yelled in shock at what was happening.

"Nigga don't want her then gets mad when she finds somebody that do on some hoe shit," Jigga said punching Micah so hard that he momentarily closed his eyes.

Micah angrily pulled out his gun not willing to ever take an *L* fighting. Micah aimed the gun at a smirking Jigga while breathing raggedly.

"I should shoot your bitch ass," Micah told him.

Jigga smiled at him as he brushed his hand over his fade.

"Niggas that kill don't do no talking," he replied lowly noticing how frightened the people were at Bahja's party. "This shit is foul as hell nigga," he said to him.

Emory and his cousin quickly pulled Micah out of the building not wanting things to escalate and Bahja sighed with relief. Jigga fixed his clothes and turned to Bahja. She was so angry that she was crying. He shook his head hating that he'd aided in placing the tears on her face.

"Let me clean this shit up shorty," he said and grabbed the flowers off the ground.

Bahja stood back angrily as he picked up everything he and Micah had ruined. Some other men began to help him including Bahja's father. Bahja was shocked to see her father actually talking with Jigga. Her parents told her they were past the color shit but to openly see him speak with a black man warmed her heart in many ways.

"I'd love to hear more about your business," Bahja's father told Jigga as they continued straightening up the room.

Jigga patted his arm.

"You definitely will. I apologize again for all of that. This night is about your beautiful daughter," Jigga said to him.

Bahja's father glanced over at her.

"That it is," he replied, and they continued to straighten up the room.

"Let's get a drink pretty girl," Vashti said walking up.

Vashti and Bahja went to the bar and grabbed a drink. Vashti sipped on water since she was still breastfeeding while Bahja sipped on some Moscato. Bahja watched the men in attendance continue to fix up the party with Jigga leading the pack and she sighed.

"I don't know what to say," she mumbled.

Vashti shook her head.

"I feel the same way. Micah was completely out of line. I don't know every detail of your relationship with him but what he did tonight was very selfish. He hasn't even been coming around," Vashti vented.

Bahja laughed lightly.

"Exactly but chooses to pop up at my party and show his ass. He only knew about it through text. I can barely get his ass to answer the damn phone. He's too busy running up behind Rian to know what's going on with me," Bahja admitted sadly.

"I just wanted to apologize for what you all witnessed. Bahja worked hard for this to happen and I don't want my actions to fall negatively on her," Jigga said stepping into the middle of the room. His eyes connected with Bahja's and he smiled at her. "I'm sorry beautiful. Don't let nothing mess up your night," he said to her.

Everyone in the room clapped still happy to be in attendance and Bahja dropped her head while still smiling. Jigga walked up on her and pulled her to his side. He stared down at Bahja intently as she held her glass of wine.

"Come to the car and blow one with me," he said and winked at her.

Bahja nodded. She grabbed a flute on their way out of the salon and Jigga took her over to his Maserati truck. He opened the door for her and she got in. Bahja relaxed in the seat as Jigga climbed into his truck. He leaned his seat all of the way back getting even more comfortable and pulled a blunt from his middle console. He sparked it up and his noir-like eyes glanced over at Bahja. Just being in his presence made her antsy. She could feel her leg jumping and was having a hard time looking him in the eyes.

"Why you do that?" he asked noticing she'd done that before when he'd pulled up on her at the shelter.

Bahja frowned at his question.

"What?"

Jigga tapped her shaky leg and she laughed. She swatted his hand away and he hit his blunt. Bahja watched the weed flow from between his thick lips and she swallowed hard. All she could think of is how good it would feel to have them wrap around her areolas.

"Stop that," he commented.

Bahja glanced down at her flute that was filled with wine.

"Stop what?"

Jigga placed his hand on her thigh.

"Stop staring at me like you wanna fuck me. I'm trying to be a gentleman with you. Looking at me like that gone bring the nigga up out of me. Unless that's what you want. Is it? You in need of something shorty? Just let a nigga know and I got you," he said lowly.

Bahja pressed her thighs together and swallowed her wine in one sip. She sat the glass down and Jigga sat up. He couldn't take it. Her presence was calling to him, tugging him her way and enough was enough. He'd sat back for months and went without her. Wondered what she was doing? If Micah was making her happy and clearly, he wasn't.

"Shorty that nigga isn't on his job. By now you should be married with a baby in your belly. Why the fuck you wasting your time with that clown ass nigga? I know he's not making you happy," he told her.

Bahja closed her eyes when she felt his hands caress her neck. Jigga put his blunt out and slowly unbuttoned her suit jacket. His hands roamed freely inside of it and they brushed against her white lace bra. Bahja moaned when he tweaked her nipples.

"*Jayvion*," she moaned calling him by his real name.

Jigga slid his hands up to her neck and turned her head to face him. The look in his eyes was commanding. Filled with so much lust and adoration. The stare was intense, so much so that Bahja had to break away from it. Jigga kissed the bottom of her chin before sliding his tongue around to her thick lips. The weed and liquor he had sat on his tongue still he tasted good as he brushed it against her's.

Bahja moaned and his teeth sunk into her lip.

"I wanna fuck you so bad. Stretch out that tight lil pussy and bust all in her," he said as he began to massage her breast again. The nipple stimulations quickly sent Bahja close to the edge. She'd never felt anything like it.

"Jigga," she said quietly as her skin prickled all over.

Jigga stuck his tongue in her ear as he squeezed her nipples. He'd squeeze them hard, then rub the tip and it was literally sending her over the edge.

"Jigga what? You wanna cum, let go and do it. Cum for me Bahja," he demanded and kissed her neck sensually.

Bahja's eyes closed tightly as her body gave way to his lusty demands. Her walls contracted, and she came from nipple stimulation. She struggled to catch her breath as she came down from her high.

"Did I just cum?" she asked quietly with a dry mouth.

Bahja's body was still tingling all over.

Jigga chuckled before kissing her cheek. He slid his hands into her pants and rubbed at the moist seat of her panties. Bahja's underwear were soaked. He stuffed two of his fingers into her opening after pushing her panties to the side and Bahja moaned when he moved them back and forth.

"Yeah, you did. That pussy came, and I didn't even touch her but when I put this dick up in you she gone squirt for me. I'ma make her do magic," he promised and fingered her so good that she came for him again.

* * *

"I don't even know what the fuck to say."

Bahja watched her sons play on the kiddie playscape as she stood a few feet away with Micah at her side. It had been a few days after her launch party and she was still pissed at him.

"An apology would be nice," she replied.

Micah cleared his throat as his eyes fell on Bahja. She looked beautiful as ever in her black leggings with her black off the shoulder tee and her black Balenciaga trainers on her feet. On her lips was a matte pink liquid lipstick while she wore her hair bone straight with a part down the middle.

Bahja was rare and Micah wasn't ready to ever watch her be with someone that wasn't him.

"I been fucking up. A lot. This whole thing with Rian caught a nigga off guard and shit. I could have found a way to still make you important in my life, but I can admit I slacked on that," he said after staring at her for a few minutes.

Bahja licked her lips.

"That's not enough Micah. I've been so patient with you. Gave you way too much leeway and that's my fault. All I did was aid in you hurting me. I made it easy for you to do the bullshit you're doing but no more. We don't have a title and for now, that's not changing."

Micah gritted his teeth. He looked at Bahja's sons before glancing her way.

"What the fuck are you saying exactly? You trying to cut me off for that black ass nigga? Since I'm not running up behind you, I'm useless to you now huh?" he asked angrily.

Bahja smiled at his anger. She was the type of person that listened to people when they got mad. People often showed you how they really felt when speaking in anger. She took a deep breath and exhaled. She refused to allow for Micah to make her feel guilty for wanting more.

"I'm saying that you've shown me what's important to you. You've been there for Rian every step of the way while giving me your ass to kiss. You weren't there for me when I went to see my parents or even when I started my blog. You don't know about what I have going on in my life because you haven't fucking been there. So, I'm saying to just stay where you're at. No hard feelings, it just didn't work out for us," she replied getting emotional.

Micah's jaw ticked at her words. He pulled his cap low to his head to shield his angry eyes. Instead of begging for another chance he walked away. Micah got into his Range Rover and sped out of the parking lot while blasting his music. Bahja glanced back at his departing truck before turning her attention back to her sons. She'd had such high hopes for Micah and herself, but it hadn't worked out. The whole situation had truly been a waste of her fucking time.

Bahja smiled to herself as she headed over to her sons.

"Dave I just want to be happy," she said quietly before joining her sons as they played without a care in the world at the park.

Eight

"Calm down, you look good shorty," Jigga told her.

Bahja smiled. She tugged at her red dress as they walked into the restaurant. They were immediately seated and instead of sitting across from her Jigga chose to sit beside her. While Bahja wore a red fitted dress that stopped above her knees Jigga was dressed in black jeans with a collared black Moncler polo. He was looking dapper as ever and because the two were so attractive they had everyone staring their way.

"Talk to me sexy," he said rubbing her thigh.

Two weeks. That was how long it had taken for her to see him again. The kids were spending the night with Vashti and her son, so she was free to get away.

Bahja licked her lips as her body once again felt that energy. The kind of energy that only he could provide.

"What do you wanna know?"

Jigga leaned over and kissed her neck. He couldn't help himself around her. She was so fucking beautiful and so innocent.

"Everything from the beginning. Tell me about your family," he replied.

Bahja relaxed in her seat and looked his way.

"My mom went into labor with me while on vacation in Paris. I grew up in Atlanta. My family owns jewelry stores and while working there at fifteen I met my late husband. He was so handsome," she said and smiled as she thought of Dave. "He really was. I had never met a man like him before. My family learned of our relationship and told me to leave him alone. By then I was gone off his love. He was my whole world, so I chose him. My parents eventually put me out. I married him and we, later on, had two sons together. He ended up dying in a car crash and well life got hard for me," Bahja stopped talking and Jigga pulled her to his side. Bahja was normally so calm when speaking about her past. Of course, it hurt but it had been a while since she'd teared up while talking about it. She relaxed in Jigga's arm.

The waitress came over and they quickly ordered their food. Bahja ordered a bottle of her favorite wine and Jigga kissed her neck. His presence was so calm.

Much like her's.

"I was homeless. I slept in the car with my kids, sometimes we could get a motel and sometimes we couldn't. I started staying at shelters and from there, I met Emory's wife Neveah. She was like my guardian angel. She helped me out in so many ways and from there, my journey to happiness began. We started working together and I even moved out here with her. I think that's it," Bahja said and smiled at him.

Jigga shook his head. He took off his glasses and set them on the table. He rubbed his left eye and Bahja leaned over to grab some lent off his beard. It was only a little still it had been bugging her since she'd sat down.

Jigga smirked at her. He kissed the back of her hand before putting his glasses back on. Jigga admired Bahja's beauty before he spoke again.

"And when do our story began shorty?"

Bahja broke his gaze.

"I don't know. This is still so new for me. I had my late husband. He was my first love. I never thought I would love someone the way that I loved him than the love was somehow gone. We didn't make each other feel special anymore. We were so distant. Friends instead of lovers and it hurt me. I'm the kind of girl that craves love. I need and want it because I don't feel like we were placed here not to have it. Dave didn't understand that about me then later on down the line I met Micah. He was with Emory when he came to get Neveah in Atlanta. We connected almost right away. He could relate to my struggle and he understood me. He was good with my sons and it felt right."

Jigga stroked his chin hairs with his eyes intently on her.

"And now it doesn't?" he asked.

Bahja avoided eye contact with him and nodded.

"I just wanna be happy. Is that too much to ask for?"

Jigga frowned at her.

"Hell nah, it's not. Don't ever feel bad for wanting peace in your life. If that nigga not providing that then it's time for his ass to go. I'll never kick the next nigga in his back to get to a woman so I'ma leave it at that. The choice has to be yours and no one else's. What I can say about myself is that I'ma go-getter. The power of positive thinking is a motherfucka. Whatever I see that I want, I work hard to have it and its mine. It's as simple as that and now that's you. Your fucking spirit is on a nigga. Calling my name and shit. I gotta have you and I would love and accept everything that came with you. He, not the only nigga that's good around kid's shorty," he said making her smile.

Soon the wine and food were being served and Bahja began to feel real nice along with Jigga. They exchanged flirty looks and gestures all night.

"What about you? What's your story?" Bahja asked Jigga feeling nice off the wine in her system. It had helped her relax tremendously.

Jigga glanced her way and licked his lips. Bahja was looking so delectable to him that he had to force himself to not be all up on her.

"I came from a middle-class family. I fell into the street life honestly because I had nothing to do. I wasn't into sports to the point where I wanted to play the shit, so I hung with the drug dealers. In my hood, them was the niggas you looked up to. They had all the women and the money so naturally, I wanted that as well. I ran into Emory on the block. Back when I met that nigga we knew him as World. His ass was young but getting it and he put me on in a big way. We were running shit but eventually, that street life started getting to me. Niggas were catching cases, snitching and popping up dead. I could feel the devil on my back, so I got my ass up out of the "D". Emory was smart. He'd left the game way before I did and was always onto some new shit, but I wasn't surprised because he'd always been smart as fuck. I eventually went into business with my people and life has been good for me since then. I'm lucky to be alive honestly but all of that is behind me. I don't have no enemies or scorned exes waiting to come out of hiding and shit," he replied.

Bahja smiled at him.

"I'm happy to hear that. What happened to your cousin and Amor? Did she ever have her baby?" Bahja asked him.

Jigga swallowed some of his steak and shook his head.

"He said she still went and got that shit. He on to the next one baby. That's just Zayne plus he got a fiancé that he done been with for a minute now. Shit, he had her before I ever heard about that Amor chick. She beautiful as hell too and in college," he replied.

Bahja couldn't believe her ears. She briefly felt like reaching out to Amor but decided against it. She was still angry with how Amor had handled things at the clinic.

"Wow, I don't know what to say," she replied.

Jigga shrugged not feeling as bad about the situation as Bahja did.

"Zayne is Zayne. You'll die from stress trying to figure out why motherfuckas do the shit they do. This date is about us. Let's go hit up a club," he said pulling some money out of his wallet. He dropped some bills onto the table. Much more than what the meal was worth and they both stood up.

They exited the restaurant hand in hand. Jigga took Bahja to a low-key club that was for the older crowd. The type of people that knew how to party without causing a fight. The kind of people that enjoyed good music, good liquor and dressing nice. Jigga's older uncle had put him up on the spot and he loved it. He could relax without having to worry about shit jumping off. He found a table in the middle of the room near the dance floor for them and they ordered more drinks. Jigga liked that Bahja could handle a drink and not get pissy drunk. That was a huge turn on to him.

Bobby Womack's **If You Think Your Lonely Now** began to play and Bahja hopped up. She *fucked* with some old school music. On some days she'd sit up in the room with Neveah and they would compare playlists.

She grabbed her glass and began to sing the lyrics to the song while swaying back and forth in front of Jigga. Jigga recorded her singing for a few before rolling up a blunt.

Another reason why he loved the small club. The only rule they had was no guns and because he'd been out of the streets for so long he rarely carried a strap on him.

Unless he felt the need to.

"Honey what you know about this," an older woman sang walking over to Bahja.

Her husband sat down in Bahja's seat and looked at Jigga.

"Don't be stingy pass that shit my way," he told him and laughed.

Jigga chuckled and did as the man had asked. He watched Bahja dance and he breathed slowly. Never had he been so content with a woman without his dick being deep inside of her.

"Wait until tonight girl!" Bahja sang staring down into Jigga's eyes.

Jigga sat up and licked his lips. Bahja walked over to him and he grabbed her hips. He wanted desperately to pull her onto his lap and fuck the shit out of her.

"Your lonely days are no more," he promised looking up at her.

Bahja leaned down and kissed him tenderly on the lips. She stared into his eyes feeling her heartbeat increase.

"You promise?"

Jigga nodded immediately.

"And I don't break them shorty," he replied and kissed her again.

Nine

"This is the second magazine and we need it to be right. It has to be perfect," Bahja said and handed her son Benji his crackers. Because she missed them so much some days she took them to work with her and today had been one of those days.

"Yum-yum," Benji said quietly and walked away in search of his brother.

Bahja smiled and when she turned around Micah stood behind her. He looked handsome as ever in his black jeans with his camo BAPE shirt. On his feet were a pair of black Maison Margella sneakers as he sported a new haircut. He gave her a small smile and held out his hand. It felt like it had been forever since she'd seen him.

"Come here ma," he said, and she took a step back.

The feeling that he'd given her when they first met was gone. She went to her office and he followed her. Micah dapped up her sons before joining her in the room. He sat across from her and took in her office space that was very kid friendly. Bahja employed nothing but moms and they often had to bring their kids to work as well so they'd created an environment that was safe for them.

"I'm proud of you. I'm happy to see you did it. I never doubted you," he told her.

Bahja smiled at him. Her cell phone began to vibrate, and Micah's eyes fell on it. Long gone was the phone he'd purchased her. Bahja was now under her own line with the same number and he had been none the wiser. She looked at him and smiled.

"Give me just a sec," she said and stood up. Bahja answered her phone as she exited her office. "*Hey,* you," she sang answering the call.

Jigga breathed into the phone.

"Tell me you're gonna bless a nigga with that pretty face today. I miss you," he said making her body tingle.

He'd been gone for two days on a business trip with his cousin.

"I miss you too. Let me call you back. Micah is here?"

"Yeah let his ass know what time it is," Micah said standing behind her.

Bahja cleared her throat.

"This nigga. Typical fuck boy shit. Lose the girl then want her back. Tell his ass it's too late now. Once you get a real nigga in your life a lame ass nigga don't even phase you. Call me when he gone baby," Jigga replied and hung up.

Bahja took Micah back into her office and they both sat down. Micah stared at her angrily as he watched her plug her phone up. Bahja was acting like shit was all good and her calm demeanor was only making him angrier.

"Yo, you really about to piss me the fuck off in here. Cause you back on money wise you think you can shit on me Bahja? Like I wasn't the same nigga doing all that I could to put a smile on your face," Micah asked angrily. He'd noticed the designer bag, the jewelry she wore and could tell that money was looking right for her again.

Bahja's head snapped back in shock. She was genuinely hurt by all that he'd said.

"Wow. That was very classless of you to say that. Please get the fuck out of my office," she told him.

Micah sighed. His anger had him saying things he didn't mean. He looked at Bahja with regretful eyes.

"I'm sorry. That was fucked up of me. I didn't mean it. I know you said you didn't want me around, but nothing has changed between us. I tried to stay away but I can't. I miss you," he said looking her way.

Bahja laughed lightly. She waved her hand around her new office.

"Micah, everything has changed. I haven't seen or spoke with you in damn near a month. We aren't even friends at this point and clearly, the feeling is mutual. Look at how you speak to me now."

Micah sighed. He sat back and cleared his throat.

"I never gave up on you ma. You was quick to walk away from me the minute shit wasn't going your way. I apologized about not being there for you before. You can't keep tossing that shit in my face. I been dealing with a lot too. My baby was born a few weeks early and not once did you call and ask me about him. He didn't do shit to you and if you got love for me then naturally you would have love for him as well. You know I fuck with your lil dudes, but did you show me that same love? Nah you been on that selfish bullshit, but I miss you and I think we can move past this. Don't keep pushing me away," he replied.

Bahja glared at Micah. He'd completely turned things around on her and she wasn't feeling it at all.

"Whatever, please just go," she pleaded with him.

Micah swallowed hard. Rian was saying all of the right things, but something kept pulling him back to Bahja. She still had a hold on him.

"I miss you. I'm not with Rian. Whenever I'm over there it's because of the baby. I apologize for not being there. I just can't let you go Bahja. Damn can't you see that I miss you?" he asked with his emotions changing the tone of his deep voice.

Bahja shook her head. In her eyes, it was too late. She wasn't looking to rehash anything that she had with Micah. Just the thought of dealing with Rian and her bullshit made Bahja cringe.

"Bahja someone is here to see you," Bahja's receptionist said peeking her head in the door.

Before she could walk away Rian was rushing into her office angrily. Micah jumped up as she tried to run over to Bahja.

Bahja's eyes darted to the other room where her sons were playing clueless to the chaos going on around them.

"I knew you would be here! The minute you heard Emory talking about her you ran over here with your punk ass!" Rian yelled and tossed her rather large cellphone at Bahja.

Bahja ducked and the phone flew through her glass wall. She'd placed the glass wall around her office, so she could see her floor space at all times.

The glass breaking caught everyone's attention. Micah held on tightly to Rian as she tried her best to fight Bahja. Never before had she felt like Micah would leave her. To think of someone else having his love literally drove her insane. She'd become someone else and although it wasn't

Bahja's fault Rian couldn't stop herself from trying to take her head off.

"Bitch come here!" Rian yelled nearly foaming at the mouth.

Bahja calmly walked around her and left out of her office. Filled to the brim with anger, she rushed over to her crying sons. Rian had crossed the fucking line.

"Maxine please call the cops. I'm filing a report on that bitch so when she runs up again I'll be able to legally defend myself," she said hugging her boys as she thought of the CCW license she'd recently acquired with the help of Jigga.

He loved guns and had her comfortable enough so that she was now shooting like a pro as well. When Bahja had disclosed to Jigga all of the things that had transpired with her and Micah he immediately knew what she needed. He'd told her that she was too beautiful to be fighting anyway. In his words, he'd said to *shoot the bitch* if she ran back up.

Bahja planned on doing just that.

Her receptionist looked at her worriedly.

"I already did! Who is this woman?" she asked.

Micah struggled with Rian inside of Bahja's office and was able to pull her out eventually. His sorrowful eyes connected with Bahja's as he walked her way with a detained Rian.

Rian had the look of the devil on her as she glared Bahja's way.

"He's mine bitch! I'll make your life a living fucking hell! You think I won't? I'll set this fucking building on fire!" Rian yelled.

Bahja let go of her sons and walked in front of Micah. Micah shook his head hating how everything was playing out.

"If he is then tell him to leave me alone. Trust I'm not the one chasing him down like you. He came looking for me, but you fucked up this time," Bahja told her.

Rian laughed like she'd told her something funny and tried to hit Bahja. She was unsuccessful but Bahja was able to slap Rian two good times before Micah shoved her back with one hand not wanting them to fight. Shock covered Bahja's face as she fell to the ground. She looked back at her sons who were watching her with teary eyes. She looked at her staff then finally at Micah. The whole scene was stupid. She didn't even want him, yet she was once again dealing with drama because of him.

Bahja jumped up and shoved Micah's arm hard.

"Leave! Get the fuck out of my life and never come back. Never, Micah!" she yelled as she started to cry.

She was hurt that she'd allowed him to pull her into his drama. Especially in front of her sons.

"I'm sorry. I really am," Micah apologized as he stared at Bahja.

Rian struggled to get free as he began to carry her away.

"Don't apologize to that bitch. You with your family let that hoe find another nigga to help her with her's," she said through gritted teeth.

Not being able to hold her tongue Bahja glared at Rian.

"Baby with a snap of a finger your man would be over here doing everything that he could for my boys plus more. That's why your confused, ignorant ass is really mad. You should be thanking me because I'm making it easy for you to have somebody that doesn't really want you. Show some fucking gratitude and get some fucking help!" Bahja said angrily.

Her assistant ran over to calm her down.

"You wish," Rian said thinking about everything Bahja had said. Still, she allowed for Micah to carry her out of the room which had been her whole point of popping up. It was to have him leave with her.

Bahja made sure they were gone before turning to her staff. She was incredibly embarrassed by everything that they had witnessed. Bahja grabbed her sons and looked at them.

"All I can say is that type of stuff will never happen again. I'm sorry," she said and swallowed hard.

Her workers nodded while some waved her off not needing an explanation. Bahja kissed her sons and took them into their play area. After making a report with the police she called Jigga who arrived at her business twenty minutes after her call to him. He showed up with his two male cousins who were beyond handsome and together the trio cleaned up her office space.

Bahja sat at her desk with her chest beating wildly. She was still so mad and contemplating calling Micah and cursing his ass out.

"Fuck them. I mean if you still hot about the shit later then I'll pull up on that nigga. I'll fuck him and her up

87

if you want me to. But that's not you shorty. He stuck with that crazy ass bitch. Let that be his karma. Trust he gone get that shit back times ten. I already hit up my man and he coming through tomorrow to fix up your glass wall. Fuck the dumb shit and I'm happy you slapped that hoe. That shit been a long time coming," he said making Bahja smile.

Jigga went over to her and pulled her up from her chair. Bahja hugged him tightly as his arms went around her waist.

"I got you, so you can relax," he assured her and Bahja did just that. She relaxes because she could feel in her spirit that Jigga was the man for her.

Epilogue

Months later

"Slow down," she panted.

Jigga shook his head. He had that look in his eyes that told her they would be a minute. Bahja moaned as his dick did sinful things to her.

Things that had her wanting to do nothing but lay in a bed with him all day.

"We need to go," she said weakly.

Jigga nodded. He grabbed her hips and pulled her slightly up. He'd shown her that he could make love to her mentally and physically. Jigga had mastered making her cum and knew just how to hit it.

"Baby, fuck! God.... slow down," Bahja whimpered as he repeatedly pounded against her spot. Her legs began to tremble and Jigga went deeper. He shifted to the left just a little and like a faucet, Bahja leaked for him.

"Shittt!" she yelled as her eyes ventured to the back of her head.

Jigga felt her wetness shooting against him and it made him bust prematurely. He leaned down and kissed Bahja passionately as they both climaxed together.

"Look at you cumming all over me. Let's go get married," he whispered against her lips.

Bahja shook her head to clear the intimate moment she'd had earlier from her mind.

"A lot can happen in a year. Children can be born, and weddings can happen," Bahja said thinking of Neveah who'd married the love of her life Emory in an intimate ceremony. "Things that make you cherish being alive. It's little pretty moments like that I live for. I'm tired. This baby just got in me and already it's giving me the blues, but I had to thank everyone for coming to our reception. We didn't want anything to be over the top plus we all promised Gunner that we would keep our nuptials simple so that he could come home and do it big." Bahja stopped talking and looked at Jigga. He was an amazing man.

He was everything she'd always wanted. He was made just for her and that's why he was now her husband.

"This man has been my rainbow. The light at the end of my storm. I'm emotional you guys for several reasons so please excuse me if I cry. For one I can't drink, and the other reason is because I am unbelievably happy. Like so happy I wanna shout it out to the world. He loves me in ways that I had never felt before. He loves me how I *should* be loved, and I promise it's getting returned. Tonight, we celebrate us and I'm appreciative of the people that wanted to witness that. Thank you," Bahja said and sat down.

Jigga pulled her to his side and rubbed her flat belly as he looked at her intently.

"I love you. The minute you feel I don't we gone have a problem."

Bahja laughed. He always said things of that nature and she believed him. The thing was she felt the exact same way. She grabbed his face and kissed his lips while gazing into his eyes.

"Same here. You stop loving me and we're making the First 48 baby," she jabbed back making him chuckle.

In the past, Micah had reached out to her several times before finally giving up. Bahja hadn't wanted to rush things with Jigga but she'd listened to her heart. He loved her and her sons. They were a team and with him things were real. She didn't care if people felt they were moving too fast. It worked for them and they didn't give a fuck about the people that had something to say about it.

Micah was now with Rian and Bahja felt nothing behind that news. She didn't hate Micah she simply wished she'd listened to her first mind when it said to cut him off. She could have saved herself a lot of time. Instead, she was trying to make something work with someone that had too much on his plate.

Jigga kissed Bahja's neck pulling her out of her thoughts and she smiled at him.

"I love you shorty, tell your man you love him back, so we can finish this dinner. I'm ready to get your ass alone again," he said with a smile.

Bahja blushed and Jigga stuck his tongue out to her. Seductively she sucked on it until she felt her panties go moist. Bahja laughed and buried her face into Jigga's neck. Jigga was nasty but she liked it. That had been how she'd gotten pregnant.

"I love you so much baby, but you already know that. You made it easy for me to love again," she whispered.

Never go in search of love, go in search of life, and life will find
you the love you seek.

Atticus

After the love is gone...

India

Prelude

2012

The tension in the room was so thick it could be cut with a knife. India stood near the doorway with her head hanging in shame. She felt like a fool but even more so than that a failure. Losing wasn't an option in her family. Everyone was expected to do great things and while her brothers had chosen to live a life on the wrong side of the law they still had taken the time to go to college and get a degree. India was the baby and the only girl.

Her life had been like a dream. Whatever she wanted she got. Whether it was a designer bag or a new car. Her father made sure of that, and all he wanted was for his baby girl to become a lawyer. Something she told him that she desperately wanted to be.

As he stood in the middle of the living room with his nostrils flaring and his honey colored eyes on India he tried to make sense of the bullshit she had just told him.

"I'm going to need for you to repeat that back to me Indie," he said calling her by her nickname the family had given her.

India tugged at her bottom lip with her teeth. She wasn't perfect. She never pretended to be. She had flaws like the next woman, but her father had placed her on a pedestal so high that it took nothing for her to fall. One wrong move and she was on the ground. Now as she stood in front of the man that was the backbone and provider of the family, she felt like a failure.

"I...I..."

"You what!"

India's mother Charlotte looked at her father. She sat up on the sofa and cut her eyes at her husband. She knew that anything involving India would set him off, but she refused to watch him yell at her daughter.

"Calm down Inez. Will you let her talk? Damn."

India's father ignored his wife while glaring at his daughter.

"What did you do for that bitch ass nigga? Cause that's what the fuck he is for letting you do the shit. A bitch ass nigga so again tell me what you did?" he questioned her angrily.

India took a deep breath and exhaled. She thought of the day everything had gone down. How afraid she was at the thought of watching Brody go to jail and how quickly she'd owned up to having the drugs. Never had she been that woman. Never in a million years did she think she would ever be in such a position but sometimes people did foolish things for the ones they loved, and India hadn't been exempted from that. It took her a millisecond to give up her dream to save her man, and now she had to face the wrath of her parents. The people who'd invested their love, time and money into helping her achieve her goals in life.

"I took a drug charge for Brody so that he wouldn't get locked up. I took a plea deal and was given a lesser charge. However, I will be on probation for the next five years. I also had to pay some fines, but Brody covered everything daddy. I spoke with my counselor, and she said that I still have a good chance of passing the bar. She said that it might be a struggle with the character and fitness application but it's not impossible. She said that even felons have become lawyers." India said almost stumbling over her words.

India gave her parents a hopeful smile until her father's disappointed eyes fell on her. She could see the anguish she caused him, and it made her tear up.

"Daddy I'm sorry. I'll still get my degree like I promised you. I swear I will."

Her father shook his head. He'd heard enough of the bullshit and had no interest in allowing for India to feed him anymore.

"Just save it. Years' worth of hard work down the drain. All those private schools were for nothing. You ruined your future for a fucking clown. I don't even know who you are right now. You're not my daughter. You're nothing to me but some dumb little girl that's clueless as fuck about what love is. I need for you to tell me why you would do something so fucking stupid? Why Indie?"

India shifted from one foot to the other. At the moment it felt like the right thing to do. She'd known Brody for most of her young life. He'd become her man and while they went through their fair share of problems she loved him and couldn't imagine life without him. She wanted to have the type of love that her parents possessed.

"I only did what mom would have done, daddy," she replied.

Inez took a step back and cocked his head to the side. His brother and even his sons chose to live a fast life, but he'd decided to go another route. After hustling his way through school, he opened up a chain of funeral homes with his incarcerated brother in law. Inez wanted long money that didn't have blood on it. With his life, he could sleep peacefully at night all while giving his family whatever they desired. He felt confused on how India could think he would ever subject her mother to a drug charge.

"Indie...baby girl. Where did I fail you? I would never even suggest some bullshit like that to your mother, and she wouldn't let me. I had no idea we were raising this kind of woman," he said and ran his hands over his bald head.

India's eyes watered.

"What kind of woman am I, daddy?" she asked with tears clouding her vision.

Inez looked her over and shook his head.

"A fucking fool. That's what you are baby," he replied coldly.

His harsh words pierced India in the heart. She'd never been spanked by her father let alone yelled at so to hear him speak to her in such a way broke her down. Slowly her tears fell while her mother stood up.

"You won't talk to our daughter like that ever. You can apologize right damn now," she demanded.

Inez moved passed India and walked out of the living room. He slammed the front door so hard that the mirror in the hallway broke. India cried harder as her mother walked up and pulled her into a hug. Charlotte rubbed her back while holding in her own tears.

"He's just upset. He'll come around baby. You go ahead and finish school and show him that you could do it. Okay?"

India nodded while continuing to cry. She cried until her tears couldn't fall anymore and eventually left her parents' home. She drove to east Seven Mile and pulled up on Brody at one of his spots. Foreign cars lined the front of the home while he sat on the porch talking to his friends. India pulled into the driveway and looked at him through the windshield. When she'd first met him, her father had told her that he wasn't shit. Brody had been the only thing they couldn't agree on, and India was clueless as to why her dad hated him so much. Sure, he had a valid reason to hate him now, but from the start Inez disliked Brody.

India, on the other hand, had been smitten with him. He was popular in school. The finest boy she'd ever seen with his tawny brown skin and steel grey eyes. It was the swag that he possessed that made her fall in love instantly. He had a street persona to him that the suburban boys lacked, and India hadn't been able to get enough of it.

She admittedly got lost in him and before she knew it years skated by while she ran the streets of Detroit with him. She fought bitches over him, and now she was fighting a drug charge for him. India shook her head as her eyes stung with tears that wanted to fall again.

"Why did you do that dumb shit India? Why?" she questioned herself.

India honked her horn making Brody look her way although he'd seen her pull onto the block. Brody stood up looking like the sexy ass nigga that he was and walked over to the car. He got in and kissed India on her cheek. His scent that usually smelled so good didn't bring her much joy that day as it blanketed the space around her. India looked at him, and the same handsome face that usually drove her wild didn't look so attractive. She shook her head trying to shake off the foreign thoughts that were filling her mind.

"You did it?"

India nodded still looking into his eyes. Brody sighed and grabbed her hand. His thick brows pulled together as he stared at her.

"I'm sorry again baby. What you did for me will never be forgotten. In fact, I got you something. I know how you like to shop so I figured you could have your own store. The building is yours baby and it's in your name. It's not no little space in the fucking mall either ma. This is a real ass building that I'm going to fill up with clothes for you. Okay?"

India nodded not as excited about having a store as Brody would have liked for her to be.

She let go of Brody's hand and stared out of her window. She didn't want a funky ass boutique she wanted to become a lawyer.

Not sell some bullshit ass clothes.

97

"I'm going to finish school, get my degree and pass the bar. I don't give a damn about selling clothes, Brody."

Brody gritted his teeth. He was pissed at how India was acting but she had held him down in a way that was unbelievable so whatever she wanted she could have. He licked his lips before speaking.

"Then I'm with you on that. If they can look past the drug charge, then you got it, baby. I'm just saying that the clothing store can be a plan b. Okay?"

India swallowed hard. Brody's words did nothing to lift her spirits.

"He disowned me, Brody. My daddy, the man I love most in this world, disowned me." India stared into Brody's eyes. She wanted him to understand the severity of the situation. "Because of you. I gave up so much for you and if you hurt me, I swear on my life that I will kill you," she promised meaning the words from the bottom of her heart.

Brody smiled to hide his uneasiness. India was placing a lot of weight on his shoulders whether she knew it or not. Still, he was grateful for all that she'd done and would do his best to keep her happy. He leaned towards India and kissed her on the lips. As he pulled back, he caressed her cheek.

"I love you too much to ever do that. I'll finish up here and close shit down so that I can take care of you. I promise that things will be okay baby," he reassured her and kissed her again.

One

"Keep 'em closed," Brody said leading India into their new home. It had been a year and school hadn't gone like India planned so she'd decided to take a break. Once her mind was right, she knew that she would return. But because going home to her family wasn't an option, India had been staying with her oldest brother while spending her free time with Brody who had been seeing more money from hustling.

India frowned as she slowly walked. Brody held his big hands over her eyes, and she couldn't see or hear a thing besides Brody's heavy breathing.

"Damn you look so sexy, baby. Daddy loves this look on you," he said and licked his lips as he admired her curvy body that was covered in tight jeans that accentuated her ass.

Brody was the flyest nigga India knew. Everything he did was in style, and she could admit that because he was so fresh with his shit that she'd been forced to step her game up as well. Now that they had a steady income coming in, India could shop without a budget, so she was wearing designer clothes that most nineteen-year-olds could only dream of wearing.

"Thank you, baby," she said smiling.

Brody admired India's round backside one more time and licked his lips. He led her into the foyer and removed his hands. Slowly India's eyes adjusted to what was before her.

Yes, her parents had money. She'd always grown up in an upper-middle-class neighborhood, but the brownstone she stood in was on another level. The décor was something out of a Glamour magazine. The home even came equipped with an elevator. India quietly walked around the plush pad with a cheeky grin on her face. Just the other night she and Brody were in his one-bedroom apartment.

The brownstone was nothing like his other place.

"You did good Brody. This is so nice, and you decorated it just like I would have. I can't wait to start sleeping over here."

Brody took India to the elevator and silently they got on. The home was so immaculate that India couldn't stop smiling. She followed him out of it once they reached the second floor and Brody took her into the master suite. For six months he'd hugged the block with no rest. No shopping sprees and no bullshitting. India had given up so much for him, and all he wanted to do was return the favor. He knew how well taken care of India was and he wanted to show her that she hadn't made a mistake by taking his charges. He wanted her to regret nothing with him.

"I know this been a shitty ass year for you. You fell out with your pops, and you dropped out of school. I know how much both of those things meant to you baby. I can't help but feel responsible. I got you the store, but you still look so unhappy. I feel like I need to do more. I feel like I need to lay more of a foundation down for us. This could be the first step baby. This is our home," he told her.

India looked around the master bedroom and noticed that all of her belongings were there. Even the things from the home she shared with her brother. India quickly walked to the closet and opened the double doors. She noticed the vast wall inside of it filled to the brim with designer threads, and her knees buckled.

This was more than she had ever expected out of Brody.

"Oh my God. Brody.... are you for real?"

Brody walked up to India and hugged her from the back. To hear the excitement in her light voice made his chest swell up with pride. *Finally*, he'd been able to do

100

something to make her happy and in return that made him happy.

"Hell yeah, I am. I told you that I got you baby and I mean it. Welcome home," he whispered.

India squealed unable to contain her happiness, and she ran into her closet to look through her new things. Brody watched her from the door while grinning. He felt better about the situation when he saw real happiness on her face still his guilt ate at him. Sometimes gnawing at him like a bug so even as India fawned over her designer bags and shoes in the back of his mind he wondered if it was enough?

If anything, he ever did for her would be enough to make her not regret taking the charge for him?

* * *

"This is the entertainment room right here," India said showing her brothers the game room she'd set up for Brody.

Paris and Kent nodded in approval. A few other people walked into the room and India stood near the door grinning. She looked like the lady of the house in her silk Versace printed dress that she'd paired with black Giuseppe heeled sandals. India's hair was done in soft spiral curls as she wore minimal makeup with a black lip.

All night people had been saying how nice she and Brody looked together. Brody was, of course, the star of the show in his black Tom Ford wetsuit. He'd been getting high all day and was once again getting lifted as India spotted him walking down her hallway with a voluptuous redbone.

India's neatly arched brows lifted as she watched Brody and the woman bend the corner headed for her kitchen.

"This place is so beautiful cousin. Show me your closet one more time," Sterling said walking up.

India looked at her cousin that was only two months younger than her and she smiled. Sterling's father was India's mother's older brother. India, Sterling and Sterling's younger sister Shia had grown up like sisters. While India and Shia rarely got along they tolerated each other because they were family.

"In just a second, let me go see something," India said and walked away. She quickly went to her kitchen and found Brody in the backyard having an intense conversation with the voluptuous woman and her brother Kent. India' relaxed the second she noticed her brother. India knew that no matter how much her brothers liked Brody they would never allow for some bullshit to go down around them.

"Can we go see the closet now? Plus, I need to talk with you," Sterling said coming up behind her.

India gazed out of her patio doors for a moment watching Brody until she sighed. She nodded and led her cousin to the elevator. They went to the second floor instead of the basement which was where the small theater room was at along with a gym. India took her cousin back to her bedroom and into her vast walk-in closet. Sterling smiled as she immediately went over to India's jewelry case. India grabbed a necklace that Brody had given her a week prior and placed it on her cousin's neck.

Sterling was her rock. They shared everything with each other and India felt like if she was doing better in life then Sterling was as well.

"Because you deserve it," India whispered clasping the $12,000 necklace around her neck.

Sterling grinned as she felt the diamond that was in the center of the necklace.

"But Brody..."

"Isn't going to say shit. Now, what did you wanna talk about?"

Sterling checked out the necklace in the standup mirror before exiting the closet with India. They both sat at the edge of India's California king-sized bed and looked at one another. They were both curvy, but Sterling's body stole the show. She had hips plus ass and it could be too much for timid men but for the man that loved a woman with meat on their bones she was perfect.

Both India and Sterling shared similar facial features including long straight noses with almond-shaped eyes.

"Shia is pregnant with twins," Sterling said with a defeated look on her face. India sat expressionless as she continued. "She's due any day now and I just couldn't hold it in anymore. She still drinks and everything India. I feel like she wants something to happen to the babies."

India broke her cousin's gaze and laughed to keep from cursing.

"Why didn't you say anything? Why is she keeping it a secret?"

Sterling shrugged.

"Daddy. You know she feels like he favors me more and I can admit that he does at times. It's all because of how fucked up she is though. He loves us both and you know that."

India nodded. Her uncle was always nicer to Sterling, but Sterling was like the perfect daughter. She'd graduated high school at sixteen and was now in college. Sterling seemed to be good at everything she did but instead of India getting jealous of it like Shia had she used it as motivation.

Sterling's success showed her that it was possible to make it in the world.

"Sterling you can't raise her sons. I know you, I know how you love to take care of Shia, but it isn't your job. If Shia can lay down and get knocked up then she can woman up and be a mother to her kids," India said finally breaking the silence.

Sterling fiddled with the necklace India had just given her.

"The babies are innocent India. They didn't ask to be here," she said quietly.

India rolled her eyes. She loved her cousin but hated how she went above and beyond for Shia.

"Who got her pregnant? You know Shia fucks a nigga from every block," India said making Sterling snicker beside her.

"Bitch, that's not funny but sadly it's true. Hell, I don't know. She refuses to talk about him. She just said that he was dead to her, so I guess that means he doesn't want the kids."

India shook her head.

"That's fucked up but it's a situation that she placed herself in. I know that's your sister, but you have to let her grow up. You have to put yourself first. I mean look at me. Look at the stupid shit I did that fucked up my future."

"Right cause life's so fucking bad for you right now and shit," Brody said stepping into the room.

Sterling stood up and Brody smiled at her. She was the only person that India hung with that he liked.

"Sterling you good?" he asked smiling.

Sterling smiled back at him.

"Yes, I'll be downstairs India and this place is really nice," she replied before walking away.

Brody closed the door behind Sterling and took off his suit jacket. India watched him intently as he went into the closet and came out seconds later with his small Louie duffle. He tossed some clothes in it and she frowned.

"Brody, what's going on?"

Brody's grey eyes peered up at her as he put a stack of money in his bag.

"This place might not be shit to you, but it cost a lot to keep this motherfucka in our possession. I gotta shoot a move to Miami for the week. I'm leaving tonight."

India swallowed hard. The worst part of Brody making more money was that India now saw less and less of him.

"You just got back the other day," India found herself saying in a low tone.

Brody zipped up his bag and took off the rest of his clothes. In nothing but his boxers, he joined her on the bed.

"Are you happy?"

India's heart thundered in her chest.

"Yes," she said immediately.

Brody leaned in and kissed India passionately on the lips. His hands caressed her breast through the Versace dress she wore, and India moaned. Brody pulled back as he began to unbutton it.

"I work really hard to make you happy India. It's nothing I wouldn't do for you and I know you feel the same way. This trip will put us in a better place financially. I need you to get me right so that I'll be good for them days. Can you do that baby?" he asked.

India's lust filled eyes stared back at him.

"I can and I'm sorry. I know sometimes I say things that might come off harsh, but you do make me happy. I love you so much," she said and got down on her knees.

Brody's eyes closed as India pulled down his boxers. Soon his smooth, thick, member was in her hands then down her throat.

One of the best places he felt it could be.

Two

"How is Chicago?"

Brody coughed into the phone.

"Cold as fuck. I can't wait to get home baby," he replied making her smile.

The twins began to cry, and India rocked both of the portable bassinets that they were sleeping in. It had been two months since her little cousins had been born and like India had predicted her cousin Sterling practically took care of them. She'd even taken off from school because of it so as a way to give Sterling a break India was watching them.

Sterling was asleep in her guest room, but she didn't mind. She was doing it for Sterling. India gave no fucks about helping out Shia who was now missing in action.

"They over there again?" Brody asked with an attitude.

India looked at the pretty little boys that looked exactly like the men in her family. India's family had incredibly strong genes.

"Yeah, I just feel so bad for Sterling. She's always stuck with them."

Brody sucked his teeth.

"Y'all need to let that hoe take care of her own kids. I told you she been on some setting niggas up type shit. I don't want her knowing where we stay at ever. Okay?" he asked with an attitude.

India was caught off guard by his tone but understood it. Shia had been linked to several different robberies by a few hustlers that Brody ran with.

"Okay and you can calm all of that down. She's still my cousin."

Brody chuckled.

"Shit you don't even like her ass but when you gonna give me some sons?" he asked changing the subject.

Talks of having kids made India queasy. She rubbed her stomach as she looked at her cousin's kids.

"Not anytime soon. We already don't have time for each other Brody. We're really young. We have all of the time in the world to have kids. Right?"

Brody sighed, and she knew she'd made him upset.

"I'll hit you back. Remember what I said India. I don't want her at the house ever. Don't even call her from the fucking phone. Call me if you need me," he replied and ended the call.

India debated on calling him back but decided not to. She'd given up a lot for Brody. She wasn't willing to give his sperm her womb just yet. Instead, India called her mom who answered almost immediately.

"Hey, baby! How are you? You've missed four Sunday dinners," she said taking the call.

India smiled. Just hearing her mom's voice made her day better.

"I know and I'm sorry. It's just so weird because he doesn't talk to me while I'm there," India replied speaking on her dad.

Her mom sighed into the phone.

"He'll be fine. This family will be fine in the end. How is the boutique going?"

India rolled her eyes. She would never tell Brody, but she hated her boutique.

"It's going. Brody hired workers and I go in a few times a day to check on them."

Charlotte laughed.

"Okay, you sound so thrilled about that. Why don't you come over tomorrow and watch the game with your dad?"

India thought of her father and her eyes watered.

"Maybe," she lied as her cousin walked into her bedroom.

Sterling's pretty face was contorted into a scowl as she cradled her cell phone in the palm of her hand.

"We have to go pick Shia up from jail," she said angrily.

"What she say?" Charlotte asked only catching the jail part of the conversation.

"Nothing mom. I'll call you back," India said and ended the call.

"What happened?"

Sterling shook her head as she checked on her nephews. She loved them as if they were her own sons. Sterling sat beside India on the bed and looked at her.

"She was with some nigga and they got pulled over. She has a suspended license and two warrants. It's going to be $40,000 to get her out because it was also drugs in the car, so they have her down for drug trafficking," Sterling replied.

India fell back on the bed and gazed up at her ceiling. A crystal chandelier dangled over her bed that she was in love with. At night when Brody felt the need to eat her to sleep she'd gaze up at it in awe.

"Sterling she hasn't seen her children in two weeks. Fuck her."

Sterling's shoulders slumped.

"I don't wanna call my dad with this mess. I have the money in the bank, but we should get her before the other county picks her up. India I'll give it back to you," Sterling pleaded in a tone that made it impossible for India to say no.

India rolled onto her side and stared at her cousin.

"Why should we do this for her?" India asked quietly.

Money wasn't an issue, she was more stuck on if her cousin was deserving of it. Which she knew she wasn't.

Sterling looked at her nephews and licked her lips.

"Because family sticks together no matter what India."

Against her better wishes, India went into Brody's safe and took out $40,000 for her cousin. They packed up the twins and took Sterling's Lexus truck to the jail. After waiting for nearly three hours Shia was released.

She rushed to the truck and slid into the backseat. She kissed both of her sons on their forehead before putting on her seat belt. She reeked of liquor and was looking like she'd stepped off of someone's corner while trying to sell some pussy. It was the middle of winter and she wore a black mini skirt that clung to her slim thick frame with six-inch heels.

"Was y'all trying to have them take me away? What the fuck, I was in there all damn day," Shia vented.

India balled her hands up into a fist and sat them on her lap. Even as kids Shia and India repeatedly bumped heads.

"How about a thank you? Yes, you should start with that," India replied.

Shia ignored India.

"Sterling, did you tell anybody else? I don't want daddy knowing about this. He already kisses your ass like you are the shit and I'm nothing."

India's shoulders shook as she laughed.

"Bitch because she is! She is not only taking care of your newborn fucking twins, she just borrowed $40,000 to get your stanking ass up out of jail. It seems like she's the shit to me."

Shia's chest heaved up and down as she sat behind India.

"Sterling you could have went into our account and got the fucking money."

Sterling glared back at her.

"How could I have done that without the other county picking you up tonight? Don't put this on me Shia. I'm so tired of your shit. You really need to grow the fuck up or I will tell daddy!"

Shia sat back in the seat angrily. She closed her eyes and when she opened them she was crying. There was no great tale of how she'd turned out so selfish. She hadn't been molested as a kid or mistreated. Shia was simply selfish. A trait many people carried.

"I hate you, two bitches," she murmured meaning the words that fell from between her lips.

While her words saddened her sister they only made India smile.

"Trust the feeling is mutual. If you don't have that money for me in the morning, you're gonna like me even less because I'ma be at your house ready to beat your ass. I'm not your sister. I don't feel bad for your lazy, trifling ass," she told her.

Shia laughed while looking out of her window.

"Since you were facing federal time like me, I really don't think you're in a position to judge. I was just with Kent the other night and he told me how your dad isn't talking to you. He's quite ashamed of you India. They all are, I mean you gave your future away to be with the modern-day G-Money but was it worth it? I know who I am India. I don't pretend to be something that I'm not. But you on the other hand love to play roles. You like to walk around this bitch like you a queen when you nothing but a hustler's girlfriend. A kept bitch and that's all you'll ever be so while you looking down on me and the shit I'm doing I want you to know that you're no better. We are cut from the same cloth my dear," Shia said vehemently.

Sterling turned on the radio to tune out her cousins but long after Shia had spoken her hateful words they still replayed through India's mind.

She'd gone from being a college student with a future in law to a hustler's girl. Her cousin was a real-life bitch but her assessment of her hadn't been too far off.

* * *

"What's on your mind India?"

India shrugged. It had been days since she'd bailed her cousin out of jail. Shia had come through with the money but still, the words she'd said to her were still on India's brain. India glanced over at Brody as he drove down the street and he smiled at her.

"Baby you worrying a nigga. What's wrong?"

India turned away from him and cleared her throat.

"I want to tell you something, but I don't want you to get upset."

Brody pulled over at the closest gas station and shut off his car. He was cool when it came to many things, but India wasn't one of them. He made sure to check out his surroundings as he mulled over what India could be holding back from him.

"Did you cheat on me?" Brody finally asked her.

India's head whipped Brody's way and she saw the look of death in his eyes. Never before had she seen him so scary looking. She quickly shook her head and caressed his hairy cheek. Gradually his grey eyes softened as he stared back at her.

"Baby what's up?" he asked again more calmly.

India sighed.

"I took some money out of the safe to bail Shia out of jail. She paid us back but while on our way to dropping her off I got into it with her. She basically was calling me dumb for taking a charge for you and how I was nothing but a hustler's girlfriend. I know Shia is full of shit but she's right. Right now, that's all I am," India replied.

Brody leaned back in his seat and gazed at her lovingly.

"I don't see it that way. You a homeowner, a business owner and more importantly the love of my life. I know Shia is your cousin but fuck her. You and I both know she ain't never had a nigga love her. She's bitter and people like her can't stand being around a happy motherfucka. I'm pissed that you would even bail her ass out of jail but that's your family. I don't know what else you want me to do to make you happy baby?" Brody said to her.

India shrugged. She didn't know either.

"I'm happy, it was just bothering me. Forget I said anything," she replied in a low, defeated tone.

Brody leaned over and playfully kissed her on the neck until she fell into a fit of giggles.

"You my world India and that's a title that nobody else got," he whispered to her before turning her head so that he could kiss her on the lips.

Three

"India your home was so nice! I wish I had a place like that. Brody must really be getting some money now," Palmer commented as they stepped into the club.

India and Palmer had been friends since high school and now viewed each other as sisters.

"Yes, your brownstone is nice as hell. That's some Sex and The City shit right there. I swear your closet is everything. I could live in that damn thing," Demi who was Palmer's older sister added with a smile.

India laughed and waved them off.

"Thanks, and yes it's cool," she replied humbly.

Although her place was off the fucking hook, she didn't like to brag about it. She'd even downplayed her new $60,000 Rolex, Brody had gotten her because she simply didn't feel the need to flaunt her wealth. Her daddy always told her real money spoke for itself and that you didn't have to speak on it.

"You don't have to play it cool for us. You know your new house is the shit!" Palmer said and they all laughed.

India smiled as she ran her hand through her dark brown strands. Her silk press had her hair feeling amazing as it fell down to the middle of her back.

"Okay I do love it but I'm really just happy to be living with my baby. How is school going?" India asked her best friend.

They went over to the bar and before Palmer could respond a tall, handsome, caramel colored man walked upbringing with him his alluring scent. India and her friends couldn't help but to smile as they gazed his way. Detroit was known for men that carried a swag like no other. Cartier frames, Rolex's and Pelle Pelle's were just a few of the things men in Detroit were known for rocking, but the man that stood before them was in a league of his own.

He rocked all white Balmain from head to toe with diamonds decorating his wrist and earrings while a Cuban link diamond chain hung from his neck. The man couldn't seem to take his eyes off of India's best friend Palmer.

"I didn't mean to break up your lil girl's night and shit but I had to come over and speak to the sexiest ladies in the club. It wouldn't be right if I didn't offer to buy some bottles. Shit as beautiful as y'all are, I'd buy this bitch out tonight just to keep some smiles on your faces. So, can I do that? What you think about that sexy?" he asked and grabbed Palmers hand. Palmer dropped her head while smiling and the charming man licked his full lips. "My bad I'm Arquez but my people call me Quez," he said with his eyes never leaving Palmer.

Palmer smiled shyly up at him and India shook her head knowing her girl was everything but that.

"It's nice to meet you, I'm Palmer. I mean we would love some bottles and whatever else you wanna give us," Palmer replied making India and Demi both snicker beside her.

Arquez pulled out his ringing cell phone and glanced at the screen before turning his attention back to Palmer.

"Cool, cool. Let me take this call, and I'll be right back. Don't let nobody come stand in my spot beautiful. They not worthy of your time anyway ma," he said and flashed her a sexy smirk before walking away.

Palmer fanned herself dramatically making India and her sister laugh.

"He's like certified fucking fine. *Damn*! I think I'm in love already," Palmer gushed while grinning hard.

India and Demi laughed again as India flagged down a waitress. India and Palmer were both underaged, but Palmer's older sister wasn't. Demi flashed her license and was able to order them two bottles of Moet.

"But what I can't understand is why this girl keeps staring at us?" Demi asked not liking the vibe she was getting from the attractive fair skinned woman that was across the room with her girls.

India glanced the woman's way and frowned. She squinted her eyes trying to see where she knew the red-haired voluptuous girl from because she did look familiar to her.

The woman continued to stare at India and her friends and it all came back to India. She'd been the woman that had been with Brody at their housewarming. She'd also seen the woman at a few of Brody's bando's and even hanging on the block with him and his boys.

The woman had always pretended India didn't exist not even looking her way when she'd come around, so India was surprised to get the steely glares from her that night.

India tried to brush it off when loud laughter came from across the room catching her attention again. India and Demi frowned as the redhead blatantly stared their way before whispering something to her friends.

"Yes, she's definitely got a problem," Demi mumbled taking off her large hoop earrings.

"Demi you and India need to relax," Palmer said not wanting India in the club fighting. "You're still on probation," Palmer reminded her.

India gave her an innocent smile. One Palmer had seen too many times in the past right before she did something crazy.

"I'm good. I've actually seen her a few times around and she didn't even breathe my way. It was like the bitch was blind so for her to be on some funny shit tonight kind of pisses me off. I'ma go see what the problem is, and I pray she answers me the right way because I'll knock a bitch in the head with this bottle if she says the wrong thing to me," India replied always the live wire and stood up.

She grabbed one of the bottles of Moet and headed over to the table.

Palmer and her sister followed her not wanting anything to pop off without her having backup.

"India please stay calm," Palmer said always being the voice of reason.

"No, these bitches are staring too hard for my liking," Demi said as they approached the table.

India walked up so close to the redhead that she could stare down into her tight black dress if she wanted to. The three women that sat at the roundtable stopped their chatter to stare at India and her friends.

The redhead with the slanted brown eyes looked India up and down as amusement danced in her eyes.

"Sweetie can you back up some and can we help y'all?" the redhead asked while waving her hand in the air.

India checked the girl out noticing she was on her shit. Her face was average, but her body was on point and so was her extensions. She wore expensive clothes and even smelled nice with the floral-toned notes floating off her skin.

But what caught India's attention the most was the diamond bracelet that sat on the redhead's wrist. It was damn near blinding India because of all of the diamonds that covered it. India couldn't help but to stare at it which in turn made the redhead put her hands on her lap under the table. Her demeanor changed almost immediately as she smiled at India and her friends.

"I was just telling my girls how cute you all were. I see you all the time and I was telling them about how fly you are. How nice your Benz is and shit. We're not the type of women to hate, shit we're happy to be partying with some cute chicks. I don't do all that ratchet shit so there's no need for the stale faces ladies. I know that none of our men would appreciate that," she said before turning back to her friends.

Palmer exhaled happy that they weren't going to be fighting and she grabbed India's arm.

"Let's go sit down," Palmer said through gritted teeth and led India and her sister back over to the table.

"Hey, beautiful can I kick it with you for a minute?" A sexy dread head asked Palmer once they were back at their seats.

India watched Palmer talk with the man before glancing back at the lady with the expensive bracelet. Everything about the redhead irritated the fuck out of India.

India went through her pictures on her phone and her heart beat increased at the photo that she saw that was taken a few weeks ago. It was of Brody palming her bare kitty with the exact same bracelet on. India took a deep breath and exhaled. Her intuition had led her to the photo and now all she could see was red.

She passed her purse and keys over to Demi.

"So, it's like this sis, I'm going to kill that bitch. I need for you to do two things for me. Give Palmer my purse and make sure them hoes don't jump me. I got faith in you," she said and quickly got up from her seat.

With the Moet bottle in her hand India rushed over to the redhead and as she turned to look back at her India smashed the bottle over her head.

"Oh my god! Oh, my fucking god!" The redhead yelled as her forehead started to bleed.

India yanked her out of the chair and threw her onto the ground angrily.

"Bitch, are you fucking my man? You actually walking through my home while fucking my nigga! Bitch, you must be crazy!" India yelled and started to smash her head against the ground.

The chaotic scene immediately caught the attention of everyone in the small club.

"*Indiaaaaa* no!" Palmer yelled running over.

"Aye beautiful chill-out!" Palmer's new friend Ishmael yelled and picked her up.

The redhead's friends rushed to her side, and he pulled a kicking and screaming India out of the club with Palmer, Demi and his boys behind him.

Once they were outside, he took her to his truck, and they all got in. He was certain the cops were on the way, and while she didn't know him, he knew of her because of Brody.

"I'ma take you to your man. You can't be hitting bitches over the head with bottles and shit," Ishmael said while frowning.

India sat in the passenger's seat with a scowl on her pretty face. Talks from the car fell on deaf ears as she started to think of every single time she'd come across old girl. India then began to think about the nights Brody would go missing or how he'd always cut off his phone once he got home and her blood ran hot.

She'd never thought for a second that he would cheat on her, but she knew that money changed people. Made them feel like they could do the unthinkable and get away with it. Hell made them feel as if they were invincible.

"Just take me home. My address is..."

"I'm taking you to Brody. He on the block," Ishmael said glancing over at her.

India pulled out her phone and called up her oldest brother. She wasn't about to play games with Brody or the nigga that was driving her to him.

"Sis, you good?" Paris asked taking the call.

The crazy thing was India's brothers were the most alpha male type men you could come across, and her mother had chosen to give them names that related to her favorite places. She swore she was in Paris when she'd conceived him and Kent when she was in England. Charlotte had never made it to India, but the name was very befitting for her princess.

India cleared her throat as she looked out of the car window. She wasn't the type of sister to involve her brothers in every situation because they never pulled up to talk, but she was hurt. Just the thought of Brody cheating on her with that bitch had her seeing red.

"Brody's cheating on me," she said quickly, and everyone in the truck looked at her.

Palmer shook her head knowing that nothing good was going to come from India's phone conversation.

"What? What the fuck you mean he cheating on you? You know what I'ma hit you back," her brother replied and ended the call.

India sat her phone on her lap ignoring the stares that were aimed her way.

"This night has gotten out of hand. India, please call him back and tell him you had it wrong. You're mad at Brody right now but you love him, and the last thing you need is for him to be beefing with your brothers," Palmer told her.

Ishmael pulled his ride onto Six Mile and Hubbard and pulled up to a two-story home. India spotted not only Brody's car but her brother's old school along with a silver Mercedes. She jumped out of the truck and rushed into the home.

"Indie, what type of shit is you on? This our homegirl. She moves shit out of state for him and you out here busting bitches in the head with bottles? Mom would whoop you up if she knew her precious India was out here acting like this," Paris scolded her.

India looked across the room at the bruised-up redhead and the girl gave her a feeble smile.

"I told you I wasn't looking to start trouble. I'm not doing your man. Brody is like a big brother to me and my name is Jenna by the way," she replied.

India looked at Brody who was sitting on the brown suede sofa nonchalantly rolling up a blunt. Although he was out hustling, he still looked at his best in his custom Pistons jersey with the snapback on that matched along with the

119

same bracelet she'd seen the girl wearing just minutes ago. India started to breathe hard as she noticed the girl no longer had the expensive item on.

India shook her head refusing to believe a lie.

"You fucking this bitch. You think you're so slick but you not. I'm done with you, Brody. I can't believe you out here fucking cheating on me!" she yelled and grabbed a nearby lamp. India tossed it at Brody and he moved just in the nick of time.

Paris led Jenna out of the house and left India alone with Brody. Paris felt like his sister was overreacting, so he'd chosen to stay out of their business from that point forward.

"India calm down. Why the fuck is you acting like this? Have I ever fucking cheated on you?" Brody asked dropping the blunt onto the table. Brody rose to his feet and walked over to India. He tried to pull her into his arms and she slapped him so hard it left a print on his handsome face. India angrily pushed him off of her and rushed to the door. Brody caught her before she could open it and hugged her tightly from the back.

India became so angry that her eyes watered, and she started to cry. Brody rocked her silently until she calmed down. India always had a fiery personality on her, so he wasn't shocked by her outburst. He'd watched India beat plenty of ass when they'd been in school and secretly he liked that she could get rowdy if need be. He definitely didn't want a scary ass woman.

Brody led India back over to the sofa, and they sat down. Brody grabbed India's chin and forced her to look at him.

It was the love that the steel grey eyes pushed her way that slowly calmed her soul.

"I'm not cheating on you. I would never cheat on you. Do you know how much you mean to me? It's because of you that I'm free right now. India, I love you, and nobody could ever take your place beautiful. What we have can't be fucking duplicated."

India gently pushed his hand away and looked at him.

"Okay so if I ask you a question you're going to be completely honest with me?"

Brody quickly nodded.

"Yeah, what's up?"

India looked down at his wrist and touched the expensive piece of jewelry. Her nails gently rubbed at the diamonds that sat on it.

"Did you let her wear this tonight?" she asked quietly.

Brody leaned in and pushed his full lips against India's. He kissed her again and pulled back to stare into her eyes.

"I don't give that bitch nothing but drugs to move," he replied and kissed her again.

* * *

"You don't like the food?"

India looked up from her plate and smiled at her mom. Sunday's belonged to Charlotte. She didn't care what any of her children were doing on Sunday they had to come share a hot meal and week re-cap with her.

India sat at the long wooden table with her two brothers, Paris and Kent and Paris's new girlfriend. India's father was in his study watching sports like always. India knew that he wasn't around because of her, but no one said anything about it.

Brody was supposedly off handling business in Texas, but India wasn't so sure of that either. Ever since the bar fight, she hadn't been able to trust a word he'd said to her. Although she didn't have all the proof, India was certain he'd fucked Jenna. She could feel it deep in her gut and was confused on what to do next.

"Mommy, I think Brody cheated on me," she replied, and Paris shook his head.

Charlotte was a live wire like India. She'd actually been the person India got her attitude from.

"What are you talking about girl? How did you come to that conclusion?" Charlotte asked with a frown.

India sat back and shook her head.

"I went out with Palmer and her sister a few nights ago and I saw this girl at the bar. Everywhere I go lately momma she's there. I noticed that she kept staring at me so I went and checked her about it. She got all scary so I went back to my seat but then I saw his bracelet on her wrist. That's when I lost it."

Charlotte looked at India in shock. Ever since she'd known Brody, he'd been India's shadow. The only thing he'd done to make her shit list was allow for India to take those charges for him.

"How do you know it was his jewelry India? Women look for any reason to act a fool," Kent said and chuckled.

India ignored her brother as she looked at her mom.

"Mommy I just know. Like I can feel that he's messing around with this girl."

Charlotte shook her head. She'd worked hard for India to be exceptional. She didn't want a regular daughter. Every day she'd told India how special she was. India was supposed to be a straight-A college student on her way to becoming a great lawyer. Instead, she was living with a drug dealer, and fighting women she felt he was cheating on her with.

Charlotte looked at her daughter and sighed. She'd begged India time and time again to come home, but India's pride always held her back.

"This is the thing. You're young, and so is Brody. That doesn't mean that he can't be faithful, but without the right mindset, it will be difficult for him. You've placed yourself in a position where now you not only need him your whole world is centered around him. You need to do a few things. For one make your life about you and not him. You need to also either accept whatever excuse he gave you and move on or leave him. Don't be one of those women that's always crying about their cheating man yet and still, they are laying down to his ass every night. Take control over your relationship and your life. It's not a hard thing to do and find happiness in yourself India. Stop looking for him to give you that joy," Charlotte told her.

India nodded still feeling the same way, and her father stepped into the dining room. He'd overheard the conversation, and it only made him hate Brody more. He walked over to India, and she stood up. His heart could no longer go without having his daughter in his life. He knew that as a father his biggest job was to be there for her. India was his princess, and although he hated the decisions, she was making regarding her life he was trying to look past them.

"Let's go watch the game princess," he told her.

India smiled and walked with him out of the room.

"Aww, shit the dynamic duo finally made up!" Kent yelled, and everyone smiled including India.

India walked with her daddy into his man cave, and they sat down. While sports played on his tv's her father looked at her. There were so many things he wanted to say but was holding back because they weren't polite.

"How you been Indie?"

India relaxed in her seat. She knew that telling him the truth was out of the question, so she chose to lie.

"I've been good. Brody got us this beautiful brownstone that I'm in love with."

Her daddy nodded. Material shit he could care less about.

"That's good but it's some things I want to discuss with you. I would like for you and Sterling to run my west side funeral home India. That could be your own income and something that you could pass down to your kids. I wanna put it in your name baby girl. How do you feel about that?"

India smiled at her dad and hugged his side.

"I'd love that!"

Inez sighed hugging her back. He wanted to give her something that no nigga could take away from her. He felt like he could sleep better at night knowing that she wouldn't have to deal with a man's bullshit for fear of being broke. Unfortunately, he knew a lot of women that did.

"Then it's settled. You'll take over that location with your cousin. I want you to know that no matter what we go through daddy will always be there for you," he promised her, and India smiled. He was one man she could always count on.

Hours later India stepped into her home full of food and happiness. She not only had a good meal thanks to her mom she was also happy because she'd made up with her father. India felt like she was floating on cloud nine as she took the elevator up to her bedroom. India walked into the room, and the lights were dimmed low. Brody sat at the edge of the bed with his shoulders slumped.

India stepped out of her flats and went over to Brody. He was supposed to be out of town so to see him in their home looking so distraught worried her.

Her thoughts ran wild as his sad grey eyes peered up at her.

"You got caught with something?" she asked in a whisper.

Brody shook his head. He stood up and pulled India into a hug. His arms held her tightly as his heart pounded in his chest.

"Nah...some other shit went down. I..." Brody took a deep breath and sighed. "I.... you know that bitch from the club that you ended up fighting?"

India tried to pull back from him, but he wouldn't let her.

"*Brody*.... let me go," she said calmly.

Brody could feel her heartbeat increase. He knew that letting her go would be a grave mistake on his part.

"Baby...she......I let her suck my dick one time after y'all fought. You haven't been giving me none, and I fucked up. I really did. She gave me Gonorrhea. That nasty bitch burnt me," he finally said, and India tried with all of her might to break free. Her eyes watered and soon tears slipped down her face as she realized that Brody *had* cheated on her. He'd given himself to someone else and in return caught an STD.

India's knees buckled, and she slid to the ground. Brody went down with her afraid to let her go. He held her in a bear hug as India cried. It was more hurtful than anything. To know that he fucked someone else and gave her something was the biggest form of betrayal to her.

"I have to go," she said while crying.

Brody vehemently shook his head.

"India I'm sorry. It was one time, and I promise it won't happen again. We can go get checked together."

India shook her head.

"You don't get it. I'm done with you. I don't give a damn about getting checked with you. I just wanna leave. Let me go, Brody," she replied.

Brody hugged her tighter.

"I can't. I don't give a damn if this house was on fire. I'm not letting you go. You my world and I fucked up once, but I'll never fuck up again. I'm serious India when I say that I won't let you walk away from me," Brody stopped talking and cleared his throat. "We'd just have to go together," he told her adamantly.

India realized what he was saying as her tears fell down her face.

125

"So, you're threatening me now? You would actually force me to be with you?"

Brody shook his head. He was but not in the way she was taking it.

"I'm simply saying that if you break up with me, then that'll be the end of both of us. They can lay us to rest together in the ground," he replied, and India closed her eyes.

He buried his face into her neck, and she stared straight ahead at the wall.

"I don't know everything, but I do know this isn't love. You don't love me, Brody."

Brody kissed her on the neck trying to ease her pain.

"I love you more than you'll ever know India."

Four

"This is really nice!" Mickey said as they toured Palmer's new home.

Every room was designed by Palmer and she'd spared no expenses when it came to decorating her plush pad. For her to be a college student she now lived in an immaculate three-bedroom townhome that she couldn't get enough of.

Palmer smiled proudly as her friends admired her living quarters.

"It's not India's palace with a damn elevator and all but it'll definitely do," she replied to Mickey.

India waved Palmer off. Her high from living in her expensive place with Brody had quickly worn off. The same home that she'd thanked God for having was now like a prison to her.

"For two dollars you can have that shit," she said making everyone, but Palmer laugh.

"Well, I'll take it. You all are like real life goals right now. From the cars to the clothes to the houses I want it all. Hell, I wish I had a townhouse like this," Palmer sister Chanel said from behind them.

Palmer smiled. She'd been with Ishmael for a year, and he'd surprised her with a new home. She was happy with him, but like all relationships, they had some obstacles they needed to overcome.

"Let's go in the family room and make some drinks. I need to talk to you guys and Chanel you need to be going home!" Palmer yelled.

Chanel rolled her eyes while pulling her keys out of her bag.

"You're no fun but have a good night ladies," she said and left out.

India quietly followed Palmer and Mickey into the family room. Mickey stretched out on the loveseat while India sat down on Palmer's plush carpet. Palmer made them Patron margaritas and joined India on the floor. Because they were close friends more like sisters Palmer could sense that something was up with her girl. Palmer had been so wrapped up with her own life that they'd all spent months apart, so she felt a little out of the loop on how India was doing.

"India why are you so quiet?"

India shrugged. Her last year had been hell honestly. Brody had pretty much forced her into being with him and while he'd become a good man to her the damage was already done. India didn't want to be with him anymore. Now she was just trying to find the courage to leave.

India dropped her head and exhaled. She couldn't believe she was about to share her horrible secrets with her friends, but she had no choice. Not telling anyone had almost driven her insane.

When she looked up at her friends her eyes were watery.

"I hate Brody. I found out right after I fought that girl at the club that he did cheat with her. He ended up giving me Gonorrhea and for the last year I've been trying to get over it, but I can't. I'm close to losing my damn mind," she said quickly almost stumbling over her words.

Mickey looked at India in shock not sure what to say while Palmer eyed her worriedly.

"Oh my God India. You didn't come over to tell us you killed him, did you?"

India had to smile at Palmer's question. Sometimes she wished she had it in her to kill him.

"Unfortunately, no. I tried to leave, and he wouldn't let me," India replied sadly.

The usually lively India lacked her normal spunk that her friends were used to seeing from her.

"India it will be fine. I'm in love with my best friend and he doesn't even know it. We're all dealing with man problems girl," Mickey told her while smiling sweetly at her.

India stared at Mickey blankly. India had faced federal charges and things such as STD's. That was way more extreme than a damn crush. She waved Mickey off because she did like the young beautiful girl. Mickey and Palmer attended college together and had grown close which in turn made India close with her as well. India could tell that Mickey was spoiled as hell, but she wasn't uppity with it. She was very down to earth which India felt was a good thing.

India now viewed Mickey as her younger sister. She was just someone you couldn't help but to like.

"I don't know about that Mickey. This is a little more intense. One minute I hate him. I mean like hate him so much that I can't lay next to him at night then the next minute he's swooping me off my feet. Making me smile but I must admit it isn't the same. It hurts me so much guys because I love him. I would never have subjected him to a disease or heartache. Never," India said with her eyes watering. She glanced around the family room while gaining control over her emotions. "I'm losing myself. I don't even know who I am anymore. I wake up some days ready to leave. I pack my shit then he comes in with all of these promises and I give in. I feel like walking away would be giving up on him. Giving up on us. Throwing all of the work I put in down the drain, so I stay but staying is killing me too," India shamefully admitted.

Palmer leaned over and gently rubbed India's leg. To see her friend in so much pain made her sad. Palmer too was in a love crisis and despite not wanting to she decided to air out her problems the same way India had.

"Well, I guess it's my turn to air out my dirty laundry. Ishmael is married," Palmer revealed and stared at her friends to see how they would react to the news.

Mickey and India's face both fell in shock. Neither woman was expecting Palmer to reveal such a thing.

"Okay y'all definitely got me beat," Mickey said trying to lighten the mood.

Palmer had to laugh to keep from crying. She was madly in love and the person responsible for all of that was someone else's husband. She was sick behind it. Had been struggling with even looking in the mirror because she hadn't left him. She'd tried and for weeks was successful until he'd shown up with tears in his hooded eyes begging her back. He was her first love. Her first relationship with a grown man. She didn't know how to shake him yet and was trying to have faith in him. Faith that he would leave his wife and be with her.

Palmer held her hand up while staring at India and Mickey.

"Before you two-judge me just know that I never signed up for this. He says that he's staying because of his kid. Ishmael grew up in a broken home and doesn't want to subject his child to that," Palmer replied robotically. Repeating verbatim what he'd told her.

Mickey shook her head as her brows knitted together. India chose to make another drink after Palmer's revelation. It was very little that India now put past men. They were always on some bullshit to her.

India looked at her friend and sighed. She wouldn't be India if she didn't keep it real with her.

"Fuck him and that bullshit ass excuse he gave you. The home is already broken if he's cheating on his wife. Palmer, please don't tell me you're staying with him," she said looking her friend's way.

Palmer's angry eyes shot to India. The two best-friends had an intense stare down until Palmer cocked her head to the side.

"India you're the last person I ever thought would judge me. Seeing how you ride for your man. I thought you would understand how love works."

India sipped her drink. She looked down at her bracelet. It had cost more money than it was probably worth. The diamonds on it sparkled with every flick of her wrist. Another *I'm sorry* I fucked you over gift and she wore it with shame. She looked at her friend and her eyes watered.

"I thought you would have learned from me. That's why I keep it real with y'all. I don't pretend. My nigga ain't shit! I want you all to see that everything that glitters isn't gold. Got damn Palmer! You can go. Shit, you all haven't even been together that fucking long anyway. You have nothing tying you to this man. I've invested so much into Brody that I have to walk away at the right time. All you're suffering from is a good dick down and puppy love. Ishmael is cute and all but he ain't all of that. Shit his boy actually looked better than him," India said thinking of the man in all white that they'd seen at the club.

They'd later found out that he was Ishmael's right hand and while it had been awkward for Palmer she'd found a way to block out the attraction that they had for one another.

Palmer's hands balled up into a fist as she stared at her girl.

"I can't believe you wanna tell me how to live. Brody ain't the shit either with his always trying to be pretty ass!"

India laughed.

"I never said he was! I'm telling you this because I love you, Palmer. Leave him now because the longer you stay the more pain you're putting yourself through. It's just not worth it," she told her.

Palmer rolled her eyes. The pain she felt at the things India said showed on her pretty slim face.

"Start loving yourself India then come tell me how to love," she mumbled.

India nodded and grabbed her keys. Arguing with her friend was pointless. They still loved one another and that would never change. She hugged Mickey and then Palmer who refused to hug her back.

"I love you and that's the only reason why I told you that. You're too fucking beautiful to be someone's mistress. Don't ever settle for that title but if it's cool with you then the shit is alright with me. I'ma love you regardless because you love me regardless. I know my man isn't shit. That's the difference between me and you. I'm not sitting here making excuses for his trifling ass. Call me when your attitude is gone," India told Palmer and left out of her new home.

India left Palmer's place and decided to pull up on Brody at his newest venture a bbq spot on West Seven Mile road. She parked in the lot and noticed Brody and his friends were on the side of the small but nicely decorated spot barbecuing and talking shit. The street was lined with luxury cars while kids played. Music blared from a few speakers and the vibe was nice. Brody always gave back to the neighborhood with free or discounted food. Did events like back to school drives and things of that nature. The reality was he made a lot of money off those same people and he believed in keeping them happy. He felt that was the best way to keep the hatred down.

India reapplied her Oh Baby lip glass before exiting her car. She spotted Brody leaning against a black Mercedes that was in the lot and talking to two attractive women. It seemed innocent but with him, she was never too sure. It also didn't help that he was looking extremely handsome in his blue jean shorts with a crisp white beater on. On his head was a Bulls Mitchell & Ness cap and on his feet were high top new Air Force Ones. A chain covered in diamonds hung from his neck while a fancy watch sat on his wrist.

His eyes seemed to spot India before anyone else as she advanced on him. Brody stood up off the car and held out his arms. India walked into them as the women both smacked their lips. Every woman to cross paths with Brody knew of India. Plus, it was hard to miss the India tattoo that ran across his forearm.

"I thought you was having a girl's night," Brody said hugging her tightly.

India sighed. She closed her eyes and even with everyone around still found herself getting emotional.

"Brody we should talk," she whispered.

Brody picked up on her mood and nodded.

"Aye tell Bloom I'm going to my car," Brody said to one of the women and led India away.

India and Brody got into his Charger and he reclined his seat. Brody made sure to place his gun on his lap and the whole scene made India shake her head. She couldn't help but wonder how she'd gotten there? When did her life go from an aspiring lawyer to the girl who dated a man that constantly needed to be armed for protection? Palmer was right in so many ways. She wasn't in a position to judge. She was dating a hustler. Yes, he had legit businesses, but they had all been purchased with drug money. She was no perfect then the next.

"Brody," India stopped talking and cleared her throat. She looked him in the eyes and swallowed hard. "I think we should take a break," she said slowly.

Brody's lazy gaze fell on her and she realized he was under the influence of a few narcotics. India sighed wanting to have the heart to heart with him while he was thinking clearly.

"I love you so much India. I still remember the first time I saw you. I swear baby that shit was unreal." Brody smiled. India looked better than ever. She only got better with time and he loved that about her. No matter how attractive a woman was she wasn't seeing India in his eyes. Them bitches simply would never compare. "You was all I could think about. You still are too. I know our past is shaky. I know this isn't the life you saw yourself having but it's ours. People would kill to be us. We might not be doing what you thought we would, but we're blessed baby. I'm trying to get all the way clean then we're really gone be on they head. Where did all of this come from?"

India smiled despite how she was feeling.

"Where did it come from? Brody did you not give me an STD?"

Brody breathed harder at her words. He was beyond tired of India bringing up his indiscretions.

"Let's not ever bring that bullshit up again. I didn't bring you shit. I made a bad decision and that resulted in someone giving us an STD. Don't say that shit like I'm just out here on some trifling shit," Brody replied with an attitude.

India's blood boiled at his words. She glared over at Brody and before she could contain herself slapped the frown off of Brody's face. Brody grabbed her wrist and tightened his grip as he stared into her eyes.

"You know I'm sorry," he said quietly.

India's jaw tensed.

"And the damage has already been done. I can't do this anymore Brody. I don't wanna do this anymore," she replied in a shaky voice.

Brody let her wrist go. He put his gun away and peered over at India.

"Okay. I'll leave the house, but can we try one last time? Can you please give me one last chance to make it right?" he begged.

India broke his gaze and he grabbed her hand. He kissed the back of it repeatedly. Brody then bit it gently making her smile.

India exhaled. She hated how much she loved him. It had really gone from a gift to a curse.

"One last chance," she whispered making Brody lean over and smother her with kisses.

* * *

"You're saying we can't have the doves in the funeral home? Is that what you're telling me?" the young lady asked angrily.

India rubbed at her temples. She was tired and had woken up feeling very fatigued. A feeling that was foreign to her.

"Mam I'm sorry but our funeral home doesn't allow that. We also won't allow for the motorcycle to be placed inside of the facility," Sterling said speaking up.

The woman grabbed her Gucci bag angrily. A displeased look covered her pretty face as she rose to her feet.

"I'll take my business elsewhere then," she replied in a nasty tone and walked away.

India watched the woman exit her office and she rolled her eyes.

"That bitch," she murmured making Sterling giggle.

"India she's grieving," Sterling chastised her.

India waved her off. She looked at her pretty curvaceous cousin and sighed.

"But that gives her no right to be fucking mean to us. Today is just not the day for the bullshit," she replied as Sterling's sister walked into the room.

For the last year, Shia had been on her best behavior, but India still wasn't convinced that she was a better person. She just felt like her cousin was better at hiding the fucked-up things that she did from the family. However, India was glad that she was somewhat taking care of her sons because it gave Sterling a chance to live her own life.

Sterling had begged India to let Shia work with them and because India could never say no to her cousin she eventually agreed to it. So far Shia had been doing an okay job.

"India someone's here to see you," she said yawning.

India looked up and a petite blond with bright blue eyes walked into her office. She smiled as she glanced India's way.

"India?" she asked politely.

India's brows rose.

"Yes, who are you?"

The woman smiled at her.

"Brody sent me to get you. I have to blindfold you to take you to him, however," she replied. India's frown deepened, and the woman laughed lightly. "He said that today is the anniversary of the first day he met you," she said making India smile.

India scooted her chair back as her day immediately got better. Brody could be arrogant, selfish and just downright ignorant at times. Then there were times when he could be prince charming. He'd do things to remind her of just why she'd fallen in love with him.

India always forgot about the day they met, and every year Brody would find a way to remind her. India wasn't one of those women that kept track of things like that.

"India this is nice. Go enjoy your anniversary," Sterling said happy to see that Brody was doing something to make India smile.

Shia smacked her lips loudly while shaking her head. India ignored her and allowed for the lady to blindfold her. She was then taken to an awaiting car and whisked away to a private landing strip on the east side of Detroit.

"You smell so good," Brody said walking up on India. He thanked the woman for bringing her and took India onto the jet he'd rented out.

Nervous jitters fluttered in her stomach as she walked slowly holding tightly onto Brody's hand.

"Brody what's going on?" she asked feeling a little anxious at what was to come.

Brody pecked her lips not able to resist them and he helped her sit down. Brody then sat in front of her and took off her black stilettos. He rubbed India's feet while gazing at her gorgeous face. Brody kissed the bottom of both her feet before pulling her big toe into his mouth.

India moaned. He'd done some freaky things to her, but he'd never sucked her toes before. Brody gave each toe a tongue lashing before pouring them both a glass of champagne.

India slightly jumped when he pressed the glass to her lips. She took a slow sip as Brody unbuttoned her blouse. He then caressed her full breast before pulling them out the bra. His long tongue flicked at her nipples making her squirm in her seat.

"Do you know how much I love you India?" he asked pushing her shirt off her shoulders. Brody then took off her bra and finally her lower garments.

He picked India up and took her to the small room in the back. Brody stripped out of his clothes and climbed on top of a still blindfolded India. India moaned when she felt him slowly ease his thickness into her body. Her body shivered at how good he made her feel.

"Damn Indie," Brody groaned. Only when he was angry or horny did he call her Indie.

India moaned loudly as he gripped her ass tightly.

"I'm not perfect. I fuck up. I hurt you and you don't deserve that. None of it. You never did. I'm pass that dumb shit. I really am. I want you to believe in me. Believe in us. Give me a baby and take my last name," he said moving slowly through her walls.

India was speechless.

The things he was saying were nice. She wanted to believe in him as well, but his past made that almost impossible to do. India loved Brody with all of her heart but slowly the power his love had over her was changing. It wasn't as strong as it was before. The hold was loosening and that frightened India. She knew that if he were to cheat again she would leave him. She didn't want it to come to that because while they had dark times they hadn't outweighed the good ones. India didn't want all of the time they'd invested in one another to be for nothing.

"You have to show me that you're really a new man Brody," she whispered as he found her spot.

Brody's heart beat faster at her response.

"No more birth control and I will. I promise you I will," he said, and a deep left stroke had her crying out in ecstasy.

Five

"I can't do this anymore! I'm tired of his black ass," Palmer vented.

India looked up from her nails and stared at her friend. They'd of course kissed and made up. The last year for her and Brody had been like a dream and despite not wanting kids she was two months pregnant. They were keeping it a secret until she hit the three-month mark.

"Palmer calm down. What happened?"

Palmer angrily paced back and forth in front of her section in the nail salon. She looked at India and her pretty face fell into a smile.

"You look different India."

India grinned at her. She loved her best friend, but she'd sworn to Brody that she would keep the pregnancy a secret for now.

"I do?"

Palmer nodded while eyeing her intently.

"You do. You look so happy too. Maybe that's it. At least Brody's got his shit together. Wait until I tell you about Ishmael's sorry ass. Everything was good with us. He told me that he had to take a business trip and that it wasn't with Rae. I believed him because lately he'd been practically living with me. All I know is that around three in the morning she started calling my phone India and I could hear him talking on his phone with someone else in the background. I was so pissed because I was believing him when he said he was done with her," Palmer replied.

India stared at her friend confused and saddened by her words.

"Really Palmer?"

Palmer looked around the salon and sighed. She was tired, and it showed all over her pretty face. Her smile wasn't bright as it normally would be, and she wasn't even dressed in her usual designer threads. Lately, she hadn't felt the need to get out of the bed let alone get pretty.

"India don't start. I know he's married."

India nodded at her friend.

"Then act like it. You're his mistress and that's what dumb ass wife's do when they know their husband is cheating. You already know how I feel about this situation and I'm not trying to argue with you. You shouldn't even be sweating her though. Clearly, she has no control over his ass. Seeing as how he can't seem to stay out of your bed. Plus, she should be on his head, not yours. It just shows how dumb she is," India said wanting her girl to feel better.

Palmer stared at her friend while frowning.

"How dumb we both are," she mumbled.

India smiled happy to see that Palmer was waking up to the situation that she was in.

"The difference is that you're not married to him, so you can walk away. And you should walk away Palmer," India replied staring into her eyes.

Palmer nodded receiving just what her friend was saying loud and clear. Her eyes watered as she leaned on India's shoulder.

"What if I can't leave him?" she asked quietly.

India rubbed her arm hating to hear her friend sound so sad.

"Then you need to stop complaining and be nice to your sister wife," India said making Palmer laugh.

Palmer hit her arm.

"That's not funny," she whined.

India nodded.

"But it's the truth. If we're going to deal with the bullshit these niggas put us through then we have no right to cry about it," she replied speaking on Palmer and herself.

"You like that?"

India moaned. Did she like it? Shit, she loved it. Her eyes rolled to the back of her head as Brody gripped the top of her shoulders. He pumped into her briskly wanting to pull every orgasm she had up out of her.

"I can't cum again," India moaned while whimpering.

Brody ignored her and grabbed her legs. He tossed them over his shoulders and went even deeper. He was so far inside of India that she feared he may rip her stomach into two. Her body convulsed as her thighs shook uncontrollably.

"*Brody,*" she whispered.

Brody licked his lips.

His nut was *right* fucking there. India's pussy felt amazing. Warmer than usual thanks to his baby and he couldn't get enough of her.

"*Shhhh.* Stop fighting it ma. Let your nigga make you feel good. This pussy deserves to cum all the time. My pussy gone stay cumming for me," he said in a guttural tone before his back stiffened. His balls grew taut. His dick got even harder and before India could stop shaking he was expelling deep inside of her walls.

Brody and India then took a shower after they'd gathered their composure and India cooked Brody's favorite meal. Fried chicken and spaghetti. It was the last meal he'd eaten at his foster parent's home before his foster mom was killed with a stray bullet while on her way to work. Brody was fifteen at the time. Because of his boyishly handsome good looks, it had always been easy for him to be placed while in foster care. Mrs. Connie had found him at the tender age of four. She'd been the only mother he'd ever known. Brody was so hurt by his mom passing that he lashed out at the world.

He turned to the streets and with hate in his heart became the opposite of his good looks. Niggas learned early on to not underestimate Brody and through that, he got a name to himself. His mom left a life insurance worth $25,000 and he spent it on taking care of the home they were living in when she passed and getting drugs. Brody knew it wasn't right, but he felt like he had no choice.

To him, hustling was a job and nothing more.

"Shit smells good fat momma," Brody said as she brought the plates into their family room.

Brody was usually always in the streets but after asking for one last chance he'd made a complete turnaround. He worked normal hours because the reality was he could do shit like that. Before he loved being on the block and in the mix of things, but India had changed all of that. They had reconnected with each other in the last year and he was happy to be in a good space with her. He also felt the need to keep her close to his side. A lot of things were happening behind the scenes and the last thing he wanted was for India to be affected by his mistakes.

Brody knew that as long as he kept a watchful eye on her their shit would be good and they were having a baby. To him, that was heaven sent.

"I love you," he said taking the plate from her.

India smiled. He'd been more affectionate, and she was loving it. She sat beside him as the movie cut on.

"I love you too. Have you thought about walking away from the streets? We have money, you have your businesses, I have the funeral home. We're not hard up for cash."

Brody smiled at her. He grabbed India's hand and kissed the back of it.

"Soon," he said dismissively and cut into his food.

India took a deep breath and exhaled. He'd been saying that for the last two years. Soon had never come and she was beginning to feel like it never would.

142

"Well, I was thinking about going back to school. I'm trying to get that off my record," she said quietly.

She could feel his eyes burning into her.

"What about the baby?"

India smiled at him. Brody was shirtless wearing Polo loungers while she wore one of his extremely big t-shirts.

"What do you mean?"

Brody leaned in and kissed her softly on the lips.

"I'm saying what about our baby? It will need a lot of your time and attention."

India nodded.

"And yours as well. Brody, I have time for school."

Brody sat back. His jaw tensed, and she could see that he was getting mad.

"You do? India you and I both know you don't. You barely have time for me. Between working and having a kid you gonna be tired as fuck. Maybe when the baby is older, but I don't want you pushing me or my kid to the side for some college shit. We living good, shit better than most. College can wait."

Brody's words burned as they fell from his thick lips. India broke his gaze and stared at the tv. Her mom never worked but that was because she didn't want to. India always had this feeling on her that she needed to be a lawyer. As a child, she would make Sterling and Shia be her clients and she would defend them. As a teen, she did mock court in school and killed it every time. As an adult, she attempted to make her dreams come true. She couldn't understand why she had to let it go? If there was a possibility that she would be able to still become one, then that's what she wanted to do.

Silently they ate, and Brody chose to ignore the attitude coming off of India. When it was time for bed he pulled her close to him and hugged her from the back. She could feel his warm breath falling over her neck as he breathed hard.

"I love you and I want the same things that you do. I just feel like school is hard and we already have a lot of shit on our plates. When the time is right you can do it," he told her and kissed her cheek.

Brody rolled over to go to sleep and India closed her eyes. When she opened them, a few tears fell from her lids. She felt like she was always putting him first in her life and was wondering just how much had he changed? The more he told her to wait on her dreams the more he began to look like the old Brody. The selfish ass nigga that did as he pleased with no regards to anyone's feelings.

* * *

"How are the boys doing? She makes sure to keep them away from me. Like I didn't practically raise them with you when they were first born," India complained.

Sterling smiled. She was tired of her sister and cousin battling with one another. Shia had for some reason decided to keep India away from her sons and while India thought it was petty she refused to call and ask her to see them. So, on the days when she really missed them, she would check on them through Sterling.

"They're good. You know you are always welcome at my home," Sterling told her.

India quickly shook her head.

"I'm good. Just bring them by whenever you can. I bought them so much stuff and I want them to have it before they get too big. When was the last time you went to see your daddy?"

Sterling looked at India and her face lit up. She was like India a daddy's girl.

"Last week. He sends his love too. You know he's always talking about you. What's going on? Today you were all quiet when the ugly bitch cursed us out for not taking payment plans. I just knew you were going to lite up on her ass."

India snickered. She shrugged feeling her days' worth of work move over her. She was beyond tired.

"I'm fine just sleepy. I'm going to leave early and go lay down. Can you lock up?" she asked standing up.

Sterling stared at her questioningly but nodded. She knew that when her cousin was ready to talk she would be calling her.

"I love you and yes that's not a problem."

India grabbed her purse and her cell phone.

"I love you too," she said before exiting her office.

India got into Brody's truck and exhaled. Her hormones were raging, and she'd woken up angry as fuck. The first few days after learning she was pregnant had been great. However, the morning sickness had kicked in and was now working her over. If she didn't have a migraine, then it was time for her to vomit until she couldn't anymore. India was close to losing her mind. She put on her seatbelt and started up the truck. India searched Brody's middle compartment for a charger before looking inside of his glove box.

"Where the fuck is this thing," India said pissed that her phone was on 2% and she couldn't find his car charger. Brody kept a charger on him *and* with him, so she knew it was somewhere in his truck. She leaned into the backseat and searched the back driver's seat pocket. India frowned when she pulled out a letter addressed to her.

She sat back and with shaky hands opened the letter. Her name had been written in pink ink and over the I's in her name were dainty little hearts. It was clear Brody wasn't the sender of the letter.

Hi, I'm not sure if this will ever make it to you. One thing I know about Brody is that he's lazy when it comes to cleaning his rides. That's why he comes to my uncle's shops. That's how I met him you know. I guess this has been a long

145

time coming. I just want you to know that he does love you. I didn't think he did. I mean all the bitches tell me that he doesn't but it's the things he does that speak volumes. I fuck and suck him better than you ever could, yet he still comes home to you. He still calls you his wife. That's love so I gracefully bow out. I can't compete with that and I'm tired of trying to. Shit, I'm 19, I can find a million Brody's, but I know for you he's the best that it gets so you can have your man back. I'm done with him.

Signed a smart bitch.

India began to hyperventilate as she tossed the letter into the seat beside her. Brody promised her on the last trip they'd taken that he was past the bullshit. After months of watching him do right, she'd started to believe him and had fallen back in love with him. Her heart was so shattered that she wasn't thinking clearly as she pulled out into traffic.

Her only thoughts were of killing Brody. India sped to his restaurant and was disappointed when she didn't see him there. She decided to go by his closest bando and was relieved to see his car sitting in front of the small home. Brody and his cousin stood on the porch talking when India sped down the street. She wanted to stop at the stop sign but she was too angry. Brody was so close and all she could think of doing was fucking him up.

"I hate him," she whispered to angry to even cry.

India drove through the stop sign at high speeds and was sidelined by an SRT Charger going faster than her. The collision caused Brody's truck to hit the corner home with India in it.

Brody and his cousin saw the accident and Brody immediately stopped talking. He recognized the truck and his feet moved like lightning as he raced towards it.

Brody's Range Rover caught fire at the hood while smoke billowed from under it. Brody and his cousin pulled an unconscious and badly bleeding India out of the passenger's side door.

"What about old boy?" his cousin asked as Brody carried India to his car.

Brody looked over at him with wet eyes.

"Fuck that nigga, I hope for his sake his ass is dead," he replied.

Brody placed India in the back of his car and got in. Brody pulled off not waiting on his cousin and drove India to the nearest hospital. He then called her family as she was being taken care of.

For hours India's family waited on an update while sitting in the lobby. Brody was so scared that he'd stood the entire time while looking at videos of himself and India. While India's father hated Brody, he was relieved to see that Brody was just as scared as they were of losing her.

"Brody she'll be good, just chill out," Inez told him.

Brody nodded but kept standing up. Brody received a text from his cousin that had been at his bando with him and he read over it.

Aye, I got the truck towed and the nigga driving the Charger is dead. This letter was also outside of the truck my nigga. I think India read it.

Brody looked at the picture of the letter and his stomach dropped. He knew exactly who the little bitch was that had written it and couldn't wait to handle her trifling ass. He put his phone away as guilt washed over him.

"Can I speak with the young lady's parents?" a doctor asked stepping out.

India's mom and dad quickly got up and went over to the doctor along with Brody. The doctor gave them all a generic smile.

"Your daughter made it through surgery without any problems. However, the accident did cause for her to lose her eleven-week fetus, but she didn't harm anything in her reproductive system, so she should be fine. She shouldn't have any issues conceiving again. She did hit her head on the steering wheel hard. The brunt force could cause temporary memory loss. That should come back to her in time as well," the doctor told them.

"Baby? My god," India's mom said and began to cry.

Brody was truly at a loss for words.

"Can I see her?" he asked in a throaty voice.

The doctor nodded.

"She's tired so only for a few minutes. The medicine she's on will make her loopy."

Brody followed the doctor to India's room. Slowly he walked in and when he saw India's black and blue face he fell apart.

"Her mom can't see her like this man," he said holding back his tears still a few escaped his eyes. The doctor looked at him.

"I'll let her father know about the bruises. It does look worse than what it is," the doctor replied before walking away.

Brody went over to India and sat in the chair beside the bed. Guilt washed over him as he stared at the woman that he loved but just couldn't do right by.

"I'm so fucking sorry," he whispered. Brody swallowed hard and slowly India opened her eyes.

She looked at him and shook her head.

"They said the baby is gone. How did it happen? I can't understand why someone would be driving that fast down a residential street," she said through her sore throat.

Sorrow covered her beautiful, bruised up face as she lay in the hospital bed.

Brody stared at her unsure of what to say.

"Baby what can you remember?"

India sighed. It hurt to even do something as simple as breathe.

"I remember leaving work and I woke up here. The doctors said I was hit in a car accident," she replied.

Brody knew it was wrong, but his body relaxed at her response.

"...And now our baby is dead. I'm so sorry. I'm so sorry baby," she whispered before falling apart. Brody hugged her as best as he could.

"Baby everything will be okay," he promised her while silently thanking God for once again showing him mercy.

Six

Months breezed by as India and Brody tried to move past the accident. India had fallen into a depression and Brody was lashing out at her. She didn't wanna touch him or even allow for him to touch her body. While Brody knew the real reasons behind the accident he still didn't care for India's sudden disgust with him.

Brody was back to running the streets and India had been basically allowing for him to do whatever the hell he wanted to.

"Thank you for bringing them," India said to Sterling.

Sterling smiled at her cousin. Everyone knew about India's loss including Shia. Shia had suddenly been really nice to India and was allowing for her to see the kids again. The boys were now very active, and India loved to take them to the park and different places which worked in Shia's favor because that gave her time to run the streets. Something she was good at.

"Anytime. I could stay with you guys," Sterling said looking India's way.

India stopped looking at the twins to look at her.

"It's fine. I was just going to cook and watch movies with them. Brody is well...actually, I don't know. He's gone, and I didn't want to be alone," India replied.

Sterling gave her an empathetic smile.

"Just call me if you need me," she said before exiting the house.

India cooked the boy's favorite meal from her, spaghetti before feeding them and putting them into the tub. She played with the boys in the room she'd set up for them until they were too tired to keep their eyes open before laying them down to rest.

India sat on her back patio with her music playing at low volume. Vodka filled up her glass as she listened to the song take her away. By the third glass, she was tipsy and checking the time on her phone.

When 4:00 AM stared back at her, her skin burned hot with anger. India called Brody and like it normally did he sent her calls to voicemail. India had been playing that game with him for the last few months but the more she sat on the patio with sadness consuming her body the angrier she became with him.

One second, she was outside and the next minute she was tossing Brody's beloved items into a trash bag. India carried as many as she could to her elevator and took it to the first floor. She drugged the bags to the door and called Brody once more. India noticed that the sun was coming up as Brody finally answered her call.

"Baby, you okay?" he asked in a throaty tone.

The voice he usually had when he'd just waken up out of a deep slumber. To hear the fake concern lacing Brody's voice made India frown.

She was genuinely hurt with the way he was playing her.

"Hey, baby I'm so much better now. It's good no one was here to kill me or take the money we have because I would have been shit out of luck waiting for you to answer the call. But get this honey, I packed up all of your shit and you have until today to get it or it's going to the closest shelter," she replied and ended the call.

Slowly India walked up her spiral staircase bypassing the elevator and went into her bedroom. She laid down on her bed as her thoughts went to the child she'd lost. India thought of Brody, the horrible space they'd somehow found themselves in and she exhaled.

"I'm tired, God. I'm so tired," she whispered, and her eyes closed.

India awoke hours later to the boys laughing in her bedroom. Her head was ringing while her stomach was knotting up in the worst way. India slowly sat up and licked her dry lips. She felt and looked like death.

"Go wash your ass baby," Brody told her sitting at the foot of the bed holding a bowl of cereal.

India frowned at the sight of him. She eyed her little cousins and saw how elated they were to be around a man. They didn't have their father in their life and because India's family consisted of mostly women aside from her brothers and father the twins were normally around the female sex.

India turned her attention back to Brody and briefly thought of kicking him off the bed. The only thing that saved him from her wrath were the boys.

"Brody you need to leave. Go take all of your shit to where the fuck you been staying at," she said quietly.

Brody chuckled like she'd told him a joke.

"Why would I do that? This where I belong. You don't even wanna touch me and now you worried about where I'm at? Since when?" he asked never looking back at her.

India slowly got off the bed and Brody eyed her body in the sexy silk and lace nightgown. Despite how much they fought he still loved everything about her.

"India..." he called out in his deep voice.

India stopped walking and when she turned to look at him he saw she was crying.

"I'm depressed Brody. Our baby is dead, and I'm hurt. Why is that so hard for you to understand?" she asked him sadly.

Brody sat his bowl on the nightstand and stood up. He went over to India in his basketball shorts and pulled her into his arms.

"Pushing me away isn't going to help shit. I love you and no matter what you think I'm out here doing, I haven't been cheating on you. I lost a baby too," he said looking down at her.

"Mama!" Shia's oldest twin yelled running over to India.

Because Shia was so seldom in their life they often got India, Shia and Sterling confused with one another. It also didn't help that all three women looked alike.

India stopped hugging Brody to grab her little cousin. Brody watched her intently as she held onto Shia's son.

"We should try again," he stated with his beautiful eyes glossing over.

India's eyes connected with his and she shook her head. She wasn't ready for anything like that.

"Not yet," she said quietly, and he walked away angrily leaving her in the bedroom with the boys.

India rushed after him with her cousin's son in her arms and followed him to the bathroom. Brody lifted the toilet seat as his eyes fell on her.

"Can I take a piss by myself?"

India sighed. She was truly tired of fighting with Brody.

"You can. I just want you to know that all that shit you were doing is done. Try me if you want to Brody and I'll make a believer out of you," she told him before walking away.

* * *

"This is cool," Palmer said as they stepped into the bar.

India gave her a slight smile. Her days were coming and going so fast that she could barely keep up. Still, she was trying to stay strong. While Palmer wore some ripped shorts with thigh high boots and a black off the shoulder top India was dressed to kill. She hadn't seen Brody in a week. He'd claimed he was working in Miami but thanks to the new app she'd discreetly added to his phone she knew better. She'd tracked him down to a club in Memphis and had taken Palmer with her. India was antsy. She was tired of fighting with Brody and wanted them to deal with the loss of their baby together but his coldness to her was making it damn near impossible.

"If he's with someone else I'm going to kill him," India told Palmer.

Palmer smiled now used to her friend's craziness. She didn't agree with it, but it no longer shocked her.

"I'm serious," India claimed and searched the club for her man.

India was turning heads as they passed the club goers. She wore a lace Balmain dress that stopped mid-thigh. It was strapless and pushed up her breast while accentuating her hips and ass. India's hair was flat ironed bone straight while blood-red lipstick stained her lips. Large diamond hoops hung from her ears as she looked around for her man.

"There he goes, and he's alone but damn there go Quez and he looks so damn good," Palmer said and smiled.

Palmer was still with Ishmael and things were at an all-time low for them. She'd been searching for ways to completely cut him off.

"And there goes that bitch Ashley," India said beginning to breathe hard. She spotted all of the women in Brody's section and shook her head. She hated how attractive he was. He already had money but to add in his good looks made it impossible for women to stay out of his face.

"She's not even close to him," Palmer said knowing that India just didn't like the girl that they both knew from back home.

"I don't care. That bitch doesn't need to even breathe my nigga's air," India replied leading them over to Brody and his crew.

India and Palmer walked up on Brody and his friends and all eyes fell on them. Brody was decked out in all black looking dapper as usual as a blunt sat in front of him. He stopped rolling it up to glance up at India.

"Palmer, what you doing here, ma?" Quez asked looking her up and down.

India noticed the way his eyes ate her best friend up, but she shook it off. Everyone knew how in love Palmer was with Ishmael.

"Nothing, with her," Palmer answered shyly and Quez grabbed her hand.

"You damn sure don't need to be in this bitch. Come here," Quez said and led Palmer over to the bar.

"What about you? How you fall off into this club?" Brody asked standing up.

India went to the app on her phone that was tracking him and flashed it at him before smiling sweetly. A few of his friends chuckled as Ashley and her girls all frowned.

India turned to Ashley wanting her to jump stupid.

"Is there a problem?" she asked her.

Ashley waved her off and walked away. Brody sat back down and resumed rolling up his blunt. India joined him on the sofa and someone with insanely bright red hair caught her attention. She looked up at Jenna and her eyes nearly bucked out of her head.

Before India could make a scene, Jenna was walking over to her. Jenna leaned down while frowning at India.

"I promise on my life I'm here for work. We just left Miami yesterday and made a stop down here. Please don't start anything in this club. You might be good, but I need to keep getting my money," she pleaded with her before quickly exiting the section.

India sat back as her chest heaved up and down. Brody decided to smoke his blunt before pulling India up out of the club. Palmer chose to stay back with Quez and his people. India knew that he wouldn't let anything happen to her girl.

India followed Brody into the plush hotel room and she went over to the designer bags that sat on the table. On top of one of the black Chanel bags was a card. India stepped out of her shoes as Brody came up behind her.

"Open it," he said quietly and unzipped her dress.

India opened the card as he took off her dress.

No matter what we go through I'ma always love the fuck out of you. This pain you feeling is temporary.

India closed the card and pulled out two beautiful purses. She went through the rest of the stuff and was indeed satisfied with all of the items he'd purchased her while in Tennessee. India thought back to seeing Ashley then Jenna in the club and cleared her throat.

They were having so many issues that she was having a hard time on which one she wanted to address first.

"I'm tired. This is a new low for me and you too. You know how I feel about Ashley's thirsty ass and you have Jenna here. Like you weren't just cheating on me with her. This won't ever end unless one of us walk away Brody. I have to walk away," she told him.

Brody turned India around and stared down into her eyes. Brody licked his lips before grabbing her face. The emotion India saw in his grey eyes was enough to make her heart pump faster.

"India, I love you. Money is money. Ashley's not even worth discussing. She fucks the homies and that's it. Jenna gets that dough. The minute she not getting it she won't be useful to me. I'm sorry for all of the shit I did in the past. I keep telling you that's done, and I mean it. We lost a lot and I can't lose you. All I keep thinking about is our baby. I would never put that shit on you but we both know that you ran that stop sign. I mean damn why didn't you fucking stop? Fuck!" Brody said and let her go.

Brody walked away from India and went to the plush bed. He sat down with his back to her and dropped his head. Never before had he voiced how he felt about her running the stop sign. He'd mentioned it once but never in an insinuating type of way.

India felt like shit as she heard him sniffle. India joined him on the bed as she thought about the things he'd said to her. She couldn't remember why she was driving so fast, but she did know she was partially responsible for the accident. The officers had even told her about the stop sign she'd run.

"I'm sorry Brody. I'm so sorry," she apologized quietly.

Brody ignored her and decided to roll up another blunt. India wanted to rub his back, beg and plead for him to understand that she didn't want any of that to happen, but she didn't. There was a huge shift with them and she wasn't sure how they would ever get what they once had back.

Seven

2016

"How did this happen?" she asked in shock.

Then as if a movie was playing in her mind India was hit with flashbacks from Vegas. Palmer was getting married to the love of her life. She'd finally been able to kick Ishmael to the side and had coincidently gotten with Arquez. India had been elated for her friend. While Mickey had chosen to stay at the room with Palmer, India chose to go to the strip club with the men. India called herself harmlessly flirting with Arquez's cousin Tarik and somehow that resulted in her having a threesome with him late that night.

India and Tarik had been given molly by the sexy dancer that was interested in doing both of them. They'd fucked all night long and Tarik made sure to cum inside of India as much as his body would allow for him too.

This pussy mine now India, you hear me? he'd told her that night while caught up in the moment.

India shook her head to clear the flashbacks of Vegas from her mind. India was ashamed of her reckless actions and also shocked. She stared at the monitor like the screen was incorrect. She hadn't been having sex with Brody because they'd been too busy fussing with one another, so the only candidate was Tarik. The last person on earth she needed to be pregnant by. Not only did he do business with Brody he was young, reckless and a playboy. India took a deep breath and exhaled. She knew she was hearing things incorrectly.

"I'm sorry doctor what did you say?" she asked again.

The doctor cleaned off her stomach that held a definite pudge to it and smiled.

159

"I said that you are twenty-five weeks pregnant. You are small, but you shouldn't have any problem picking up some weight. I'm also prescribing you iron pills because you battle with anemia. Do you have any questions?"

India sat up with her mind reeling. She knew. When she'd missed her first period she'd known but she didn't want to accept it. She had too much going on to do that. Her best friend had just gone through a multitude of bullshit including shooting a man that she'd once loved so India had ignored her problems to be there for her. Now months later her skeletons were falling out of the closet. She couldn't hide them even if she wanted to.

India looked down at her stomach that no longer looked like a gut but more like a baby bump and she exhaled. She'd gone through most of her pregnancy in the blind all because she hadn't wanted to hear the truth.

"Is...is everything okay with the baby? I haven't been drinking but I still want to make sure."

The doctor nodded while smiling at her.

"Everything looks and sounds fine. You will have to come in for some tests but as of now I'm not concerned, and I don't want you to be either. Don't forget to set up a follow-up appointment. It's very important to keep them on time," she replied before walking away.

India robotically did as she was told before going to her car.

"What did they say?" Sterling asked from the passenger seat.

India passed her the papers and rested her head on her steering wheel.

"Oh my god...Indie...he's going to kill you. Like what the hell are you going to do?" Sterling asked in a whisper.

India shrugged.

"I don't know. After losing my baby I never thought this would happen again. Especially with someone else.

God! I can't believe his little young ass did this to me. I could go kill him," India vented.

Sterling sat back with a frown on her face.

"You always say you're done with Brody but you and I both know you love him. Just how do you plan on taking another man's baby to him? Huh?"

Before India could reply a small hand tapped on her window. India's brows knitted together as she slowly rolled the window down. Outside of her car was the woman she was certain was Brody's mistress.

India just had no proof. So, whenever she brought up Brandy and how she seemed to go starry-eyed whenever he was around, Brody always shot her comments down. With time Brody had gotten very good at keeping the dirt he did under wraps. India hadn't had to deal with any real disrespect since before the loss of her child. But even with things looking perfect India knew they weren't. She felt so disconnected from Brody that it was scary. They'd long ago lost the spark that they once possessed as a couple and were both hanging onto a love they once had. India stayed because she did once love him with all of her heart but also the guilt from losing his baby kept her home. Brody, of course, stayed because he knew that no other woman would love him how India had.

"You must have lost your fucking mind? Why exactly are you at my car Brandy?"

Brandy took a step back and smiled. She was pretty India couldn't deny that, but India had never been threatened by her looks. Brandy was artificially attractive which meant she needed to have a ton of shit on for her to look like something. She could not rock Forever 21 or Target and turn heads. India felt like she could wear a dollar store outfit and still shut shit down.

"I think it's time we talk. I saw you in there and I felt like enough is enough. Brody has been sleeping with me for

161

the last year on and off and I want you to know that," Brandy revealed as she stared down into the car.

India smiled as she took off her obnoxiously large earrings.

"And you're telling me because you're a side bitch with a conscious? Or you feel like telling me that will make me leave him so that you can take my spot? Which one is it because I'm confused?" India asked pushing the door to her Mercedes open.

"India no," Sterling said getting out of the car with her.

Brandy took another step back and glared at India.

"I'm telling you the truth because he's too scared too! He doesn't want you anymore India. He said it's more loyalty than love. I mean he's only with you because he feels like he has to be. You need to let him go," Brandy said getting emotional. She was dealing with a heavy period which was why she'd been at the doctor's office in the first place.

India looked at Brandy like she was crazy.

"Let him go?" India laughed. She looked around her body then back at her car. "Bitch even if I gave him to you he wouldn't stay. I'm not forcing that man to be with me just like I didn't make you hate me. You getting played by *my* nigga because you a dumb bitch is what makes you hate me. And that's what he is. He really can be a motherfucka when he wants to be but he's mine. That's why you're really mad," India said and slapped Brandy so hard her head whipped to the other side.

Sterling grabbed India before she could hit Brandy again and Brandy ran to her car crying. Sterling let India go and glared at her. India had always been the firecracker between the two but now that she was pregnant things were different. She needed to think of her baby and not just herself.

"India you really need to calm down. Fighting while pregnant is not only reckless but ratchet as hell. I'm telling your momma on you."

India stopped looking at Brandy's car that was speeding out of the lot to glare at her cousin.

"I swear if you do that I'm not talking to your ass for a month. You play too much."

Sterling walked around the car.

"I'm serious. You will not be out here on Mike Tyson status while carrying my little cousin. Act like the woman that almost went to law school."

India smiled as they both got into her car.

"That India you're referring to is beside you. I'm just fed the fuck up. I can't believe Brody was fucking her old ashy hand's ass. I'm so done with him!"

Sterling looked at her cousin, thought of the predicament she was in and had to laugh.

"Bitch you pregnant by someone else and you're upset with him? Both of y'all need to let the games go or call it quits."

India started up her car as her phone began to ring. She saw Brody's name and rolled her eyes.

"He started it and I only cheated twice, I fucked that prince in Fiji because I mean he was a damn prince and well you know how the last one happened."

Sterling nodded while still staring over at her cousin.

"You should call him and at least tell him about the baby India," she suggested.

India looked at her like she was crazy.

"I'm not doing that. I've got too much going on right now," she replied not ready to face Tarik.

Sterling grabbed India's phone and unlocked it using her code. She went to Tarik's name and called him. India snatched her phone out of her cousin's hand as the call picked up.

"Hello," an angry feminine voice said taking the call.

India's eyes connected with her cousins and India sighed.

"I was calling to speak with Tarik," she said in the nicest tone that she could muster up.

"He's not here but it's good you called. I was actually looking over his messages to you the other day and I want you to know that whatever you two did in Vegas is the past. We've decided to try to make our relationship work and it would be great if you could lose his number. Okay, thank you so much bye, bye. *Bitch*," the woman said and hung up in her face.

India smiled to keep from calling the girl back.

"Today just isn't my day cousin. Can I at least get some Patron wine while we're out?"

Sterling snickered in her seat.

"You know damn well they don't make no Patron wine."

India laughed as she pulled out of the lot.

"No, I'm for real I think I saw it somewhere near the Moscato," she replied making Sterling laugh again.

After spending the majority of her day with her cousin India finally stepped into her home. She could smell Brody as she took her shoes off. Soft music flowed throughout the lower level of their brownstone while the aroma of soul food filled the air.

India walked into the kitchen and found him standing near the island making a drink. He wore nothing but denim pants with a pair of blue boxers sticking out the top of them. He was bare feet as his rose gold Cuban link diamond chain hung from his neck. Brody's grey eyes looked at her pensively as she walked over to the stove and studied the food that she knew he hadn't cooked.

"I missed you, baby," he said quietly admiring her beauty.

India used a nearby fork to taste the mac and cheese. The last thing she planned on doing was playing with Brody. She was sure he knew all about her altercation with Brandy.

"I love you too so much. I know lately we been going through it but we nine years into this. We came too far to let this shit go," Brody spoke walking up on her.

India's chest started to heave up and down at the thought of her leaving Brody. He was right they did have nearly a decade in the game but what did it mean if they didn't have trust?

"I can't do this with you anymore. This isn't love Brody. I guess what your little side bitch said is true. We're with each other out of loyalty and that's it. I've gotten so immune to this. The cheating, the lies, none of it even hurts as much as it once did. That right there is disturbing. It's sad that my heart is used to you hurting me," India said to him.

Brody spun India around and pulled her into his arms.

"Let's go to counseling. I know it can help me, baby. I fuck up. I know I do but I love you so much." Brody stopped talking to stare down into her eyes. They'd grown up together. India was his life and he didn't know who he was without her.

"You don't deserve that. Somewhere down the line I lost sight of what was important but I'm telling you right now that shit is gone," he declared.

India pushed Brody back and faced the sink.

"Brody just save it. You've said this same shit for a hundred years now. We're both fools you know? You're a dummy for cheating on the best thing to ever happen to you and I'm the fool for staying. I've been so damn dumb. Instead of facing what we are I've been ignoring the truth. We aren't good together and our past has pushed me to do some horrible things Brody," India said thinking of the baby growing in her belly. She took a deep breath and exhaled. "I cheated twice trying to take away all the pain that you caused me, and it still didn't work," she revealed quietly.

Brody took a step back with anger and anguish washing over him. His chest heaved up and down as he processed what India had just told him.

"So, you fucking somebody else? Is that what the fuck you saying to me India?"

India glanced down at the knife block praying she didn't have to use it on Brody.

"You fucked Ashley, that ugly hoe Jenna that you still have trapping for you even after she burnt us! Brandy and a host of other bitches that I will never know about. Does sleeping with someone two times really make me the bad guy?" she asked choosing to put both of her cheats on Tarik instead of revealing it had in fact been two men between her legs at separate times.

Brody became so angry his skin darkened.

"Hell, fuck yeah it do! You out here fucking niggas like that shit cute!" Brody yelled and grabbed India by the back of her neck.

India snatched a butcher knife out of the block and held it near Brody's neck after he spun her around. Brody's eyes narrowed as he looked down at the knife.

"You was gone fucking cut me? What the fuck is wrong with you?" he asked and shook her shoulders.

India let the knife fall from her hand as her eyes watered.

"Brody, I need some space. This has just gotten to be too much. You hoeing around, I'm hoeing around and we've both forgot about the love. I can't keep dealing with this shit and especially now that I'm...um older I think." India shook her head. She wasn't ready for him to know of the baby. "I just need to clear my mind for a few days. Okay?"

Brody let India go and walked away. He wanted to beg her to stay. He wanted to proclaim his love for her, but his ego wouldn't let him. No matter how many women he fucked, he couldn't accept India doing the same thing.

"Get the fuck on then with your trifling ass," he mumbled heading towards his man cave that was on the lower level of the brownstone.

India nodded. Wounded by his words and nonchalant attitude she rushed upstairs.

"Fuck you too Brody. After all of the shit I put up with you wanna try to flip this shit on me? Fuck you nigga!" she yelled walking into her bedroom.

Brody walked to the bottom of the steps angered even more by her outburst.

"Just get your shit and go! Fuck you doing all of that talking for? Go to that other nigga and get the fuck up out of here before I hurt your ass!" he yelled and rushed up the stairs.

India grabbed her carry-all off her closet floor and tossed as many things as she could into her bag. India started to grab her shoes as Brody stepped into the closet. His angry grey eyes searched the bedroom space that they shared as a blunt hung from his long fingers in his left hand.

"India, I thought you was leaving. What the fuck you in here doing?" he asked glaring at her.

India grabbed a few pairs of shoes then some jewelry.

"Brody don't come in here fucking with me. Just go smoke your blunt and leave me alone," India said trying to play it cool.

She was slightly worried he might strike her. The fact that her two brothers no longer lived in Michigan also made her uneasy.

"This my shit too. I'll do what the fuck I wanna do India. Don't get shit confused around here. Just cause you done fucked me over don't mean you running shit now," Brody said angrily.

India shook her head still packing her bag. The silence that greeted Brody only made him more upset.

"I really can't fucking believe your ass. You ain't shit for this right here!" he said with his voice rising so loud that it made India jump.

Brody hit the closet door so hard that it nearly came off the hinges.

India's hands shook as she zipped her bag up. Her only objective was to leave the brownstone in one piece.

"So, who is this bitch ass nigga? Who was stupid enough to fuck with my bitch?" Brody asked angrily.

India moved faster not looking to ever go there with Brody.

"It's not important who he was," she said calmly.

Brody advanced on India and dropped down to her level. India tried to remain calm as he gripped the back of her neck.

"Don't fucking play with me India, who was he?" he asked through gritted teeth.

India had never seen him so mad. She shook her head refusing to say a name and Brody let her go. He stood up and before India could stand he kicked over the glass jewelry desk that sat in the middle of their closet.

India's body shook in fear of what he would do next. She wasn't trying to involve her father, but she knew that if Brody was to hit her that was exactly what she would have to do.

"India I could fucking kill you," Brody said angrily.

"Well it doesn't feel good does it?" India asked standing up. The more Brody acted an ass the more it angered her. She looked up at him as he glared her way. "All the times you hurt me, that was how I felt but worse because I didn't deserve any of it. I never did and those were your words so don't sit here and act like you the victim. Do good shit to people and good shit will come your way," she told him.

Brody cracked a smile on his handsome face.

"Keep talking shit and you won't be walking up out of here," he warned her.

India looked him up and down in disgust.

"I fucking hate you. I mean I really hate you, Brody," she said and grabbed her bag.

India walked by Brody and he grabbed her arm. Sometimes he hated her too. He hated that he couldn't let her walk away from him. He hated that he loved and needed her so much and he hated that no matter how many women he fucked he couldn't get her out of his system. They were young. They had a lifetime to be tied down to someone yet at twenty-three he already felt married to her. Brody hated the power she possessed over him and if he could have he would have walked away from her years ago.

"I understand that you mad. Shit, I am too but we both know that leaving each other isn't an option. I don't know how I became the bad guy considering you been fucking cheating on me, but I'll be that if that's what it takes for us to get past this shit we going through. I won't let you walk away from me. I'm only giving you two days India. Two days then I'ma be expecting your ass back here," he said and let her go.

India walked out of her bedroom and eventually out of her home. She got into her car after putting her luggage in the trunk and thought about calling her best friend Palmer. Palmer had recently gotten married and had a baby, so the last thing India wanted to do was worry her. India started up her car as Brody walked to the door. Not able to look at his face anymore she quickly eased out of her driveway and drove off.

India's phone rung as she pulled onto Thirteen Mile road. She picked up the call on her blue tooth in her car.

"Look I'm not in the mood for no bitch playing on my phone. I promise you I will pull this truck over, find your address through this phone number and pull up on you bitch," India said angrily.

Tarik chuckled through the speakers in her car.

"Well, it's a good thing I'm not a bitch. Somebody got you mad as fuck right now. But ma, I miss that sexy ass face and I actually want you to pull up on me. Fall through," he said showing her what his intentions were with his voice going husky in the call.

India sighed hating the effects that his deep voice had on her. Tarik was part of the problem.

"I shouldn't. Your girl picked up when I called you earlier. She let me know what was up so why are you calling me?" India asked with jealousy peeking through her light voice.

"And I talked to her about that stupid shit. We trying to see what we can work on, but you got that nigga Brody, so you understand how it is. Right?"

India cleared her throat. She knew better than anyone how it went.

"Unfortunately, I do. Look I got a lot going on right now and...."

"And you need to let me take care of that. Meet me at the MotorCity. Let's get a drink and do some grown up shit that's gone make you feel better."

India laughed.

"Can you even get into the casino?"

Tarik chuckled at her question.

"You know I'm talking about the fucking hotel with your smart-mouthed ass, but I got something for you. I'ma find a way to make that motherfucka snap shut. You gone meet me up there India?"

India shook her head. The last thing she needed to do was meet up with him but what she wanted to do was get an escape from her reality and she knew he could provide that.

"Okay I'm on my way," she reluctantly relented.

Tarik smiled.

"That's music to my ears sexy. I'm already down here on Jefferson so just hit me up when you in the hotel," he said and ended the call.

India shook her head as she headed to downtown Detroit. Tarik was Palmers husband's younger cousin. India of course was attracted to Tarik but because he was only nineteen she'd refused to take him seriously. But once they got acquainted with one another on a personal level she quickly assessed that the only thing young about him was his age.

India had never in her life been fucked so good. Tarik was not only long, he was thick and knew how to stroke her in ways that could immediately get an orgasm out of her. India wasn't sure if the food was growing the men up quickly or what, but she'd been very pleased with Tarik in Vegas and still secretly fantasized about the night they'd shared together.

It took India no time to make it to the hotel in downtown Detroit. She valet parked her car and went upstairs to the hotel room number that Tarik had sent over to her as she was driving. India made sure her clothes were in tack and ran her hands through her hair before knocking.

The door opened minutes later, and Tarik stood on the other end with a sexy smirk on his handsome caramel brown-skinned face. He was just as sexy as India remembered him being. His left hand that had a lion's face tattooed on the front of it swept across his taper fade as he stared India up and down. From the fullness of his lips that were outlined with a mustache down to the slanted dark eyes, he possessed India was happy with the man that stared down at her.

Tarik's gaze set her body on fire as he looked her up and down.

"Damn. Why the fuck you so fine?"

India rolled her eyes. Silently she prayed that he hadn't noticed how his presence affected her.

"Too damn fine," Tarik commented and slapped her ass as she walked by him.

Tarik shut the door then he followed India into the room and hugged her from the back. India closed her eyes as he kissed her on the neck sensually. Tarik smelled like cologne mixed with a little bit of weed. His soft lips felt heavenly as they tantalized India's skin.

"I missed your sexy ass. You missed me?"

India ignored him as he led her over to the king-sized bed.

"I see you still on that fronting shit. I know you missed a nigga. I mean you showed up," he said and pushed her up on the bed. Tarik licked his lips as he pulled down her leggings and before India could register what was going on he was filling her up. India moaned when he thrusted his big dick into her.

"Oh my god! Ugh...shit," she moaned out in ecstasy.

Tarik continued to pound into India as he took off his shirt. His tongue got lodged in his throat at how good she felt. The night he'd entered into her he thought it was the pills they'd popped but now as he tore down her tight walls he knew it was more than that. Not only was India incredibly wet she was also insanely tight.

His hand gripped her hip tightly as he reintroduced her to his dick. It had been some long gruesome months without her and he couldn't imagine himself going that long without the feel of her again.

"*Damn...* you wet as fuck baby. Shit dripping. Did you miss this dick India?"

Smack!

His hand went to her ass before he pushed himself all of the way inside of her again. India's eyes rolled into the back of her head.

"I did. I missed it so much," she confessed, and her legs started to shake. As she clamped down harder on him Tarik dug deeper into her.

He leaned down and started to suck on her neck. India could feel him releasing inside of her as his teeth sunk into her skin. If she hadn't been already pregnant by him she would have gone off on his ass.

"Damn, you feel even better than last time. Gone make a nigga fuck around and drop a baby off in you," he joked and immediately India was brought back into reality. She squirmed beneath him until he reluctantly pulled himself out of her. Tarik pulled off her shirt as she slowly stood up.

"Let's go shower sexy," he demanded and without saying another word he pulled her into the connected upscale bathroom. Quietly Tarik finished undressing India then himself. India stepped into the shower with his semen seeping from between her legs. She turned on the water as Tarik stepped up behind her. His hands went between her legs and he gently massaged her clitoris.

"I'm in love with this already. She make a nigga feel all warm and bubbly on the inside India. You need to let that nigga of yours know that he's on borrowed fucking time," he told her.

Just thinking of her current situation with Brody brought tears to India's eyes. She shook her head as the hot water sprayed against her skin. Tarik's hard on pressed into her ass as he played with her delicate pearl.

"What's wrong India?" he asked hearing her whimper but in a different way than the one he was looking for. India turned in his arms and gazed up at him. She didn't know much about him besides the way he fucked yet she was carrying his child. A child she didn't ask for. A child that was undoubtedly going to change her life forever. Now the biggest question was just when would she tell him?

"My life is so fucked up right now. One minute things were going well. Then something shifted, and I woke up in hell. I don't know what to do," she confessed.

Tarik picked India up and she wrapped her legs around his waist. Slowly he inserted himself deep into her warm walls and India moaned. Tarik kissed her on the lips while looking up into her eyes.

"Fuck the bullshit. None of us are perfect so all we can do is try. Stop letting shit that you can't change stress you out. Stop doing that," he told her and rose her up and down on him.

India moaned as she wrapped her arms around his neck. Tarik felt like he was splitting her into two.

"Slow down...you're so big," she moaned.

Tarik groaned deep into the back of his throat before kissing her again. He just couldn't get enough of her.

"Stop whining and cum on this dick. That's what I need you to do," he commanded and like she was the puppet and he was the master her body exploded for him.

Hours later India rested on the plush bed with Tarik. They were both spent from the hours of none stop fucking they'd done and India was content with lying in his arms. Tarik, on the other hand, was looking to be inside of her again as his member rocked up against her.

"I'm sore boy."

Tarik chuckled.

"Yeah okay. How you been sexy? You just stop fucking with me and shit."

India closed her eyes. She was so tired from the life she was living.

"Do you ever think about just up and leaving?"

Tarik smiled at her question. Gently his hands rubbed up and down her back.

"I'd run away with you," he replied.

India laughed lightly. He was so charming the shit really was ridiculous.

"I'm serious, Tarik."

Tarik slapped her ass gently.

"I am too but yeah. You know I was in school in DC. That shit wasn't working for me, so I dipped out. My parents didn't like it, but I had to live for me."

India inhaled his sexy scent as she rested her face on his chest.

"And that was hustling?"

Tarik nodded.

"It was hard to be in someone's fucking class when I watched my people buy Ferrari's and shit. I held out for as long as I could then I woke up one day like fuck this bullshit. I'm working a hundred hours to get a fucking Louie belt when I could make that shit in an hour. The decision wasn't hard at all. It hurt me more to have to tell my mom that shit. She wanted me to be a college graduate. She be on my head now thinking I'ma end up dead but I'm good. I might be young but I'm ahead of my time India. Hustling forever was never my goal. I came into this shit with a plan and I still will go back to school. I'ma do that for myself you know?"

India cleared her throat. Tarik really was so much more than his good looks and tender age. He was also about to become a father. He just didn't know it yet.

"I'm not happy Tarik. I haven't been for a while now," she admitted to him.

As Tarik exhaled at her words India began to cry. Tarik pulled her onto his lap and stared up at her pretty face. India gazed down into his eyes as she carefully sat on his erection. The intrusion initially hurt as it filled her walls to the max. Tarik groaned before pulling her face close to his. Slowly he moved beneath her without breaking eye contact.

"India you too beautiful to be so sad. If a person not putting love into you then all they doing is draining, you dry. Don't ever give nobody the power to do you like that ma," he whispered before kissing her passionately on the lips.

India moaned deep in her throat as Tarik fucked her from the bottom. His movements were calculated, so smooth that she didn't know she was cumming until the immense pleasure was on her. India's eyes widened as he gave her body the greatest pleasure she'd ever felt.

"It feels good. My god," she whispered as her walls contracted then creamed for him.

Tarik swallowed hard as his member was drenched with her wetness.

"Fuck, you got the best baby. You hear me India?" He asked making her eyes connect with his. India whimpered as her body twitched and Tarik gripped her hips. "This the best pussy I done ever had and I'm not about to let that shit go," he told her before she cried out in pleasure.

* * *

"India what the fuck is going on? I need to know why Brody is in my living room losing his damn mind over you," Palmer said into the phone.

India closed her eyes as the wind kissed her skin. The California weather was the shit. Warm breezes, beautiful sunsets, and limited rain. She was in weather heaven.

"I needed a break. For nine years I've played this game with him. I needed to see if it was time to let him go. I think it is," she revealed to her best friend.

Palmer grunted having heard India say those words a thousand times before.

"I don't know India. You always say you're done with him. What did he do this time?"

India thought back on Brody's dealings with Brandy and rolled her eyes.

"Slept with Brandy old casket ready looking ass. Bitch gotta have a face full of makeup on just to go to the damn mailbox yet that was appealing to him. I'm over it. I won't keep dealing with his infidelity then when we were arguing you know that light skinned ass nigga had the nerve to act stupid on me. I really thought for a minute that he was going to hit me, and it just made me angrier. All of the things we're dealing with is because of him and I'm tired of it!" she vented.

Palmer sighed taking in all that India said to her.

"I get it I do. I won't make excuses for his cheating but the past you have to let go of. You took them charges India and you never forgave him. I mean why did you take them in the first place?" Palmer asked.

India sat up on her lounge chair and gazed out at the pool.

"*Palmer* I love Brody. That's why I took the charge. Don't make me the bad guy," India said defensively.

"Look I love you. I'm always on your side so don't be getting an attitude with me. I'm just saying that I feel like you hold a lot of resentment towards Brody for something that you chose to do. Eventually, you will have to let that shit go if you want to be with him. Or maybe you don't. You said you were through this time, right?"

India's heart beat faster as she looked up at the clear blue sky. She felt like she was through but now that she was miles away from him she wasn't so sure. Brody had been a huge part of her life for years and she'd grown used to his presence.

"I don't know," she said quietly.

Palmer smiled.

"Then you should try to figure it out while you on this break and don't stay away too long. You know I'm pregnant and I need you here for the birth," Palmer said and laughed.

India's hand went to her own stomach. She thought about the life she was carrying and shook her head.

"I promise I won't."

Eight

"This is nice as hell and where did this baby bump come from?"

India's narrowed eyes glared Shia's way before they fell onto Sterling.

"It's a baby in my stomach Shia. You know like what happened to you when you had the twins or did you forget? I mean you never have them any damn way so maybe you forgot you were a mother," India quipped.

Shia smiled pushing down her nasty reply. She'd fought India plenty of times when they were kids and she had no interest in doing that again.

"Oh okay. So, who are you pregnant by? Must not be Brody since you're out here hiding," Shia commented and glanced around the spacious living room. Shia sucked her teeth at how lavish India's temporary living quarters were. "I see you're still using him to take care of you though."

India's face fell into a frown as she eased off the blush pink leather sofa.

"Bitch," fell from her lips softly as Sterling walked towards her.

"Can y'all please play nice? Dang it's not that serious and Shia I didn't bring you out here to talk shit," Sterling said and pushed India back down.

India looked at Sterling as she thought back to the first time she'd gotten into it with Shia.

"The minute I got the pink Barbie bike that she wanted she started hating on me. Like damn, your daddy bought you two one as well, but she was still mad because I got mine first," India replied.

Shia sat down on the loveseat and rolled her eyes. It was crazy because she did love and hate her cousin at the same time.

"I'm sorry. I wasn't trying to be funny and I don't give a damn about that bike. How long do you plan on staying out here? This place is really nice too. Maybe I could stay at your brownstone since you said Brody hadn't been there since you left?"

Sterling shook her head before India could.

"No what about the twins?"

Shia smiled.

"I could bring them with me but forget it. It's not that serious."

India rubbed her small baby bump. Six months in she was finally getting a stomach that seemed to grow every time she looked in the mirror.

"Shia, I do plan on going back home. This isn't a forever thing," India told her.

Shia looked at India.

"And Brody is? I just want you to make the right decision. We might not get along, but we are family. I would hate for you to be in the same situation that I'm in," Shia sighed actually looking concerned for India. "I don't know maybe things will work out for you. Have you told him about the baby?"

India shook her head.

"He's flying out here in a few days and I plan on telling him then," she replied ignoring the look Sterling was giving her.

"Well, I wish you nothing but the best. I have a friend picking me up in a few. I'll catch you hookers later," Shia said and stood up.

Sterling waited for her to be out of the condo before looking at India.

"India you haven't told Tarik or your parents about this baby. What are you doing? This is dumb and selfish," she told her.

India nodded. Sterling knew her in ways no one else did and she valued her opinion. She also knew her cousin would never steer her wrong.

"I know. Palmer doesn't even know," she mumbled feeling ashamed of her actions.

Sterling sat back while shaking her head.

"You just plan on popping up in Detroit with a whole child like it fell out of the damn sky? Eventually, they will have to know. Why are you acting like a fourteen-year-old? You're a grown ass woman with your own clothing store. You don't need anyone's approval of this pregnancy and you need to tell the real father India. It's not right to hide this."

India looked around her spacious living room. She was subletting from an old classmate that was traveling through London for the next year on her own eat, pray, love type thing so she wasn't spending a grip of money. The break was more for her than anyone else. India wasn't ready to tell everyone about her baby that she'd produced with a man that she didn't love and barely knew.

India's cell phone vibrated on her lap as Sterling turned on the TV. India saw it was a video call from Tarik and she smiled. They'd been keeping in touch via phone and he had become a friend to her in some ways. He still, however, didn't know about the baby.

"Hey, how was New York?" she asked him as she went upstairs and into her bedroom.

Tarik popped up on the screen with a frown on his handsome face. His usually well-groomed hair was in need of a lineup and his beard was longer as well begging for a trimming. India took in his looks as she sat down on the bed. She made sure to not show him her baby bump.

"Shit's all bad for a nigga Indie," Tarik replied calling her by her nickname. He'd heard Sterling call her it one time over the phone and after that, he was drawn to the nickname her family used for her.

India watched his dark eyes look back at her with gloom lingering in his orbs and her heart raced at what could be wrong with him.

"What happened? Is Quez okay?" she asked.

Tarik quickly nodded. Not wanting to scare her.

"Yeah, that nigga good. Shit for one I dropped dirty then I got into with your nigga in the hood and we ended up shooting at each other. Shits crazy right now," he replied.

India's eyes grew wide at his response. She talked with Brody every day and he hadn't mentioned anything of the sort. Because they both hold significant places in her life she needed for them to get along. India loved Brody and she was pregnant by Tarik. She didn't want them shooting at one another.

"*Okay*, why exactly did you shoot at him Tarik? I mean you have no reason to not like him."

Tarik chuckled. He licked his lips and the small gesture drove India wild.

"I don't? I never envied no man but I'm a little mad that he gets to have you all of the time while I can only see you when you pissed off at him. He don't even appreciate the woman that he has but you know I never fucked with that nigga like that. He was Quez boy, but I always saw the bitch in him. He fucked me over on some money shit then lied to my cousin about it. I had to check his ass because I don't play about my money. Shit got serious and I ended up shooting at him. Somebody called the cops and they took us all in. Brody was smart enough to not press charges, but I had some shit on me so they sending me away. I feel like I should have just stayed my ass in DC. At least there I was in school and not in the streets."

India wanted desperately to rub her stomach. Everything she was hearing was making her sick.

"When are you leaving?"

Tarik sighed as he fired up a blunt.

"Shit my P. O violated me, so they want me to turn myself in now. It's only two years but still. A cell ain't never been for no nigga like me. My momma won't even take my calls cause she so mad. I'm the black sheep of the family and shit," he said and shook his head. India smiled because she could relate. "I want you to come see me before I go in. I need to see your face sexy. Tell me you gonna come," he demanded.

India could have fallen off the bed at his request. She slowly shook her head.

"I'm in another state."

"And you can catch a flight. I wanna see that pretty face and feel that warm ass pussy one more time. I thought we was friends Indie. You gone leave your man hanging like that?" he asked and pushed the blunt to his lips.

India took a deep breath. Tarik was so much more difficult to deal with then Brody because he always demanded something that pulled her out of her comfort zone.

"I don't know. My cousins just flew in to see me," she said with a pout.

Tarik blew smoke out his mouth as he looked at her.

"You see Sterling all the fucking time ma. Jump on a flight today and call me when you touch down," he replied and ended the call.

India rolled her eyes at his demanding ways as she pulled her laptop onto her lap. She booked the quickest flight that she could catch to Detroit and got off her bed. She started to breathe heavy as she walked to the walk-in closet. Lately, anything that she did caused her to have shortness of breath.

"I'll just have to tell him the truth. Maybe I can convince him to not say anything until after the baby is born," she said to herself.

India grabbed her Fendi book bag and tossed into it an outfit and a pair of thongs. She went to grab her Chloe sunglasses and Sterling barged into her room. A look of worry covered her pretty heart-shaped brown-skinned face.

"Hey, we need to go get Shia. She's at some dude's house fighting his baby momma. Because she's on my plan and using an iPhone that's under my name I have her on that app, so I can track her down. Do you have a gun out here?"

India looked at her cousin and sighed. That was the exact reason why she didn't fool with Shia. She was always in some shit and they were forced to run to her rescue.

"I don't but I think my friend has a stun gun. I was about to catch a flight to see Tarik. It's leaving in two hours," India replied.

Sterling nodded while pulling up her baby sisters location.

"This shouldn't take long. She's only thirty minutes away. I know she's irritating as fuck but she's family. We look out for each other, right?"

India thanked god that she was smart enough to get ticket insurance because she was positive that she would miss her flight. She pulled her phone out of her pocket and sent Tarik a text.

Sorry, can't make it today. I promise I'll book a flight for tomorrow.

Tarik's message came through seconds later.

It's all good. Just do you and I'll hit you up when I go in. Don't start acting funny on me either ma. You be good Indie.

"Come on India," Sterling said and left back out of the room.

India's baby kicked, and she found herself getting emotional. She knew Tarik's two years would fly by but still, she felt a way about him getting locked up. She texted him back as she exited her room.

You will do that time standing on your head pretty boy, but I do need you to hit me up. I have something very important to tell you.

Tarik text her back immediately.

I got you and I will once I'm good.

India wanted to say something else, but no words came to mind so she put her phone away and walked down her stairs. India and Sterling tracked Shia to a home deep in the Bay.

India pulled her car up to the home that had fifteen or more people surrounding it and India quickly assessed the situation. In Detroit, they were protected. Both India and Sterling's father were known throughout the city then they had men in their family that would fight the world for them, but they weren't in Detroit. They were in another state alone and without real protection. India was usually down to act a fool but her unborn baby had slowed down her feisty spirit.

"Damn, let's just grab Shia and go. These motherfuckas look ignorant," Sterling said and got out of the car.

India grabbed a small thing of pepper spray that she kept in the car and put it in her purse before getting out as well. Shia's loud yelling could be heard as they walked up.

"Bitch I don't even know you! I have been knowing Ken since middle school. I had the dick before you!"

India shook her head as she walked in between people to get a better view of her cousin.

"Shia let's go," Sterling said sounding more like her mother than her sister.

"Nah, this bitch wants to fuck my baby daddy then throw the shit in my face like I'm going to let that shit slide. Bitch, you gone get it today," a pretty fair skinned woman said and ran up on Shia. They began to fight, and India looked around as a few women start to move towards them.

The last thing she wanted to do was fight while being pregnant, but she refused to let them jump her cousin.

"Shia let's go!" Sterling gritted and grabbed Shia by her arm. Two girls tried to run up on her and India ran to Sterling's side as Shia continued to talk shit.

"Bitch what's up!" Shia yelled and spit at the girl that stood behind Sterling.

India quickly went into her purse knowing what was about to go down.

"Bitch, did you spit on me? I got yo ass!" the girl yelled and punched Sterling trying to hit Shia.

Sterling let Shia go and began to fight the girl. Shia began to fight the baby momma again and out of nowhere, India was hit in the back of her head. She felt like everyone in the crowd was attacking them as she struggled to fight two girls. India flipped the cap on her pepper spray and held her breath as she sprayed wherever she could.

Still, the pepper spray stung her eyes as everyone was affected by it including her cousins. India began to cough as she grabbed Sterling off the ground. She noticed her cousins pretty face was bruised and anger moved through her. India sprayed the crowd again not giving a damn who she hit in the eye with the mace.

"Come on, Shia," India said walking Sterling to her car.

They quickly got in as two women ran towards them with glass liquor bottles.

"Oh my god just hit them," Shia muttered while rubbing her own eyes.

India quickly pulled away but not before one of the bottles connected with her back windshield making it shatter.

India's skin grew hotter as she silently drove home.

"I swear that nigga better not call me unless he's talking money. Got me fighting his ugly baby momma and shit while he hides in his house," Shia said smoothing down her tangled extensions.

Sterling said nothing as she rubbed her busted lip. She was fuming mad at how she'd been brutally attacked by bitches that she didn't even know.

"You know..." India took a deep breath and sighed. "For this reason alone, I don't mess with you. It's always some drama. You got me and Sterling putting our life on the line for you over a man that's not even yours. Don't you get tired of this? What you're going to do is pack your bag up and catch a flight home because I'm done with you," India told her.

Shia stopped rubbing her eyes to glance India's way.

"Wow. You really think you're better than me? You always going off on someone India. I had to defend myself! That bitch was trying me."

India waved her off not trying to hear shit she was saying.

"What you should have done was take the L and keep it moving. You could have gotten us all killed my baby included then I would have had a serious problem with your ass. You need to grow the fuck up. Doing stupid shit like we sixteen. Act like a mother and less like a hoe."

Shia sat in the backseat with her heart pumping wildly in her chest. She hated the way India talked to her.

"Fuck you India I have my sons and my sister. You have no one but that cheating ass nigga of yours and that bastard ass baby that you scared to tell people about. Fix your own life and leave mine the fuck alone," Shia replied not looking to spare feelings.

India pulled her car into a nearby gas station. Sterling stopped touching her face to look at her cousin and her sister. Since the sandbox, they couldn't seem to get along and Sterling was tired of it.

"Can y'all just let this go? We're already fighting the world now y'all wanna fight with each other? This is silly," she vented.

India got out of the car after parking at the pump and went to Shia's door. Shia's first thought was to lock it, but her ego was too big for her to do that so instead, she pushed her door open and got out. Shia could tell by the way India looked that she was on one. India was an Aquarius. She had a lot of love in her heart and would do for anyone but once she got mad she could be downright scary. She became someone you didn't want to catch in a dark corner and Shia was now the recipient of her wrath.

India glanced at her shattered back window then her cousin.

"Did you just call my baby a bastard?"

Shia wanted to take a step back, but she couldn't because she was already leaning on the car. She placed her hands on her hips and frowned.

"We both said things we didn't mean but yeah I..."

Wop!

India couldn't hit her cousin quick enough. Up against the car, she tore Shia new asshole. Sterling jumped out of the car and attempted to pull India off her sister.

"India stop!" she yelled.

A man ran over and helped her as India slapped Shia repeatedly hoping to beat some common sense into her.

"Bitch," India gritted and slapped Shia one last time before she was pulled away.

Blood leaked from Shia's nose as she frowned at India. She was in a state of shock as Sterling pulled her into the back seat. Sterling sat next to her as India pulled away from the man.

Feeling so much better than before India got into her car and drove off. Shia held her head back to keep her nose from bleeding. India glanced back at her and smiled.

"And every time you disrespect my baby you'll get that treatment bitch," she said and turned on her radio.

* * *

India kept her eyes trained on the monitor as the cool gel slid across her belly. She could feel the heated gaze from Brody as he sat next to her.

"You have three months left to go. You've already decided to do a natural birth but just in case you change your mind medicine will be available to you. Do you have any questions?"

Brody cleared his throat.

"Is the baby okay? Does she have a good heart and shit like that?" he asked still staring at the monitor.

The OB-GYN smiled.

"Yes, the baby is progressing at a good rate. India doesn't have any complications which is good. This should be an easy birth for her. She just needs to gain a few pounds. Lately, her weight has dropped," the OB-GYN replied and took the device off India's stomach. She wiped India's stomach clean and shut off the monitor. "Make a four-week appointment with the clerk and like I said before try to put back on the pounds that you lost. Okay?"

India sat up and smiled at her.

"Okay."

The OB-GYN discarded her used gloves and left out of the room. India quietly began to get dressed as Brody stared her down. He'd flown in that morning and India had shown up at the airport with her baby bump on display. She'd then taken him to her appointment and now that her OB-GYN was gone she knew that she had to own up to her shit. She stood to her feet and Brody gently caressed her stomach.

He'd been begging for another baby and she'd flat out refused. He was pissed that she hid it from him, but he was elated to have a child with her on the way.

"I can't believe you hid this shit from me. You was that mad at being pregnant again baby?"

India swallowed hard as she took a step back.

"Let's go so we can talk."

Brody nodded, and they left out of the room. India made another appointment and they exited the doctor's office. Brody drove India's car to her condo. As they got out of the car he glanced over at her.

"Why you acting so weird? You not trying to give the baby away or no crazy shit like that are you?"

India quickly shook her head. She led him into the condo and up the stairs to her bedroom. Brody stood by the door as India took off her clothes.

India looked at him once she was down to her undies and he could see that her eyes were watery.

"*I love you.* Despite the drama, despite me saying that I hate you whenever you piss me off I do love you, Brody. I've loved you for as long as I can remember," India stopped talking and ran her hands through her hair. She was so scared that her hands were starting to shake. "I um..." she stopped talking and closed her eyes. When she opened them, Brody was still staring at her intently. "Remember I said that I slept with someone? Well, it was Tarik and um he's um..." India cleared her throat and Brody stepped off the door.

His brows furrowed as he walked up to India. Brody grabbed her hand and led her over to the bed. India sat down, and he stood over her. With his grey eyes staring down at her he grabbed her face.

Slowly he applied pressure on it.

"He's what India? You fucked a nigga I hustle with and he's what?"

India tried to turn her head and he tightened his grip on her face.

"Tell me that nigga got you pregnant, so I can kill your ass right now," he said angrily, and his hands went down to her throat.

"Brody!" India yelled, and Sterling came running into the room.

While Shia was immediately sent home after the yard fight and gas station altercation Sterling stayed behind. She wanted to make sure that Brody wasn't on no crazy shit with her cousin.

"Brody she's pregnant," Sterling said pulling on his arm.

Brody ignored Sterling as he stared down into India's eyes. To learn she was carrying another man's child had to be the worst thing that ever happened to him. Just to see her swollen with another man's baby made him lose his shit.

Brody let India go and was tempted to slap the taste out of her mouth. He glared down into her watery eyes and shook his head. He desperately needed to clear his thoughts.

"We good Sterling. Give us some space," he said never taking his eyes off of India.

Sterling looked at her cousin and made sure she was good before leaving out of the room. Sterling pulled the door up but refused to close it. Once she was gone Brody cleared his throat. He started to think back on all of his encounters with Tarik and everything started to make sense. He had never been buddy, buddy with Tarik but once he noticed that Quez and Palmer were on some funny shit he saw a change in Tarik. Tarik all of a sudden was always griming him on some hating shit and recently they'd been in a shoot-out over money that Brody fucked him out of.

Brody had honestly lost the money in the casino on some drunk shit while gambling and was going to pay Tarik back, but Tarik didn't have any understanding and instead chose to shoot his car up. Brody was ready to put a price on Tarik's head now that he'd learned that the young nigga had gotten his woman pregnant.

Brody went over to the chair that was in the corner of the room and sat down. He pulled out a cigarette. Something he only smoked when he was very stressed and sparked it up. Usually, India would ride him about it but knew when to pick her battles, so she said nothing as he filled her room up with the awful smell of smoke.

The more India realized how serious the situation was the sadder she became. She slowly stood up and walked over to Brody. His eyes never connected with her as she stepped in front of him.

"I'm sorry. I know that what we have isn't perfect, but it's ours and I'm sorry. Brody, I'm so sorry," India apologized and climbed onto his lap.

Brody made sure to blow the smoke the other way so that the smoke didn't get in India's face. India sat on Brody's lap and hugged his chest. She listened to his heartbeat as he smoked his cigarette. There were so many things that Brody wanted to say but he didn't. The thing that angered him the most was that India was having a baby that didn't belong to him still he couldn't just say fuck her.

Brody knew his lies, he knew his secrets and more importantly, he knew that his love for India ran deeper than anything else he'd ever experienced in his life. Yeah, he could walk away from her, but would he find someone that he loved more than her? He wasn't sure, and he wasn't willing to take that chance. He'd put in too many years to watch India go be great with the next nigga. The man in him just couldn't allow for that to happen.

"Have you told your family?"

India sighed and shook her head.

"No," she said quietly.

Brody chuckled. He finished his cigarette and India pulled back from the hug to stare into his eyes. Through his glare, she could see the pain she'd caused him, and she wanted to make it right. She wanted to show him that no matter what he would be the man in her life.

"I'm sorry. I love you, Brody," she whispered and kissed him.

Even with the taste of cigarette lingering on his tongue, India kissed Brody passionately. She closed her eyes and his hands went down to her ass. Slowly she grinded on him as she attempted to kiss away his pain. Brody's hands gripped her ass hard as he pulled back. His eyes seared into her in a heated gaze.

"You belong to me India. I won't let you be with anyone else. No fucking body but me," he told her willing to catch a case to keep her apart from the next man.

India nodded.

"I only want you. This will be your daughter too baby and you'll love her like she's your own. This will be our family and he won't get in the way of that. I want to be with you baby," she assured him.

"You got into that accident and my baby didn't make it. I been begging, you to try again and you didn't wanna do it. Now you carrying this hoe ass niggas baby and that shit hurts. How could you do this to me?" Brody asked hitting below the belt. He was hurt beyond words. He knew he was wrong, but he had to say it. He needed for India to feel guilty.

India blinked rapidly as her eyes watered.

"I'm sorry, I'm so sorry. I love and wanna be with you. Brody, I'm sorry," she apologized repeatedly staring him in the eyes. She still couldn't remember the accident, but she knew that she'd been in one that resulted in her baby dying.

"And you'll never leave me?" he asked quietly.

India smiled at him lovingly.

"Never," she whispered.

Brody swallowed hard before nodding. He kissed her again and stood up from the seat while still holding India. He carried her over to the bed. Brody laid India on her back and took off her underwear while she stared up into his eyes. Brody kissed her big belly pulling off his own

193

clothes. While licking his lips he opened India's creamy caramel thighs and stuck his head into his favorite place.

His tongue lapped against her clitoris making her eyes roll into the back of her head. India gripped his head as she started to roll her hips. Her pregnancy made her extremely horny and she was glad to be getting some real action. She was tired of using her rabbit to quench her thirst.

"Right there, baby. Eat your pussy," India moaned feeling the ecstasy began to take over.

Brody worked his tongue faster as his thick fingers massaged her walls. India's legs began to shake, and he ate her out through her release. Brody came up for air with wet lips. His grey eyes peered down at India as he climbed between her legs. Slowly he pushed his hard dick into her and it felt so good India climaxed again. Her mouth fell open as Brody started to long stroke her.

Brody leaned down to suck on her puckered nipples while rocking in and out of her. India clamped her muscles down hard onto him and his back stiffened. After years of being together, they knew how to bring one another to their knees almost immediately.

The harder India squeezed his member the harder he pounded into her. Brody stuck his face into the crook of her neck and pounded out her wet walls.

It wasn't long before they were both climaxing.

Two days later India sat inside of her car in the plaza mall with her phone in her hand. All day she'd been sick to her stomach and was out buying crackers when Tarik had called her collect.

"You good Indie? How shit hanging baby?" he asked her.

India sighed as she gazed out of the window. She wasn't sure how to broach the subject, so she'd decided to just come out and say it.

"I'm pregnant Tarik. Like seven months pregnant with your baby. That's how shit is hanging with me," she replied.

Tarik chuckled.

"Aye, you funny as shit but now isn't the time to joke with a nigga like that. You back in the D? I want you to come see me."

India cleared her throat.

"I'm not joking Tarik. I'm having your daughter....... we are having a baby."

Tarik was quiet for a moment while he processed what India had told him. They'd fucked more than once, and each time had been unprotected. Reckless on both of their parts but they also weren't exclusive, so he wasn't sure what to believe.

"You sure it's mine?"

India's nose flared as she frowned.

"Yes, I wasn't having sex with Brody at that time. We were on a break. Don't come at me like that Tarik."

Tarik breathed hard into the phone.

"Come at you like what? You got a house with your nigga. Been with his ass for a fucking lifetime and shit so hell yeah, I'm gone ask if it's mine. Are you sure India?"

India rolled her eyes. Her issues with her troubled relationship may have given her hoe tendencies but she did know who her baby father was.

"Yes, I'm sure. We can take a test. I wouldn't lie to you. I need for you to understand that I'm going to stay with Brody and he will be a part of our daughter's life as well. Because he's found it in his heart to forgive me I want you to respect what we have. Kalila will love both of you so this little beef thing you two have should be over for her. Okay?"

Tarik laughed. India was funny to him and she didn't even know it. He could have said some shit to fuck her *whole* life up but hating was never his style, so he kept it to himself.

"Kalila huh? I like that. My nana passed away last year, and her name was Cecily. Can you make that her middle name?"

India palmed her belly.

"Um sure. That's not a problem. Can you just let whatever issues you have with Brody go? I can't be worried about you two while trying to be a new mom."

"Look as long as he stays the fuck out of my face then he good and India if she is mine then let it be known that she's my daughter. She won't need that pussy ass nigga for shit. Don't have people thinking that's his daughter and it's not. Jail or not I'll have somebody pull up on his ass," Tarik said angrily.

The phone beeped, and they were notified that they had two more minutes to talk.

"Look you need to come see me. You coming?" he asked wanting to speak with her in person.

India promised Brody that they would have a fresh start. She promised him that the baby wouldn't push them further apart. She also promised that Tarik wouldn't be a problem. India said a silent prayer that Tarik didn't make it hard for her to keep them.

"I guess I can do that. I'm flying home to tell my parents, so I'll see you then. And Tarik don't tell Quez or Palmer. I'm not ready for everyone to know just yet. Please," she begged.

Tarik groaned not liking all the secrecy shit she was on. To him it was silly as hell, considering soon enough everyone would know of the baby.

"Yeah, alright. So, if you staying with that hoe ass nigga then what am I to you? Your baby daddy?" Tarik asked not liking the way that sounded.

India frowned not caring for the sound of it as well.

"My friend. Just like how you call me every day nothing has to change. We're about to have a kid together so it's only right for us to be cool with each other. I mean you still wanna be my friend, don't you?"

Before Tarik could reply the call ended.

Nine

India snuck into Detroit on a mission. She was jet-lagged and cranky but more nervous than anything.

As Brody turned the rental down the block to her family home her jitters only got worse. India looked at herself in the mirror and exhaled. Her best friend had been glowing for both of her pregnancies. With her son and daughter, she'd looked like a million bucks. India wasn't feeling the love from her pregnancy at the moment. Her skin was extra dry while her hair was battling two different textures and on top of that she couldn't pick up the pounds that the doctor wanted her to have because of stress.

Brody was slowly starting to lay more and more rules down to her about Tarik and the whole situation was a big fucking headache for her.

"If you take her to see him, make sure that nigga put me on the visitor list. I see he always hitting you up too. Start putting that shit on speakerphone. I'm not about to play with his ass," he said with an attitude as he pulled into her parent's driveway.

India rolled her eyes behind her oversized frames. She loved Brody and knew that she had fucked up still his attitude wasn't helping any.

"India you hear me?"

India took off her seat belt.

"Yes, Brody I do."

Brody stared at India for a moment before nodding. He brushed his waves and moisturized his face before turning his attention back to India.

"You look beautiful baby, but you need to fix your hair and your skin is patchy as fuck. Let's get that shit together," he said and exited the car.

India's face fell into a frown as she watched him walk up the driveway. She'd always loved how clean Brody was.

How much pride he took into looking good but damn he'd taken his pretty boy shit to new heights.

She glanced down at her black leggings with her off the shoulder pink top and laughed.

"This nigga thinks he looks better than me," she said and laughed again.

India exited the car and met Brody at her parent's door. He rang the bell twice then smoothed down his white collared Givenchy shirt before it was pulled open.

Charlotte stood on the other end of the door looking like a beautiful older version of India. She quickly stepped outside and pulled India into her arms. It had been months since she'd seen her and they both weren't used to that.

"I don't even know what to say about this belly girl! I could kill and kiss you all at once," she said hugging her tightly.

"It damn sure didn't come by itself," India's father said walking up.

India hugged both of her parents and they went on to greet Brody. India walked into her family room and was caught off guard by the family members that filled up the room.

India was only expecting to see her parents.

"You better act like you happy to see me and where that belly come from?" her granny Nancy asked standing up.

India's granny was in great shape and looked like older versions of India and her mom. India quickly hugged her granny then her aunts and cousins. When she made it to Sterling she pinched her arm hard.

Sterling winced before laughing.

"I tried to call you twice and you sent me to voicemail bitch," Sterling said knowing just why India was upset.

India waved her off as shame moved over her. She stepped into the middle of the room and her older brother Kent smiled at her. She could tell everyone was happy to see her with child. Especially after watching her lose a baby.

"I didn't expect for you all to be here," India said and laughed nervously.

A few of her family members laughed while the older generation stared at her intently. Brody walked over to India and lovingly kissed her cheek. They'd been going at it, but India loved him so much at that moment for being there for her. She leaned into him and he gently caressed her round belly.

"As you all can see I am with child. It's a girl and while she isn't biologically Brody's she is still his daughter."

A few people clapped not catching on. India's parents and even her brothers watched on in shock. They had never seen India with a man beside Brody.

"Kitchen now," Inez said and walked away with his immediate family trailing behind him.

Brody grabbed India's hand and took her into the kitchen with her family. India looked at her parents nervously as she leaned on Brody for support.

"Talk," her father said with a scowl on his handsome face.

India cleared her throat, but it was Brody who answered her father.

"India and I took a break and while that was going on she hooked up with somebody named Tarik. We back together now and despite the circumstances is trying to make it work. India loves me unconditionally and I love her just the same. I won't treat this baby no different than if I made her myself," Brody said calmly.

India's father stared at him for a moment before nodding. He walked over to Brody and pulled him into a hug. It was the only time he'd ever done it before.

"Thank you," he said quietly before pulling India into his arms. India began crying as her father hugged her.

She felt like she was continually letting him down. He had such high hopes for her and she hadn't lived up to any of them.

"I'm sorry for disappointing you daddy," she said into his shirt.

Inez took India into his man cave and they sat on his sofa. He touched her round belly and she smiled at him with blurry eyes.

"This other man Tarik. Do you have any feelings for him?"

India looked at her dad shocked by his question.

"Daddy no. I love Brody."

Inez's question was answered by her response. He chuckled as he looked at his beautiful daughter. His only baby girl that was worth more than she thought she was.

"I love you princess. You know how I am about you. Brody is better but I'm team you. Whoever makes you happy is who I like. Brody has been putting you through it for years now. Maybe this other fellow is who you're supposed to be with," he suggested.

India thought of Tarik and sighed.

"Brody is all I know," she admitted quietly.

Inez stared at her.

"And that's the problem because I'm sure you're not all he knows. You're worth more than a car and a house. Some bullshit ass purse or a trip. You deserve real love. You deserve to have all of the love you've been giving him. Put India first and watch how happy you'll come to be. It all starts with you baby," he told her, and they began to talk about the baby.

* * *

"This what's up. A little family reunion and shit," Tarik said sitting down.

India was so nervous that her leg shook. He'd honored her request and she was shocked but happy to see him comply. By doing so he was making her life so much easier.

Brody sat beside her angry as fuck. His light skin was two shades darker. Anger swirled in his pretty eyes as he glared across at Tarik who was looking cool as a cucumber.

Tarik stopped smirking at Brody to look at India. Pregnancy enhanced her beauty into something serious. From the glow gracing her melanin to the fullness of her lips. Her body was thicker, and it looked good on her.

"You look nice Indie," he commented making Brody sit up in his chair.

India grabbed Brody's hand to calm him down.

"You promised," she mumbled

Brody didn't break Tarik's gaze as he kissed the back of India's hand.

"It's like this lil nigga. Any visit with her is a visit with me. All that calling her daily and shit is dead. Call your bitch, this mine. All that extra shit gone get you touched," Brody warned him.

Tarik sat back, and his eyes fell on India. He couldn't understand her at the moment. He knew what they were, and India did too. Obviously, Brody didn't, his insecurities were showing, and it only made Tarik smile. Clearly, he was threatened by him.

"India how you feel about this shit? You cool with this nigga handling your every move? He telling you how to deal with your baby daddy and shit. Do you oversee him and his hoes? I'm curious," Tarik said and stared at Brody daring him to get up.

Brody chuckled lowly and India sighed. The back and forth shit she could do without.

"Tarik I just want you and him to get along. Nothing more. I won't keep you away from your daughter."

"You damn right you won't!" Tarik said getting loud and Brody glared at him. Tarik placed both of his hands on his head. "You got something to get off your chest nigga? Let's not get shit twisted my cousin fucks with you but I don't. You already know how I feel about you. If a nigga not on his job, then that leaves room for another one to step in. You know the drill. Don't get righteous cause India sitting down with us. You know how this shit goes," he told him.

Brody cleared his throat. He decided to stand up to walk off his anger and India looked at Tarik with pleading eyes.

"Tarik..."

Tarik shook his head. He was so pissed at her that he could have yanked her ass up.

"Why the fuck you letting this nigga control you like this? You can't be fucking serious, but I don't give a fuck. Long as he's good to my kid he safe. You and I both know your pussy gone be on my dick the minute it gets the chance to. Brody knows it too that's why he on this possessive ass shit. You need to get your shit together. You acting weak as fuck and I don't like that shit. Send me some pictures of the ultrasound pictures too," he said before standing up.

India watched Tarik walk off and her heart raced in her chest. She was clueless as to how she would deal with him and Brody without losing her mind.

"I'ma fuck around and kill his ass," Brody vented as she stood up.

He'd walked back up as Tarik was headed to the guard. India grabbed Brody's hand and looked up at him. His angry eyes glanced down at her and that was it.

She felt nothing. So many times, in the past she'd felt butterflies, electric shocks hell something but it was gone. India wasn't sure when it left but it wasn't there anymore. However, from the short time she'd sat across from Tarik, she felt at peace. She felt the tug, the hold he had over her and to realize that Brody didn't have that same effect was like a shock to her system.

Ten

She's big as shit now. How you been feeling? Quez told me you been MIA on Palmer. When you taking your ass home? You can't hide a baby, running around like your ass is fifteen and shit. Let your girl know what's up India.

XXX

Real funny and I just need time. How is it in there? Are they on you and yes, she is. She won't stop kicking my side. I can't wait to have this girl. It's so close to the time and I called your family. Your parents are really sweet. I was able to email your mom the photos I sent you.

XXX

On me? India this not no movie. Niggas are chill in this bitch until you fuck with them. She told me you did and that's what's up. I been thinking about finishing school when I get out. Why didn't you go back ma?

XXX

I love that! You should go back. Now just isn't a good time for me. I have a lot going on.

XXX

That's that bullshit. If you don't wanna go back just say it. For our daughter, we need to be the best versions of ourselves. You change for the better for the people you love. I miss that pretty ass face too. Send a nigga some pics or something. Damn. At least let me get some pussy shots. Shit.

XXX

I had the baby and she's so beautiful. I know we talked but it felt right to write you also. I still can't believe I went over my due date. It was like she wasn't ready to come out but I'm glad she did. Having her has changed me in ways I never imagined. She looks so much like your baby pictures that your mom showed me. I can't wait for you to meet her. Her name is Kalila Cecily Royale. Not sure if I told you but her name means a heap of love. I hope you like it. The delivery was so smooth and I'm just so happy. I'm praying that my happiness jumps off the pages and invades your world. You've become a real friend to me Tarik and I thank you for that. I thank you for giving me this beautiful angel. Our beautiful angel.

* * *

"Look at you, hey baby. Damn, she's beautiful," Tarik said holding his daughter for the first time. His daughter looked so much like his baby sister that the shit was insane. He was still going to, however, get the test just to ease his nerves since India did have a man at home.

India sat across from him with a seething Brody. India tried to sneak away by herself, but Brody was on her ass. He'd even made connects in LA and was handling business out there. Anything to keep her within arm's reach.

"She's so, pretty isn't she?" India asked still swollen from the childbirth.

It had only been three months and while she didn't want her baby around so many strangers for Tarik she took the chance and flew her out.

Tarik stared at his daughter in awe.

"Yeah she's fucking gorgeous," he replied. He kissed her forehead tenderly. "Daddy love you already baby," he said, and Brody shifted in his seat.

Brody had also grown extremely close to the baby and was not happy with Tarik holding who he viewed as his daughter.

"India we gotta go," Brody said and stood up.

Tarik's eyes shot up to him as Brody tugged down his fitted cap. Tarik had been very patient with India. The phone calls were always on speaker and every visit had been with Brody. He didn't give a fuck about the way Brody controlled India but the last thing he was gone let him do was control his time with *his* daughter.

"You didn't have to come, nigga. The shit you do with India is on y'all. I'm letting you know right now you not running shit Kalila's way. It would be a motherfucking war if you even tried it. This is my daughter. You walking round this bitch bragging to your peoples like she all you. You can front for them but we all know the truth. India you better let this nigga know," Tarik said angrily.

Brody glared down at him.

"She ain't gotta let me know shit. Last I checked everything Kalila has come from me. India don't need that bullshit ass money you sending her. We good over here motherfucka and whether your bitch ass like it or not that's both our daughter. I was the nigga that cut the cord, I'm the nigga that feed her at night and I'ma be the nigga to give her a fucking sibling. Dumb lil nigga," Brody said and walked away.

India sat down embarrassed and angry. She looked at Tarik and before he could bitch at her she began to cry. She was still emotional and to watch Brody and Tarik argue hurt her. She just wanted peace in her life.

Tarik calmed down at the sight of her tears.

"Indie calm down," he said still holding his daughter.

India shook her head.

"I'm tired of it Tarik. You two don't know how hard y'all are making life for me. I can't take too much more of it," she announced.

Tarik sighed. It was only because of her that he dealt with Brody's bitch ass.

"We gone be good but you gotta put your foot down. This is our kid and I'm not about to let him control nothing concerning our daughter. I'm coming home soon and when I do shit gone be different. He can get on board or get his ass killed. It's as simple as that," Tarik said and went back to loving on his daughter.

A few days later India rested in her bed as she spoke with her mother on the phone. The baby had been sick, and India was positive it was from traveling from LA to Michigan and being around so many strangers. Brody was in Detroit for a week and India was happy. She needed a break from him.

"How did it go?" India's mom asked.

India thought back on the way Tarik had smiled when he'd seen their daughter and it warmed her heart. She'd been waiting for months to see that moment.

"It was nice until him and Brody got into it. Things are getting worse between them."

"And just why was Brody there with you?" her mom asked.

India cleared her throat. She was close with her mom but felt that her parents didn't need to know every single detail about her relationship.

"Because he flew into town with me. He's touchy when it comes to Tarik, so I try to do things to ease his mind," she replied.

Charlotte was quiet for several minutes before speaking.

India this is some soap opera shit right here. What you have going on with Tarik is between you two. You aren't married to Brody. He needs to back up some and allow for you to build a healthy relationship with the father of your child. He might feel like Kalila is his daughter but biologically she belongs to Tarik. Enough is a fucking enough. Shit. You need to bring your ass home," she told India.

India shook her head.

"I know. It's just so peaceful out here but I know that I have to return. I haven't even told Palmer about the baby and I missed her baby shower. I know she's pissed at me. I'm just so stressed out ma. It's crazy," India replied.

The baby began to cry, and India picked her up from her bassinet. She noticed that the baby's cheeks were extremely red, and it frightened her.

"Ma she's really sick. Maybe I should take her to the doctor," she said beginning to worry.

India's mom sighed in frustration.

"This is why your ass needs to be home. Take her to the emergency room and call me as soon as you know what's wrong. India, I know you love Brody, but you have to let him know that he can't run your relationship with Tarik," Charlotte told her before ending the call.

Before India could set her phone down it rang again. She looked at the screen and frowned.

"Quez is everything okay?"

Arquez sighed into the phone.

"Nah, Palmer in labor and she crying and shit. Where you at?" he said sounding stressed.

India's heart beat faster.

"I'm in LA but I'm on the first flight out right now," India replied and ended the call.

She rushed to pack a small weekend bag with the baby's stuff and rushed out of her place. India put her daughter into the car and glanced down at her. Her baby was still red in the face and crying hysterically.

India rubbed her soft baby hairs before closing the door. She loved Palmer, but her daughter would always come first in her life. India took her daughter to the closest hospital and she was immediately seen. For two hours they checked on Kalila before prescribing her some cough medicine. She had a small viral infection that would clear up within a few days.

India was then able to catch a flight to Detroit three hours later. She rushed into the hospital after taking her daughter to her parent's home and went up to the birth center. India spotted Arquez and she exhaled.

This was home. These people were her family and she felt extremely bad for shutting them out of her life. She ran over to him and he hugged her tightly.

"She's here! She so damn beautiful man," he said happy that his daughter was born with no complications.

India let him go and smiled up at him. She'd always like Arquez. To her, he was the better man for her best friend Palmer. In fact, he adored Palmer in a way that India felt all men should.

"What room is she in?' India asked nervous to see her friend.

"Back this way," he replied and took India to the room.

India rushed into Palmer's room and came face to face with Palmer and Mickey. She looked at both of them nervously.

"Where have you been?" Palmer asked angrily.

India shifted from one foot to the other. She glanced at Mickey and gave her a small smile. Mickey was usually so well put together but that day she looked stressed. India wasn't sure what was going on with her, but she could tell she was going through some things.

"I'm late because my baby was sick," India said nervously.

Palmer and Mickey looked at her like she was crazy. Mickey quietly excused herself from the room and India went over to Palmer. She sat down in Mickey's chair and took a deep breath. She exhaled and stared at her friend.

"I was unhappy with my situation Palmer. I got pregnant by Tarik while we were in Vegas for your wedding. I found out months later. It was too late for an abortion but after losing my baby I wouldn't have gotten one anyway. I ran. I'm sorry because that wasn't fair to any of you, but I did. That was why Brody was over at your place acting an ass. Of course he found me, and he asked me what was up. I wanted to lie but I kept it real. For the last year, we've been dealing with it. Whenever I go see Tarik in jail he tags along. He's very hands-on with this whole thing," India said trying to spruce up the situation.

Palmer shook her head. She was extremely hurt by India's actions. India pulled out her phone and showed Palmer a delivery video. Palmer watched it while smiling then gave India the phone back.

"I don't know what to say. I mean, of course, I'm happy that you had a beautiful, beautiful baby girl. Our kids will definitely be best friend's like us, but I'm hurt India. You hid this from me. I would never hide anything from you. No matter how serious it was," Palmer replied.

India nodded. Her eyes watered as she stared at someone that she considered family.

"And I know that. I'm so sorry. Please forgive me. I mean I was saving the godmother spot for you."

Palmer cracked a smile.

"Who else were you gonna fucking pick? We all know you don't have any friends," she said and they both laughed.

It was very true that India kept a small circle.

"But even if I did it would still be you now where is the baby?" she asked and looked around.

Palmer smiled at the thought of her daughter.

"She's being checked on. She's so gorgeous India. I can't believe we both have little girls. Are you coming back home?"

India nodded. She didn't want to but felt it was needed. Plus, Tarik was close to the end of his sentence and she did want him to be hands-on with their daughter.

"Yes, I am. You know Tarik is getting out soon. He says that his boy is having him a welcome home party. He wants me to come," India replied.

Palmer nodded. Of course because of her husband she knew all about the party.

"Yes, it was originally in Florida but because he will be on probation they chose to keep it here. Whenever me and Quez go see him he always talks about going to school and things like that. He's grown up so much India. Him and Quez are going in on a chicken wings franchise and everything. I now see why he's so determined to change his life around. For his daughter," Palmer said to her.

India smiled. She talked with Tarik a lot but didn't know about the wing business. She looked at her friend and exhaled.

"Palmer does he have someone?"

Palmer looked at India and frowned.

"Indie don't. This could end very badly. I think that you two should co-parent for as long as you can then maybe years from now give it a try. And that's only if things with you and Brody don't work out."

India laughed.

"Palmer I don't need your permission and it's not like that. I wanna know just so I won't be blindsided by it. Does he?"

Palmer nodded, and she could see the sadness fall over India.

"She was pregnant by him as well, but she lost the baby. She's nice too, I won't lie but I mean you know I'm always team India. No matter what."

India smiled kind of sad at Palmer's response.

"No matter what boo," India told her.

Eleven

"She's so adorable. We're so happy to have your ass back!" Sterling said holding India's daughter.

India smiled but didn't take her eyes off of her cousin Shia. Shia sat beside Sterling with an ugly mug on her pretty slim face. India figured she was still in her feelings about when she'd beat her ass in Cali.

"Shia, you good?" India asked her.

Shia shrugged before running her small hand through her soft strands. She looked at India and gave her a fake smile.

"So how does Brody feel about this? Is he actually taking care of her? Like he calls her his daughter?" she asked.

India's brows knitted together. Shia was the only person that was more concerned with someone else's life instead of her own.

"Yes Shia. You would think you would be more interested in why the twins daddy doesn't give a fuck about his own kids," she said angrily.

Sterling gave both of them a look as Shia briskly stood up.

"You know what, that was childish as hell for you to say that India. I'm gone," Shia said looking extremely hurt by India's words before she walked away.

Sterling shook her head as she handed India her baby back.

"You two have been doing this mess since you all were kids. Its childish as hell," she reprimanded her.

India smiled. She kissed her baby's chunky cheeks.

"That's on Shia. You know how she is. I don't have time for it. You have to deal with her. I don't but how have you been? You need a man," India said changing the subject.

Sterling gave her a bashful smile, and India's eyes widened.

"Who is he?"

Sterling giggled, and her cousin could see the happiness covering her face.

"This guy named Brando. He's a Yaasmin," she replied.

India clicked her tongue and grinned at Sterling. Yaasmin's were considered Detroit royalty. They had long money and it wasn't anything fake about them. They were also known for being very handsome men.

"Bitch I'm impressed. What's the tea? I need it now," India said making Sterling laugh.

"Well, I went to a party with Celine. You know she works at the Eastside location with me now. That's Elsie that died a while back little sister and he was there..."

India sat on the edge of her seat in anticipation.

"And...."

Sterling covered her face and India squealed making a few people in the sushi spot glance their way. Sterling was always so selfless. Beautiful inside and out and she was happy for her cousin. Glad to see that she was finally out dating and had done so with a Yaasmin. Shit, it didn't get any better than them.

"I can't wait to meet him. Maybe he has a cute, wealthy cousin for me. Somebody that wanna take me to Dubai and shit," India joked. She'd already been there twice with Brody.

Sterling waved her off.

"You got your plate full as it is with Brody and Tarik. Are you really ready for him to come home?"

India shrugged. She glanced down at his daughter and saw nothing but him. She was like the female version of Tarik. She even had his skin complexion.

"I have no choice but to be. Brody is like the perfect fucking man now and that pisses me off. I wish he could have been this man years ago then maybe we wouldn't be in this situation. I'm losing my damn edges stressing over him."

Sterling nodded.

"I can only imagine. You're dealing with two dominate men and they both want you. It has to be hard on you."

India grinned at her cousin.

"What makes you think Tarik wants me?"

Sterling smiled at her.

"I mean why wouldn't he? You two were drawn to each other from the start and now you have his child. I'm sure he wants the hell out of you and that's why Brody is all of a sudden, the perfect man. I just hope his efforts can be enough to keep you out of Tarik's bed because I don't see this ending well."

India nodded with sad eyes.

"Palmer said the same thing but I'm not doing anything wrong. Tarik and I will be friends and get along for her. Nothing more." India stopped talking and smiled to herself. "Yes, nothing more," she repeated.

After having sushi with her cousin India took her daughter to see Tarik's mother Collette. She was a lively young grandmother because she'd had Tarik at the ripe age of sixteen. Collette had two more kids a boy and a little girl and Tarik was the oldest. Despite being a teen mom, she now owned a chain of massage parlors with her husband Cedrick.

"Oh my gosh, she gets gorgeous every time we see her!" Collette said holding the door open for India.

Tarik's parents lived in an immaculate part of Novi in a gated subdivision. Their home was decked out and the second India walked in it made her smile. It was truly gorgeous from the decor to the wall art.

"Wow this place is amazing," she murmured slipping her shoes off.

"Thank you, sweetie," his mom said grabbing the baby from her.

India followed his mom into the family room and she saw that they were alone. Collette held the baby as she sat next to India.

"Thank you so much for keeping us up to date with her. This is my first grandbaby and I'm just in love with her already. Tarik told me about your family business and I think that's amazing. As you can see we have something in common with that as well. He also said that you wanted to study law, but your record was affected by past mistakes. I had my friend downtown look you up and she was able to get it expunged. We're line sisters and she's been a judge for over ten years. I hope you don't think I was being nosey or overstepping my boundaries," his mom replied.

India was hit with a wave of gratitude. She was so happy that she began to cry. She hugged his mom tight as she could, and his mom hugged her back.

"I didn't always have my husband. We separated after I had Tarik. He chose to do other things and I was left to raise a kid while being a kid. I want my grandbaby to have the best life possible and that can only be achieved with the help of parents that can give her that. Anything else you need just let me know. Whether you two are friends or not you are a part of this family. You gave me this little angel here," she said and began to play with a very alert Kalila.

India spent hours at Tarik's mother's home before retiring to her own place. She bathed her daughter and breastfed her before taking a shower herself. With extra time on her hands, she decided to write Tarik an email because she felt Brody had been intercepting their letters. Suddenly they had stopped and when she asked Tarik about it he'd looked at her as if she was crazy. It was then that she realized Brody was keeping them.

India sat in the middle of her bed in her satin pajama short set and opened her MacBook. She went to his email and typed away.

Hey. I saw your mom today and she's gorgeous. Like fly as fuck. I hope I can look like that when I'm a granny. You know what forget I said that. But she was really nice, and I can see how much she loves Kalila. She also helped me out a lot about my past and I have you to thank for that. You really do care for me. J/K but for real it's nice to know that I can count on you. I hope you're in there being good. Your daughter needs you home.... we all do;0

Twelve

A year later

"You ready?"

Kalila smiled and it made her slanted eyes nearly disappear. She was wearing a pink romper with pink jelly's and her curly brown hair in two ninja buns. She looked adorable with her rose gold jewelry on that Tarik had his mother send over.

She clapped and when Brody stepped into the room her eyes lit up. Yes, she saw Tarik regularly, but the facts were she was living with Brody. In her eyes was her father. She held up her arms for him and he picked her up with ease while smiling.

"Hey daddy's baby," he said making India stare at him.

India grabbed Kaila's bag and went over to Brody. He looked and smelled amazing as he stood before her. For the last month, he'd become distant and she knew why. It still didn't give him a right to stay out at night.

"Brody is everything okay? You know that staying out shit will never work with me."

Brody glanced down at India and licked his lips. She'd lost all of her baby weight and then some. She was now the slimmest he'd ever seen her, but she still had all of the assets that drove him wild. He kissed her lips before smiling at her.

"It was one time and I told you I got too bent to drive. My fucking phone died and..."

"You were on that bullshit. Don't play with me," India said cutting him off.

Brody grinned at her. Even through his Cartier wired lenses, his pretty eyes stared at her in amusement.

"And that nigga coming home so I gotta behave huh? India you know a nigga better than that," he said and walked away.

India followed him.

"What does that mean?"

Brody walked out of their home. In the last year, he'd given her a bigger place with a large backyard for Kalila although she couldn't use it yet.

"It means if you couldn't leave me back then what makes you think some shit done changed," he replied coldly.

India was caught off guard by his words. Outside of his one stunt of staying out late, she hadn't had any trouble from Brody. They had been good, he had also been very loving to her. She didn't like how he tossed a threat out into the air so casually.

"Brody I can do whatever I want. Trust if I stayed with you it was my choice. You didn't make me do shit," she said and hit the locks on her Porsche.

Brody opened the back door and glanced over at India. She could see that his eyes were slightly zoned out. It was a look on him that she'd never seen before.

"Brody, what's going on? Are you high on pills?"

Brody smirked at her.

"Chill out Indie. We all grown and shit," he replied. He put the baby in the car seat and strapped her in. He then closed the door and went over to India. Brody picked her up and instantly her legs went around his waist. India stared down into his handsome face with her heart racing. He was a fucking asshole whenever he wanted to be but damn he was always handsome while doing it. That could never be denied.

"You still love me?" he asked looking up at her.

India nodded.

"Of'course, she whispered.

Brody licked his lips.

"Then skip that party bullshit he having and come with me. Take our daughter to his momma and come back. I wanna take you somewhere," he replied.

India stared into his eyes.

"Where?"

Brody grinned at her.

"Come back and you'll see. Okay?"

India wanted to object but, how could she? Brody was her man and well Tarik was just her child's father. She had to keep the peace in her home.

"Okay," she relented making him smile.

India gave him a quick kiss before he put her down. She got into her car and took her daughter to Collette's home. Most of Tarik's family was over for his welcome home dinner. The food had been catered by Tarik's favorite restaurant and his mom had gone all out with the décor. India spoke to the family members she knew before bumping into a petite thick girl with long naturally thick hair that was in curls. India smiled as she held onto her baby.

"I'm sorry," she said and walked past her.

India found Tarik's mom in the kitchen. His mom smiled when she saw her and took the baby along with the bag.

"You're not staying?" Collette asked with her smile dropping.

India shook her head as the same girl she bumped into walked up.

"Momma is this the baby?" the woman asked.

Collette nodded but didn't hand over the baby.

"India this is Tarik's girlfriend Sabrina. Sabrina this is India," Collette said introducing the two.

Both women just stared at each other before Sabrina turned her attention to Kalila.

"She looks just like him," Sabrina gushed.

India smiled slightly amused by Tarik's woman.

"And me too," she added.

Sabrina ignored her and held out her hands.

"Can I?"

Collette shook her head while smiling.

"When Tarik gets here. Can you go check on the kids in the back?" she replied.

Sabrina stopped smiling but did as she asked. Collette turned to India and smiled at her.

"I'll keep her with me at all times. See you later baby," Collette said and hugged India.

India left out of Tarik's mom's home agitated. She rushed back to her place and was greeted with rose petals at her front door. A big smile covered her face as she noticed candles all around her foyer. Soft r&b music played as she stepped out of her sandals.

"Brody!" she called out very surprised by his romantic gestures. India followed the rose petals throughout her home. In the kitchen, India picked up a photo that she'd taken with him in front of his cousin's home on Murray Hill and she smiled. They were so young. So full of love. She missed the young Brody and India.

India kissed the photo before following the photo trail into the family room. Inside of the room were photos of the first time they'd taken a trip out of the states together. Money was starting to really come in and they were recklessly spending it. India picked up the first Gucci bag Brody ever bought her, and she laughed.

"I was so damn happy to have this thing," she mumbled.

India put the hobo bag on and followed the rose trail up the stairs and into her bedroom. She opened the door and standing in the center of the room wearing all white and holding a red box was Brody.

India's eyes watered as he opened the box. Inside of the cushioned Cartier box was a diamond solitaire ring. So big, so beautiful. Like nothing, India had ever seen before. Brody dropped down to one knee and peered up at her lovingly.

"I'm far from perfect but you love me. What we have is real love India. I don't want a minute to go by without you being my wife. Marry me," he said emotionally.

India seemed to float over to him. Slowly she nodded, and Brody smiled up at her. He placed the ring on her finger and she leaned down to kiss him.

"I love you, baby," he whispered.

India's tears fell as she gazed back at him lovingly.

"I love you too," she whispered back.

Thirteen

"I'm just so worried about her. Easton keeps calling and asking me what's up with her and I don't have anything to tell him. I feel so bad!"

India rubbed Palmer's arm. The waitress brought over another round of shots and India thanked her.

"But Palmer they treated Mickey like a damn kid. They had to know this would fucking happen. Shit, she's probably tired of their shit and on some vacation. Knowing Mickey, she's probably in Paris or something," India said and smiled.

Palmer shook her head. She wished it was that simple.

"India, she suffers from this mental disorder. She needs help and that's why she's running because she doesn't want it. I already lost Chanel and I don't wanna lose anyone else," Palmer said, and India stood up to hug her friend.

They were both free from the kids and enjoying a night out on the town. They'd been sipping Patron and like usual it had them emotional.

"I know she'll be fine. If you want we can go look for her in the morning," she suggested.

Palmer nodded. Anything was better than waiting for her to pop back up. Palmer said a quick prayer for her girl before wiping her face. She then took her shot and India did the same. Palmer looked at India's hand and shook her head. India's ring was fly as hell. There was no denying it.

"He gave you some shit like Kobe Bryant's wife, but you deserve it. I can't believe you're getting married!"

"Shit me either. It took that nigga long enough. What's good India?"

India froze up at the sound of Tarik's deep voice. She spun around and found him standing behind her along with her best friend's husband. India glared at Palmer and Palmer looked at her innocently.

"I swear I didn't know! He said he was alone," Palmer replied.

Tarik brushed his hand across India's ass before walking up behind her. He reached around her and grabbed one of the extra shots off the tray. Tarik tossed it back as India breathed heavily in front of him.

"He was alone. I met him up here. Aye, India let me holla at you real quick," Tarik said and pulled her away. He took her into the VIP section and they sat down. India chose to look through her phone as he sat beside her.

"You on some childish shit right now. You couldn't come to my dinner?"

India sighed. She started to check her emails as she responded to him.

"That was about you. I made sure our daughter was there."

Tarik calmly grabbed her phone and placed it in his pocket. India's head shot up and she glared at him. He licked his lips as he smirked back at her.

"Can I get a hug?"

India smiled nervously at him before leaning over. Tarik hugged her tightly and she noticed that he'd gained some muscles while away. Muscles that she hadn't been able to see while sitting across from him in the visiting room. He tenderly rubbed her back as she closed her eyes.

"What happened to you?" he asked her quietly.

India's arched brows furrowed

"What do you mean?"

"The India that had my dick hard on sight was confident as fuck. Always in charge of her own lane. I don't know you different now. Shy and shit. Scared to even look a nigga in the eyes," he replied.

Tarik let India go and they both sat back. While Tarik soaked in her post-baby body India admired his good looks. Tarik sat in all white besides her looking sexier than she remembered. Sexier than he did the last time she'd seen him.

His creamy brown skin was flawless as his various tattoos covered his skin. He wore a white cap that was pulled low to his head almost shielding his almond-shaped eyes. In his left ear was a diamond earring while a rose gold chain hung from his neck. The alluring scent of Blue De Chanel wafted off is skin as he peered over at her.

"What's good? I see you lost some weight ma," he commented. India nodded not looking very happy about his assessment of her and he licked his lips. "But it looks good on you. Where the baby at?"

"With my mom," she replied.

Tarik nodded again. He grabbed her hand and tugged her over to him. His eyes fell on her huge engagement ring and he chuckled.

"Got damn that nigga must be frightened that I'm out now. All it took was for you to have a baby by another nigga, but I understand. If I was him I'd be doing everything in my power to keep you too."

India pushed Tarik's hand away and frowned at him.

"Brody and I are good. I need to get back to Palmer."

She tried to stand up and Tarik was right behind her. He pulled her back to his front and he gently placed his hand on her stomach. India's chest tightened as he pressed himself against her.

"She good. She with her husband. Come take a ride with me sexy," he whispered.

India's walls creamed at his words. She wanted to do more than take a ride with him. She wanted to take a ride on him.

"Tarik, please," she begged not wanting to cheat on her fiancé.

Tarik shook his head. He slid his hand up the center of her chest and grabbed her breast through her black lace top. She wore a demi cup bra but felt as if she was bare as he toyed with her round nipples. He played with them until she began to leak through her clothes.

"Stop fucking playing with me India. Let's go," he said and let her go.

Tarik grabbed India's hand and led her out of the club. They went to his car in the lot and quietly got in. India's leg shook nervously as she rode with Tarik to the MGM grand hotel. While Tarik got them a room Brody called her phone repeatedly. It was as if he knew or could sense she was about to do him wrong.

India chose to go grab a drink at the bar before finally going up to the room. When she entered into it she found Tarik sitting on the edge of the bed with nothing, but a towel wrapped around his waist. A blunt was pressed against his lips as his eyes fell on her.

He blew smoke from his mouth and smiled.

"I really thought your ass had dipped out on a nigga. Come here sexy," he said and gave her a look drizzled in lust.

India stepped out of her heels and slowly walked over to Tarik. He grabbed her waist and peered up at her. He'd put out his blunt and was giving her all of his attention.

"Did you miss me?"

India sighed.

"Tarik this is wrong. You clearly have someone, and I'm engaged."

Tarik's eyes widened in surprise.

"No shit? Let me see your ring," he said making her laugh. She hit his arm and he chuckled. "If we didn't wanna be here we wouldn't be. You don't have to put on for me. Now I'ma ask you again did you miss me?" India slowly nodded, and an appreciative smile graced his face.

"That's better. Get naked," he said and gently pushed her back.

India took off her clothes and he took her into the bathroom. Although he had just showered he wanted to make her feel good, so he got in again. India stood by quietly as she watched him lather her up. The strength that emanated off of him told her that he was no longer the young nineteen-year-old that had made her immediately smitten with him. He was now a grown ass man. It showed in all of the things that he did.

Tarik made sure to take his time washing off India. She looked like she'd been getting no love from Brody. It was all in her eyes. India may have been able to front for other people, but Tarik saw through the fake smiles and could see nothing but despair when he looked at her.

Tarik wanted to make her happy and he knew that he could. She made him feel things he never felt before. He was gone put some shit on her so good that she had no choice but to wake up to the connection that they shared.

"Face the wall baby," he said pulling her out of the haze his wash had put her in.

India quickly obliged, and he came up behind her. Tarik kissed up and down her wet back before slapping her ass. He slowly pushed into her opening and India closed her eyes. He felt even better than she'd imagined.

"Oh yes," she moaned.

Tarik held in his groan and swallowed hard. They'd gone from fucking to having a kid together. She'd given him a real reason to live. Whether they got together or not he would forever fuck with her because of that.

"This is it right here. You got what I been missing Indie. You happy I'm home?" he asked pumping into her.

India nodded like her life depended on it.

"I am," she admitted with a whimper.

Tarik dug deeper into her and her body instantly climaxed for him. He smiled at his handy work. Happy to see that he still knew how to make her get off.

"This still my pussy, don't forget that shit," he told her and bent his knees a little so that he could really get deep inside of her.

India cried out and Tarik slid his hands up her body. Gently his hand gripped her neck as he slid in and out of her. Tarik was fucking India so good that tears were beginning to fall from her eyes. India's head fell back against his chest and he let her neck go.

Tarik's thick member twitched as he felt his nut rising up.

"India, you feel so fucking good. Pussy was made for me baby. I know you love this dick but now I need you to love me," he said surprising even himself.

India's body shivered and seconds later he was coming inside of her. Tarik then pulled her out of the shower and took her back into the bedroom. He laid India on her back and slid back inside of her.

India moaned as her legs went around his body.

"Tarik, please pull out. I'm not on birth control," she told him.

Tarik nodded. Shit, he wasn't trying to have back to back kids anyway. One was enough for him.

"I got you. We gone have to get that plan c shit in the morning," he said making her laugh.

India hit his arm while smiling.

"Plan b," she corrected him, and he leaned down.

Tarik kissed her lovingly while gazing into her eyes.

"I missed the fuck out of you," he whispered pulling back and the way that India felt while being under him as he filled her up was unexplainable.

She smiled weakly and her eyes once again grew wet with tears. Tarik kissed them away while pumping in and out of her.

"Why you crying?"

India shrugged.

"I'm scared," she replied quietly.

Tarik nodded. He hiked up her legs so that he could get deeper inside of her.

"Scared to be happy?" he asked, and India shook her head.

"I'm scared that he won't let me," she revealed, and Tarik had to bury his face into her neck to calm himself down.

Some things he would have to discuss with her when he wasn't inside of her body.

* * *

"What is this?"

Tarik smiled as he held their daughter. To see Kalila with her dad did something to India. They were blood and it showed with all of the similarities that they possessed. While Tarik was decked out in blue jeans with a white short sleeve Burberry tee, Kalila wore the matching shirt with blue leggings and Burberry slides. It was adorable, and she hadn't stopped smiling since she'd been in her daddy's arms.

"What the fuck this look like? Your ass about to sign up for school. Come on," he said and smirked at her.

India broke eye contact with him and stared at the building. They were outside of Wayne State and while she passed the university a million and one times she'd never thought of going in and applying for school.

"But I'm not ready," she said nervously.

Tarik walked over to India and kissed her cheek. She tried to pull away from him not wanting her daughter to see her be affectionate with two men, but he only held her tighter by the hand.

"Come on, this scary shit not you. Let's get that confidence back. We can sign up together," he suggested.

India stopped staring at the school to look into Tarik's eyes.

"You would sign up for me?"

He licked his lips before shaking his head.

"Nah for her. We both need to do this shit for her. Have some degrees hanging on our walls and shit," he replied.

India grinned, and a nervous energy filled her belly.

"Okay," she said quietly and Kalila started smiling almost like she knew what the situation was.

"See even she's happy for us. Kalila like, get y'all degrees up. I don't want no uneducated ass parents," Tarik joked.

"Whatever come on," India said and walked into the college with Tarik and their daughter following after her.

Hours later India and Tarik left out of the admissions office both enrolled for the fall classes at Wayne State University. India had two years left of undergraduate school before she could take her LSAT. Then she could enroll in law school. Tarik had three years to go for him to have a business management degree.

After leaving the college Tarik took India and Kalila to his cousin's barbecue. After introducing India to everyone that didn't know her they sat down at a small table in the back of the massive backyard. India couldn't help but notice a pretty petite girl staring her way. She smiled at the girl and began to eat some salmon before noticing that the girl was continuing to look at her.

"Who is that Tarik?" she asked him.

Tarik glanced across the yard at the pretty woman and shrugged. His cousin had plenty of bitches, so he wasn't sure who the fuck she was.

"I don't know. Why?"

India sighed.

"No reason. So where is your girlfriend? Is she okay with you doing all of this?"

Tarik licked his lips and grabbed his baby from India.

"We just friends. She got her own situation with some nigga and I'm cool with that. I'm not trying to lock her ass down, so I told her to be his problem. I got enough on my plate with your engaged ass," he said making India snicker.

"We're co-parenting Tarik," India told him.

Tarik leaned towards India and discreetly stuck his tongue in her ear. She held her breath as his soft tongue caressed her lobe.

"Stop. I'm serious I can't go there with you again," India said pushing him back.

Tarik sat back in his seat and looked at his daughter.

"We don't have to try hard to be happy India. The shit just feels right. Why the fuck is you so determined to be with that hoe ass nigga? He ain't shit," Tarik said with an attitude.

India glared at him when someone tapped her shoulder. She looked up and her eyes fell on the pretty woman who had been staring her down minutes ago.

"Yes?" India said smiling.

The woman looked from India to her baby and cleared her throat. While she wore a face full of makeup that was beaten to perfection India could still tell she was young. She gathered the young woman was around twenty if that.

"Hi, I really wanted to say sorry," the woman said quietly.

Tarik looked her way and frowned. He wasn't for the shit at all.

"Sorry for what? Don't come over here on that bullshit ma," he said to her.

"I'm not. I don't even know you. I'm talking to India. Years ago, Brody jumped on me because you read my letter and I guess it made you have an accident. That was when your baby died. I mean I never thought that something like that would happen. I was so in love with him and when he didn't leave you I was angry. I'm really shocked to see that you're here with someone else but that serves him right. I mean how low down is he to have two damn kids on you," she went on.

India's heart stopped once the young woman mentioned her accident. It was like she was taken back in time. Right before her eyes, she saw herself in his truck. She'd decided to leave work early and was searching through his console for a charger.

India saw herself finding the letter in the backseat. Her eyes watered. Her face grew a shade darker and her tears quickly fell. The words hurt her. She knew it was true because she knew her man. Every woman knew deep down what her man would and wouldn't do. India knew Brody had once again been unfaithful.

She saw herself angrily driving to his bbq restaurant and him not being there. India remembered that she'd then went to his bando at the time and spotted him outside. Instead of stopping at the light she'd driven faster, and it happened.

"Oh my god! Oh my god!" India cried out making everyone in the backyard stare their way.

Tarik looked angrily at the girl and she quickly walked away.

"Tarik, what's wrong with India?" Collette asked rushing over with her husband.

Tarik handed his mom the baby and helped India stand. She was staring off into space and it was worrying him.

"She just needs to lay down. Can you keep the baby? I'ma take her to my place," he replied.

His mom nodded while eying India worriedly.

"Yes, of course. Just go and call me later," she replied.

Tarik carried India out of the backyard and to his vehicle. She began to weep again as he placed her in the passenger's seat.

"All this time he made me think it was all my fault. All of this time," she murmured sadly.

Tarik quickly got into his car and pulled away. It took him half an hour to get to his place. He parked in his carport and carried a sleeping India into his home. Once Tarik laid her down he called his cousin and let him know to have Palmer come through.

India woke up two hours later drenched in sweat. Her eyes strained to make out the dark room that she was in. She wiped the sweat from her forehead and sat up on the bed.

Brody.

It was like he was set out to destroy her. She felt that he was, and it hurt her. She'd done everything that she could to make him happy. In return, she'd lost herself. In return, she'd made him too comfortable. So much so that he repeatedly did selfish bullshit with no regards to how it would affect her.

India rose off the bed and discarded her damp clothing. She put on a pair of Tarik's sweatpants with a beater of his. She found Tarik downstairs in his brownstone smoking on a blunt with Quez. Palmer sat next to her husband with her eyes glued to her phone.

Everyone glanced up when India entered the room.

"India you okay?" Palmer asked standing up.

India raised her hand. She wasn't in the mood to talk and the person who she did have words for was not present.

"Where's my baby?" she asked quietly.

"With my mom. She came over and got her bag so she's good. You want me to go get her?" Tarik asked.

India shook her head. She glanced around for her purse.

"I need to get to my car. Palmer, can you drop me off to it? It's at the funeral home," she said calmly.

Palmer made eye contact with Tarik and he slightly shook his head.

"Palmer!" India said raising her voice. "I'm no fucking kid. Regardless if you take me there or not I'm going. Now can you drop me off to my car?"

Palmer swallowed hard. She didn't want India to do anything that would make her catch another case.

"India you should stay the night here and calm down. He's already been calling me looking for you and I don't want you two to do this. He fucked up then just let him go. I'll help you pack and you don't have to ever look back," Palmer told her getting teary eyed.

If India was hurting, then so was she. They were just that close.

India shook her head. She didn't wanna cry. She wanted to fuck some shit up. She closed her eyes and swallowed down her emotions.

"Fuck it I'll walk," India said and walked away.

Tarik jumped up and grabbed his pistol off the table. Palmer and Arquez followed suit and together they went to India's home that she shared with Brody.

Tarik was there for India and his cousin was there to make sure he didn't catch a body. Palmer was of course there for her best friend.

"India please calm down," Palmer whispered as they pulled up to the big home.

Brody's Maserati was parked in the driveway next to India's birthday gift that she'd driven only a few times.

India pushed the door open ignoring Palmer and damn near power walked up her driveway. She was so mad she honestly could have run up it. She unlocked the front door and walked into the home. It smelled fresh and had the aroma of home-cooked lasagna wafting through the air.

"Why haven't you been answering your phone baby!" Brody yelled from the kitchen.

Every once and a while he would cook. It wasn't shit he did on a daily basis. India ignored him and went into his man cave. She grabbed his gun from under his desk and found Brody in the kitchen.

"India, please calm down!" Palmer said running behind her.

Brody's brows bunched together at the sound of Palmer's voice. He turned around and was face to face with the love of his life. India pointed the gun at him with pain in her eyes and hatred for him in her heart.

"Brody, how did I get into that car accident?" she asked him quietly.

Brody's heart began to race. He watched Tarik and Arquez step into the kitchen and he looked back at India.

"What the fuck is going on? Why the fuck you bring this hoe ass nigga with you?"

India ignored his question. She moved the gun slightly to the left and let off a round into the wall cabinet. Palmer jumped and Arquez walked over to her. He ushered her behind him as everyone stared at India.

"Don't let this nigga put you behind bars ma. Just pack your shit and we can go," Tarik said walking over. He touched India's back and the way he handled her made Brody angrier.

"*Nigga* get the fuck out of my shit! India why the fuck is this nigga here?" he asked again.

India took a deep breath and exhaled.

"Brody you lied to me. You made me believe that it was my fault. Yes, I ran that stop sign but we both know why. Your dog ass, nasty ass, cheated on me again. When you begged and pleaded for one more chance. It's because of you that I lost our baby, Brody! How could you do me like that? After everything I've done for you," India said with pain hanging onto her every word.

Brody took a step back and he dropped his head. Shame came over him like a blanket. When his eyes peered back at India they were watery.

"I fucked up," he said lowly. "It was my fault and I'm sorry. I'm so fucking sorry that I did that shit, but I'm done now. Baby, we about to get married. We got a daughter together. We're a family," he pleaded with her.

Tarik's head snapped back in amusement and he chuckled.

240

"We? Nigga that's my fucking daughter. I didn't hate when you did all of that bullshit you did to keep me away from her because she was with you first. So, I didn't open my mouth and say shit but enough is fucking enough. You stressing her the fuck out behind your shit and all that's gone do is make life hard for Kalila. Tell her all the shit now nigga and let her decide what she wanna do," Tarik told him.

Brody looked at Tarik and gritted his teeth. His large hands balled into a fist as he stared his way.

"You on that pussy ass shit nigga? I don't give a fuck who you connected to, your ass is dead," Brody threatened him.

"Brody throwing out threats like that ain't gone work for me. This some shit you created. Be real with her so she can finally know what's up," Arquez said looking his way. "Cause you was my nigga but Tarik family. You know how this shit go. You take his life then you gone lose yours," Arquez told him while staring into his eyes.

Brody knew what time it was, but he really didn't give a damn. His back was so far against the wall that the fucking bricks were bruising his skin. He knew that it would be no coming back for him if his secrets got out.

"I suggest y'all niggas leave right now. I'm licensed to carry, and I have the right to end y'all shit. India show them to the door then we can talk. I'm not about to discuss shit in front of them," he said and glanced around the room looking for his gun.

His life was very relaxed and had made him not as paranoid as he once was. In return, he didn't have weapons all over like he once did.

"India let's just go. Please," Palmer begged as a bad feeling moved over her. She hadn't felt that feeling since she'd had to kill her ex-boyfriend Ishmael. It scared her and the last thing she wanted was for her friend to do something that she couldn't take back.

"I'll leave as soon as Brody tells me this big secret that he's been hiding. A secret that I see everybody knows but me. Brody, what is it?"

Brody shifted from one foot to the other. He ran both hands over his haircut and looked India in the eyes. He couldn't say it. His love for her wouldn't allow for him too. He knew that the news would ruin everything that he'd worked so hard for them to have.

"I love you India. No matter what I have always loved you. You know that, if you didn't you wouldn't have stayed. You love me too. We can get past whatever issues we have," he replied sincerely.

India stopped looking at Brody to glance over at Tarik.

"What is it?" she asked him needing to know.

Tarik sighed. He hated he'd even brought it up. He didn't wanna win India by default. That wasn't a win at all to him.

"India let's be out or you can stay here with him. Which one is it?" he asked putting her on the spot. "But I'ma let you know that if you stay then I'ma fall back. I'ma really let you go cause all this young and the restless shit is for the birds. I can't do it," he replied.

India shook her head.

"I just need to know," she said getting emotional.

Tarik wasn't happy with her response. He grabbed the gun from her and took the clip out. He placed it in his back pocket before kissing her forehead.

"All the shit this nigga done did it shouldn't even fucking matter. No matter what I'ma still be your friend ma but I'm done," he said and walked away.

His cousin followed after him as Palmer stayed behind in the kitchen. India looked at Brody and saw that he was staring at her sadly. Years she'd given him, time, tears, moments she could never get back. It was all a waste. He wasn't the man she needed him to be and he never would be. The man for her was trying to walk out of her life.

India licked her lips as her shoulders slumped.

"*Brody*...I'm done," she said quietly finally tossing in the towel before walking away.

Palmer followed her, and they found the men in the driveway near the cars smoking on a blunt. Tarik spotted her coming his way and his eyes widened in surprise, but he held his smile in.

"Did he tell you?" he asked with smoke falling from between his lips.

India shook her head. Tarik nodded coolly.

"And how you feel about that?" he asked.

India shrugged.

"I don't care. For the first time in over ten years, I feel free Tarik. I feel like I can maybe be with the man that's going to love me right," she said and wrapped her arms around his waist.

Tarik grinned down at her. He couldn't help it. He'd fallen for India the second he entered her body years ago.

He was glad to see that she was willing to take a chance with him.

"India baby come here," Brody said stepping outside.

"Palmer get in the car," Arquez said spotting Brody's gun that was sticking out the back of his jeans.

"India come on," Palmer said in a pleading tone and grabbed her arm.

India gave Brody one last glance before getting into Tarik's car with her. They sat in the backseats together as Brody talked with Tarik and Arquez. India was a ball of nerves not wanting any bloodshed to occur.

"India tell this nigga what's up," Tarik said opening the back door.

Brody stood a few feet behind him breathing heavily.

"Yeah tell me what's up? After all of these years, you gone walk away from me? For him? This lil nigga can't give you shit that I haven't given you already. Don't let that baby daddy shit play into your head. I'm trying to make you a fucking wife India. You don't wanna marry me?" he asked with more pain in his tone then anger.

India couldn't fall for it. She'd done that too many times before.

"Brody you had a fucking decade to get it right. A decade. I can't do this with you again. I really can't," she replied and when she shook her head she was crying.

Brody nodded solemnly.

"I'm guessing these bitch ass niggas told you about Shia then? That shit was so fucking long ago. I don't even give that hoe no real money because she did that shit to trap me. She gotta live with that decision she made and she ain't never been a problem for us because she knows I'll kill her ass," he replied.

India's mouth fell open in shock. Palmer sat beside her shocked as well. The hood knew. Especially the men. However, it was their code that kept them silent. It wasn't their business to tell. India was detached from the city life outside of her funeral home. She didn't hang on the blocks, so she didn't know about the rumors and shit like that.

Betrayal hit her like a brick in the face as she stared back at Brody. Her cousin. He claimed to love her with all of his heart, yet he'd had twin sons by her fucking cousin.

Twin sons that she'd watched, bathed and cared for out of love. India felt a level of betrayal from him that she wouldn't wish on her worst enemy.

"Palmer I can't," India said breaking down and hugging her best friend.

Brody stood speechless. He was positive that Tarik or Arquez had told her of his scandalous ways. The painful cry that erupted from India was enough to let him know that they hadn't.

Tarik patted his arm as he passed by him.

"You did that shit all by yourself my nigga," he told him before getting into the car. His cousin followed suit and soon they were pulling away from the home India once shared with Brody.

* * *

Months skated by as India tried to adjust to not being with Brody. It wasn't that she missed him it was more so India letting go of the anger that she had in her heart. It had affected her so much that she wasn't even with Tarik sexually. Tarik had given her his place and was in an apartment in downtown Detroit.

"They just wanna talk," Inez said walking into his family room with his sons following behind him.

India stopped watching TV with her mom to gaze up at her brothers. Kent and Paris both stared down at her with apologetic looks on their handsome faces.

"We didn't want that shit to hurt you, sis. We honestly didn't know until we left the "D". He had them niggas shook for real and I feel like people didn't speak on it because its Shia. We all see that he gave no fucks about her ass," Kent said.

India waved him off. She looked back at the movie as her mom rubbed her leg lovingly.

"Get the door," Inez told Kent as the bell rung.

Paris sat next to India and tried to pull her into his arms. India brushed him off not ready to forgive the two men she felt would always have her back.

"Hey family," Tarik said walking into the room with a sleeping Kalila in his arms.

India smiled up at him. Tarik was so handsome, so loving and India was saddened at how stupid she'd been to overlook him. In his black jeans with the black crew neck on he looked sexy like always. He smiled down at her and she saw he was wearing a bottom grill that was covered in diamonds. Something he did whenever the mood struck him.

He'd also been kicking it with his down south family tough lately and India had noticed how the Florida niggas were rubbing off on him and in a good way.

246

"Hey Indie, where you want her?" he asked staring at India intently.

India shifted on the sofa. She'd gained fifteen pounds from stress eating and Tarik loved the added weight on her.

"I can put her upstairs Tarik. How is your mom? She was supposed to come over the other day," Charlotte said standing up.

Tarik smiled at India's mom and kissed her cheek. He passed her Kalila and joined India on the sofa. His hand went to India's thigh and India unconsciously found herself resting her head on his shoulder.

"She's good ma. She has been sick, but I'll let her know you were looking for her," he replied.

Charlotte nodded before stepping out of the room. Seconds later Sterling walked into the house and India took a deep breath.

What was once a close-knit relationship had quickly crumbled. Shia was missing and had left her sons with Sterling. Sterling was hopeful that she would pop back up and in good health while India was waiting for her to come back so she could beat her ass. While Sterling didn't know about Brody being the kid's father she still found excuses for Shia and India resented her cousin for that.

They hadn't spoken to each other in months.

"Hey family, its Sunday," Sterling said and gave everyone a small smile. She hugged Inez then India's brothers. Sterling went over to India and India lifted her head to glare at her.

"India, please. I miss you," Sterling said and swallowed hard.

India exhaled, and Tarik nudged her side.

"Come on ma. This your Thelma right here," he said making the men in the room laugh.

"Yeah, India at least forgive her. Y'all been close since before you could fucking walk," Paris said, and Inez nodded.

"India talk with your cousin," Inez said staring their way.

India sat up and slowly stood up. Tarik couldn't help but to gaze at her ass and lick his lips.

"You looking good ma," Tarik said oblivious to the fact that all of the men in the room were watching him.

India smiled as she gazed back at him.

"Thank you," she said quietly and followed Sterling out into the hallway.

India leaned against the wall as her cousin stood before her. Sterling looked beautiful and appeared to be in good health as well. India was happy to see she was doing fine.

"I'm sorry India. I can't go another day without us being good. From the moment we could talk you've been my best friend. My sister and the one person I could depend on no matter what. I love you and I'm sorry that she did that. There is no excuse for what she's done, and I'm done with her. It took me a while honestly because you know how I am about family but if I have to choose I choose you India. You've always chosen me, and I don't wanna not have you in my life. Please forgive me," Sterling begged her cousin needing her back in her life.

India's hard resolve cracked. She walked up to Sterling and they embraced each other tightly. Sterling began to cry as India hugged her.

"It was never about you choosing sides. I just wanted you to understand what she did to me. That's your sister, not mine. I'll forever have your back Sterling," India told her sincerely.

Sterling cried harder.

"Same here," she whispered extremely emotional.

Later that night India laid in her bed with Tarik and their daughter. Kalila was once again sleeping as Tarik laid his head on India's lap. They hadn't had sex in so long India had lost count but at the moment Tarik appeared to be okay with that. India was happy that he was letting her heal without any added pressure.

"That nigga still coming by the funeral home?"

India cleared her throat. Brody was relentless in trying to get her back. She'd given him the store back and he didn't want it, so she ended up selling it. She'd changed all of her numbers and now he was popping up at every place that he felt she would be. Not only had her brothers both paid him a visit her father did as well still he searched high and low for her.

"Yes, but I didn't open the door for him. I called my dad and he was able to make him leave. Eventually, he'll get the picture," she replied.

Tarik nodded. He didn't care if he did or he didn't. As long as Brody didn't put his hands on her he was good.

"Yeah okay. Do you regret leaving him?" he asked.

Because they were friends India wasn't thrown off by his question. She rubbed Tarik's fresh haircut and he closed his eyes.

"Sometimes my heart will get confused and I'll have all of these what if moments, but never do I wake up sad that I left him. I regret staying for as long as I did but I'm learning that even that was a good thing. If I would have left him sooner who's to say I would have ever run into you? I could have left town or been with someone else. I see now that everything happens for a reason. I'm more focused on learning from my mistakes. I wasted a lot of time with him and I won't ever do that again. I'm learning to really love myself so that when you give me your heart I can know what to do with it. You can't trust your heart to someone that doesn't know how to take care of their own heart. You just can't so I'm trying to be better," she replied.

Tarik sat up and climbed on top of India. She giggled as he kissed her nose. The way he made her feel was so unreal at times. India never knew that a man could make her so happy.

"You already got my heart. I want you to get better so that you will trust me enough to give me yours. It's like my mom always tells me. What's to come is better than what has gone," he said and kissed her lovingly on the lips.

Epilogue

Two years later.

"Hi," I'm nervous so you must forgive me. There was a time when I never thought I would be on this stage. A time when I never saw myself going after my dream. I have a business and it's successful. I had no reason to pursue college. However, I was blessed with people especially a person that saw more for me. There is nothing wrong with wanting more. I wasted years that I can't get back because of fear. I allowed for fear to control me. Fear of being single, fear of being an old college student, fear of not being good enough. We weren't born with the spirit of fear inside of us. This is only the beginning for me. I will become a lawyer. I will have a practice and I will be a woman that my daughter can be proud of. I'm honored to be the student commencement speaker. It took hard work and dedication for me to get up here. You have to fight for your dreams. You have to fight like you've never fought before. Be proud of the steps you've taken fellow graduates and know that it only gets better," India said before everyone clapped for her.

India smiled and went back to her seat. Soon the students were called up to get their degrees and India found herself on the bright lawn taking photos with her loved ones. The last two years had been hard for her. She had to deal with heartbreak, betrayal, and college along with being a mom. She tried to jump headfirst into a life with Tarik, but it didn't work out that way. She was still too hurt by Brody's lies and secrets. They decided to become friends and just three months prior decided to really be a couple. India felt good. She wasn't angry, she was in a good place and that had taken time.

India loved where she was with Tarik and couldn't wait to watch him walk across the stage. He was really her biggest supporter.

"Can I talk to you?" Brody asked walking up with a single red rose. He was donning a black Tom Ford suit looking handsome as ever. A sexy rotten soul was all he was.

India stopped smiling at her mom and looked his way.

"Don't make a scene," India's mother told her father who was still angry with how Brody had broken his daughter's heart.

India handed her belongings to Tarik who was close by with their daughter and she smiled at him.

"I'll be right back," she whispered.

Tarik who was looking handsome himself in some black slacks with a red Gucci buttoned down shirt on nodded. India walked with Brody to a tall tree that provided ample shading for them and Brody handed her the rose. He looked her over and licked his lips at how beautiful she was.

India now rocked her hair in a sexy short pixie cut. The style complemented her high cheekbones and slanted eyes. She was wearing a fitted black dress that stopped above her knees with black Christian Louboutin heels. Her decorated cap was in her hand and on the top of it was *Still Standing* written out in pearls.

"You did it," Brody said and sniffled. He took off his Cartier sunglasses and India could see his pretty eyes were red. India nodded feeling no remorse for him.

"That I did."

Brody put his glasses back on and licked his lips.

"I miss you. My life hasn't been the same since the day you moved your shit out. I don't have a reason to live anymore. I done tried to take myself out a few times and chickened out," he said and chuckled to keep from crying.

India shook her head.

"How about living for your sons? With everything that's happened with Shia passing away, they really need you now."

Brody shrugged. Talks of Shia was the last thing on his mind. Shia was never important to him.

"I remember when we used to live for each other," he said not wanting to discuss the reason why they were no longer together. Brody still hadn't made any effort to be in his kid's lives.

He didn't plan on it either although he was now sending Sterling monthly checks for them.

"And I'm glad I woke up. Have a good day Brody," India told him and walked away before he could take her down memory lane.

India rejoined her family and Tarik pulled her to his side. He gazed down at her in a way that made her weak in the knees. He wasn't shady. He wasn't a user. He loved her in such a sweet way that it made her a better woman. Tarik was a go-getter and in turn, it made India a go-getter. She now owned two more funeral homes. He owned a chain of wing restaurants with his cousin and money wasn't an issue for them.

They communicated sometimes even without words. They were best friends so much so that it made Palmer and Sterling jealous at times. Most of all they were lovers. They loved each other through the good and the bad days. They were a power couple. They handled everything with each other by their side and when times got too hard for them they prayed together. The real definition of goals and now that they were officially an item they were a force to be reckoned with.

And I'd choose you;

In a hundred lifetimes

In a hundred worlds

In any version of reality,

I'd find you

And I'd choose you

Has Our Love Gone Away?

Rocky

Prelude

"You wouldn't," Rocky said smiling at him.

Kesaun smirked at her and his handsome face sent her body into overdrive. She watched him make a dash towards her and she ran as fast as she could to the other side of the pool. Kesaun picked up her curvy body and tossed her in.

Rocky closed her eyes as she was submerged under water. She swam to the top and wiped the water from her eyes.

Kesaun chuckled as he swam over to her.

"Damn you sexy when you mad," he commented, and she splashed water in his face. Kesaun pulled her into his arms and kissed her soft lips. Rocky tried to resist but it was no use. He was too sexy; his lips were too soft and the way he held her in his strong arms made her weak for him.

"You know I like it when you wet for me ma," he said and kissed her again. Rocky closed her eyes and he swam them to the wall of the pool. He propped Rocky against it and his fingers went to the middle of her thighs. Kesaun stared at her with lustful eyes as he slid two fingers into her snug opening.

"Baby," Rocky moaned as her eyes rolled into the back of her head.

Kesaun sucked on her neck.

"Love me Rock," he demanded with so much yearning in his deep voice that it tugged at her heart.

Rocky breathed heavily.

"I want to," she admitted and Kesaun worked his fingers harder. "Just not yet," she replied and Kesaun snatched his fingers from her body and swam away from her.

Rocky watched him get out of the pool as her heart thumped in her chest. She closed her eyes as her once happy mood became gloomy.

"Damn you, Bucks," she mumbled hating that after so long he still held the key to her heart.

* * *

"Shit won't be easy, but I believe in you. You got the spirit of a hustla on you plus you come from that life. I'll never forget about your pops and all he did with us," Bucks said and pulled out his vibrating phone. His eyes scanned the text and he had to take a second to smile.

We need to talk in a few days. You can't keep taking over my life while in another state Bucks!

Bucks chuckled as he responded to Rocky's text.

The only way to change that beautiful is for you to bring your ass home. I'm coming to you this week.

Bucks put his phone away and looked at the young man before him. He was loyal, a thorough bread and a go-getter. Because of those things he'd become the person Bucks passed the connect down to. Bucks was done with the streets. He was ready to move on to other shit and to him, Bibby was next up. Bibby's father once hustled for the

Matins and long after he went to prison the Matins still looked out for his family.

Bibby now ran the streets at nineteen and Bucks had taken him under his wing.

"I appreciate this shit for real bruh. You already know how I view y'all. We family," Bibby said and slapped hands with Bucks.

Bucks nodded until two men entering his bar garnered his attention. The aggression jumped off the men. From the way they walked to the grim looks on their dark faces they screamed trouble.

Bucks, Bibby and Bucks security for the bar all pulled out their weapons. Bucks sat his pistol on his lap wondering who the men were. He was lowkey, so quiet you wouldn't notice he was there unless he wanted to be seen so enemies were something Bucks could proudly say he didn't have a lot of.

"What's good?" Bibby asked as the men walked up.

"Where Denim at?" the tallest man with the thick brows and unkept fade asked glaring at Bucks.

Bucks smiled as he sat up.

"The only man to ever question me is the one that spit me out. He don't look shit like you. It's best for you to exit the same way you came in my nigga," Bucks replied and grabbed his drink.

The man that had just questioned him gritted his teeth before the man with him patted his arm. They shared a knowing look before departing the bar.

Bibby stared at the door long after they were gone with a frown on his face.

"They checking for your girl?" he asked Bucks.

Bucks typed away on his phone before giving Bibby his attention.

"It's her ex-nigga. He was on some stalking type shit and she moved here. I guess he done found her, but I'll handle it."

Bibby shook his head.

"Them niggas look shiesty. Let me take care of them for you," Bibby suggested.

Bucks patted his arm to calm him down. Bibby was a real street nigga. He didn't do any talking. Just the thought of someone being a threat to him made them a target and he never missed a shot.

"Relax, I got it covered. Just hit up them storages and get that shit. You watch your own back. I'm good over here nigga," Bucks told him, and they dapped one another up again before Bibby left.

Bucks had a few more drinks before leaving the bar. He called up Rocky as he headed home, and she didn't take his call, so he put his phone away. He was buzzing on a strong ass strain of marijuana and desperately wanted to be sliding up in Rocky. He missed everything about his baby but especially how she felt.

"She coming home this fucking week. I'm done playing with her ass," he said as his tire went out.

The big tire began to deflate, and Bucks immediately pulled over. He chuckled at how he hadn't had a flat tire in a very long time.

"Fucked up ass roads," he complained pushing his car door open.

Before Bucks could step out of his car the cold hard steel of a gun was coming into his view. A low chuckle fell from the man's mouth who was holding it.

"Now I'ma ask your bitch ass again. Where the fuck is my girl at?"

Bucks sat stunned for a moment wondering if he could grab his gun before the man let off a round into him? Bucks tried his luck and the man shot him in the chest off instinct. The man shot at Bucks again and Bucks held up his hand to shield his face. The bullet tore through the skin on his left hand and Bucks fell back in pain.

The man with the gun went through Bucks pockets making sure to grab his phone before running off to the awaiting car.

Bucks breathed slowly as his eyes grew heavy with exhaustion. A state of shock came over him as he thought of the one woman he loved.

Rocky.

One

"What's good, beautiful?"

Rocky shrugged. She was mourning a kid that she had no clue she was carrying. The feelings were confusing to even her. What Rocky did know was that it hurt to no longer have the baby that she'd made with a man that she was falling in love with.

"When I was twelve one of my friends died. He had an allergic reaction to some food right in front of me. The shit was mad crazy because I thought he was joking. I didn't realize how serious it was until it was too late. That fucked with me for a while. My parents got me counseling and the therapist told me that I was holding on to a death instead of accepting that my friend was dead. She said I was stuck in phase one which was shock or denial shit I can't remember but I think that's what's going on with you. I'm just as hurt behind this as you are. I'm making it though because I know that what's meant for us, is meant for us. If we supposed to have a family together then it'll happen, baby. Be thankful that you still alive. I know I am," he said with his words filling up the void she had deep inside of her.

Rocky hugged his waist tighter feeling a bit calmer than before.

"Do you love me?" she asked in a light voice filled with more need than she liked for it to have.

Bucks looked at her and a genuine smile covered his handsome face.

"More than I ever loved a woman in my whole fucking life."

"You can now take your seat belts off," a deep voice said over a speaker startling Rocky out of her sleep.

She gazed at the man she held onto and it wasn't the man that had just been in her dreams. Suddenly she was emerged back into reality.

Bucks has been shot! You have to come home Rocky.

Rocky read over the text that changed her life. The text that canceled her vacation and had her on the first flight to Detroit. The power of words never ceased to amaze her. They could change your life in an instant whether it be good or bad.

"Ladies and gentlemen your flight to Detroit has just landed. Thank you for flying with Delta. Enjoy your stay in Michigan."

Rocky felt like a zombie. She was certain she looked like one in her disheveled sweats and frizzy curly hair that had once been a silk press. Between sex, crying and stressing over Bucks that style had long ago left her. Rocky attempted to pull herself together as she smoothed out the navy tee while licking her chapped lips.

"Come on Rocky, we up ma," Kesaun said and stood up.

Rocky rubbed her tired eyes and gazed up at him. It hadn't been easy when she'd first left Detroit. She was dealing with heartache along with losing a child. Seattle had been a breath of fresh air for her. Meeting him had been the icing on the cake. Kesaun had been nothing she wanted but everything she needed to have, in order to deal with not having Bucks in her life.

She forced herself to stand up and she grabbed Kesaun's hand. She watched him toss his red hood over his head to shield his handsome face and he led them out of the cabin. They entered into the Metro Airport and Rocky sniffed the air. She exhaled as it hit her.

She was back home.

The last place she wanted to be but the very same place that she had to be. It took them no time to find their bags considering it was only ten people on the early flight. They then rented a car and Rocky relaxed in the seat while Kesaun headed to the hospital. She wasn't anywhere near ready to see Bucks, but she had to. Her heart needed for him to be okay.

"He's gone be good. You look so fucking tired. I want you to promise me you'll get some rest while you out here. Can you do that baby?" Kesaun asked.

His relaxing deep tone made Rocky smile. He was always so gentle with her. Nothing like the tough as nails MMA fighter that he was known to be. Kesaun was nothing like Bucks but they did share the same laid-back demeanors. It took a lot to piss Kesaun off and no matter how many times they'd gotten into it not once had Rocky ever felt threatened by him or his strength.

"Yeah, I just hate he had to get shot. This is crazy but I'm so happy he's alive. It could have been worse."

"Hell, yeah it could have been. I don't speak on the next man or his lifestyle, but I will send some prayers up for him Rocky."

Rocky glanced over at Kesaun surprised by his words. She'd been seeing him for a while now. Even while she'd gone on a Christmas trip with her best friend Pia who just so happened to be married to someone close to Bucks. Rocky had slipped up and had sex with Bucks. Feeling riddled with the guilt she'd told Kesaun the second she'd touched down in Seattle. He went a month without calling her before showing up on her doorstep. They'd found a way to move past it, but she knew Bucks was a soft spot for him. Hell, if the roles had been reversed she'd surely felt some kind of way.

"Thank you and I mean that," she said staring into his eyes.

They rode in silence the rest of the way to the hospital and with Rocky's help, it took Kesaun forty-five minutes to get there. While he parked she rushed through the emergency doors in search of a familiar face. Bucks had been shot two times the previous night, but Rocky knew for a fact everyone was still up there. He was receiving two surgeries and she wanted to be at his bedside when he woke up.

"Rocky!"

Pia's strained voice made her turn around. Rocky ran towards her at full speed and they embraced each other tightly. The tears Rocky didn't want to fall broke through and escaped her eyes as she hugged her best friend. Pia rubbed Rocky's back in soothing motions trying to get her to calm down.

"He's fine Rocky, I swear he is. We were just shaken up, but things will be okay."

Rocky nodded still sobbing into her grey shirt and a small hand grabbed her arm.

"Pia let me talk to her."

Rocky let go of Pia and looked wearily at Bucks, mother Ann. Her eyes were tinted red and swollen. She still looked her same regal, beautiful self but her appearance was off kilter because of her unmade face. She pulled Rocky into a hug and she sighed. Ann smelled like Bucks and just being in her presence gave Rocky a huge sense of relief.

"He's fine Rocksana. I missed you dearly sweetheart and I got the gifts you sent me. I never forgot about you and neither did Braylen. Do you wanna see him?" she asked.

Rocky nodded. Of course, she wanted to see him.

"Yes," she replied trying to calm down.

"Rocky, you good?" Kesaun asked walking up.

Rocky pulled back from Ann to look at him. She didn't want him to see her like that but knew eventually he would. His thick brows dipped into a frown as he took in her disheveled appearance. That fast she'd come apart.

"Yes, his mom is going to take me back there to see him. My sister will take you to the waiting area."

Kesaun looked at Pia and gave her a quick head nod. Pia walked up to him and she grabbed his hand.

"Hi Kesaun, I've heard so much about you. The waiting area is this way," she said giving him a genuine smile before leading him towards that area.

Kesaun glanced back at Rocky always so overprotective of her and she gave him a reassuring smile. Ann pulled her away and back to her side.

"He's very handsome sweetie. I see Braylen has some competition," she said and they both smiled.

The room Bucks was kept in was cold and dark. It took Rocky back to when she'd lost her baby and it made her hug his mother's small arm for support. Ann led Rocky over to the bed and her heart dropped. Bucks was sleeping with his chest bandaged up along with his hand.

"They shot him in the hand and in his chest. Two inches from his heart. My God, he had angels with him that night. I'll leave you alone with him," Ann said and left out of the room.

Rocky stared at Bucks for a moment before taking a seat. He looked so peaceful and even after being shot he still looked handsome. His caramel brown skin barely had any marks covering his face as he rested in the bed. Rocky touched his thick lips before running her hand over his face.

She leaned towards Bucks and sniffed him. When the same alluring scent he always had to him greeted her nostrils it made her smile. Rocky kissed him gently on the lips and sat back in her seat.

"Bucks, what are you doing with your life? You told me I could leave to get my shit together and you just went buck wild, huh? Are you trying to leave me?"

Rocky's eyes swelled again with tears as she licked her lips.

"Because I'm not ready to say goodbye to you. I will never be ready for something like that Bucks. You have so much more, life to live and I refuse to watch your mom cry over a casket."

"Or me," A deep voice spoke walking into the dimly lit room. Rocky looked up and smiled at his father. She'd had the chance to meet him once but even then, he was extremely nice to her.

She stood up and they shared a quick hug before their eyes both found their way back to Bucks.

"We all do things in life that we regret, and my biggest regret is not shielding my son from the life I was living. Can you give me a minute?" he asked somberly.

Rocky looked at him and saw just where Bucks got his handsome looks from. His father was tall with a mocha complexion and didn't look old at all. In fact, he was aging beautifully considering he had a grown son. Rocky nodded and gave Bucks one last look before walking out of the room.

"Hi, were you in the room with Braylen?"

Rocky swallowed down the emotions she was feeling to look at the pretty girl standing before her.

"Yes, he's still sleeping."

The girl sighed and hugged herself. The small act made Rocky pay attention to her small baby bump that seemed to jump off her petite frame. Another type of emotion crept into Rocky as her thoughts started to run wild.

"I'm sorry who are you?" Rocky asked trying to not overreact.

The pregnant girl shook her head and glanced behind Rocky at Bucks hospital room door.

"I'm Denim. Braylen and I don't have a title but we're having a baby together," she said with a shrug and her eyes watered up before she fell apart.

Denim caught Rocky off guard when she hugged her tightly. Rocky stood still in shock as Bucks baby mother hugged her. Rocky was too hurt to cry. She'd lost her baby and now Bucks was having another one with someone else. Rocky always envisioned them having another child together. She'd never added other people to that equation.

"You should probably get something to drink so you don't get dehydrated," Rocky told her pulling back.

They both loved the same man and no matter how much Rocky felt her pain she still had no interest in sharing a hug with her. The reality was she was about to have something with Bucks that Rocky didn't.

That was a very hard fucking pill to swallow.

Denim looked at Rocky and wiped her face.

"Yes, I should. Could you come with me? His family doesn't treat me bad, but I can tell they have their walls up because I'm not *her*," she said with an eye roll.

Rocky cleared her throat and smoothed down her hair. When she'd decided to start going weave free she had Bucks in mind and even when the cut had been done she'd sent him a picture. He, of course, loved it and so did she. Rocky did indulge in extensions whenever she wanted to, but she was happy to no longer be a slave to them because at one point she'd spent thousands for them. Rocky was now wearing a blunt cut bob that she kept parted down the middle.

"Uh, sure"

"Cool, it's this way," Denim said and walked off.

Because Rocky did still love Bucks she unashamedly checked out Denim as she walked behind her. Denim was smaller than Rocky and didn't have much of an ass or breast, but her face was a type of gorgeous that Rocky couldn't deny. She also had a nice wavy lace front in that was practically undetectable but because weaves were something Rocky knew all about she could still see it was a wig.

"So how do you know Braylen?" Denim asked much calmer than she was seconds ago.

They'd gotten some coffee and Denim had purchased a sandwich as well. Rocky sat across from Denim with a fake smile on her face. Rocky wanted to be upset with Denim but the vibes she was getting off of her were cool. Plus, it wasn't Denim's fault that she and Bucks were no longer together.

"I'm *her*, his ex," Rocky replied and laughed nervously.

Denim's smile fell.

"Oh."

Denim let out a nervous chuckle as well and she sat back. Her hands went to her stomach and Rocky watched her check out her looks the same way Rocky had done her just minutes ago.

"You're beautiful. He always said that you were and now I see he wasn't lying. I love your hair as well. Braylen is always ragging on my weaves. I know he has a thing for natural girls," Denim replied while smiling.

Rocky returned her smile.

"Thank you and you're beautiful as well but I guess we shouldn't expect anything less from Bucks. Right?"

Denim's brows knitted together.

"Are you referring to Braylen?" Denim asked.

The way she freely used a name Rocky only called out when he was making her float to the heavens did get under Rocky's skin.

"His street name is Bucks. You didn't know that?"

Denim shook her head.

"I suspected that it was, but he never talked about it, so I didn't either. I rarely went around his family or friends. We always stayed in our own little world although we did go to Vegas with his friend Aamil and his wife. That was fun," she replied and smiled at the last part.

Rocky nodded because Denim was living a life with Bucks that she had wanted to live. They, however, couldn't find a way to get it right.

"Also, he told me about the baby and I'm so sorry about your loss. When I told him, I was pregnant he was angry, but he warmed up to the idea like a month ago. I moved here for work. I don't have any support besides my work family and Braylen. So, when I found out he was shot it was like I had been pierced with that bullet as well. I could have died when I got that call from his mother."

Rocky looked away from her and her eyes watered.

"Yeah, me too," she mumbled feeling that exact same way.

The women shared an awkward silence until Pia stepped into the cafeteria with Kesaun following behind her. Just seeing his handsome face look her way brought Rocky comfort. Kesaun had a body built similar to Floyd Mayweather only he was much taller than him.

Rocky stood up as they approached them and so did Denim. Rocky watched Pia give Denim a generic smile and she wanted to laugh but she didn't.

"Kesaun this is Bucks um..." Rocky stopped talking and looked to Denim for clarification on just what she was to him and Denim giggled.

"His girlfriend," she said quickly and held out her hand to Kesaun.

Rocky did her best to hide her irritation with Denim's greeting that she'd just given Kesaun. Instead, she turned her attention to Kesaun and he pulled her into his arms. Rocky rested her head against his hard chest as he spoke to Denim.

"Nice to meet you and you good Rocky? Should we go back to the hotel cause I'm tired as hell?"

Rocky sighed not wanting to go but knowing that maybe leaving was best for them at the moment. She also knew that she had to be mindful of Kesaun's presence. She knew that he wasn't looking to sit in the hospital all night while she checked on her ex.

"Uh...yes we can leave. Just give me a chance to see everyone and tell him goodbye."

"Okay I'll be over here getting something to eat baby," he said and walked away.

"I'll sit here for a little while longer," Denim said and rubbed Rocky's arm as her own eyes watered again.

Because they shared so many things in common Rocky did relate to her. Rocky pulled some paper out of her crossbody and wrote her number on it for Denim. She passed Denim the paper while staring at her.

"Call me if you need anything," she told her.

Denim took the paper and smiled.

"I will. Thank you," she replied.

Rocky walked off with Pia and Pia glanced over at her with questioning eyes.

"Sister wives?" she asked quietly, and Rocky shoved her shoulder. Pia laughed and shook her head. "But no that was mature of you Rocky. Denim is cool, but she isn't you. You and Bucks are really taking a page from me and Ahmad's book right now honey with these fake ass relationships y'all are in. The only word of advice I can say is don't play this game for too long because its time you can't get back."

They stopped at Bucks door and Rocky looked at Pia. Her girl looked good in her black leggings with her cut off cream hoodie on. Her hair was touching the top of her shoulders and had this tousled look to it while her pretty face was free of makeup and shining with a natural glow to it. Rocky had missed the hell out of her, so she hugged her again and spun her around so that she could slap her fat ass that she knew Ahmad was loving on all of the time.

"Why didn't you tell me about her? And she's pregnant by my Bucks, what the fuck Pia."

Pia shook her head and licked her heart-shaped lips.

"I'm sorry I just wanted you to keep focusing on you. I knew all of that would make shit worse and he's not in a relationship with her."

Rocky's eyes rolled as she looked at Pia.

"But they're about to have a baby together though. She's giving him something that I couldn't, so he'll love her even if she thinks he won't. You know he will because that's the kind of man he is." Rocky exhaled and rubbed her eyes. "I should have never left. I practically gave him to her."

"I been telling your ass to come back but what's done is done. You and I both know who he wants to be with," Pia replied and pulled Rocky into a hug.

Ann stepped out of the room and yawned as she looked at Rocky and Pia.

"He's up but he's very weak. He wants to see you, Rocky. Pia could you show me some more pictures of them beautiful kids of yours?" his mom asked.

"Yes, you can even take them with you for a few weeks if you'd like," Pia replied, and they shared a laugh as they walked away.

Rocky stood at the door for a minute collecting herself. The last time they'd seen each other she'd lost all sense of thought. They'd fucked like dogs in heat at the cabin and she'd taken so much of his dick down her throat that she'd been hoarse for days after that. She'd run back to Seattle and cut him off again.

Bucks had been angry with her and told her that it was the last time he was gone let her do that shit.

His exact words were *your time is fucking up beautiful.* Rocky believed him, so she'd been trying to see if she could walk away from Kesaun, her life in Seattle and be back in Michigan with Bucks.

Rocky took a deep breath and entered Bucks room. His TV was on and the curtain was pushed up blocking his bed so Rocky couldn't see anything but his feet.

"Ma? Beautiful is that you?" he asked weakly.

His voice, *God* it did something to Rocky. Her tears flowed as she walked closer to him. Rocky walked around the curtain and he looked up at her. His left eye was bloodshot red like he'd busted his blood vessel and to just see that someone had brought harm to him in such a brutal way broke her down.

"Rocksana, come here ma. A nigga good, you can believe that," he said in a hoarse voice and opened his arms.

Rocky walked over to him and hugged him gently. Bucks breathed into her hair and she closed her eyes while reveling in his touch. She'd almost lost him, and it had been one of the scariest things she'd ever experienced.

"Damn, a nigga missed the fuck out of you girl. You know that? Huh, Rocky?" he asked and ran his good hand through her hair.

Rocky nodded as she continued to hug him.

"Am I hurting you?"

"Nah, you good. You wanna get in the bed with me?" he asked making her smile.

The thought crossed Rocky's mind until she remembered that what they used to be wasn't what they were at the moment. It was no longer her place to get in the bed with him and that saddened her.

Rocky forced herself to pull back from him and she sat in the chair closest to his bed. Bucks looked at her endearingly as he grabbed her hand.

"I had to get shot up to get you back home?"

He smirked at his question, but Rocky didn't find a damn thing funny about what he had said.

"Bucks please tell me you're done with the streets. Can you do that?" she asked staring at him intently.

Bucks pulled his bottom lip into his mouth and stared straight ahead. Rocky soaked in all of his pretty boy features as he did so. Bucks looked *exactly* the same just in bad conditions because of the circumstances he was in.

"Rocky," he said, and Rocky shook her head.

"If not for me then at least for your unborn baby," Rocky told him, and that made Bucks look her way.

"Bae...I'm sorry. I didn't want you to find out like this. I wanted to be the one to tell you. We not together though and I don't see that changing anytime soon," he said in a sincere tone.

Rocky shrugged wishing things could be different.

"Neither are we, so you don't owe me an apology. I was just shocked is all. She's beautiful and nice. You did good."

Bucks squeezed Rocky's hand and flipped his arm over. He pulled on Rocky's hand and she looked down at his right wrist. On it was a cursive "R" that was very beautiful with a small crown near the top of the letter.

"I told you I would never forget you. You thought I was playing?" he asked staring into her eyes. Rocky broke his gaze not able to deal with the emotions she was feeling, and Bucks licked his lips. "Come here, come give me the kiss I been waiting on since your ass snuck up out of the cabin," he said and still her body worked for him better than it worked for herself. Rocky leaned in and Bucks passionately kissed her on the lips.

Bucks slipped his tongue into her mouth and her body came alive for him. His strong hand roamed freely over her landing in-between her legs. He cupped her sex possessively through her grey joggers and rubbed it back and forth in a slow teasing motion.

"I missed the fuck out of you Rocky. You here to stay?" Bucks asked and pulled her bottom lip into his mouth.

Rocky wanted to protest and tell him no but, how could she? Bucks was all consuming. With her, he never played fair. He wanted all of the love, time and energy that she had to give, and Rocky didn't know how to not give it to him.

Weak for his love she nodded, and he grinned at her.

"I love you ma," he said against her lips while rubbing at the sweet spot between her legs.

"Braylen?"

Denim's soft voice was like a bucket of ice water being tossed onto Rocky. Rocky quickly pulled back from Bucks while he took his time moving his hand from between her legs.

His eyes stared at Rocky for a moment before he looked over at Denim.

"Give us a second beautiful," he told Denim.

Beautiful. The sweet word falling from his lips while aimed at another woman hurt Rocky. She thought that was what he'd reserved for her.

Clearly, she was wrong.

"...Okay and Rocky your boyfriend is waiting for you at the door," Denim said and walked away.

Rocky tried to stay calm as Bucks' head snapped her way. He cocked his head to the side as a frown marred his face.

Rocky knew she hadn't done anything wrong still she felt guilty as he looked at her.

"Boyfriend? What the fuck," he said and chuckled which made him cough. Rocky handed him some water and he grabbed her hand. "Who is this nigga, Rocky?"

Rocky nibbled on her bottom lip while staring at him.

"He's that fighter from Seattle. We talked about him," she said quietly.

Buck's eyes narrowed at her.

"Not really. You said you and this nigga was friends. When the fuck did that shit become a relationship?" he questioned her not hiding his disdain about the fake title Denim had given her friendship with Kesaun.

Rocky shifted from one foot to the other.

"Bucks...you have someone pregnant."

Bucks nodded.

"And we not together. You left me ma. I been fucking waiting on you. You already know this shit not about to ride beautiful," Bucks told her.

Rocky smiled to keep from going off on Bucks. Yes, she loved him and was often a slave to that love, but she was still Rocksana. She would always speak her mind.

"Bucks you already in the hospital, you might wanna watch how you're talking to me. Kesaun is a friend. I guess like the same way you and Denim are friends," she responded with a bark to her light pretty voice.

Bucks smirked at her. He licked his lips as his eyes slid up and down her body. Bucks waved her over and Rocky walked up on the bed.

"I told you about Denim on the trip. We was never in a relationship. Truthfully, I'm just opening up to the fact that I got a baby on the way beautiful. The shit isn't easy for me either. You know I always thought it would be you still that's not my woman. I need you to stay here with me. Can you do that?" he asked.

Rocky sighed. Bucks was being Bucks. Always demanding more from her. More than she was comfortable with giving him.

"Bucks I have a life in Seattle."

Bucks broke his gaze and stared straight ahead. He was tired and still in a lot of pain but his talk with Rocky couldn't wait.

"Rocky I fuck with you. You know that, and I never hid that shit. What happened to our baby was fucked up. Still, that didn't have to be the end of us. I gave you time and I was being patient, but that time is up. Do what you feel you need to do but if it's not concerning me then we can stop playing this game right now," he told her before getting comfortable in the bed.

Rocky watched him began to doze back off as she pondered over what he'd said to her. She swallowed hard before giving him a gentle kiss on his forehead.

"I love you, I'll see you in the morning," she whispered.

Bucks exhaled as she walked away from the bed.

"I love you too beautiful," he said quietly.

Rocky exited Bucks room and went back to the waiting area. As she stepped into the small space she was greeted with familiar faces. She embraced Aamil who was Bucks best friend and his wife Drew that she was close with.

Rocky noticed Denim sitting off to the side by herself, but she didn't go over to her. Rocky was still low key pissed at how she'd called her out to Bucks over Kesaun. Rocky went on to hug the rest of Bucks family before Pia pulled her to the side of the room.

Pia looked at her with tired eyes as she held her cup of coffee.

"What happened?"

Rocky shook her head. She couldn't take her eyes off of Kesaun who was having a conversation with Ameer who was Aamil's older brother. She watched Ameer grin at him and they slapped hands. Rocky shook it off figuring they were discussing boxing.

Men were easy like that. It didn't take much for them to get along.

"He's mad and basically said that if I leave that's it. Like this is some crazy shit because I can't just walk away from my job and Kesaun," Rocky replied.

Pia nodded.

"I know but if that's the case then why not just let Bucks go? Its clear Denim would love to have him."

Rocky's eyes briefly connected with Denim's then her belly. Just seeing her pregnant made Rocky uneasy.

"That won't work either. This is Bucks...*my* fucking Bucks," Rocky said to her.

Pia grinned at Rocky and licked her lips.

"Then do what you have to do to get your man back. *Steal her man, steal her man,*" Pia chanted in a joking manner fucking with Rocky.

Rocky laughed before hugging her again. It had been a YouTube Video they'd gotten that saying from.

"You know that's always been my man," she replied in a low tone making Pia laugh.

"Then your ass better start acting like it."

Long after they'd left the hospital Rocky rested in the hotel bed with Pia's words on her mind. Kesaun rested beside her with his eyes on the sports channel. He lived and breathed his sport and was always checking out the latest news and gossip concerning the MMA business.

Rocky admired his fair brown skin. The way it seemed to melt over his muscular body. Then there were his tribal tattoos that slid across his biceps then up his neck and they were sexy as fuck to her. Rocky knew his story. How he'd hustled in DC before running into a fight promotor that saw something in him that he hadn't seen in himself.

Kesaun was twenty-four but he'd found a way to dominate the sport he was so good at. Rocky respected and adored him. She loved how he could make her laugh then cry out while fucking her passionately. He was one of a kind and she didn't wanna lose him still in the corner of her mind was Bucks.

They were two very different men that both meant something to her. However Rocky couldn't lie to herself. Bucks possessed a huge part of her that Kesaun didn't. But he came with things that worried her. He was in the streets and was now expecting a baby with someone else. Kesaun was legit and had no kids. Hell, he didn't even have a dog. All he had was his passion for fighting and his love for Rocky.

"What you thinking about baby?" he asked glancing over at her.

Rocky smiled at him and touched the soft jet-black hairs on his head that had been cut into a curly taper. Kesaun's hooded eyes peered at her curiously as he licked his lips.

"Do you still love him?" he asked.

Rocky's heartbeat quickened at his question. She closed her eyes and he leaned into her. Kesaun kissed her tenderly on the lips calming her down.

"I get it. I know how this shit goes but see me and him not the same. While he made it easy for you to walk away from him I won't. Lay back," Kesaun instructed her and climbed on top of Rocky.

Rocky did as he'd told her to do and he took off her t-shirt and underwear. Kesaun took off his boxers and grabbed a Magnum before joining her in the bed. Rocky's chest heaved up and down in anticipation as he sheathed his thick member with the latex.

"We not together but we both know this is where you should be Rocky. I won't fight with no nigga over a woman, but you know in your heart who makes you happier. Who gives you the most peace," he said before sliding inside of her.

Two

"It's a girl. I want to name her something with a "B". You know something that's close to his name. I hate my name, so you can trust she won't be named Cotton or no mess like that," Denim said and smiled.

Rocky's lips pressed together as she quirked them up at Denim. Rocky typed away on her laptop as they both sat in Bucks cold room. Bucks was once again resting, and Rocky was trying to get as much work done from Detroit that she could.

"Did you know what you were having before your baby passed away?" Denim asked nervously.

Rocky glanced up from her screen. She took a deep breath and exhaled.

"Denim I would rather not talk about that."

Denim nodded.

"I didn't mean anything by it. I can understand why you would say that and I'm sorry. My ex boyfriend was very abusive. He jumped on me when I was four months pregnant and I lost our child, so I do know how that feels," Denim revealed making Rocky feel bad about snapping at her.

Rocky's hard resolve relaxed a bit as she closed her laptop.

"I'm sorry that happened to you as well. How long ago was that?"

Denim's dark eyes filled with sadness.

"Two years ago. That was the last time I saw him. I pray he's dead," she replied.

"If he was that horrible to you then I hope he is as well. Is that why you're up here alone?"

"Yes, and the job I have pays me good. I work for a leading loan company. It's okay, I just get lonely at times. I know I've been working your nerves these last two days," Denim said and laughed.

Rocky gave her a genuine smile. She had but she wasn't terrible company either.

"You're good. This is just weird to me," Rocky admitted.

Denim nodded feeling the same way. The beautiful women both found themselves staring at Bucks before Rocky decided they needed some fresh air.

"We should go grab some food," she said putting her laptop up.

Denim smiled, and it showed off the small dimples in her cheeks. She stood up and rubbed her protruding belly as Rocky put her work stuff away. They exited the hospital and Rocky noticed a tall, handsome man staring at them. He watched them for a moment before going to a new black Charger.

Rocky thought nothing of it as she led Denim over to Bucks G-Wagon that she was using while in town. Rocky took Denim to her favorite shawarma spot in Dearborn and they ordered food before grabbing a table. Rocky answered text messages while Denim hungrily licked her lips.

"I'm starving," Denim said quietly and they both laughed.

Rocky glanced up to smile at her and she noticed that the same attractive man from the parking lot was now in the shawarma spot at the counter. Someone with a more serene lifestyle would have thought nothing of it but Rocky was immediately on alert. She didn't wanna scare Denim still something in her gut was telling her that he knew who they were.

"Don't look back but I think this nigga is following us," Rocky said quietly to her.

Denim's arched brows pulled together.

"Is he dark skin with a sponge fade?" she asked fearing it was her crazy ex-boyfriend.

Rocky shook her head before laughing.

"What the fuck is a sponge fade? Is it shaped like SpongeBob or some shit?"

Denim snickered.

"No, it's just shaped like a sponge at the top. It sounds crazy but it's nice to look at."

Rocky nodded and her heartbeat increased when the handsome man advanced on their table. He carried not only his food but theirs as well. He sat their food down and his honey colored eyes fell on Denim and Rocky.

"I'm Bibby. I work for Bucks. I saw you looking and I didn't need for you to call in the cavalry. He has me watching y'all," he explained and sat next to Denim.

Denim smiled shyly at him as Rocky blatantly stared his way. She pulled out her phone and called Aamil.

"What up sis?" Aamil answered in a groggy tone.

They'd all been coming to the hospital around the clock to check on Bucks, so she was certain that he was catching up on his rest.

"Hey, it's this nigga here named Bibby that said he works for Bucks."

Bibby chuckled as he unwrapped his food.

"Yeah, that's my little nigga. It's some shit happening behind the scenes and until its handled we need eyes on you and her. You good?" Aamil replied.

His answer made Rocky very uneasy. She had a lot to say but knew it wasn't the right time.

"I am. Can you tell Drew I'm stopping by today?"

Aamil cleared his throat.

"Yeah I got you," he replied before ending the call.

Rocky put her phone away and smiled at the handsome Bibby. He was a looker with his creamy brown skin that was red-toned brown with his bedroom honey colored eyes and his low-cut fade that was lined up like Mitch off of Paid In Full. His clothes were simple yet stylish and he wore no chain but on his wrist was a Rolex that was shining even in the restaurant that had horrible lighting due to the blinds on the windows being shut.

What made Bibby stand out the most was the confidence that oozed off his 6'3 frame. He was built like a ballplayer and had a few scattered tattoos here and there. He had a full mustache with a small goatee, full lips, and a straight nose. He was a pretty boy but had an aura to him that made you aware of his dark side.

When he caught Rocky looking he shot her a smirk before opening the bottled water.

"I wasn't trying to scare y'all. That's why I smiled outside of the hospital ma," he told Rocky.

Rocky relaxed in her seat and grabbed her food.

"I wasn't scared more like on alert. I've been through some things so I'm always watching my surroundings. Even before Bucks, I was known to be around street men. My father hasn't always been straight laced if you know what I mean."

Bibby nodded.

"I know, and I know your old man. He's an OG for real. He's also a good dude. You good ma?" Bibby asked turning to Denim.

She'd been cradling her food while frowning. Her eyes glanced his way and she nodded before exhaling.

"I have heartburn," Denim divulged to him.

Bibby turned back to his food and Rocky tore into her's. For several minutes they ate in silence before Denim spoke again.

"All of this is new to me. With Braylen we just dated and hung out. I never saw this part of his life before," she said and looked down at her food.

Rocky's eyes connected with Bibby's and he shrugged.

"I gotta say this ladies and I mean this with the uttermost respect. To watch two women that have been with the same man be so nice to each other is fucking amazing to me and shit. Bucks always been like a father figure. He is the one person that I know will give me good advice whether I wanna hear it or not. I have nothing but respect for that man and I see now that other people feel the same way. It's not too many niggas out here like him," Bibby said and both women nodded agreeing with him.

Later that day after Rocky took Denim back to the hospital she went to Aamil and Drews home. Drew met her at the door with a huge glass of wine.

"A woman after my own heart," Rocky said with a smile.

Drew laugh and pulled her into a hug. They then went into Drew's living room and sat down.

"Where is everyone at?"

Drew pulled out a rolled up blunt and lit it up. She didn't indulge in marijuana like she once did. Now her days were filled with motherly and wifely duties along with running her boutiques but when she had a break from it all she did have a smoke.

"Aamil took them to their afterschool bullshit," Drew replied making Rocky laugh.

Rocky grabbed her glass of wine and kicked off her slides.

"Drew it's so much going on. I don't know if I'm coming or going. I have my mom and Kesaun blowing me up asking when I'm coming back then I have Bucks and his shit load of baggage. I wanna hate Denim you know but I don't. She's sweet, kind of irritating at times but she means no harm. However, in the back of my head, I'm still like this is the chick that's about to have a baby by your man. Do you fuck with her like that? And why do we have someone tailing us?"

Drew looked at Rocky and shook her head. While Rocky was dressed in tight jeans that had been cut at the knees with a white graphic top, Drew had on a pair of leggings with a black cami. Her body still looked amazing and although Rocky didn't know about the surgeries she'd had in the past to acquire her look what Rocky did know was that Drew was gorgeous as hell to her.

"Girl you just said a lot of shit. I don't even know where to begin," Drew said and they both laughed. "No, but for real let's start with Denim. She is sweet. In the beginning, I was very mean to her because hell she wasn't you but Aamil got on me, so I did start speaking but it's never gone past that. I always knew you and Bucks would find your way back to one another."

Rocky's eyes lifted from her glass and fell onto Drew.

"How did you know that?" she asked quietly.

Drew smiled at her.

"Because real love never goes away. And look at you right back here. As far as your job and your special friend I would say to keep it real with them. You have to do what's best for Rocky. Not work to please other people. Not even Bucks," Drew told her. Rocky nodded taking in what she was saying and Drew continued. "Now this stays between us. I know you're becoming best friends with Denim but don't forget she's not family yet. From what we know it was her ex-man that shot Bucks, so you know the Matin men are losing their damn minds. We haven't had drama on us like this since Ahmad's little ass so yes, we're kind of stressed right now. It's not so much as anyone is scared they just want it handled. You know how they feel about Bucks so just keep an eye on her. Watch her moves and while I feel like she doesn't have any contact with him you can never be too sure. Also, don't tell her about who did the shooting. Aamil was adamant on that," Drew replied.

Rocky nodded feeling very overwhelmed with the situation. She drank some of her wine and looked at the woman that she considered to be like a big sister to her.

"Drew I love him. I love him so fucking much but I'm scared. I don't know if I can handle any of this. I don't know if I'm ready to leave everything that I build in Seattle. I just don't know," Rocky admitted.

Drew sat up and rubbed her leg endearingly.

"But how will you ever find out if you don't take a chance?" she asked her.

* * *

Its rainy as fuck here. When you coming back?

Rocky glanced up from her phone and her eyes fell on Denim. Denim was asleep in the chair by Bucks bed while holding her stomach. She looked back down at her phone as someone knocked on the room door.

Soon Kesaun. I'll call you later.

Rocky put her phone away and answered the door. The woman that stared back at her was drop dead gorgeous. She had a curvy body and was of average height. She had inky black hair that hung past her shoulders with a pretty smile. She waved at Rocky and the ring on her finger immediately caught Rocky's attention.

It was big as shit.

"You must be Rocky. I'm Salem a friend of Bucks," she said and pulled Rocky into a hug.

Rocky dropped her guard and gave the pretty woman a hug back. They separated, and Rocky stepped to the side so that she could walk in. It was then that Rocky spotted a sexy ass dude standing in the hallway frowning. He wore a black two-piece suit and was so attractive that she momentarily lost her train of thought.

"Salem make this shit quick," he said in a deep tone.

The woman glanced back at him and sighed.

"I will Huss, calm down," she replied, and Rocky's eyes connected with the man's.

He gave her a quick once-over before walking off. Rocky followed the woman into Buck's room and watched her stare at him as he rested in bed. He was due to go home the next day and Rocky was ready for him to leave.

"I'm so happy he's okay," Salem said sincerely.

Rocky could tell that she was itching to hug him. Rocky walked to Salem's side and nodded.

"You and me both. How do you know him?" she asked.

Salem turned to her and licked her lips.

"We ran into each other when we were both going through it. I was beefing with my husband who was my boyfriend at the time and he was well, he was hurt over you. We were there for each other. We tried to make something work but it didn't. It was clear to the both of us that we were both in love with other people. He's so special and the way he spoke of you did something to me. It made me love my man more," Salem replied.

Rocky stood by not sure what to say. Salem glanced over at her and smiled.

"Can you all tell him I stopped by? We like to stay in touch when we can, and I don't want him to think I didn't come through to check on him," she said and laughed.

"Of course," Rocky said and led Salem to the door. Before Salem could open it all the way she turned to Rocky.

"He loves you so much, Rocky. I would love to sit down and talk to you. Please take my number down," Salem said quietly, and Rocky passed her the phone.

Once Rocky locked her number in she gave her another hug and left out of the room. Rocky went back to Bucks bedside and sat in the chair closest to his bed. She stared at him for a few minutes and slowly his eyes opened.

Even with all of the bruises on his handsome face his masculine beauty still shined through. He licked his lips as he stared her way.

"Who was that beautiful?" he asked in a throaty tone.

Rocky grabbed his water and passed it to him. Bucks grabbed her hand and kissed the back of it.

"I'm ready to get the fuck up out of here. A nigga ain't never slept this fucking much," he complained and drunk all of his water.

Rocky smiled taking the cup from him.

"That was Salem."

Bucks nodded while giving her an indifferent look.

"Okay. How you doing?" he asked changing the subject.

Rocky sat her hands on her lap. She wasn't ready to leave just yet, but she needed to go back to Seattle. The days were flying by while her new life was calling her around the clock seeing if she was ready to return to it.

"Bucks...I..." Rocky took a deep breath and closed her eyes.

Bucks sat up as best as he could and grabbed her hand. He wasn't in as much pain as the doctors kept telling him he would be. His biggest issues were that he would find himself short of breath along with small pains in the hand he was shot in.

Bucks eyes seemed to penetrate into Rocky as he gazed her way.

"I love you, Rocky. You know that but if you leave, you don't have to come back ma. I won't hate you, shit I love you too much to ever do that any fucking way but I can't keep doing this shit. I just can't," he said somberly and let her hand go.

Rocky briefly glanced Denim's way and when she saw she was awake Denim cleared her throat. She stood up and glanced around the room before looking at Bucks.

Bucks continued to hold Rocky's hand as he stared back at her.

"Would you ever love me like you do her?" Denim asked becoming emotional.

Bucks exhaled, and Rocky was able to pull her hand from his grasp.

"Denim...beautiful did I ever say I was looking for love from you? The minute we met what did I tell you?" he asked her calmly.

Denim broke his gaze and grabbed her mini Celine bag. She put the crossbody on and grabbed her phone. Tears fell from her eyes as she looked at Rocky.

"Can you please drop me off at home?" she asked.

Bucks frowned her way.

"Nah, Rocky she good. Can you give us a minute?"

Rocky looked from Denim to Bucks.

"Please," Denim begged and headed for the door.

Rocky ignored the glare that Bucks sent her way as she grabbed the truck keys and honored Denim's request.

Rocky took Denim to her apartment as Bibby tailed them. This time she wasn't worried when she saw his Charger and instead felt at ease. Rocky stood in the doorway of the nicely decorated two-bedroom pad as Denim stepped out of her sneakers.

Denim sat on her sofa and grabbed her throw blanket. Softly she cried as Rocky watched her.

Rocky nibbled on her bottom lip as she felt mixed feelings. While she felt bad for Denim she had to admit she still loved Bucks, so she was happy that he still loved her as well. Rocky found herself joining Denim on the sofa. She rubbed her back until Denim calmed down.

"He's right you know? He never sold me a dream, but I always envisioned myself being with him. I guess I was so caught up on what we could be that I didn't take the time to see us for what we were. He's always talked about you, even spoke with you around me. I just can't understand how he can be with other women sexually and still only have love for you? It's like he's locked himself up for you and you don't even want him," Denim vented.

Rocky was offended by her words.

"Why would you say I don't want him?"

Denim sat up. Her pretty face contorted into a frown as she stared at Rocky.

"Because you don't! You have been playing games with him since you left. He's told me about it a million and fucking one times! If you don't want him then let him go. I would love to be with my child's father," Denim said before laying back down on the sofa.

Rocky stared straight ahead as her heart pumped faster in her chest.

"Bucks is the only man that I have ever loved," Rocky said to Denim.

Denim closed her eyes.

"Then love him or leave him alone," Denim replied.

Three

Denim found herself sitting alone in the park. She watched the small children play without a care in the world and her eyes welled up with tears. She wiped a few away as Bibby took a seat beside her.

Bucks had been released a week prior and was still getting his rest. Rocky was back home packing up her apartment with the help of Pia and Denim was hurt. Rocky was choosing to leave Seattle and Denim knew in her heart that any shot she had with Bucks was now gone.

Because she had pride and wouldn't beg anyone to be with her she was trying to give Bucks space. She needed for him to be out of her system.

"You good miss lady?" Bibby asked and passed her some apple juice.

Denim glanced his way and took the small bottle. She smiled at him and nodded.

"As good as I can be. Thank you."

Bibby shook his head. He took off his cap and brushed his hand over his waves before turning his attention back to her. His eyes did a quick scan of the park and he decided to stand so that he could have an even better view.

"It's nothing. I know you grown and shit, but this park is kind of hot ma. Let's find a better place for you," he suggested and grabbed her hand.

Denim allowed for him to help her stand and she stretched her neck to stare up at him. Bibby was much taller than her.

"I don't wanna go home. I'll go to the mall. I need to walk anyway," she replied and walked away.

Bibby followed her and soon was trailing her as they headed for the mall. Denim and Bibby both valet their cars and he walked beside her as she began to purchase items for her daughter.

"How far along are you?"

Denim grabbed a dress off the Nordstrom rack. She looked at Bibby and sighed. She wasn't necessarily in the mood to be cordial, but she appreciated his efforts, so she told herself to not take her anger for Bucks out on him.

"I'm seven months pregnant. I know I look bigger than that," she said with a smile.

Bibby shook his head. He grabbed the extra clothing that she had for her daughter and continued to follow her around the store.

"So, where your people at?" he asked again breaking the silence.

"My family is from down south. We've never been close like that. I fell out with my mom years ago because of this family secret that I would rather not repeat, and she hasn't called me since then. My father is older and retired. I see him every once in a blue moon and I'm an only child. I've always been a loner. What about you?"

Bibby opened his mouth to respond and a tall, thick, scantily clad dressed woman approached him with her friends.

"Bibby, what is this?" she asked angrily.

Bibby stepped in front of Denim and glared at the woman.

"Don't even play yourself out like that in front of your girls. Turn the fuck around ma," he replied, and the woman did as she was told without causing a scene taking her friends along with her. Bibby turned back to Denim and he chuckled. "I like bad bitches, that's my fucking problem," he joked, and Denim laughed.

It was the first time she'd laughed in weeks.

"I thought bad guys like good girls?"

Bibby licked his lips and once again scanned the store with his eyes.

"I'm not a bad guy," he said still looking around the area they were in.

Denim nodded.

"And I'm not a good girl," she said before walking to the other section.

Denim missed the intense look Bibby gave her before he followed after her.

* * *

"You did so good!"

Kesaun nodded but didn't give Rocky back the same energy that she was tossing his way. Rocky stood near the door in his changing room nervously. She watched him change into a black Champion sweat suit before turning his attention her way.

"It's been a minute baby. You said a few days and you stayed in the city for weeks. I'm glad to see you okay," Kesaun said in a clipped tone.

Rocky stepped off the door and walked over to him. He tried to move past her and she hugged his side. Kesaun had been good to her. Shit perfect but he wasn't Bucks. It was as simple as that. Rocky prayed she wasn't making a mistake by choosing Bucks, but she had to follow her heart. Something was telling her that if she didn't then she wouldn't get another chance to be with the man that she still loved with all of her heart.

"I'm so sorry," she apologized getting emotional.

Kesaun took a deep breath and exhaled.

"Why Rocky? That nigga is an old ass hustler. I don't get what the fucking appeal is. He got a pregnant ass woman and you walking away from your life to be with him. This shit is stupid," Kesaun vented.

Rocky closed her eyes. She had no interest in debating with him about who was the better person for her.

"You're a good man. I know you're going to make some woman very happy. Like you did me," she replied and swallowed down her tears.

She might not have been in love with him, but she did care for him.

Kesaun finally hugged Rocky back. He looked down at her with his dark eyes and frowned.

"I wanna be with you though. The first sign of trouble you call me ma. You know I'll drop everything for you," he said making her smile.

Rocky nodded and he kissed her forehead.

After leaving Kesaun Rocky went to her mother's home. She'd packed up her apartment earlier that day with the help of Pia and Drew who'd decided to tag along wanting to see Seattle and of course the Fifty Shades of Grey building that was talked about in the famous book series. They were back at her place waiting on her so that they could hang out before catching an early morning flight. Rocky was slightly sad at the thought of walking away from Seattle. She'd come there at her lowest and made a real home for herself. Now she was heading back into the lion's den and it did frighten her. The fear of the unknown was killing her.

"So, this is it?" Rocky's mom asked answering her door.

Rocky's mom lived in an immaculate home on Mercer Island. Rocky loved everything about the grand place and knew that her mom worked hard to stay there. Rocky's mother's public relations firm was one of the most profitable firms in the states.

"I guess it is. I'll be back though."

Rocky's mother nodded while staring at her sadly. She pulled Rocky into a hug and swallowed down her tears. Rocky's mother had left her when she was younger and chose to make a life somewhere outside of Michigan. Rocky's father wouldn't let Rocky go and her mom didn't put up a fight. Rocky's mother wasn't cut out for the street life. She also didn't want that for her daughter, so she'd been elated when Rocky chose to come to Seattle after losing her baby.

Now Rocky was leaving to go be with Bucks and it hurt her mom. Made her fearful for her daughter's future.

"Kesaun is so sweet. Such a gentleman and he loves you," she said pulling back from Rocky.

Rocky smiled at her mom.

"And I love Bucks. I tried. Even when I wanted to come back after the Christmas trip and you talked me out of it. I tried to be happy here. Something was always missing mom. It was him."

Rocky's mom shook her head. She hated Bucks and she didn't even know him.

"Rocky you have to be with a person that can offer you more than love. Can he give you safety and a peace of mind? I don't think he can then your father tells me that he's also expecting a child with someone else and that worries me. He sounds like a hot damn mess. History has a habit of repeating itself, honey. His lifestyle was too much for you back then and I don't see how much has changed now. He was just shot, he's a hoodlum and yet you're leaving your life behind to be with him. It scares me because we both know bullets have no name. I just want the best for my child," she told her earnestly.

Rocky blinked away her tears and hugged her mom again.

"I know but this is my life. Bucks isn't my daddy and well I'm not you. I walked away from him twice. I can't do it again. I just can't," Rocky said, and her mom cried as she hugged her back.

"Then all I can say is good luck and I'm here if you need me," her mom offered as she hugged her back.

After Rocky returned to her packed up apartment she changed clothes and took Pia and Drew to a local nightclub. The Seattle nightlife was very different from Detroit still the women had fun and even indulged in harmless flirting as they danced their night away.

"Listen you keep dancing with that fine ass white guy and Aamil is gonna feel it in his bones. He gone hop on a plane and be waiting on us outside of the club," Rocky told Drew and laughed.

Drew smiled while shaking her head. It had been so long since she'd gone on a trip without her kids or husband.

She welcomed the two-day vacation and was partying it up. She chugged down her D'usse and smiled at Pia and Rocky.

"Tonight, I'm like ain't no momma, ain't no wife," she said jokingly and they all laughed.

Pia smiled as she stared at Rocky and Drew.

"No, but for real it feels good to get this break. Seattle is nice, but I don't see how you stayed here so long. It's so different from Detroit," Pia expressed and Rocky smiled.

"It is but I wasn't clubbing or no shit like that. I went to work and went home," Rocky replied, and the music changed.

I can do anything, yeah
Hell nah, hell nah, hell nah, hell nah

Blared through the speakers and all three women rushed to the dancefloor. Jay-Z and Beyoncé's song Nice had everyone on the dancefloor as the music filled up the club.

Rocky closed her eyes as she swayed her sexy body to the music. She rapped the lyrics as the liquor gave her a nice escape from the worries that plagued her mind.

"*I'm so nice, I'm everybody type, goddamn right*
I'm so nice, Jesus Christ, I'm better than the hype, I give you life!" Rocky rapped and Drew pulled her into a hug as they all danced close together.

Rocky listened to the lyrics of the song and felt that same way. There were no limits to the things she could do so she was following her heart and going home to her man.

Four

"You didn't have to come."

Bucks sat up in his seat and glanced over at Denim. His dark eyes stared at her intently as he sat beside her. He was back moving around despite the doctor's orders and as long as he didn't overdo it he was good. He was more focused on making sure Denim was good and making Rocky the happiest woman alive.

"Why wouldn't I come?" he asked.

Denim shrugged. Her disdain for him was growing by the second. She knew it was misplaced anger. He'd never sold her a dream still it was easy to hate him. She'd accepted that he wasn't going to ever love her but that didn't mean she had to like it. Denim preferred to not be up under him.

It made it easier for her.

"I just figured you would be somewhere with Rocky. I know she was out looking for jobs today."

Bucks licked his lips as his eyes scanned over the chilly doctor's office. Denim was rocking a black maxi dress with side pockets and wedge heels while he wore black jeans with a collared Polo. He glanced down at his black Buscemi sneakers and sighed. Life had gone from being simple too stressful as fuck for him.

"Denim don't make me out to be the bad guy. You know I care about my child. Don't you?"

Denim swallowed hard. She hated how he effortlessly turned things around on her.

"Just stop it Braylen," she murmured as the doctor walked into the room.

The doctor smiled at Denim and Bucks as she stepped into the room. She sat at the foot of the examining table Denim laid on and lifted her skirt. Denim shifted on the padding as the doctor checked her cervix.

"Denim, wow," The doctor said looking up at her.

Bucks sat up with his eyes on the doctor.

"Is anything wrong?" he asked with a hint of worry in his deep tone.

The doctor shook her head.

"No, she's dilated. Seven centimeters to be exact. You're in active labor," she notified Denim and Bucks.

Denim smiled nervously as Bucks sat back in his seat.

"So, this is it?" he asked looking at Denim.

Denim broke his gaze not wanting to get lost in it.

"Yes, this is it. I'm going to have her admitted and prepped and we'll see how long this princess is going to take to come out. It's time parents and she is early but she's at a great weight. Actually, the size of some full-term infants so she won't need NICU as long as it's a smooth delivery," the doctor replied before sitting back and taking off her gloves.

She discarded them, and Denim pulled her dress down. She sat up and Bucks rose to his feet. He let his mom and people know that it was time before texting Rocky.

Bucks then went over to Denim and rubbed her arm. She'd been frowning at him since he'd told Rocky to stay in Detroit at the hospital. While Bucks didn't wanna be with Denim it was never his intentions to make her hate him. He wanted to have a healthy relationship with the mother of his child.

"I know this isn't ideal. I didn't walk into your life to hurt you. You might not see it like that, but I was trying to get over her. I just couldn't. I love her too much, but I apologize Denim if you feel I did you wrong. We don't have to be together for me to have love for you," he told her.

Denim closed her eyes. She was scared and heartbroken. The last thing she wanted to hear was that the man she wanted had love for her. She turned her head towards the wall and licked her lips. She would never want sympathy affection from anyone.

Bucks made it clear who he wanted and now she was good on him.

"Just be there for our daughter. You don't owe me anything," she replied, and Bucks rubbed her stomach.

He gave her forehead a chaste kiss and it made her heart hurt.

"I'm sorry," he apologized before Denim stood up and exited the office with him.

For two days Rocky hid out at the penthouse not ready to visit the hospital before Bucks picked her up and took her to see his daughter.

Rocky walked beside him nervously as he entered into the nursery section. They were both filled to the brim with emotions. Bucks felt that it was best to show Rocky from the start that she too was a part of his child's life. His daughter that he did get a test on just to be sure.

"Come here," Bucks said and pulled Rocky over to his daughter's crib.

Bucks pulled Rocky to his side and she stared down at the brown-skinned beauty that was a day old. Bucks daughter was gorgeous with her noir like hair that covered her head. She was big for her to be born early and already she had facial features like Bucks.

Rocky's eyes grew wet with tears as she gazed at the sleeping beauty.

"She's beautiful," she said quietly.

Bucks sighed. He kissed Rocky's forehead before letting her go. He washed his hands before grabbing his daughter. She stirred in his arms but remained asleep. Rocky and Bucks sat in the two chairs near her small crib.

"Her name is Braille. She's so damn pretty," Bucks said still looking down at his daughter.

Rocky nodded. She was filled with all kinds of emotions. She felt it was only so many times that she could say the girl was beautiful before it sounded generic.

"Yeah," she mumbled and pulled out her phone.

Bucks glanced up at Rocky and cleared his throat.

"You wanna hold her?"

Rocky shook her head.

"Not now. I'm going to go get some coffee and wait for you in the waiting area," Rocky replied and walked away.

Rocky made a beeline for the closest bathroom and she fell apart with tears the second she was in her stall. She closed her eyes as she held her flat stomach.

"She's just a child. An innocent kid," she told herself quietly.

Rocky exited the stall once she was intact and washed her face with the harsh bathroom hand soap. Rocky dried off and exited the bathroom. Bucks leaned against the wall with his eyes on her.

In his all black clothing with his 508 Bugatti frames covering his eyes, he looked beyond sexy. Nothing like a man that had been shot twice. With so much going on they hadn't had a chance to spend any real time together.

"You good?" he asked stepping off the wall.

Rocky gave him a huge, fake smile.

"I am."

Bucks grabbed her hand and led her out of the hospital. They went to the market to grab some groceries before going back to the penthouse. While Bucks rolled up a blunt Rocky took a quick shower. She then tossed on a silk, long, black nightgown and began to cook.

All week she'd been eating takeout and was eager to have a home-cooked meal.

"You know nothing could ever take away the love I have for you. Right?"

Rocky stopped beating on the steaks to glance back at Bucks. She admired him in his jeans with his bare chest on display. His tattoos like always stood out on his skin while his small yet expensive chain rested against his chest. Bucks hit his blunt once and walked over to Rocky. His hands slid across her round ass in the nightgown as he admired her beauty.

He leaned down and kissed her on the lips.

"I'll die loving you," he promised before kissing her again.

Rocky went back to the food and Bucks leaned against the counter in the kitchen. Everything with Rocky felt right.

He was so relieved to have her back home with him.

"Rocksana, what's good?" he asked not liking her silence.

Rocky shrugged. Whenever he said her full name it made her walls contract.

"I'm tired Braylen," she replied.

Bucks chuckled.

"Ma, my hand better and my chest not hurting. I'm putting that work in on you tonight beautiful," he declared.

Rocky shook her head.

"You should be up there with your daughter. I'm good, plus I need to catch up on some sleep."

Rocky didn't want her words to come out harsh still they had a bit of anger to them that didn't sit well with Bucks.

"Rocky we both know that was unnecessary beautiful. I will go back and check on her but right now it's your time. I'ma always make sure the women that I love is good."

Rocky rolled her eyes. Bucks was being his normal charming fucking self while at the same time making it hard to be mad with him.

"And you have so many women that love you back," she rebutted.

Bucks hit his blunt a few times.

"Did I leave you? Last, I fucking checked you walked up out this bitch like the love we had wasn't shit. I let you go because I knew you needed that break, but your ass didn't wanna fucking come back. What the fuck was I supposed to do!"

Rocky waved him off.

"Come for me," she replied getting emotional. Rocky dropped the meat beater and it clanked against the marble countertop. She turned to the man that owned her heart and swallowed hard. "You were supposed to fucking come for me! Not fuck other bitches, make them fall in love with you and definitely not get them pregnant. What the fuck Bucks! We lost our kid!" she yelled.

Bucks put out his blunt and shook his head.

"You so fucking selfish Rocky. We lost our kid then I lost you. I lost every fucking thing and you wanted a nigga to be lonely. Sitting up begging you and shit. Don't put this one on me. I didn't mean for any of this to happen, but I won't apologize for having my daughter. We could have had two fucking kids by now with as long as your ass been gone!"

Rocky glared at him before looking back at the food. She picked the large T-bone steaks up and tossed them at Bucks. He ducked, and she shook her head.

"Fuck you. I know I left but you could have tried to come and convince me to come back. You made a couple of calls and that was it. I left everything to be here. A good ass job. A man that was falling in love with me."

Bucks nose flared at the things Rocky said to him. He gave no fucks about Kesaun.

"You want me to say thank you? Beautiful don't get this shit twisted. I always ride for you and you know that. But this shit will be mutual, and I won't thank you for doing some shit that you supposed to be fucking doing. You belong here with me. I love you and I'm still hurt we lost our baby, but I won't let that shit control my life, Rocky. You need to stop letting that shit control yours!" he yelled before walking off.

Rocky slid down to the ground and her first thought was to pack her things and leave. She smiled as she realized that she had no home to run to. Plus, she'd been running for a while now. Running had gotten her and Bucks in the predicament they were in.

"God help us," Rocky mumbled as she stared down at the steaks that were across from her on the tiled floor.

Five

"She's so beautiful," Bucks mother said as she held the baby.

Denim was now home from the hospital and for reasons unknown to her Bucks had relocated her into a nicer, bigger condo that was in a gated complex.

Bucks and his family was very hands-on with Denim's daughter and Denim was glad to have them. So far only three of her family members had tried to come to Detroit to see her daughter.

Ann passed baby Braille back to Denim and she sat next to her on the sofa.

"So how are you, sweetie? Braylen told me that you rarely take his calls and he pretty much communicates with you through text messages."

Denim stared down at her daughter wondering how something so beautiful and perfect could exist?

"I don't wanna love him Mrs. Ann so yes I've been distancing myself. It's clear that he will only ever love Rocky. When I first met him, we did talk about Rocky, but she was never the focal point of any conversation between us. He showed real interest in me. If he hadn't I wouldn't have fallen for him. I feel like I've been duped and maybe a little blind to what's going on but that's done with now. I don't hate him I just don't like him right now," Denim said being honest with Ann.

Ann smiled at her.

"I'm happy that you're doing what's best for you. My son has his way with women. If you feel like it's a dead end, then you're doing the right thing. To see how you're handling this makes me proud of you sweetie. It's not easy to walk away from a man you love and just had a child with."

Denim snorted.

"No, it isn't," Denim admitted with a small smile, and Ann laughed lightly.

"You'll get through this sweetie. What doesn't kill us will only make us stronger. Its cliché but very true," Ann told her.

Denim talked with Ann for another hour before walking her to the door. Denim laid down the baby after breastfeeding her and took a long bath. Once she was done she exited her bathroom and screamed out when she found her ex-boyfriend Nico sitting at the edge of her bed.

On his lap was a gun while a big smile sat on his handsome face. He wore all black and even had on gloves.

Denim pulled the plush pink towel tighter to her slim body as she stared at him.

"Damn baby look at you. Don't even look like you just had a bastard ass baby," he commented.

Denim's chest heaved up and down in fear. Nico wasn't a friendly man. In the beginning, he'd been prince charming however with time she was able to see he had a dark side that often controlled him. Nico would verbally and physically abuse Denim without giving it a second thought. Denim's breaking point was losing her baby. She'd snuck out of the hospital and never looked back. She was very clueless as to how he found her.

"Your mom. She'll tell me whatever for some dough. You know she can't stand your ass. Ever since you lied on your uncle," Nico said reading her thoughts.

Denim broke his gaze.

"He did molest me," Denim said quietly not wanting to revisit her horrid childhood.

Nico licked his lips.

"And that's why I took care of him."

Denim's angry eyes flashed Nico's way.

"And she blames me for his death, yet she tells you about my whereabouts? Unbelievable," Denim expressed.

Nico chuckled as he stood up.

"Nah she just not shit. Much like the daughter, she pushed up out of her. How could you walk away from me Denim? After all the shit we've been through then you have this niggas baby. He don't even want your slut ass!" Nico yelled, and his deep voice made Denim take another step back.

"Nico my kid," Denim said trying to reason with him.

Nico's eyes narrowed into slits as he aimed his gun at Denim.

"Fuck that kid. If you didn't have mine you won't be able to live to take care of his," he said and before he could pull the trigger two shots to his chest sent Nico flying back on the bed.

The gunshots had come out fast and sounded low because of the silencer that was on the end of Bibby's weapon. Bibby stepped into the room with two of his men standing behind him. He looked at Denim and glanced back at his crew.

"Go grab the shit from the trunk," he directed them and closed Denim's door.

Denim's body shook as she watched him grab her some clothes from her dresser. Bibby passed the clothes to her and she dropped her towel. Bibby looked away as Denim quickly put on her pajama set. She touched his arm when she was done and when his honey colored eyes looked her way she fell apart.

Denim hugged Bibby as her heart thundered in her chest.

"Thank you," she whispered as tears fell down her face.

Bibby rubbed her back and soon his boys was coming back into her room. Denim let him go and went to check on her daughter as Bibby and his people cleaned up her condo.

"You good?" Bucks asked rushing into the room thirty minutes later.

Rocky stood in the hallway quietly and their union didn't hurt Denim as much as it once had. She was happy with knowing that she'd been given a break. She could have been with a man that secretly vined for another woman, even cheated on her to have that woman but instead, he'd been honest and spared her feelings. Although she'd still been hurt Denim was glad that it hadn't been prolonged.

She knew that would have made it hurt worse in the end.

"I'm good," she replied, and her eyes fell on Bibby. He stepped into the room shirtless and wearing black gloves.

Denim noticed things about him that she had never seen before. He was very attractive in a masculine way. His eyes were insanely pretty, and his lips were so full you couldn't help but imagine kissing them. Bibby was also well toned with his muscles and abs on point. Even the few tattoos he had on his chest looked appealing on him. He was a looker for sure.

She rose from the chair with her daughter in her arms and went over to Bibby. Denim hugged him again and he stood still as a board as she hugged his body.

"Thanks again," Denim told him, and Bibby stepped back.

He avoided eye contact with her as he replied.

"It's nothing ma," he said and walked over to Bucks.

Denim watched Bucks and Bibby speak in hushed tones before Bucks came back over to her.

"You gone have to stay with me while I set you up in another spot," he said and grabbed the baby.

Denim's face fell into a frown and she didn't miss the angry look that Rocky also sent Bucks way. Denim walked out of her baby's room and found Bibby in her bedroom. Her ex-boyfriend was gone, and her floor carpet was being pulled up by two men that she'd never seen before. Instead of watching the men tamper with evidence she walked up to Bibby. He stopped searching through his phone to glance up at her.

"You good miss lady?" he asked before licking his lips.

Denim smiled weakly at him.

"If I could come stay with you until my place was done I would be. I'm a neat person and I don't mind cleaning and things of that nature. I could even say I'm staying with you and get a hotel room. Anything but going to his place," Denim said stumbling over her words.

Bibby's demeanor quickly changed. Looking after Denim was one thing but letting her live with him was something very different.

"Ma, that's not my place to say yes to that. Bucks is my guy. I told you that and if this is some get back shit then you barking up the wrong fucking tree. I don't play them kind of games," he replied.

Denim's shoulders fell. She was too tired and still in shock from everything that had just transpired to put up a fight.

"Forget I said anything," she said and walked away.

Denim packed her things along with her daughters as Bibby discreetly watched her.

* * *

Rocky sat at the bar angrily. She had a new job to prepare for but instead of doing that she was out drinking.

Her eyes looked up at the scantily clad women on the stage and memories flashed through her mind at all of the times that she'd danced on a pole.

Rocky had once taught women to pole dance along with Pia. They'd thoroughly enjoyed teaching women to dance and Rocky did miss the sport.

"What you doing in here Rocky?" Hayward asked taking a seat beside her in the booth.

Hayward ran in the same circle as Bucks and was insanely handsome. He also owned the strip club that Rocky was sitting in.

Rocky smiled at him as she grabbed her drink.

"Nothing but I'm sure that fun is about to be ruined. You called up your boy, right?" she asked.

Hayward chuckled. His green eyes scanned the club before falling back to her.

"Something like that. Just to let him know what's up and shit. You good?"

Rocky nodded not wanting to see Bucks.

"As good as I'ma be Hayward," she mumbled.

Rocky's despondent mood had Hayward leaning over to rub her shoulders. He then got up from the booth and Rocky was given a bottle of champagne on the house of course.

Rocky smoothly tossed back drink after drink.

As her eyes slightly closed and the liquor moved through her giving her the relief she needed from the stress in her life Bucks sat beside her.

Smelling like a loud ass marijuana strain he grabbed her bottle and took it to his lips. Bucks drunk down the rest of the champagne and sat back. His eyes bored into her as he stared her way.

"Why are you here?" Rocky asked him with a slight slur.

Bucks hated how fucked up she'd gotten.

"You don't need to be out here doing reckless shit like this ma. You know better," he said calmly.

Rocky smiled. Her actions were exaggerated because she was buzzing.

" *You know better,*" she mimicked him before grabbing the champagne. Rocky tried to turn it up and her eyes narrowed when she realized he'd drunk the rest.

"Damn you just gone drink my shit?"

Bucks smirked at her. She was really pissing him off. He waved over a waitress and ordered another bottle. Rocky relaxed once she realized more liquor was on the way. Her eyes went back over to Bucks as her phone vibrated on the table.

"Your phone beautiful," Bucks told her.

Rocky picked it up and they both saw that it was Kesaun calling her. Rocky immediately declined his call. Bucks jaw tensed as he stared her down.

"Why the fuck is he still calling?"

Rocky shrugged as the waitress sat down the bottle of champagne along with two glasses. The waitress poured them both a glass and smiled at them before walking away.

Rocky grabbed her glass and smiled at Bucks. It was silly, downright grade school shit but she marveled at making him jealous for the small moment. Without trying his actions had made her jealous numerous times.

"Maybe he wants that old thang back. I mean you did," she replied sweetly with a shrug and sipped on her champagne.

Bucks had to chuckle to keep from fucking Rocky up. He decided to roll up again and Hayward joined them along with his cousin. Rocky downed her champagne and water that Bucks forced her to drink. She then ate some delicious shrimp alfredo while Bucks kicked it with his people.

"I love this song!" Rocky announced as they began to play Cardi B's *She Bad*.

Rocky tried to stand up and dance and Bucks shot her a look that let her know she was pushing it. She smiled as she sat back down. Bucks friends then left the table and he pulled Rocky close to his side.

Rocky gazed up at him lovingly as he caressed her face.

"You been here for weeks and I haven't felt you," Bucks told her.

Rocky nodded. She gave him a lazy grin.

"And with the shit, you been doing you won't be touching me anytime soon," she said with a smile.

Bucks smirked down at her.

"Whatever you say, baby, come here," he said and pulled her face close to his.

Rocky closed her eyes as they shared a passionate kiss. She tried to stick her tongue into Bucks' mouth and he pulled back.

"Drink some more water Rocksana," he said and pulled out some money.

Rocky rolled her eyes.

"Now I can't tongue kiss you?" she asked and grabbed the champagne instead of the water.

Bucks placed two hundred dollar bills on the table and smirked at her.

"It's clear that you do whatever the fuck you like beautiful. Let's go I need to show you something," he said and stood up.

Rocky sipped some water and finished off the champagne. She stood with him and tugged at her jeans that fit her body snuggly.

Bucks gave her a quick once over and licked his lips. She was thick in all of the right places and he couldn't wait to feel her again. He slapped her ass before grabbing her hand.

Together they exited the club and went to his truck. Rocky thought nothing of her car that had recently been shipped to Detroit as they rode out of the lot.

Bucks kept a sly smirk on his face as he took Rocky to his cousin's business.

Rocky looked at the sign as he parked, and she giggled.

"I know exactly what I want! How did you know I wanted one?" she asked quickly taking off her seatbelt.

"I always know what you want and need baby," Bucks told her exiting his truck.

Rocky pursed her lips as she stared at the newly re-decorated building.

"You used to," she mumbled still talking shit.

Bucks chuckled as he advanced on her. He pulled Rocky to his side and smiled down at her.

"I see you on one tonight. Let's go in here ma," he said and pulled her into the building.

"Look what the fucking cat drug in!" Bucks cousin Remy said as he walked towards her with a highly intoxicated Rocky.

Rocky cheesed at the beautiful dread headed girl with a silly grin on her face as she hugged Bucks side tightly.

"I want a butterfly on my ass," Rocky said, and Bucks smirked at his cousin.

"Aye, Rocky go grab some more water beautiful while I talk with my people," he said looking down at her.

Rocky waved him off and instead went to the other side of the room to look through some photo albums that were on a table.

Fifteen minutes later Rocky sat on Bucks lap in her underwear. The left side of her ass was exposed as his cousin Remy tattooed her.

Rocky couldn't stop staring up into Bucks' eyes as the tattoo gun pressed against her fat butt cheek.

"It kind of hurts baby," she whined.

Bucks licked his lips. He kissed her nose before swiping his tongue gently across her lips.

Rocky pulled his tongue into her mouth and sensually sucked on it.

"I'm so horny...I wanna suck the skin off your dick," Rocky said feeling *good* off the champagne in her system.

Bucks member rocked up immediately at her nasty words.

"Shit I want you to do that too," Bucks said quietly.

Bucks female cousin Remy laughed as she wiped off Rocky's new tattoo.

"Let me get y'all horny asses up out of here," she said while shaking her head.

Bucks ignored her as he kissed Rocky on her lips once more. He paid his cousin and Rocky put her jeans on once her butt was taped up.

"I can't wait to see it!" she said excitedly as they exited the tattoo parlor.

"Get me, right baby," Bucks said as he pulled his G-Wagon out into the traffic on Livernois Road.

Rocky glanced over at him and knew she couldn't say no. She was too horny, and he was too attractive.

She unbuckled her seatbelt and leaned towards him. Bucks grabbed her chin and made her look up at him.

"Who you love with all of your heart?" he asked in a husky tone.

Rocky swallowed hard.

"You," she whispered.

Bucks nodded.

"And who loves you back with all of his fucking heart?"

Rocky smiled at him.

"You do."

Bucks caressed her chin.

"Stop acting like you forgot that shit," he said and let her chin go.

Rocky grabbed his Ferragamo belt and un-looped it. She unbuckled his denim jeans and went into his black boxers. Her hands quickly found his thick erection and she pulled it out.

Rocky licked her lips as she eyed his veiny member. It wasn't discolored or shaped funny. No, it was perfect in size and shape and it smelled divine.

Even his penis smelled so fucking good.

Rocky licked her lips as she lowered her head. She sucked the small pre-cum that was leaking from it before putting as much of him into her mouth as she could.

Bucks groaned in pleasure as she began to work her mouth on him.

"Damn," he said quietly as he drove a little faster to their home.

Rocky closed her eyes and thought of nothing but pleasuring him. She allowed for his grunts and groans to guide her and within minutes he was sputtering out semen and spilling it down her throat.

"Fuck," Bucks cursed having to pull off at a nearby lot not wanting to crash.

Once he was good he drove away, and they went to the penthouse. The minute they stepped through the doors Bucks attacked Rocky. He pushed her against the wall as he sucked and licked on her neck.

Rocky moaned as she lowered her jeans taking her underwear down with them. Bucks then picked her up and took her into the kitchen. He laid Rocky out onto their black marble island and she kept her legs open as he walked over to the fridge. Bucks grabbed the strawberry sauce that Rocky used for her pancakes and took it back over to Rocky. He stared down at her with lust blazing in his eyes as he licked his lips.

"Take the rest of this shit off," he said opening the jar.

Rocky quickly took off her top and her bra and stared up at him. She was so hot and bothered that her wetness was seeping from her opening.

"Bucks," she said in a whisper and he shook his head.

"You been showing your ass lately but I'ma get you together. Did you really miss me Rocksana?"

Rocky nodded eagerly. Her chest heaved up and down as Bucks rubbed strawberry sauce on her clitoris.

"I did, and this is where I belong," she whispered to him.

Bucks leaned down and with the tip of his tongue slowly licked her clitoris. Rocky moaned as her thighs shook. Her feet were planted firmly on the island and his head was between her legs.

"You leaving me again Rocksana?" he asked pulling back to look at her.

Rocky shook her head.

"I couldn't even if I tried to," she replied and could see him visibly relax.

"And I wouldn't let you," Bucks told her before lowering his head again.

Rocky cried out as he attacked her clitoris with no remorse. He sucked the sauce off before taking his tongue down to her opening. Bucks held her lower lips apart as his tongue went in and out of Rocky. All the while he rubbed her clit with his thumb.

Rocky's thighs began to shake, and he replaced his tongue with his fingers. Bucks slid up Rocky's body and sucked on her nipples until she fell apart for him. He then pulled out his dick that was back hard and thrust into her.

Rocky's eyes closed as her mouth fell open.

"Oh....my.... God...yes baby. Yes," she said taking everything he had to give her.

Bucks grabbed onto Rocky's shoulders and rammed his member in and out of her as he sucked on her bottom lip.

"Oh my god! I'ma cum again," Rocky announced and soon her juices were wetting him up even more.

Bucks groaned and sped up his pace. He slid himself in and out of Rocky until he was letting off deep into her walls.

* * *

"I was really caught off guard by the accident and need a few days to recover. I am so thankful that you all understand," Rocky said with her eyes closed.

"No, we're just glad that you weren't severely injured in the accident Rocksana. How about you take five days off and we'll see you then?" her new manager suggested.

Rocky sighed with relief as her stomach rumbled and not in the *I'm hungry* kind of way.

Rocky slowly sat up.

"That would be perfect. Thank you again," she replied before ending the call.

Rocky slowly got out of her large bed and trudged to her bathroom. She looked at herself in the mirror and shook her head.

Hickies adorned her neck in a way that made it seem as if she'd been attacked by mosquitoes. Rocky ran her hand through her matted-up hair and sighed.

"I look a hot fucking mess," she said and smiled at herself.

She went to the toilet and sat down. She was naked and had woken up with her alarm. Rocky exhaled as she began to relieve her bladder. Soon came liquids from her rear end then soon after she was wiping herself. Rocky flushed the toilet and washed her hands before turning on her shower. Her ass kept stinging, so she rubbed at her cheek. She frowned when she noticed it was a band-aid over her ass.

"What the fuck was I doing?" she asked herself having no real recollection of her previous day outside of Bucks fucking her silly.

Rocky pulled off the band-aid and rubbed over her stinging ass. When she felt the raised skin, she frowned deeper. Rocky went back to her mirror and turned with her ass facing it. She glanced back to look at her butt and her knees buckled.

In clean, crisp calligraphy was **BUCKS** tattooed on her ass cheek. Rocky's jaw fell slack as she stared at the freshly done artwork.

"Bucks!" she yelled letting her ass go.

Rocky rushed out of the bathroom and tossed on the first pair of clothes that she came across. She put on a pink baseball cap and searched for the keys to her car.

Her hands shook as she called up Bucks.

"What's up beautiful?" he answered then chuckled.

Rocky could tell from the loud commotion in the back that he was at Aamil's barbershop.

"...Hey, I was looking for my car keys," she said as calmly as she could.

Bucks chuckled again, and it had Rocky seeing red.

"Ma, I got it. I had to go pick it up this morning. That nigga Aamil swooped me up from the house. You okay? Did you call your job?" he asked.

Rocky sighed. She ended the call on Bucks and grabbed the keys to his G-Wagon.

Rocky quickly exited the building and drove to Aamil's main barbershop location. She parked in front of the door and hopped out of Bucks truck.

Laughter and the smell of soul food greeted Rocky as she stepped into the barbershop. Aamil was the first one to spot her as she searched the room for Bucks.

"What's good Rocky?" he asked sitting up in his seat.

Aamil was a lot like Cedric The Entertainer from the movie *Barbershop*. He never cut hair but had his own station for him to sit at, so he could be in the mix of things.

Rocky ignored Aamil and her eyes fell on her ignorant ass man. Her extremely handsome ignorant ass man.

Bucks sat in his barber's chair with a big grin on his face. He wore all black and was giving her a knowing grin.

Rocky smiled back at him and headed his way. Bucks held out his arms for a hug and Rocky greeted him with a slap to his face.

The chatter in the vast room immediately went quiet as everyone watched the scene unfold.

"What the fuck was that for!" Bucks asked not used to anyone putting their hands on him.

Rocky turned around and pulled down the jogging pants that she wore.

Even with her wearing thongs, a big part of her bottom was exposed for everyone to see.

"Look what you did to my ass, I can't fucking believe you!" she yelled, and Bucks jumped up from his seat.

His jaw tensed as he yanked up her jogging pants and led her to the backroom. He leaned against the door as Rocky stared him down angrily.

"What do you have to say about this Braylen?"

Bucks shrugged while glaring her way. He was still angry with the way she'd walked in and slapped the shit out of him.

"Nothing. You wanted a tattoo, so I took you to get one. We need to discuss you putting your fucking hands on me then showing my shit off to the whole fucking barbershop. Let's talk about that bullshit you just pulled," he replied.

Rocky was not happy with his response and his anger towards her wasn't making the situation any better.

"Fuck that slap. Why did you do this Bucks? I can't have your name tattooed on my ass!"

Bucks looked down at Rocky and smirked at her.

"Why not?" he asked holding back a grin.

Bucks attitude had Rocky ready to slap the shit out of him again. She closed her eyes and counted down from ten. When she opened them, she saw Bucks was cheesing while looking her way.

"Get the fuck away from me," she told him aggressively and because she was so riled up he stepped to the side so that she could exit.

Rocky walked away from Bucks and the men waited for her to exit the doors before they all roared with laughter.

Six

"When do you plan on going back to work?"

Denim looked up from her phone and smiled. Instead of going to Bucks penthouse she'd gotten a hotel and was finally in a new place. It had taken him only a week to set her up in a new pad. This condo was even nicer than the last one and Denim loved it.

"I have a lot of vacation time saved up and I still have time off because of the birth so at least another month," she replied.

Drew nodded as she held baby Braille. They were always just cordial, but Drew was trying to put in a real effort to get to know Denim because the baby was, in fact, Bucks daughter. Also, Bucks was with Rocky, so she saw no reason to be salty towards Denim.

"Well since you didn't have a shower I would love to throw you one. It would be at my place in the backyard and the family will show up and show out for you guys," Drew told her.

Denim smiled touched by her suggestion.

"I would love that, but I don't necessarily have to have one. Did Braylen put you up to this?" Denim asked.

Drew frowned as she shook her head.

"No, he didn't. I will admit things between you and me was never super friendly, but things are different now. Braille is a part of this family and I want you to feel welcomed as well. Denim, you can ask anybody about me and they'll let you know just who I am. I don't do fake and phony, so I kept it real in the beginning because I didn't like that Bucks was bringing other women around. Aamil told me to calm down so I did find ways to be cordial but the type of person I am kept me from grinning all in your face you know? However, things are different now and I don't want you to feel excluded. A baby changes everything, right?"

Denim sighed. She didn't like how Drew had played things between them but she kind of understood where she was coming from. Denim also didn't have time to hold grudges, so she accepted her reasons behind it.

The reality was she didn't plan on being Drew's new best friend, so it really didn't matter to her.

"Right."

Drew smiled and glanced down at the gorgeous baby. Braille was like a doll baby to her.

"Are you okay concerning the shooting?" Drew asked breaking the silence.

Denim pulled her knees up on the sofa and licked her lips.

"The crazy thing is I'm okay. I feel like I've been through so many bad things in my life that something like that wasn't shit. I guess if I can get past my uncle molesting me something like that is a walk in the park," she replied and shook her head.

Drew was caught off guard by her words. Drew rocked the baby for a few minutes before speaking.

"Well, I guess we do have something in common. I was molested as well and like you said after a while you become numb to the pain. If you ever need anyone to talk to I'm here. I was concerned about you because you saw the shooting then went to a hotel by yourself. I just knew you would have been at Bucks place or flying home to be with your family."

Denim shrugged.

"I'm used to being alone. My family has never really been there for me and Bucks has Rocky. I know he would have gladly taken us in, but I don't wanna be in the middle of that. It took a lot of strength for me to even stop calling him. I know you all see him, and you immediately think of Rocky, but I had built something with him as well. Granted he never sold me the dream. He also didn't make me feel unwanted," Denim stopped talking and smiled at how things once were between her and Bucks.

"He had a way of making me feel so beautiful, so lucky to have someone as caring as him around. I fell for him without even knowing it. The baby was a shock to both of us but definitely my greatest blessing. I don't have to have him in my life, but I can't go a day without her. All I need is for him to be a father to her and I'll be good," Denim replied confidently.

Drew nodded very impressed with her reply.

"I can tell you will be," Drew said smiling, and someone knocked on Denim's door.

Denim stood up and checked the peephole. When she spotted Bibby's handsome face her stomach knotted up.

"Is everything good!" Drew called out.

Denim licked her lips.

"Yes!"

Denim made sure her hair was smoothed down before opening the door. Bibby glanced up and down the hall before looking at her. Wearing navy jeans that were tattered at the knees with a black crew neck on that said *Making Moves* in the center of it, he looked sexy as ever. Bibby seemed to scope out the scene before finally turning his gaze her way.

He licked his full lips as he looked down at her.

"For the baby," he said and cleared his throat. "I wanted to get her some shit," Bibby told her.

Denim took the bag and smiled. She stepped to the side and his hand grazed her hip as he stepped by her to walk in.

From just his small touch Denim felt her body come alive for him. Denim smiled to herself before closing the door. She then led Bibby to her family room and Drew smiled as surprise flashed across her face. She had laid the baby down and was gathering up her things to go. Drew gave Bibby a quick hug before he took a seat on Denim's leather sofa.

"*Bibby* it's always a treat seeing you," Drew said smiling at him.

Bibby dropped his head and smiled bashfully. All of the women knew he was attractive and the attention sometimes made him uneasy. He was a street dude. He didn't give a damn about looking good.

"Mrs. Matin," Bibby said looking back up at her.

Drew smiled and headed for the door with Denim trailing behind her.

"He's a lil sexy ass dude. I remember when I first met Bucks we would all crush on him," Drew smiled and they both snickered. Drew looked at Denim. "He was like Bibby in so many ways. They both have that commanding presence to them. I'm not saying you looking for Bucks in him I'm just saying that I can see how they both would attract your attention. Have a good night and I'll call you with the details about the shower," Drew said before leaving out of the door.

Denim made sure to lock up and set her alarm before going to her hallway bathroom. Denim's heart pumped a little faster as she stared at herself in the mirror. She'd pretty much lost her baby weight. Denim had always been slim with subtle curves. Nothing like Rocky or the woman that had approached her and Bibby at the mall. Denim had a high metabolism, so it was hard for her to hold on to weight still she had a small thumper with c-cup breast. It was also Denim's beautiful face that always brought attention her way. She'd always heard that she had a face for modeling. She had the perfect bone structure with the straight nose, heart-shaped lips and thick brows.

Denim did a breath check and smiled at how silly she was being.

"Relax, girl damn," she scolded herself before leaving out of the bathroom.

Denim found Bibby watching the sports channel on her TV. He looked at her when she took a seat beside him and he cleared his throat.

"I swear I'm not on no stalker shit. I just wanted you to know if things would have been different you could have come to my spot. That wouldn't have been a good look though. Bucks is like my damn father in some ways and you just had this niggas baby. That shit makes me very uncomfortable and we don't know each other on that level," Bibby explained to her.

Denim pulled her knees up to her chest and tried to keep a smile on her face.

"And you found out where I lived and came over just to say that to me?"

Bibby picked up on her attitude and sat back. He bit down hard on his bottom lip as he gazed her way. His eyes peered at her so intently that Denim chose to stare at the wall facing her instead of him.

"You're beautiful as hell. The minute he showed me who you were I was like damn, she bad as hell. Not even bad in that superficial kind of way. You have that natural beauty to you that's rare as fuck now. I was thinking about you so hard that the shit made me mad. I knew I couldn't have you. So, when he asked for me to follow you and his woman I really got pissed. I was forced to see you every day and not even talk to you. I'm a loyal person ma. I don't do grimy shit. Even me being here makes me feel like I'm out of pocket."

Denim took a deep breath and exhaled.

"He's with someone else."

Bibby nodded.

"Still it's the respect you know? You can't call a nigga your people then go after the woman that had his kid," he replied.

Denim looked over at him.

"Then you should leave," she told him.

Bibby smirked at her. He grabbed her hand and placed a kiss on the back of it. Denim ignored the way her body felt as he held her hand.

"Have a good night," he said lowly before standing up.

Denim stood with Bibby and took him to her door. She avoided eye contact with him as he exited her condo. Denim closed the door as her heart raced. For a brief moment, she felt sad until her daughter began to cry. Denim smiled as she was brought back to reality.

"The only thing that matters is you," Denim said thinking of her daughter as she headed for her bedroom.

Seven

"Damn, that is big as hell," Pia said and laughed.

Rocky rolled her eyes as she pulled her leggings up.

"Keep laughing and I'ma help Ahmad get your ass drunk so we can have matching tattoo's," Rocky replied.

Ahmad chuckled as he made himself a plate of the food Pia had just cooked for all of them.

"Yeah sis I'm feeling some kind of way cause she don't have my shit tatted on that ass," he joked.

Pia rolled her eyes. She looked over at her husband and pursed her lips.

"Nigga do I look like Rocky?" she asked him.

Pia and Ahmad cracked up laughing and Rocky glared at the both of them.

"Y'all get on my fucking nerves. Ramsey and Parker are the only two people in this house that I like but I'm serious Pia what he did wasn't right," Rocky complained.

Pia looked at her friend and smiled.

"I can admit what he did was slick as hell but hiding out from him isn't the answer either."

Rocky rolled her eyes.

"It isn't?" she asked quietly.

Pia shook her head. Pia glanced over at Ahmad and was hit with their shaky past. They'd gone through a multitude of things to be together, but they had come out on the other end. Pia knew that Rocky and Bucks could as well as long as they worked together.

"A relationship, be it a marriage or just something you all place a title on is hard work Rocky. All of this running is a waste of time. Didn't I tell you that at the hospital? I know it's a lot," Pia said and found herself getting choked up. "When I came home to Ahmad and Ramsey I was cut deep. I was so fucking hurt Rocky," Pia expressed, and Ahmad swallowed hard himself.

They'd been happy for a while now, so it was hard for him to hear his wife speak on the things he'd done to her.

"And I'm sorry," Ahmad said still cradling his plate of food.

Pia nodded. She knew that now.

"Rocky love won't always be easy. You have to decide who's worth loving. I knew in my heart that no man would love me like him. I knew that he could be better, shit that we could be better. We just had to apply ourselves. I didn't give up on him that time around. I made the decision to love all of him and once we got on the same page miraculous things started to happen. Yes, he took that jail time and it was hard but love wise, family wise we are at our best. He still works my fucking nerves but its everyday problems. Don't you want that with Bucks?" Pia asked her.

Rocky took a deep breath and exhaled.

"I do. I love him, I was just hurt by his actions. We already have so much shit going on and him doing that was like a slap to the face. He's too grown to be acting like that."

"And you two grown to be running every time we have a problem. We gotta get past that juvenile shit beautiful," Bucks said walking into the dining room with a bouquet of red roses.

Rocky's eyes narrowed as she looked at Ahmad and Pia.

"I see you two are snitches as well," she murmured.

Ahmad shrugged.

"Pia got's some shit she needs to handle tonight. I'm not bout to let your angry ass fuck that up for me," he replied and dapped up Bucks before leaving out of the room.

Pia smiled apologetically at Rocky before following after her husband.

Bucks handed the roses to Rocky and she smiled as she took them. He sat across from her and Rocky was able to admire his good looks in his designer threads. Cartier wood framed glasses covered his eyes as a Detroit Mitchell and Ness cap sat on his head.

Bucks stared at Rocky for a minute before finally speaking.

"I could have handled that tattoo situation better. It's like since you came back we haven't been on the same page. I want you to know that I appreciate you and I love you, Rocky. I know watching me have a baby had to be hard as fuck, but I thought I was making it clear where my heart was. I'm not here to fight over how we got here. I'm here to say all of this end today," Bucks told Rocky.

He stood up and glanced down at her before walking off. Rocky wasn't sure how to feel anything other than worry as Bucks exited the room.

When he entered minutes later with her family in tow along with his family she couldn't stop grinning. Rocky even spotted her mom who she knew didn't care too much for Bucks but had come out of loyalty to her.

"Hey baby girl," her father said looking her way.

Rocky's eyes watered and slowly tears fell down her cheeks. She waved at her dad before Bucks walked up on her. Bucks dropped down to one knee and pulled out a red velvet ring box. He cleared his throat before speaking.

"Hey beautiful," he said in a gentle husky tone. Rocky smiled at him and he leaned up to tenderly kiss her lips. "I love you. I can admit I was fighting it at first. I never wanted or felt I needed to have a main woman in my life. Especially not somebody younger than me but you came in and changed me forever. When we're long and gone from here all we'll leave behind is our legacy. The way we affected people and how they felt about us. Me..." Bucks stopped talking and took a deep breath.

Aamil was there to pat his back. Everyone from Bucks side of the family was over elated to see the moment finally happen.

"Me, I have to have you in mine. I see a life for us, I see kids and I see happiness. Only you can give me that kind of joy that I need. Rocksana will you marry me?"

"Aww Rocky," her mom whispered becoming emotional.

Rocky ignored the happy whispers from everyone around her and stared at Bucks. Slowly she nodded her head and he opened the ring box. He chuckled as he lifted the lid.

"I was so nervous I forgot to open this shit," he said with a nervous energy moving through him.

Rocky's jaw hit the floor as she stared down at the beautiful diamond.

"I helped him pick it out," Pia said proudly with her own tears falling from her eyes.

Rocky grinned as Bucks slid the ten carat Bulgari solitaire diamond ring onto Rocky's finger. The diamond was huge, but it wasn't in a gaudy way. It was stunning and very much so Rocky's style.

"I love it, come here," Rocky whispered and kissed Bucks on the lips.

Everyone in the room began to clap, cry and whistle. The loudest cry, however, came from Ramsey who was Ahmad's son. He maneuvered through the crowd and his wet hazel eyes glanced up at Rocky.

"Here's all my money. Be with me," he said crying.

Rocky smiled as she took the $2 from Ramsey. Bucks chuckled as he looked down at him.

"You just like your pops man, just like your pops," he joked, and everyone started laughing again as Rocky pulled Ramsey into a hug.

She covered his face with kisses making him laugh.

"You'll always be my first love," she promised him as her eyes once again connected with Bucks. Rocky blew him a kiss and he grinned back at her.

* * *

"Thanks for meeting up with me. How is he doing?"

Rocky smiled at the pretty woman that sat across from her.

"Bucks is Bucks. He did get some rest, but he was up and moving around way too soon. He's good though. His daughter was born early, and this happened," Rocky replied and flashed her ring.

Salem squealed at Rocky's reply. She grabbed her hand and admired the stunning diamond.

"Wow! Congratulations!" Salem told her excitedly.

There wasn't any fakeness to it and Rocky could tell she was genuinely happy for her.

"Thank you! We were really going through it when I first got back. It was a huge disconnect. Then his daughter was born, and I was hurt. I, of course, could never hate a kid but I'm not going to sugarcoat things. I was very upset that it wasn't me giving him a child. I've even backed off from Denim because of it. She still calls and texts me and I just don't know what to say. Bucks is great with his daughter and we're back good now, but I can tell that he's even watching my every move. I know he loves me but if he feels like I can't accept his kid then we won't be walking down that aisle. I recently started back going to my family's church and the pastor is helping me a lot. Especially with forgiveness and acceptance. Accepting things, I can't change," Rocky replied.

Salem went into her bag and pulled out her small photo album. She'd gotten it as a gift from her husband.

"They call this a brag album, so I put all of the things I hold dear to my heart in it. The first photo is of my daughter. She died in a car accident that we were in. I..." Salem stopped talking and her eyes watered. Rocky's hand began to shake as she held the photo album.

"She's so beautiful," Rocky told Salem.

Salem smiled weakly at her.

"Thank you. I was placed in prison right after she passed away because they felt I was at fault for the accident.

Sometime later the truth came out. The photographer I modeled for had given me a sleeping pill in hopes of raping me but none of that mattered. I knew my truth and I still didn't have my child. Rocky my own family was against me. All I had was my cousin in my corner then Huss. Even Bucks for a moment. Like I said he and I related to pain. We were both in mourning. He spoke of the baby you two lost and he was hurt, Rocky. That's not something that you forget. However, people deal with pain differently. Don't think that because he isn't as vocal as you are that he's not thinking of the what could be. Bucks is also mature enough to separate the two. His daughter isn't a replacement if that's what you're thinking. I have a child by my husband and I still love and think of my angel every single day. I also have another daughter through Huss. She's on the third page. She's my baby for real," Salem said and smiled.

Rocky smiled at the beautiful photo of the pretty girl.

"And how do you get along with her mom?"

Salem laughed.

"I fucking love her. She's on the fifth page with her little family. I'm actually the godmother to her newest baby," Salem revealed making Rocky frown.

"I'm shocked," Rocky admitted.

Salem smiled.

"I know. I tell people that and they look at me just how you are right now. Toy is special. Even when Huss and I broke up she was on his head like you gotta go get our girl back. They understood that being together wasn't going to work for them and they remained friends. They have a nice blended family and now collectively we all do. We spend holidays together and everything. Toy is like a second mom to my own son. We genuinely love each other and I'm never ashamed of that. When adults get along the kids always reap the benefits of that. I feel lucky to have been blessed with a situation like that. I can't speak on Denim, but I can say that it's nothing wrong with liking her Rocky. The better you all get along the more blessed and happy the baby will be. Give it a try, I mean who knows she could be the friend you've been looking for," Salem told her.

Rocky sighed as she handed the photo album back to Salem.

"Because I've suddenly been so cold to her I don't want it to come off as me being fake."

Salem nodded.

"Just tell her how you feel. Tell her how this isn't easy for you. Communication is key and if it doesn't work out then at least you know you tried. Don't you love him enough to give this a real go at it?" Salem asked her.

Rocky nodded without having to think about it.

"I do," she replied, and Salem put her photo album away.

"Then be that beautiful, strong woman that he fucking loves the shit out of and fix the family. You know nothing is done right until a woman handles it," Salem said and they both laughed.

After leaving lunch with Salem, Rocky felt compelled to go visit Denim. She even stopped and grabbed the baby some things.

Rocky went up to Denim's condo and knocked on the door nervously.

"Hey!" Denim said answering the door and holding the baby.

Rocky smiled at her and held out the bag. She passed it to Denim and smiled at her before walking in. Cardi B's new album was playing on low volume and Rocky found herself humming along to the song as she stepped out of her heels. She took off her Off White crossbody and sat it on the end table as they walked into Denim's living room.

"I'm happy you came by. I've been calling you to say congratulations and you didn't pick up," Denim said sitting down with the baby.

Rocky smiled as she chose to sit beside Denim. Rocky admired the beautiful baby as Denim looked through the bag.

"Thank you so much. That's why I came by. I felt like it was time for me to clear the air. I know when we first met we were cool then I kind of fell back once he was released from the hospital. I was just dealing with a lot Denim and I didn't know how to handle everything," Rocky admitted to her. Rocky played with the baby's small foot and smiled. "It hurt to know that he was having women and all of these things without me. I had to realize that my leaving did play a part in that. I needed to accept it, but it was never like oh fuck Denim. You've never done anything to me but be nice. I wasn't even there for you when Bibby had to shoot your crazy ass ex. I've really been cold, so I will apologize for that. I want us all to be a family because that's what we should be."

Denim stopped sifting through the clothes in the bag to look at Rocky.

"I know you're hurting. Hell, imagine how I feel. I had to accept that the man I'm having a child with doesn't want a future with me. That was a huge freaking pill to swallow but I never took it out on you. I had no one to be mad at but myself and him. More so me though. I thank you for coming by. I do feel like we could be friends, I just didn't want you to be weirded out by it. The reality is you're marrying her father. I really do want us to get along Rocky," Denim said to her.

Rocky stared into Denim's eyes and could feel the sincerity in her words.

"Me too," Rocky whispered.

Rocky stood up to wash her hands before sitting back down. She grabbed the baby from Denim and the baby smiled at her. Rocky cooed at Braille as a peaceful filling washed over her.

Since she'd come back to Detroit and learned about Denim's pregnancy she'd been afraid. Hurt even but as she looked at the precious baby she felt them fears wash away.

Braille was a gorgeous little girl that only wanted love. Love that Rocky would abundantly give her.

"Hey princess B," Rocky sang to her while smiling.

Denim took a picture of them and decided to send it to Bucks with the text that read *look at your girls.* Bucks immediately text her back, *Y'all just don't know what seeing this pic does to me.* Denim showed Rocky the text, and Rocky felt even better about stopping by.

"This was needed," Rocky said, and Denim nodded agreeing with her.

"So how have things been going for you?" Rocky asked as Denim turned on the TV.

Denim looked at Rocky and shook her head.

"I think I like someone, but he doesn't wanna go there with me," she revealed.

Rocky grinned at her. She was surprised but happy to see Denim was moving on.

"Oh really, who?"

Denim went to Bibby's very dry social media page and showed her his photo. Rocky smiled as she popped her on the leg.

"Bitch what!!! Bibby is everything. It was my first time meeting him at the resturant with you and all I kept thinking was that this dude looks like he's the man. It's the way he carries himself. But even when he walked up on us when we were about to eat, I could see him checking you out," Rocky said, and Denim smiled.

"But he doesn't wanna talk to me because of Braylen. I won't be fake with it Rocky. I have very few words for him. I feel like as long as he spends time with Braille that's all that matters. I don't run behind him, so I don't wanna call him. What do you think I should do?"

Rocky sighed.

"I could talk to him," she suggested.

Denim nibbled on her bottom lip before shaking her head.

"You know what don't. Being with Braylen has shown me so many things. If a man wants you he will make it clear. I'm not going to make anything easy for Bibby," Denim replied and Rocky smirked at her.

"Well if he wants you bad enough he'll find a way to make it happen," Rocky said before they both began to watch the TV.

Eight

"Shit been smooth nigga?" Aamil asked walking up

Bucks held his daughter in his arms as he looked at his longtime friend that had long ago become family.

"Yeah, these niggas pissing me off. They should have been done with this fucking building months ago. I got shot and these niggas started sitting on they ass. I fired them motherfucka's," he replied angrily.

Aamil chuckled as he grabbed Bucks daughter from him.

"Nigga you better load up the Glocks right now," Aamil told him staring down at the beautiful Braille.

Bucks chuckled.

"Glocks? Nigga, I'm cleaning out whole cities if some stupid shit pops off concerning her," he said in a serious manner.

Aamil nodded in understanding. He had a daughter and there was no limit to the things he'd do for her happiness and protection.

"I can feel that because I'd be right beside your ass. How Rocky doing with all of this now?"

Bucks looked down at the contracts sitting on his table and shook his head. He needed another contractor as soon as possible for the movie theater he was building in the heart of the city. The venture was big for him and was taking up a lot of his savings but for his family, he felt it was worth it.

Bucks had become popular thanks to the Matin family, so he knew a lot of celebrities and people in high up places. It was nothing for him to get backed by them and already he had celebrities ready to promote the theater for him.

"It's been good with us lately. Denim sent me a picture of Rocky and my daughter a few weeks ago and I swear that shit did something to me. All I need is peace in my life. When the time is right Rocky will push out a baby but until then I need her to be cool with the one we have already. Shit, they ain't gotta be best friends but I need them to get along. We on some Will and Jada shit over here because being united is always better than being divided," Bucks preached and Aamil chuckled.

"You ain't never fucking lied! I tried that shit with Mina, but it didn't work plus she was on some snake shit. Denim different though and she seems cool. I was glad to see Drew even warm up to her. It's not easy coming into a family that's so close but she got your kid, so we gone accept her with open arms nigga," Aamil told him and Bucks nodded.

"I appreciate that shit too," he replied as Bibby stepped into his penthouse with a small frown on his face. Bucks picked up on his gloomy mood and shook his head. "What's good nigga? Why you looking so down?" he asked him.

Bibby dapped up Bucks and Aamil and took a seat at Bucks dining room table. He took off his cap then his glasses and Aamil chuckled.

"Oh, shit nigga you worrying us up in this bitch," he joked.

Bibby chuckled. He respected Bucks and Aamil very much so the last thing he wanted to do was cause any drama.

"I needed to speak to you about Denim," he finally said.

Aamil smirked and passed his goddaughter back to Bucks. He grabbed his key fob and his bottled water.

"I'll fuck with y'all niggas later," he said before leaving out of the penthouse.

Bucks held his sleeping daughter as he looked Bibby's way.

"What's good?" he asked again this time with a slight attitude.

Bibby sat up straight and stared him in the eyes.

"I wanted to talk about Denim with you. First, let me say we never kissed or no shit like that. The only time I hugged her was when we was at her place after I took care of that nigga. It's just this vibe we got." Bibby stopped talking and shook his head. "It's hard to explain the shit but I feel this connection with her. Like I wanna see what she about, but because I respect you I never took it there. Let's be clear I never did," Bibby replied.

Bucks nodded. He glanced down at his daughter and placed a kiss on her soft, hairy forehead. Braille was covered in hair.

"Denim is a good woman. When I started fucking with her she was always so quiet and shit, but I liked that about her. It didn't work out with us, so I would be a bitch ass nigga to try to hold her back from being happy. If you feel like you can put that smile on her face than who am I to stop you? All I ask is that you keep her and my daughter away from that street shit. You knee deep in it so anything that affects you will affect them. Make sure they always good and we'll be straight," Bucks told him.

Bibby sighed with relief before chuckling.

"Shit we haven't even talked about being together nigga. I just couldn't make any moves with her without consulting with you first. I'm not with that shady shit," he said, and Bucks smiled at him.

"Nah, I feel you. I would have done the same thing. Just try to do right by Denim, you see how shit played out with us. She looks at a nigga like he ain't shit now and it does fuck with me sometimes. I never wanted to be a nigga that she hates. Life just played out that way and I couldn't play both of them. I want her to be happy. She's a good ass woman, just don't fuck her over," Bucks replied.

Bibby thought of Denim and licked his lips.

"Hurting her is the last thing I plan on doing nigga," he assured Bucks.

* * *

Denim smiled as she watched Bucks open up a gift from his mom for their daughter. Drew had gone all out with the help of the other ladies in his family and given her a beautiful baby shower in her backyard. Pink and purple décor was all over the yard. Drew had managed to get all of Denim's favorite foods along with Bucks and they had a huge turnout.

While Bucks sat down the gold gift bag Aamil pushed a pink Range Rover truck towards him. Bucks and Denim both smiled as they looked at the adorable kids play vehicle.

"When she turns sixteen I'll cop her a real one," Aamil said and Bucks laughed.

Bucks stood up and dapped Aamil up before looking around the large backyard for Drew.

Drew stood near the food with a wine glass in her hand.

"Good looking," Bucks told her, and she smiled at him.

"Please, you know we love this little girl already," she said waving him off.

Denim admired the truck before the handsome nicely dressed Bibby caught her attention. He'd stepped into the backyard with two large bags filled with girl clothes. He sat them at the kid's table and found a seat with Aamil and his brothers.

Denim stopped staring at him and noticed Bucks was watching her closely. She decided to drop some of the anger she had directed his way and she smiled at him.

Bucks was shocked to see her smile his way. All he wanted was to get along with her. The arguing and extra shit he could do without. Bucks thought of the good times he did share with Denim and he sighed. He hated the way shit had gone down but he had to choose Rocky.

On any day of the year regardless of the circumstances, he would *always* choose Rocky.

"You enjoying yourself ma?" Bucks asked noticing how happy she looked.

Denim nodded. A few of her family members had flown out and she was happy to see them.

"I actually am. This is really nice," she admitted to him.

Bucks nodded.

He sat back and brushed his right hand over his freshly cut hair. His eyes admired Rocky as she stood beside

Drew in her tight jeans smiling. Bucks loved how she seemed to be enjoying the shower as much as him and Denim. Shit like that meant a lot to him. He turned back to Denim and before he could speak Salem walked up holding her husband's hand.

"Hey, we just stopped by to bring our gift," Salem said, and Bucks sat up.

Bucks took the gift as Denim gave Salem a pleasant smile.

"Congrats nigga," Salem's husband Bucks told him.

At one-point Bucks had been Huss's connect. Things turned sour when Huss found out Bucks was pursuing Salem and Bucks gracefully bowed out. Salem was taken, and he was man enough to accept that.

"Thanks," Bucks said and dapped up Huss.

Salem smiled down at Bucks like she wanted to say more but she didn't. The situation still didn't sit well with her husband, so she knew how far to take it.

"We'll be going now. Congrats again," Salem said before walking off with her husband following behind her.

Denim turned to Bucks and saw he was already staring at her.

"How is it that you dated so many women after Rocky, yet you remained deeply in love with her?" she asked really wanting to know.

Bucks shrugged.

"The kind of love I feel for her doesn't just go away ma," he replied speaking bluntly hoping she didn't take offense.

Denim sighed. Her eyes fell to her lap and Bucks grabbed her hand.

"I will always be there for you because of Braille and you know that," he said lowly.

Denim nodded. She lifted her head and her eyes connected with his.

"I'm not worried about that. I know that as long as you're alive you will be there for her. I just want to have that kind of love for myself Braylen," she replied.

Bucks let her hand go. His eyes landed on Bibby who had managed to speak to almost every man in attendance yet still keep his eyes on Denim.

Bucks smirked as he peeped the scene. It was clear Denim and Bibby was feeling each other.

"You will when it's meant to happen, and I pray that nigga gives you all the love you want and need beautiful," Bucks told her sincerely and pulled her to his side.

His eyes connected with Rocky's as Denim hugged him and Rocky blew him a kiss.

Hours after the baby shower Denim walked into her condo tired beyond belief. Braille was spending her first night with Bucks and Denim was worried sick. She'd pumped like silly and sent over things when they weren't needed. Now all she could think of was what was her baby doing?

Denim stepped out of her shoes and called up Rocky.

"She's sleeping Denim. I promise I'm watching her like a hawk. Nothings in the crib with her. I even swaddled her like you showed me. I promise she's fine," Rocky assured her.

Denim took a deep breath and exhaled.

"Call me if you have any worries. Okay?"

"Promise," Rocky replied.

"Okay," Denim murmured and ended her call. She set her phone down and jumped when someone began to knock on her door.

Denim went to it and when she noticed Bibby on her doorstep holding a black bag her heart raced.

"Why should I open this?" she yelled through the door

Bibby chuckled. He licked his lips as he stared at the peephole.

"Because you just as curious about me as I am about you miss lady. Open this door with your pretty ass," he replied smoothly in his deep tone.

Denim nervously opened the door. She walked away and soon he was with her in the living room. Denim sat quietly on the sofa as Bibby sat down beside her. She opened her mouth to speak and he caught her off guard by kissing her passionately on the lips.

Denim closed her eyes as Bibby kissed her like he loved her. Like it was going to be his last fucking kiss. The *passion*, the *aggression* mixed with the *lust* was almost too much for her to handle.

Slowly his tongue played with her's as his hand caressed her neck sensually. Denim moaned into his mouth and he bit down hard on her bottom lip.

"Please don't do that shit," he said with a groan and kissed her again.

Bibby kissed Denim for several more minutes before trailing his long tongue down to her neck. He even kissed her chin before taking his attention back to her sexy lips. He sucked on the top and bottom one as Denim held on for the ride.

Bibby finally pulled back and Denim swallowed hard. He'd kissed her for so long she was parched.

"Wow," she said quietly with her lips tingling, and he chuckled.

"I been wanting to do that shit for a while now ma. Can I speak real quick?" he asked politely in his deep voice.

Denim watched him pull some dark Cîroc from the plastic bag and she smiled.

"I'd like a drink and yes you can."

Bibby pulled out some plastic cups.

"You not breastfeeding?"

"I am but I can pump it out. You have to be lit for the liquor to affect the milk. And look at you talking like you know what's going on," she jabbed at him.

Bibby chuckled as he made both of them a drink.

"Shit I know a little something. I spoke with Bucks and I let him know how I felt about you. I didn't need his approval Denim, but it was important for him to be understanding of this. I don't step on people's toes. Especially people that look out for me. That's not who I am. I took a chance by even talking to his ass, but I couldn't stop thinking about you. I'm interested in seeing where this goes miss lady," he revealed to her.

Denim took a sip of her drink as she stared at him. Bibby's gaze was placing her in a trance.

"I am interested too in seeing what you're about, but I wasn't going to chase you. I mean I don't even know what your real name is," Denim said and smiled.

Bibby leaned towards her and touched one of her long individual braids that had been wrapped in a white cord to decorate it. The Poetic Justice braids looked good on Denim and he was feeling the fuck out of the look on her.

"It's Bakari," he replied and brushed his finger across her full lips.

Denim smiled. His name was *cute.*

"I don't know what to say. This is so close to home but still, I wanna give it a try," Denim replied.

Bibby tossed back his drink.

"Betting on me is the best thing you can do miss lady. I just wanna put a real smile on that pretty ass face of yours," he replied, and Denim smiled hoping she was making the right choice.

Epilogue

Two years later on a cold Christmas morning

"Stop running from this dick," Bucks said and slapped Rocky's ass.

Rocky moaned. She closed her eyes and dropped her head.

"But baby..."

Smack!

"I don't wanna hear that shit. You know this pussy good, you know I'm bout to stretch it out. You don't want your dick to cum?" he asked talking so nasty that it made Rocky climax in return.

Rocky's legs shook as she released all over him and Bucks pumped harder into her.

"Damn this is the best pussy," he said and groaned.

Seconds later he was filling her up. Bucks waited a few minutes before pulling out and he slowly got off the bed. He grabbed a clean washcloth and ran it under warm water in their connected bathroom in the lodge.

They'd once again vacationed with the Matins. Christmas at the cabin had become their thing but this time it was extra special. Rocky had just discovered she was pregnant and they were overjoyed at the news.

"Baby I gotta take a nap," Rocky said as he stepped back into the room.

Bucks cleaned off Rocky and kissed her tummy that was still flat.

"Baby let's do this breakfast thankful shit Sophie has us do then you can go back to bed," he said and kissed her lips.

Rocky nodded and rolled her eyes. She begrudgingly got up and put on her onesie that Sophie had given them. Bucks then put on his pajamas and when they opened the door they spotted Braille coming their way

Bucks and Rocky both smiled as she raced towards them.

"Da-da!" Braille yelled excitedly.

Bucks picked up his daughter and kissed her chunky cheeks. Denim wasn't too far behind her with Bibby on her heels.

Rocky smiled when she saw they were wearing the same cheesy ass pajamas.

"Girl she's been on one all day. I'm so tired," Denim said, and Rocky smiled at her.

"You and me both," Rocky replied.

Bibby and Bucks dapped each other up and everyone headed downstairs.

In the dining room was the Matin family along with some extra people that they also considered family.

Rocky chose to sit next to her bestie who'd just found out she was pregnant as well. They were both excited to be going through their pregnancies together.

"This has been an amazing holiday," Sophie said standing up.

Sophie was Pia's mother-in-law. She smiled as she gazed in Rocky and Pia's direction.

"We have some new babies on the way. Rocky was also recently married along with this man over here," Sophie said and pointed to the Matin families longtime friend Hayward.

Hayward saluted Sophie as he sat next to his beautiful wife. Sophie then looked at Rocky. "So, I think it's only right that we let Bucks go first. He's been blessed tremendously, and I know he wants to shout it out to the whole damn world," she said before sitting down.

Bucks kissed Rocky on the lips before standing up. He still held his daughter and she clung to him tightly as he looked at his friends and family.

"I'll keep this short. Y'all know I don't do too much talking but Sophie is right. These last few years have been the best years of my damn life. I got hit with some bullets and for a second I thought I might die but God saw something else for me. I was blessed with my beautiful baby girl and Rocky came back to me," Bucks glanced down at Rocky and she smiled lovingly up at him. "Then to see her holding another one of my kids makes me feel like it was all worth it. All that drama and shit was worth it if that was what was needed to get me to this moment in my life. I love you beautiful," Bucks told Rocky before sitting down.

Aamil's brother Kasam always known as the jokester of the family smacked his lips and everybody looked his way.

"I don't know who the fuck gone follow up after that shit," he said seriously, and everyone laughed.

However Rocky couldn't stop staring at her man. Her husband and soon to be father of her child. Bucks was right all the pain and tears had been worth it. They'd made it to their happiness because the love they shared was so strong that it had brought them back together.

Rocky knew that with Bucks at her side there wasn't anything that they couldn't face and not overcome. She leaned towards him and smiled.

"We finally got this thing called love right," she whispered, and he chuckled before kissing her tenderly on the lips.

"I was never bad at it, that was all you," Bucks joked pulling back and Rocky punched his arm playfully before kissing him again.

Book Discussion Questions

1. Do you think Bahja moved on too fast from her late husband?
2. Do you think Micah ever loved Bahja?
3. Was Jigga a good pick for Bahja?
4. Did you understand why Rian was so angry with Bahja?
5. Was India stupid, confused or in love with she took the charge for Brody?
6. Was India and Brody too young to be in such a committed relationship?
7. Was Brody going to ever stop cheating?
8. Was India at fault for the way Brody behaved?
9. Did you like Tarik for India?
10. Was Rocky stupid for moving back to Detroit?
11. If you were Denim would you have been upset with Bucks?
12. Do you think Bucks ever loved Denim?
13. Which man did you like better for Rocky?
14. Was Bibby a good choice for Denim?
15. Do you think Denim should have fought for Bucks?